# Sands of Sirocco

## Annabelle McCormack

This is a work of fiction. Names, characters, organizations, places, events, and incidents are products of the author's imagination or used fictitiously. Any resemblance to an actual person, living or dead, or actual events is purely coincidental.

Copyright © 2022 by Annabelle McCormack

All rights reserved.

No part of this book may be reproduced in any form or by any electronic or mechanical means, including information storage and retrieval systems, without written permission from the author, except for the use of brief quotations in a book review.

Published by Annabelle McCormack

Cover by Patrick Knowles

Cover photography by Richard Jenkins Photography

Other images by Shutterstock

www.annabellemccormack.com

*For Cora, Andrew, Evie, Victoria, and Graham...without you, this book may have been finished a year earlier. Just kidding. I love you. (It's probably closer to ten months.)*

# ALSO BY ANNABELLE MCCORMACK

**The Windswept Saga**

A Zephyr Rising: A Windswept Prequel Novella

Windswept: Book 1

Sands of Sirocco: Book 2

Whisper in the Tempest: Book 3

**The Brandywood Small Town Contemporary Romance Series**

All This Time

I'll Carry You

Once We Met

**Stand Alone Contemporary Romance Novels**

See You Next Fall

To find out the latest about my new releases, please sign up for my newsletter or join my Facebook Reader's group! I love hearing from readers and have some great offers lined up for my subscribers.

# Sands of Sirocco

# PREFACE

*November, 1917:* After three grueling years of war and a particularly bloody and demoralizing year in France, the British are in desperate need of hope. The Americans, who have entered the war on their side, have yet to mobilize troops to Europe in significant numbers. On the Eastern Front, their former allies have fallen apart as the Russians have dissolved into chaos and been taken over by the Bolsheviks. Their enemies, the Germans and Ottoman Turks, are as exhausted as they are, but with the Russians withdrawing from the war, they are free to concentrate their troops on the Western Front in France.

The only glimmer of hope that the British have is in the Palestinian campaign. General Edmund Allenby has successfully battled his way up the Palestinian coast and is at the gates of Jerusalem. Victory there is seen by the British government as a potential Christmas present to hopeless troops and an opportunity to decisively smash the remaining Turkish resistance.

But the British have made huge diplomatic miscalculations in the Arabian Peninsula and the Transjordan. In their attempt to find allies, they have made conflicting promises to: 1) Sherif Hussein, who has helped T. E. Lawrence with the Arab Revolt, 2) the French government in the Sykes-Picot Agreement, with promises to divide the region between the French and British after the war, and 3) the Zionists, to whom they have pledged to help make Jerusalem a national homeland in the Balfour Declaration.

This explosive information has the potential to make already strained diplomatic relationships with their French and Arabian allies a powder keg. The published Balfour Declaration has already ignited the ire of Muslim nationalists in the region, who see the British as displaying the imperialism they had hoped to escape.

But the British have a larger goal in that region, one that has been intrinsic to their presence there since the beginning of the war and one which trumps all their other promises: finding and dominating the rumored oil fields which could help them win the war.

# CHAPTER ONE

## KANTARA, EGYPT

NOVEMBER, 1917

*Men never seemed to tire of finding the most idiotic ways to kill themselves. Even if by accident.*

Ginger Whitman stepped back from the operating table, taking a pause from the gruesome work in front of her. The accidents, like this one, stood out amongst the deliberate bloodshed. Given the time she'd spent at operating tables, she may as well be a surgeon. As it was, she wasn't even assigned as a nurse for this train.

She wiped her hands on her apron, leaving streaks of blood. The patient on the table wasn't dead yet but would be soon if she didn't work quickly. He moaned, though his cries had lowered to a rolling boil of pain since she'd given him morphine. However, any slight shift or touch was likely to cause an eruption of screams again … and being on a train that jostled easily didn't help.

The operating theater of the train was dimly lit. Windows on either side of the carriage reflected the fading light of the surrounding desert beyond the walls of the train. They'd stopped in the middle of the wilderness unexpectedly. The stillness also ushered in the stifling heat.

Whatever the reason for their stop, the poor soul in front of her had suffered for it. And the men who had stopped the train on a slope had been the idiots—not him. The manner of his injury had been horrific. He was a brakeman for the railway and had been on top of a train car before they'd completely come to a stop. His leg had slipped between two train cars, then got crushed when the cars had slammed together.

The bleeding tangle of bone and flesh below the knee no longer resembled a leg. Neither would it ever again function as one. If he survived. *Poor man.*

The soldiers she'd spoken with often feared this type of injury most of all.

She turned to the waiting stare of the nurse who oversaw patients on the train. Sister … Ginger blinked. *What's her name again?*

The last few weeks had been such a blur of people. And when the nurse had come through the carriage reserved for the Queen Alexandra's nurses, Ginger had been dozing. Weeks of fourteen-hour shifts at the front had caught up with her. They'd woken her since she was the most senior nurse.

"I think we'll have to amputate." Ginger kept her voice low. "The bleeding is too severe and the leg too mangled."

"No!" the man cried. "No, please, not my leg! Sister, please … save my leg." His eyes were dark and wild, his Australian accent like that of many other soldiers who served in this region.

The other nurse's face paled. The operating theater was empty, most noticeably, of its surgeon. Even during the transports, a surgeon was normally present on the train. But in this case, they were nearing the end of the line and the surgeon had disembarked at the last stop, at Romani. "It can't wait until we reach Kantara?" the nurse asked.

More than anything, Ginger wished it could wait. Amputations weren't usually in her purview. But she'd assisted in more than she could count. *And if I do it wrong?*

The man would end up suffering for it. The haste of field hospital amputations often resulted in several more surgeries to the same limb, trying to correct the lingering issues, including pain.

And there wouldn't be the benefit of chloroform and ether. *Bloody Royal Army Medical Corps.* She'd trained as an anesthetist for a few months earlier in the summer. Then they'd forbidden it for English nurses. Because women shouldn't do such things.

Bristling with irritation, Ginger shook her head. "The train cars crushed his leg—it could lead to contracture and worse and his bleeding is too severe." Her eyes went to the window on the opposite wall of the train car. The horizon of the desert landscape was darkening, the fading light of the sun streaking the sky with blazing ochre and maroon. Skylights on the roof of the car added more light, but that wouldn't help now. Once the sunlight was gone, they'd have to work by candlelight.

"Do you have any idea why we stopped here in the first place? Or when the train will start moving again?" Ginger asked. Unscheduled stops were rare, but perhaps the engineer had seen something on the tracks up ahead.

"None."

"All right." Ginger squeezed her eyes shut, trying to shake the fog of sleep lingering in her mind. If there was no one else and no time to waste, she didn't have any options. She settled her shoulders back.

She could do this. He would die if she didn't.

She cocked her head, indicating the nurse should follow her to the far side of the carriage, out of earshot. Their footsteps echoed across the wooden floor. "Can you get the guillotine? We'll need an orderly to hold him down."

The nurse's eyes widened. "Are you going to perform the surgery?"

"Yes. We have to hurry." It would be laborious if she wanted to leave the man as good of a stump as possible. Multiple surgeries on a stump were horrific—months, sometimes years of suffering. Some men would wake in the night screaming with the pain they felt in the limbs they no longer had.

How many times had she been at their sides during those times, helpless to relieve their agony?

As the nurse left, Ginger rushed across the room, looking for the anesthetic. Her pulse ticked faster.

*RAMC be damned.*

She wasn't about to torture the man. Her hands trembled as she lifted the mask for the anesthetic.

Would she remember her training well enough?

A soft grumble from the patient steeled her resolve. Her fingertips grazed over the smooth glass bottles stored on shelves until she found the ether.

She checked over her shoulder. If she hurried while she was alone, she could administer the ether before anyone could stop her. There wouldn't be time for a combination of ether and chloroform—the safer method. She found a clean towel in a supply cabinet, then folded it over the mask.

Nervous energy tingled up her spine as she hurried back to the patient. "This should help with the pain." She placed the mask over his mouth. He stilled as she opened the ether.

A few drops and he'd be ready for surgery in minutes.

Ginger used her most soothing tone. "Breathe deeply with me and count. One ... two ... three ..." As the patient's breath steadied, Ginger surveyed the operating theater. The car was sparse in its outfitting. Two sturdy metal operating tables. Then, smaller tables holding basins and towels. Shelves of surgical equipment.

The car was peaceful as the patient drifted to sleep. *Thank goodness.* She needed a moment to think clearly. Her fingers felt dry and stiff, the skin on her hands rough with unending days of exposure to the solutions before her: iodide, alcohol, antiseptic, carbolic lotion.

Despite the heavy workload, the days after the third battle of Gaza had been thrilling—the British Army had pushed through the line at last, forcing the Ottoman Turks and Germans back to Jerusalem. The stalemate broken, the spirits of the troops and the medical staff had been high.

And during that time, Noah had found her, giving her the Claddagh ring she now wore on her left hand with the promise they'd be together soon. Learning Noah was still alive and loved her had been a singular bright spot in the most heartbreaking year of her life.

She pushed thoughts of him away. There would be time enough later for warm memories. Right now, she had a patient to tend to.

She'd assisted in surgeries on the trains before but never imagined she'd direct one. Back in Alexandria, her inquiry to the London School of Medicine for Women remained unsent. She'd resolved to move forward with it so many times, but something had always held her back.

To think if she'd had the gumption to do it ages ago. How differently she'd approach this situation. With confidence, certainty.

Now, the only thing she was certain of was the soldier would bleed out if she didn't hurry. His leg was practically detached above the kneecap, and the hastily applied tourniquets were only doing so much.

The door to the room clicked open, and a medical orderly

strode in. "Sister Wilson said you'd need me in here." He eyed Ginger warily. He probably hadn't expected her to be so young.

*Sister Wilson.* That must be the nurse who had fetched her.

*Think clearly, Ginger.* She ground her teeth. This was too important for her to be sluggish. "We need to amputate immediately. If you'll wash up—"

Footsteps sounded, followed by the bold shove of the door. A stench came from the three men who entered: sweat and body odor of days spent in the hot, merciless sun, and stale cigarettes.

The men hauled a soldier between them who bled from a wound below his collarbone. The injured man's head lolled—he was unconscious—a large dark bruise shadowed his face. His hands were bound in front of him.

Without ceremony, the three men dumped the patient on the empty operating table. One of them, a lieutenant, scanned the theater. His eyes settled on the orderly. "Who's the surgeon here?"

"For the moment, I am." Ginger frowned. "You can't come bursting into thi—"

"I didn't know they had lady doctors on the train." The lieutenant wrinkled his nose. "But I guess you'll have to do." He laid a thick hand on the injured man. "Patch him up. Now."

*As though he's not interrupting another surgery.*

Without waiting for a response, he gestured to the other two men that they should follow him out of the operating theater.

She was used to men dismissing her but she rarely let it bother her as much as it should, used to orders.

But the lieutenant's behavior was so appallingly brash that her jaw dropped. She exchanged a glance with the orderly, and his sheepish expression only furthered her determination to challenge the lieutenant. "Just a moment." Ginger set her hands on her hips. "I'm treating a patient whose injuries can't wait. I've already prepared him for surgery."

The lieutenant scowled and raked dirty fingernails against his temple. "Well—this private here can't wait either."

The operating theater felt crowded, the air thick. Ginger scrutinized the injured man. His uniform shirt was open at the collar, and he was missing a shoe. As she stepped closer, the pungent stink of urine rose from his clothes. They had covered a wound on his neck with a rag. "What happened to him?" From the bruising on his face, she imagined he'd been in a fight.

"He tried to shoot himself. Get out of what was coming to him." His lips held a twist of contempt as they focused on the injured man's face. "We had to wrestle the pistol away from him."

The nature of this unfortunate injured man's situation became clearer. "A deserter?"

"Aye. Now, patch him up. We'll want him back to health so he can get the punishment he deserves."

Squaring her shoulders, Ginger gave him a look of disbelief. "You want me to 'patch him up' so you can execute him later?" The Australian soldier she'd been preparing for surgery mumbled. He couldn't afford this waste of time. "My good sense and my ethics prevent me from participating in your sense of justice, sir."

Ducking his chin, the lieutenant reddened. "You won't treat him? That doesn't conflict with your 'ethics'?" He loomed over her. "You think you can meddle because you're a lady doctor, but you can't. We stopped this train for this traitor here"—he pointed a finger at the deserter—"to get treatment as soon as possible. And this train will sit here until he does. I have my orders. Now do it. We'll be right here."

Arguing with him would be useless and only cost her precious time. The irony of it all was that if she *were* a doctor, her rank equivalent would be to a captain—above this man. Not that the RAMC had done female physicians the courtesy of bestowing them a true rank. They faced even more trouble than the nurses did.

The lieutenant would have to go. Then she could do whatever needed to be done.

At last, she nodded stiffly. "But you can't stay in the operating theater. You can stand guard outside if you wish. You're filthy and could expose this other patient to infection." Would he listen? She'd hedged her only chance on doing this her way on the cooperation of a disobliging man.

The lieutenant scanned her face with wary eyes. Sucking in a breath through his teeth, he left, accompanied by his men.

They left a vacuum of stale air. Ginger glanced at the orderly and motioned toward the deserter. "Give that man a shot of morphine." Her voice was low, her nerves high. How much time did she have before the lieutenant checked in?

She returned to the Australian. Putting her fingers to his wrist, she felt for his pulse, which was faint. "We need to hurry with the amputation."

The orderly leaned over the deserter, syringe in hand. "And this one?"

"Let's make him as comfortable as we can for now. Unbind his hands, to start." Ginger lifted her head as the door opened once more. The other nurse had returned with the guillotine on a cart.

The nurse gaped at the deserter. "And this new one?" She wrung her hands. "This is the oddest stop, wouldn't you say? Two patients for surgery all at once?"

"We'll carry on as best we can. The amputation first. You can disrobe the new one. Then compress his wound." Ginger swept the stray strands of her flame-colored hair behind her head into a tight knot as the nurse moved toward the equipment.

"Do you need sterile gloves?" The nurse looked at Ginger, her face pale.

Ginger bit her lip. "Do you have any that will fit me?"

The nurse shook her head.

"Then, no. They'll only get in the way." The rubber was too thick and cumbersome if she used gloves meant for a man. She'd be more accurate with her fingers.

She went to the washbasin and scrubbed her hands with soap before sterilizing them. The barren wall of the train, whitewashed after the British Army had commandeered it from passenger service in Egypt, reminded her of how many people it took to help the troops. She'd worked in tents, in hospital ships, on islands, in hospitals, in former hotels, and under the light of the moon with no cover at all.

"This soldier has a chest wound," the nurse said, peeling back the rag from the deserter's injury.

"Compression. Quickly, Sister."

A chest wound. In a blink, her mind was back in the desert, with Noah struggling to breathe as she sought to keep his lung from collapsing. And, nearby, the bodies of her father and brother...

But she couldn't let her mind wander there.

They worked at a brisk pace, the urgency of the procedure weighing equally heavily in Ginger's mind as the thought of that lieutenant stalking outside the room. If he came in and saw her neglecting the deserter, would he make a scene? She couldn't allow herself to be distracted by him. The poor Australian brakeman wouldn't even be in this situation if it hadn't been for the train stopping.

The orderly worked as her assistant as she tended to the wound above the laceration first. She'd need to clean and cauterize the wound, to staunch the bleeding, then cut the flap of skin for the stump. The guillotine would be last.

When she'd trained as a nurse, she'd never expected to do work like this. Noble thoughts of tending to soldiers had included visions of holding hands, wiping brows, and spooning soup to lightly wounded men in proper hospitals.

How different it had all turned out to be.

The wounds had been macabre and the tactics of warfare, horrific. When the nurses had first arrived at the "hospitals" in Egypt, they'd found dirty buildings unfit to sleep in, let alone treat patients. They'd had to start by scrubbing floors.

And the tropical diseases—brought about by flies, heat, mosquitoes, lice—she'd never even considered those. She'd had malaria once. Seen orderlies and nurses die of typhus. The destruction had been immeasurable and unforgettable.

She'd learned techniques for wound irrigation the RAMC had considered too complex for them at the start of the war. Those hesitations by the brass had vanished when nurses became a necessity.

And though she didn't want to admit it to herself, part of her hesitation in applying for medical school lay in all the awfulness she'd experienced. She was exhausted—and not just physically.

Before this, she'd scoffed at the idea of being destined for marriage and motherhood. Now, that sounded like a wonderful future. She'd had her fill of war.

"Sister ..." The other nurse caught her attention. "His pulse is slowing."

Before Ginger could give the nurse any further direction, the door to the operating theater pushed open once more. The lieutenant marched inside. "Well?"

Ginger felt all the eyes of the operating theater on her. The nurse didn't know about the lieutenant's orders, but the orderly did. He busied himself with cleaning the instruments Ginger had set to the side, his head down.

The lieutenant focused on her work with the amputee. His

eyes swiveled toward the deserter. Then, his hands clenched, a vein throbbing in his neck. "You disobeyed me?"

Ginger focused on her work, heat rising to her cheeks. *Steady hands, now.* "I'm going to have to ask you to leave, Lieutenant. I'm in the middle of a critical surgery, and you're interrupting." Her voice sounded calmer than she felt.

"He's fading, Sister," the other nurse said.

"Did you hear? The private is dying! Do something, you useless baggage!" The lieutenant stepped toward the deserter, his hands flailing helplessly.

She could only save one man. Ginger gritted her teeth. And it wouldn't be the one the army intended to shoot. The soldier had been through enough. Deserters didn't deserve the death sentence they received. But as she was in no position to change that, she could do this.

Ginger didn't respond, but her heart pounded. The lieutenant's presence made her fingers feel more slippery as she held a suturing needle in her fingertips and his body quivered with fury.

The other nurse no longer held the deserter's wound under compression. Her face was grave. "This one didn't survive."

"You bloody woman!" A stream of curses followed, and the lieutenant came toward her.

The orderly stepped between them, keeping the lieutenant away.

The lieutenant shoved a small table set up with equipment, metal clanging. "Do you have any idea what I went through to catch that man? Or what his desertion cost my men?"

The scent of burned flesh filled the space as Ginger began the cauterization. "Lieutenant, I already had a patient. One who didn't deserve to die at your whims."

The lieutenant backed away. He studied her, his gaze unnerving.

When she'd finished with the amputation, she directed the other nurse to bandage the wound, then turned her attention to the deserter.

Ginger didn't want to feel relief, but it came in a slow trickle through her chest. His jaw was slack, the scruff of a few day's growth on his face. Bruises hid his youth. He couldn't be too old—in his young twenties, at most.

She prayed the morphine had helped ease his suffering. The bindings that had held him had torn his wrists. He must have struggled to raise the gun toward himself. He'd probably missed his intended target and given himself a much more painful death.

And to think they'd wanted her to prolong his torment. She covered him with a bedsheet to give him some dignity.

"Satisfied with your dereliction of duty?" The lieutenant's eyes blazed.

Ginger folded her hands in front of her apron. "There was nothing we could do for him." She gripped her fingers even more tightly.

The lieutenant's face deepened to a dark flush of scarlet, his lips puckering under his thin moustache. He stepped toward the deceased soldier. The other nurse gave Ginger a questioning look. Ginger shook her head slightly, hoping she would understand not to speak up.

"Women doctors aren't worth their weight in spit," the lieutenant said as he started toward the doorway, and Ginger relaxed.

"How dare you?" The nurse stamped her foot with indignation. "To begin with, this nurse is one our finest. And there was little to be done when we had two emergencies at once."

Despite the nurse's desire to defend her, Ginger felt a trill of alarm go through her. The lieutenant had been about to leave, which Ginger would have welcomed. She lifted her hand to prevent her from speaking further. "Not to worry, Sister. Emotions are always high when a soldier perishes."

The lieutenant turned back, his eyes narrowing at the Australian, who slumbered after his surgery. He looked back toward Ginger. "You're not even a doctor?"

Ginger lifted her chin. *Damn it.* She set her lips to a line.

With a sneer, the lieutenant pulled a notebook and pencil from his pocket. "I want your name, the hospital where you're posted, and the name of your superior," he said to Ginger.

Ginger repressed a sigh, then gave him the information. *Just what I need.* The train ride back home was, in theory, supposed to be a respite of relaxation.

The lieutenant stared at her name on the notebook, then gave her a menacing look. "There will be consequences for you soon, Sister Whitman. Mark my words."

Then he left, slamming the door behind him.

## CHAPTER TWO

### JERUSALEM

The downpour made the nighttime landing more difficult, but Noah Benson didn't mind. Rain also provided cover from the watching eyes of the Turkish Army. The skiff bounced in the sea's choppy waters, wet season threatening in earnest now.

The salt spray stung Noah's nostrils, and he wiped his eyes with the backs of his fingers. Rain dripped down his chin, clinging to the stubble of several days' growth. He hadn't had the time to grow a full beard. He squinted, looking toward the land for the signal from Fahad, his friend behind the Turkish lines. The storm would make it difficult to see, and Noah couldn't afford to miss it. With as many vessels as there were out in the waters, they'd agreed the light would only flash three times.

When he'd first come to the Levant years ago, he'd never imagined he'd spend so much time sneaking into it someday. Noah vastly preferred going by land, an impossibility now with the mounting British offensive drawing closer to Jerusalem by the day. Noah hoped he wasn't too late to retrieve the information they had sent him for. The numbers of Turkish and German officials fleeing had grown over the last week, according to their contacts. Any Ottoman ally was likely growing nervous—including Abdullah. And only Abdullah could help him.

A flash of light flickered three times, then it extinguished. *Time to move.*

Noah guided the skiff through the waters as he tried to focus. He'd much rather be working on the offensive. After a year of hard-fought battles up the coast of Palestine from Egypt, the British were at last on the brink of success—one the Allies desperately needed. Jerusalem was in their grasp. Noah's frustration at being pulled away from the front extended through every stroke of the oar into the water.

As he drew closer to the shore, the skiff felt more like a block of wood floating in the rapids of a river. The fragile hull caught the swell of the waves, which pushed it toward the surf. He braced himself as sand scraped the bottom of the vessel and then Fahad was in the water, grabbing the skiff's side and dragging it inward. Noah hadn't even been able to see him on the shore. Noah hopped over the side, and the two men pulled the little boat up the sand until they safely beached it against the brush of the dunes.

"*Akhy Nuh.*" Fahad embraced Noah. Both were out of breath. The rain pelted them in the strong wind. "It does my heart good to see you alive. I heard rumors."

"They weren't entirely unfounded." Noah grasped him by the forearm. He'd spent two months at Lord Helton's house in early summer, where Victoria's fussing over him had made him want to flee. He'd never seen her so emotional. Not even when he'd told her there could be nothing between them.

The promise he'd made to Ginger as he lay dying in her arms had been the most honest words he'd ever spoken. Victoria seemed to sense it wasn't the time to convince him otherwise, even if his life wasn't in his hands right now. But since he'd promised Ginger they'd marry someday, an unnerving sense of caution had crept into his actions. A caution he couldn't afford, especially when he had to keep his wits about him.

More than anything, he wanted to return to Ginger, live the life he had never dared to dream of. But what if he'd only put her in a position of further heartbreak? What could he really offer her right now?

A crack of thunder drew his mind to the present. He followed Fahad from the beach, hurrying. The storm continued to provide cover from curious eyes, but the residents of Jerusalem were likely watchful, waiting for the war to reach them.

Fahad's motorcar was parked a short walk from the beach, and they climbed inside it. The covered top wouldn't protect the seats from Noah's sopping-wet clothes. Despite being grateful for shelter from the rain, Noah was cold, the night bitterly chilly. He shivered, wishing he had the time to stop at Fahad's home for dinner and sleep.

Then again, his discomfort was nothing compared to that of the poor soldiers who'd been battling for over two weeks straight, wearing their summer uniforms of twill shorts and short-sleeved shirts. Noah had the benefit of a trench coat and long sleeves. The soldiers were out in the elements with no relief in sight. He gave Fahad an apologetic glance. "By the time this war is over, I'll owe you a new car."

Fahad grinned at him. "Marry one of my daughters, and you'll owe me nothing."

Noah chuckled. "I'm engaged. And still Catholic." Fahad wouldn't ever allow a daughter of his to marry outside of his Islamic faith.

Noah had lost count of the number of children Fahad had by

now. He didn't seem twenty years his elder, especially not after some of the adventures they'd had together. That he could have any daughters old enough for him to marry was the only reminder of the age gap between them. They were a long way from Luxor, where they'd met so long ago, when Noah had first joined their mutual friend Jack Darby for an archeological expedition.

Fahad gave him a neatly tied package. Inside was a change of clothes comprising a simple cotton tunic and darker *aba*, open in the front. Fahad had also packed trousers and a *keffiyeh* head-dress, with a corded *agal* band to hold it in place. The passenger seat was cramped, but Noah changed quickly, leaving his wet clothes folded on the floor.

"How is your family?" Noah asked.

Fahad lifted one hand from the wheel to gesticulate with his palm up. "They are well. As well as can be expected."

"And Nasira?" It had been at least a year since Noah had visited with Fahad and his wife while coming through Jerusalem.

"Worried about you." Fahad gave him a grim look. "She says this isn't the time to be sneaking about the streets of the Old City. The Turks are sleeping with one eye open, looking for spies."

"Jack will be within reach."

"She's just as worried about Jack as you." Fahad grunted and reached an arm back again. He brought forth a basket covered with a faded blue cloth. "She sent dinner for you."

Noah's stomach growled at the scent of warm bread. He unscrewed the container's metal top to find lentil soup, still warm. The scent of mint met his nostrils. It wouldn't have mattered if it were stone cold. "You may have the best wife in Jerusalem." He tore a piece of bread, then dipped it into the soup.

"I *do* have the best wife in Jerusalem." Fahad gave him a fond smile. "Next time, you'll have to stay for a few days. When your people have liberated the city." He said the last part with a sardonic smirk. Many local Arabs welcomed the idea of the British rather than the Turks, whose policies had been oppressive. But trust them? That was another matter altogether.

"And the Turks and German citizens? We've had reports of refugees on the road to Nablus."

"The refugees are so thick, the road is impassable. Most head to Damascus." Fahad shook his head. "How did the evacuation go?"

"About the same." Noah took another bite, the taste heavenly. He chewed and swallowed, trying to pace himself. As the Ottoman Turks had fled Gaza and the surrounding villages, they'd left every sign of an army in full retreat. Buildings reduced to rubble. Piles of ammunition, wagons. Smoking vehicles. Dead animals. More pitiable had been the animals abandoned alive and still attached to heavy loads.

The looting had been as horrific. Bedouin and locals had trampled the wounded Turkish soldiers in their efforts to get to the supplies left behind. And the dead women and children …

Noah drew a sharp breath, then studied Fahad's profile. "But the government has promised to keep the fighting outside the city. Keep the holy places from harm."

Fahad's lips twitched. "The holy places which they plan to give to the Zionists?"

Noah grimaced, a heavy feeling growing in his heart. For years, he and Fahad had discussed this, with Noah assuring him the British had no intention of coming in and building nations. The Balfour Declaration, issued just weeks earlier, had changed everything. All his local allies and contacts had been regarding him with worry, wanting a clarification of the new promises the British government had pledged in their support of the Zionists, who wanted to make a homeland in the Levant.

If they only knew about other secret deals that had the potential to erode their trust altogether. The government had promised to help make Sherif Hussein a leader and king among a group of tribal nations with little in common. They'd also promised the French some of the same lands they'd pledged to Hussein, who was still being deluded about their honesty by T. E. Lawrence.

That the Cairo Intelligence Bureau had sent him here to learn about the oil concessions in the area told Noah they had another aim that might trump all those promises: securing oil fields in the interests of Britain.

He eyed Fahad and swallowed another bite. "Nothing is decided."

"When our options are the Zionists or Bin Hussein, it appears a great deal has been decided." Fahad sighed. "I don't blame you, *ahky*. You might do better in charge than those men, but you're one of us." Fahad put a hand on his shoulder, his grip strong. "I'm certain your mother would be proud."

Noah's throat thickened. He met Fahad's gaze and gave a small, thankful nod.

Fahad released his shoulder. "Eat. You have little time."

They continued in silence, the heaviness of their conversation weighing in the space between them. When he'd enlisted, none of Noah's loyalties had felt divided. Britain, king, and country. And it was the army that had wanted him to be here, to live and breathe and become what he was now.

Yet, what he was now was a liar. A killer. Someone willing to look his friends in the eye and tell them what they wanted to hear rather than the truth. Just like the sycophant diplomats in Cairo. *"The great thing about you Brits,"* Jack had said the last time they were together, *"is that you do a swell job of making everyone feel heard. Which is a problem when you're not listening to anyone but yourselves."*

A problem indeed. Noah didn't even know if there was an official position on any of it. But the British government had certainly put a target on the backs of men like himself, who they commissioned to make promises he couldn't keep.

The rows of cactus hedge and rocky walls soon gave way to dark and narrow stone streets. An occasional cedar or olive tree rose among the buildings, but with the rain and darkness, it was hard to see much. As they passed through the gap in the wall near the Jaffa Gate, Fahad slowed.

Noah tensed. A Turkish guard stopped them, and Fahad handed travel papers over to him. The guard scanned them, then thrust them back into the window. He hurried back to his cover, away from the rain.

Noah released a breath as he waved them through. One more reason to be thankful for the storm.

When the car stopped, Noah met Fahad's awaiting gaze. "Thank you. As always. And give my regards to Nasira."

Fahad wagged a finger. "One more thing." He handed Noah a gun, which Noah recognized as the Mauser parabellum the Turkish officers carried. Fahad held his hand out, palm up.

Noah removed his own service pistol and traded the Turkish gun for it. Fahad always worried about those details. If Noah was stopped and searched, his British-issue weapon would give him away. Noah had even lost a pistol that way, forced to dispose of it before they could search him. Still, he preferred a gun he'd had a prior opportunity to fire.

He left Fahad and went back into the rain, darting through an alleyway. When he looked back, Fahad had already pulled away, his car lights off. Even though their time together had been brief, seeing Fahad had been good for him and erased some anxious thoughts clawing in the back of his mind.

Noah sidled up to a doorway on a stone building and rapped sharply. The door opened a minute later. Jack Darby stood behind a crack in the entrance, the yellow glow of electric light behind him. Jack eyed him, then opened the door fully, ushering him through. "I thought you might not show up."

The door closed behind Noah. Jack wore a similar outfit to his, and his dark beard had fully grown in—it seemed wild, in fact. Had it only been a month since they'd last seen each other? Noah tipped a smile at him. "When have I ever failed to appear when I said I would?"

Jack didn't comment, going toward a window high enough from the ground that even a man as tall as Jack—over six feet— had to stand on his toes to see out of. Raindrops battered the window, running in rivulets down the pane. Thunder trembled in the distance. "Not a great night for going out, but it'll have to do. How was Fahad?"

"He seemed well enough. Frustrated." Noah rubbed his hands together, his skin still cold, grateful that Jack had a fire going in the small room. The cramped space featured only a makeshift bed on the floor and a rickety table with two chairs. No running water. A chamber pot was in the corner, under the washstand. Hard to imagine someone with as much money as Jack had accumulated over the years would live like this for an extended period.

Jack came back from the window. "We're all frustrated. It's high time this damned war ended already." He sat in one chair, inviting Noah to take the other.

As a seasoned cryptographer, Jack's services weren't likely something the army wanted to let go of—even with America having joined the war. Jack had confessed to Noah he'd been tempted to ask his government to help him get out of his commitments to the British. But with the Americans, Jack would probably end up in France. Jack's knowledge of the languages in this region—both present-day and ancient—were more useful here.

Noah went to the fireplace instead, to ease the chill. He'd found nothing but a hot bath could dispel the cold that came from being wet and miserable for an extended period—but that wouldn't be a possibility tonight, of course. The fire helped. He checked his watch. They had only minutes before they'd need to be on their way.

Jack observed him in silence. "You look better than the last time I saw you. Not so thin." He cocked his head. "Maybe even less tormented?"

Noah met Jack's dark-brown eyes. They'd been friends for too long for Jack not to inquire, and the last time they'd seen each other, Jack had made him promise. "I saw her."

A pleased smile settled on Jack's features. "When?"

"In Gaza. She was at the clearing station. About two weeks ago."

"Good. Now—don't you feel better?"

"Not much."

Jack leaned back in the chair, and it gave a tremulous groan. Noah braced himself, waiting for the chair to snap, but it held steady.

Of course Jack was interested. Jack had been there when Ginger had saved Noah's life. He'd seen them together. He knew how Ginger had changed Noah, even in the brief span they'd been together. And what Ginger had sacrificed in the end: she'd promised Lord Helton to stay away from Noah, something Victoria had neglected to relay to Noah during the months he'd been recuperating.

Noah had been sure she'd stayed away out of hate. Why wouldn't she hate him?

Jack had been the one to tell him differently.

Noah rested his shoulder against the wall, his skin feeling

unnaturally hot from the fire. "If I'd left well enough alone, she might have found someone who suited her better. Someone equipped to give her a life."

Jack stood and rolled his eyes. "Right. Because you'd be able to live with yourself if she ever married anyone else." He picked up a canvas bag by the bed and slung it over his shoulder. "Well, since you've learned nothing, there's nothing more to say. Except you might want to keep an eye out. I intercepted a message from Sir Reginald Wingate to Lord Helton asking about details regarding what happened with her father."

Noah stiffened. He'd dreaded that possibility for months now—that someone with a higher level of authority than Lord Helton would want to know more about the matter. Sir Reginald Wingate was one of the worst possibilities as he'd recently been named high commissioner to Egypt. "When did you intercept it?"

"About a week ago." Jack drummed his fingers on the tabletop. "Which is why I brought the whole thing up. She may need your help with it if they dig too deep."

"I worry about what other secrets Lord Braddock hid that may come back to haunt his family." Noah had unraveled much of the man's underhanded dealings, and yet it felt as though he'd barely scraped the surface. The ring of smuggling Lord Braddock had operated was deeply underground. Without Stephen Fisher, their hopes of discovering the key players remained stalled.

His gut clenched at the thought of Fisher out there. Lord Helton's refusal to let Noah hunt for him still infuriated him.

The conversation was doing little to bring Noah the calm he'd craved before his meeting this evening. "Shall we move on? I'm not sure this mental exercise is doing me any good."

Jack seemed to understand he'd struck a nerve. "You got it." He stood. "Ready for this?"

Noah smirked at him. "Do I ever have the choice?"

They left and headed back into the rain. They were matched in height, which had never worked to their advantage when they were undercover—both were several inches taller than the average Arab or Egyptian. Noah ducked under an archway, the dark enveloping them. With the rain, the baked ancient dust of the limestone buildings had settled, giving way to an earthy smell. He exited the covered arched passageway, following Jack into a narrow, curved side street.

He'd never dreamed his aptitude for languages would lead him to years of this.

Jack stopped. Noah crouched beside him. Jack pointed to a building across the way, where a candle shone in a second-story window. "Abdullah is in there. If there's trouble, knock the candle over."

"And if I can't?"

Jack shrugged. "Then improvise. I'll do my best to help. He should only have one or two men with him tonight, at most. At least, based on my sources. But hopefully it won't come to that."

Noah crossed the street and knocked on the door. The door opened, and he nodded to the petite man who stood there. *"As-salaam alykum,"* he said. Then he continued in flawless Arabic, "Karim Sayed. Abdullah is expecting me."

The man stood on his toes to look past Noah, toward the street. Then he ushered Noah through. He directed him up the staircase and then down the hall to a doorway. He opened the door, folding his hands in front of him.

Abdullah, a large, solid man with bushy brows so thick they nearly joined above his nose, stood from a desk in the back of the room. He wore a fine gold-embroidered maroon caftan with gold tassels. Spreading his hands, he gave Noah a toothy smile, greeting him in Arabic. "Karim, my friend. It's been too long.

I'm surprised to see you out of Aleppo. All your friends seem to flee the city, and here you are."

Noah embraced him like an old friend. Most of the times he'd met with Abdullah, it had been safely within firmly held Ottoman territory. He'd only visited him in Jerusalem once—in the house of a Turkish diplomat. "And you? Don't you fear the regime change? Yet you stay."

Abdullah pursed his meaty lips. "They profane our gates. But they have showed their true face now, with their promises to the Jews. They will not chase me out of my homeland."

Abdullah's Ottoman loyalties were no great secret—more than many, he'd profited from rubbing elbows with the Turks and Germans in Jerusalem.

"Do you have the papers?" Noah asked. His gaze flickered to the candle at the window. He'd have to take a few steps to make it there if necessary. Knowing Abdullah, he and the man at the door were both heavily armed. He produced from his tunic the bag he'd strapped to his torso during the sea voyage. The one thing he couldn't afford to lose—the money they had given him for this exchange.

Snapping his fingers at the man who'd shown Noah in, Abdullah rubbed the well-groomed beard along his jawline. The man came forward and Abdullah whispered in his ear. The man left the room, closing the door behind him.

Abdullah held out his hand for the bag. Noah gave it to him, thankful to have his hand free if he needed to reach for his gun. Abdullah opened it and sifted through the contents, then lifted dark eyes toward Noah, a satisfied look in them. He pulled out a rolled paper from his robe. Sucking air through his teeth, he unrolled the paper on his desk, revealing a map. He gestured Noah to stand beside him.

The map was of the entire Palestine and Transjordan region and Arabia, as well as Syria. Abdulla pointed to some shaded areas, which had names and dates written above them. Noah had spent so much time staring at maps of these regions he could practically draw them from memory. "These are the concessions granted, to the best of my knowledge. There are two areas of interest not represented here."

He pointed to an area near Mosul. "There are rumors of good conditions in Kirkuk."

"Seepages?" Noah scanned the map. He'd heard of oil seepages in Kornub, and recently, but not of that area. He'd have to send a message to Gertrude Bell in Baghdad.

"Perhaps." Abdullah shrugged. "The rumors conflict."

He pointed to another area, much further south in the Arabian Peninsula. "The second area of interest is here. My men tell me Ibn Saud granted a secret concession to an Englishman —a Lord Braddock. I can't tell you more of it, but I have someone who can."

An icy feeling hit him in the core. Lord Braddock had been granted a concession? What had happened to it?

As Noah tried to process Abdullah's claims without reacting, the door creaked open behind him. Abdullah looked over Noah's shoulder and straightened. "Karim. Let me present you with *Oberleutnant* Stephen Fisher."

Noah froze. Of all the people who might be in Jerusalem, only Stephen could give him away instantly. Several thoughts assailed him at once, his eyes glued to the map in front of him. He'd have to remember as much of it as possible in case it didn't make it out of this room with him.

Whatever Stephen was doing here, Noah had only seconds to react. Abdullah and his men would easily overpower him. No candle would help. And if he left, they'd alert the Turks to his presence.

Noah pulled his gun from its holster. He fisted the map in his other hand, crumpling it, then fired three shots toward the window. The glass splintered and burst, shards tinkling against the stone street below.

Abdullah cried out and Noah glanced back. His eyes met, for a split-second, with Stephen's icy blue gaze. Then Noah hurled himself toward the window, arms over his face. Shots rang out behind him.

## CHAPTER THREE

Dusk settled on the streets of Alexandria as the wooden tram rattled forward on the steel tracks in the street. The windows of the narrow streetcar were open, and Ginger leaned toward them, waving air onto her face to deter both the heat and the smell of body odor from the packed car. She'd been fortunate to find a seat on a bench. Men and women, mostly European, left standing room only.

Ginger wanted to attribute her unease to the dark, but ever since she'd gotten off the train in Kantara the evening before, a taut feeling had gripped her in the chest. The sides of her neck hurt and she rubbed them under the bottom edge of her boater hat.

The lieutenant from the train had failed to reappear, but his threat lingered. She couldn't force herself to feel the fear he'd intended, though. She'd make the same choice. Again and again. She had to live with her conscience. She was too tired, too weary of the agonized bloodshed she'd witnessed these last three years. *Enough.*

Still, it was a wretched way to end her time at the clearing station frontline hospital. She'd kept her head down for several months now, gone about her business without bringing notice to herself. With the deaths of her brother and father in the spring, her meager wages had transformed from pocket change into a necessity. Her mother and sister depended on the money she sent them each month while they stayed in Egypt.

The breeze from the window pushed her hair into her eyes.

*A terrible crack. Henry slumped forward.*

Ginger startled, grabbing the arm of the wooden bench seat. She searched the street for the source of the sound but saw nothing. Just street traffic, horses, wagons … yellow light from the streetlamps.

What had made her jump? Had the sound been in her mind this time?

She gulped a deep breath, trying to steel herself into composure. As she'd done so many times over the last few months, she pushed the images out of her mind. *Bury them deeply*. Where she couldn't find them.

Her eyes darted past the other passengers on the tram. In a far corner, a man caught her attention. He didn't look out of place for this quarter of Alexandria—though he didn't wear a uniform and he appeared to be European. His suit seemed expensive, and he smoked a cigarette.

He looked up, his eyes meeting Ginger's. She glanced away.

An unsettled feeling rose. He seemed to watch her. Then she laughed at herself. *Ridiculous.* Her imagination must be as exhausted as she was.

The tram turned onto the main street in front of the Eastern Harbor, which curved beautifully along the sea. When the rains and storm were fierce, the waves came right onto the street, stopped only in some places by a sea wall. A promenade, called the New Quays, stretched alongside the seawall and was a popular location for tourists to stroll. Tonight, the mild weather and moonlight cooperated with the soldiers attempting to court the women they'd met while on a pass. The corners of Ginger's lips turned up and she was glad to see them enjoying themselves.

In Egypt, the British soldiers had much to celebrate—after the victory at Gaza in early November, General Allenby had pushed the army closer to Jerusalem. The campaign seemed to be the sole bright spot in what had been a terrible year for the Allies in the war.

A strong, fetid odor crept into the tram, and she wrinkled her nose. Lovely as the promenade was, with the swaying palm trees, the Mediterranean views, and jeweled sand—the stench of dead marine life and the rubbish produced by humans marred the space.

They passed the Kait Bey side of the promenade, heading toward the residential area of the cosmopolitan city. Ginger strained her eyes, trying to see the old fort at the end of the promenade. No matter how many times she passed the location, she thought of it with a sense of admiration. Thousands of years before, the area had been the site of the famed lighthouse at Alexandria—one of the Seven Wonders of the World. Now, what little remained of it had been incorporated into the fort.

Something about Alexandria broke her heart. So much rich history of the city seemed crumbled and faded—but the knowledge that she passed landscapes viewed by Alexander the Great and Cleopatra gave her chills.

She didn't have much time to play tourist now though. With the British offensive, there was an ever-steady stream of wounded soldiers entering the military hospitals. The men were often the most seriously wounded, too ill to board the ships heading back home.

The tram stopped at a cross street. Despite herself, Ginger glanced back. The man was gone. When had he gotten off?

Ginger disembarked. When she'd arrived at the hospital from the front and found a note from her mother requesting she come to dinner, the matron had warned her she shouldn't be out late. Tensions with the locals had been rising.

The heels of her shoes clacked against the pavement as she increased her pace.

She reached the three-story narrow house Lord Helton had loaned the Whitman women for their use. Nestled among a row of similar homes, it wasn't in the poshest neighborhood of the European quarter of Alexandria. Many of the homes provided shelter for the local British officers and their wives—at least, the women who'd come into Egypt before the government had banned the practice.

Unfortunately, as the war had gone on, the enlisted soldiers who had risen in the ranks were not the upper class, polished officers from war's beginning. Even the local Egyptians, who had at first looked at the officers with admiration, disliked this new crop of ill-mannered men.

Her mother, a dowager countess, bore the surroundings with as much dignity as possible. Lucy never ceased complaining about the neighbors.

Her mother's maid from Cairo—the only servant whose service Lady Braddock had kept—greeted her with a smile when she opened the door. "Good evening, Bahiti," Ginger said, breezing past her and into the foyer.

Bahiti led Ginger back toward the dining room. Ginger nearly tripped as she entered. Her mother and Lucy stood by the table, each wearing stylish evening dresses fit for one of the many white tie dinners they'd attended at their home in England. Ginger hadn't expected this level of elegance.

Her mother smiled. "Ginger, darling! It's so good to see you safe and sound." She wrapped her arms around Ginger's neck. "Though you're barely on time. We'll speak more at dinner.

Hurry, go upstairs and change." She wrinkled her nose at Ginger. "That scarlet hat clashes terribly with your red hair."

Ginger removed her boater hat and turned it in her hands. "I—" She frowned. "I wasn't planning on changing, Mother."

Her mother gaped at her. "You can't meet William looking like that."

*William?* Ginger blinked, her brain slogging.

Lucy poured a glass of wine from the crystal decanter on the buffet. "Mother told you about this dinner two months ago." She sipped her wine, and her eyes narrowed. "And don't say she didn't because I heard her. It doesn't matter to you."

Ginger adjusted her collar. *Don't start, Lucy.* She wouldn't let her sister dampen her good mood. "What am I supposed to change into?"

"I have a dress in your room." Her mother slipped her hands into hers. "Don't you remember? William is coming tonight. He arrived in Alexandria this morning. He's come to tour the house in Cairo."

*Oh.* Ginger nearly groaned. Since her father's earldom had passed to a distant cousin after his and Henry's death, all Lucy could talk about was "Cousin William Thorne" and how he'd stolen Penmore out from under them. He'd planned a trip to Egypt to settle her father's estate and review the details with the Whitman women. "I forgot he was coming."

"Hurry now. William will be here at any moment." Her mother waved to Bahiti to take Ginger upstairs.

Her mother's sudden need to impress him seemed strange. "I don't think I really need to change. I must be back at the hospital in a few hours. It's a dinner. And I'm tired, Mother."

"Clearly. You look terrible." Lucy glared. "You'll never impress him with bags under your eyes and that dowdy outfit."

*Ah. There it was.* Leave it to Lucy to be so blunt, both about Ginger's appearance and the goal of this dinner. This was to be a matchmaking occasion. William was a distant cousin and a bachelor. If he married Ginger, her family could regain their home. Ginger was the logical choice, considering Lucy's age. Lucy hadn't even debuted into society yet.

"I don't want to impress him." Ginger studied the twinkling crystal decanter on the buffet. Where had the crystal come from? "My outfit is what I'm allowed to wear while traveling. I've seen nurses reprimanded for wearing pastel-colored blouses and pearls—they're quite strict with what we can wear."

"Go and change." Her mother shooed her from the room. "Bahiti will see to your hair."

Too tired to argue, Ginger allowed Bahiti to lead her up the tight staircase in the back of the house. Frustration throbbed at the base of her skull, but she couldn't be angry with her mother over this. She didn't know any better. They moved past the two larger bedrooms, which her mother and Lucy occupied, to a small one facing the alley behind the house.

As Ginger ducked into the room, she sighed. She shouldn't have had to ask why her mother went to such trouble. Or why a fancy gown they couldn't afford lay on Ginger's bed.

She'd turned twenty-five in October. In her mother's mind—really, in the eyes of society—she was an old maid.

She looked at the ring Noah had given her. Her mother would have to be disappointed twice over. Once when Ginger refused to display an interest in William Thorne and again when she learned Ginger intended to marry Colonel Noah Benson, whom her mother despised so much. The last time her mother had mentioned Noah, it was only to discuss the ruin he'd brought to their lives and her reputation.

Noah had promised they'd marry as soon as they were able. Their encounter in Gaza had been like a dream—one she'd thought of often. Her heart had been so light for the week after she'd seen him, she practically felt as though she'd floated through some of the more gruesome parts of treating the wounded from Gaza.

Still, she pulled the ring from her finger and switched it to her other hand. It was better not to raise questions.

She disrobed quickly, and Bahiti came up behind her. As the beaded navy frock came over her head, Ginger stiffened. The dress's square neckline barely covered her scar. She shielded it with her hand, hoping Bahiti wouldn't see it. The Egyptian woman hesitated before pulling Ginger's hand away. Bahiti's expression didn't change as she took in the jagged letters S.A.F.

In her nightmares, she never revisited the day she shot her brother or the way Stephen Fisher killed her father. She revisited this. The knife at her breast. The smell of cigarettes. Stephen carving his initials and blood on his mouth. When she thought of this, the dull reality of the nightmare she'd lived came back to the surface. No sudden jolt or opening of her eyes could reduce the cold sweat that broke out on her neck. Time, they said, would help.

But it hadn't.

She pulled the neckline's gauze-like fabric over the scar. Bahiti's dark eyes met hers. *"Ana asef."* *I am sorry.*

"You don't have to be." Ginger swallowed. "It's a war wound. I have many."

She sat at the vanity as Bahiti swept her hair above her head. It took only minutes before the maid transformed her appearance. The upper-class lifestyle of her youth felt so distant, especially during moments like this. And what would her mother say if she told her she was considering leaving the nursing service to train as a surgeon?

She sighed and stood from the vanity. As she reached the dining room, she heard the deep baritone of a male voice, followed by the laughter of her mother and sister. William must have arrived while she'd been upstairs. She sucked in a deep breath and entered the room. She was capable of polite, practiced smiles.

Her mother and sister looked up from their seats. A man, only about ten years older than her, stood. He wore an olive military jacket and matching trousers, the Royal Flying Corps insignia on his left breast. To Ginger's surprise, his left arm was in a sling.

He gave Ginger a sheepish grin, his light-blue eyes warm. "You must be Cousin Virginia. I've heard so much about your beauty and kindness from the servants at Penmore." He came forward and took her hand, then pressed a kiss to the back of it. "William Thorne. At your service, my lady."

At least he seemed friendly.

He led her to the table. Ginger briefly met her sister's eyes. William clearly wasn't what Lucy expected. No doubt Lucy had vilified him in her imagination to the point of making him a rude country bumpkin. While Ginger doubted he'd been blessed with the same upbringing Henry had, who her father had prepared to be the next Earl of Braddock, William was likely from a polite background.

He ran his hand through his jet-black hair, shifting in his seat. A dimple showed in his cheek as he smiled again. "I'm quite nervous, you see. It's an odd thing, filling the shoes of another man you know little about."

"You don't need to be nervous. We're all eager to learn more about Penmore. How are you enjoying it? I miss home," Lucy said. Her thinly veiled contempt tinged the features of her oval face.

Why was Lucy so determined to be rude? Whatever William had been before, it wasn't his fault that the title and house had fallen to him. He was the rightful earl, and Lucy should know that. Ginger's mother shot her youngest daughter a sharp look.

William reddened and looked down at his empty plate. "Penmore is beautiful. I can't imagine a lovelier place to grow up."

Living in Penmore felt like another lifetime ago. Her family longed for it … sometimes Ginger did, too, when she let herself think about it. But those memories were linked with Henry. And Stephen lurked in them also.

Her stomach tightened as she settled back into her seat. As Bahiti came by with the first course, she sipped her wine. "Where did you grow up, Lord Braddock?"

"Sussex." He spread his napkin on his lap. "And—William. Please." He shifted in his seat again. "I'm aware of the complexity of my presence. My most sincere condolences, Lady Braddock. And to all of you. Losing your closest family members is horrible enough without having to dine with an upstart who took the family home out from under you."

If she was honest, William wasn't what Ginger had expected either. She hadn't given too much thought to the man who was now master of her former home. Thinking about him was too fraught with the guilt of what she'd done to her family. But he seemed to be a gentleman.

"That's very kind of you." Her mother bowed her head. Ginger could tell her mother was seething at Lucy for her rudeness. "We don't consider you an upstart at all."

"Regardless, I'm here to assure you of the honor of my intentions." William thanked Bahiti as she served him a soup. The familiar smell of cream of potato made Ginger smile. It was the one dish Bahiti made well. She was no cook.

William sipped a spoonful of soup. "I want to do right by you all. I've gone through the books, and it doesn't appear much was put aside, but I want to do my part to rectify—"

"How do you plan to do that?" Lucy interrupted, quirking a dark brow.

Ginger wanted to pull her by the sleeve over to another

room and tell her to behave. Even if Ginger had no intention of entertaining William as a suitor, she'd still treat him politely. Lucy's failure to do so seemed baffling. Then again, Lucy had asked what they all wondered. But asking so plainly was rude.

William held his spoon over the soup bowl, awkward and frozen. "Ah, that is—"

"Is there a Lady Braddock waiting for you at home?" Lucy asked.

"Lucy," her mother said in a scolding tone. Her mother wouldn't spare words for her later, Ginger was certain of it. It was entertaining, seeing Lucy be the one to clash with her. Just like life had been before the war. Ginger presently held the title of troublesome daughter.

"What? If inappropriate topics are dinner table fare, there's no harm in asking." Lucy smiled as sweetly as she could at William.

Ginger resisted the urge to cover her face. Someone needed to save William from his lack of experience. And from Lucy's impertinence.

He reddened further. "Of course, of course. I apologize. You're correct, Cousin Lucy. This is no time to discuss finances." He tugged at his collar. "And, sadly, no, I've never had the good fortune of marrying. But I'd very much like to."

Lucy's expression changed, a hint of a smile in her eyes as she looked at Ginger meaningfully. "Well, you've come to the right house."

Could she kick Lucy under the table? A marriage to the new Earl of Braddock would solve many of her family's financial issues. And it would put Penmore in their hands once again. Unfortunately, it wouldn't be something Ginger could help them with.

Silence settled on the table. Ginger felt sorry for William. His attempts at congeniality only resulted in the cringe-worthy nature of the conversation. Ginger tasted a spoonful of her soup, then asked, "Are you excited to see Cairo?"

"Delighted. Antiquity has always fascinated me. I'm hoping to spend several days seeing the sights." William sat back in his chair. "You ladies should come with me. I'd love the company and the chance to spend more time with you. I plan to stay in Egypt until the summer."

"Oh, that sounds wonderful." Lucy's face brightened. "I'd much rather be in Cairo. And maybe Angelica will finally be up for company."

Ginger stared at the creamy soup. *Angelica.* The thought of her made Ginger feel ill. The news of Henry's death had devastated his former fiancée. But she was also Stephen's sister. Stephen had disappeared that day too, and Angelica mourned him. Did she have any idea what a monster her brother had been?

Lucy missed her friendship with Angelica and wrote to her often. She didn't know Lord Helton's men intercepted those letters or the threat Stephen Fisher was to their family. It was too dangerous for Angelica to know how to reach the Whitman women. With no response from Angelica, Ginger had hoped Lucy would get over the friendship. She would rather no one in her family go near the Fishers again. But the more time that passed without a reply from Angelica, the more determined Lucy seemed to be to contact her.

Maybe Ginger and her mother had made a mistake by not telling Lucy the full truth of what had happened in the spring. But Mama had been determined not to spoil Lucy's memories of her father and Henry—or frighten her about Stephen.

"Are you certain it wouldn't be too much of an imposition?" Her mother touched her temple, where silver streaked her red hair. Ginger could only guess at her mother's embarrassment. She would be loath to turn down William's generous offer, but she still wasn't comfortable with the appearance of accepting charity.

"I'm certain. It would be an honor." William returned Lucy's eager smile. "I'd be a very fortunate man indeed, with three lovely travel companions."

"Just two." Ginger's eyes moved toward the clock on the mahogany buffet. They'd need to speed dinner along if she was to make it through the entrée. She hadn't planned on a full-course dinner. "I'm with the Queen Alexandra's Nursing Corps at one of the local hospitals. I'm afraid my work won't allow me the ability to leave. But thank you."

"That's very noble of you." William tapped his fingers on the chair's arm. "One of my biggest regrets is being unable to serve further during the war."

"If you don't mind my asking, how were you injured?" Ginger eyed the sling.

William noticed the direction of her gaze. He leaned back in his seat. "I was with the First Wing of the Royal Flying Corps—shot down during the Battle of Aubers. My left arm has been quite useless since then, I'm afraid. The doctors aren't sure if I'll ever regain the function."

"Oh my, how difficult that must have been," her mother said, a sympathetic look on her face. Lucy's lips twitched. Knowing her, Lucy was likely considering whether marriage to a cripple was something that would deter Ginger.

"I'm sorry to hear it." Ginger forced herself not to look at his arm, curious about what exactly had left him disabled. "I'm certain it's been quite a change for you."

William gave a disingenuous smile. "What I miss the most, to be honest, isn't the use of my arm. It's that I'll never be in the cockpit of an aeroplane again. I don't quite know how to describe the experience, but it's incredible. Being up there"—he pointed skyward—"surrounded by the blue heavens, with the birds and the clouds beneath you. It's breathtaking."

Lucy scrunched her nose. "That sounds terrifying. You should consider yourself lucky you're still alive."

Ginger bit her lip. But Lucy was also right, for once. He was lucky. All the countries of Europe faced a drastic reduction in the male population of her generation and many of those who survived were scarred beyond recognition, both physically and from shell shock. To redirect the conversation, Ginger met William's gaze. "I had the privilege of going on an aeroplane once last spring. You're right, it was magical."

"Really? You're one of the few people I've met—and perhaps the only woman—who has." William rested his good arm against the tabletop, seeming to relax with the topic. "Before all this, I would have considered myself somewhat of an adventurer. I thought it might be marvelous to try to cross the Atlantic Ocean in an aeroplane. Imagine the boundless possibilities for the future with all these new inventions they keep coming up with."

William gestured lazily toward his left arm. "Which is why I'm not entirely worried about my arm yet. I'm sure within a few years they'll come up with something to fix me too."

Ginger smiled. Whatever flaws William had, his optimism and enthusiasm were infectious.

After Bahiti cleared their entrée course, Ginger stood. "I regret to have to leave so quickly, but the matron asked me to return by the beginning of curfew."

"So quickly?" Her mother fiddled with her serviette. "Can't you stay longer?"

"I'm afraid I can't." Even in the European quarters of town, the threats to a young woman out alone past dark were serious. Especially after the Balfour Declaration. "Tensions with the locals have been increasing by the day."

William and her mother stood. "I hope I can spend some more time with you, Ginger. Perhaps in the weeks to come, you'll find some leave?"

She didn't want to encourage him. "Maybe so." Ginger nodded a good-bye at them. She hurried to change back into her uniform and then her mother walked her to the door.

"Cairo, then?" Ginger embraced her mother. "Are you sure it's wise? I worry about you going there. Stephen Fisher still hasn't been caught."

"I understand your concerns, but I must resist the temptation to avoid the ghosts of the past," her mother said, then kissed Ginger's cheek. "Besides, I'm certain it would be beneficial for us in the long run. If I'm not mistaken, William appears to have come to Cairo to find a wife."

Ginger gave her a tight smile. "Then perhaps he should look at Lucy."

Leaving the house, she pushed her guilty feelings aside, then walked back to the tram. The mild winter weather ensured a pleasant breeze from the nearby Mediterranean Sea. She turned back to glance over her shoulder at the house. William presented a problem she hadn't been expecting. The consequences of her father's actions continued to hang over her like a dark cloud.

Ginger tried to tell herself—as Noah had—that the government would have executed Henry for treason. Henry would have died even if she hadn't shot him. Unlike her father, who had shown some remorse for his actions and made a deal with Lord Helton, Henry had reneged on the deal when he'd tried to kill Noah. But a part of her wondered if allowing Henry to escape wounded would have been enough to save her family.

And she *missed* him. Her throat was instantly thick, her eyes misting with tears at the thought of her brother. They'd been close most of their lives. His teasing smiles and ability to understand her were unmatched.

She swallowed tearfully. *Damn it, Henry.* She was still angry at him too. He'd been so sure he was doing right by the family. Doing what he could to protect them. He'd lost sight of everything, including basic morality. She blinked her tears away. No matter how much she tried, she couldn't forgive him for what he'd done. No more than she could forgive herself.

Turning, she continued her trek. Up ahead, a figure disappeared into the shadows around a nearby alley. Her heartbeat fluttered. She could have sworn the figure looked like the man she'd seen on the tram.

Matron's warning about being out late rang in her head.

She quickened her steps. She'd almost reached the tram stop when she heard a voice call her name. "Lady Virginia Whitman."

Ginger's breath caught. A few feet from the stop, a motorcar idled at the curb. Leaning against the motorcar's door stood the man from the tram.

She swallowed, then looked around. A few people lingered in the streets. But her experience with Stephen had made her more cautious. She gripped her handbag. "Who's asking?"

He gave her a congenial smile. "Peter Osborne. At your service." He tipped his hat. "Sir Reginald Wingate has sent me to speak to you. Can I trouble you for a conversation?"

The commissioner of Egypt? What on earth would he want with her? Ginger blinked at him. Could this have to do with the deserter from the train?

His words made her step back from him. "Perhaps another time? I'm expected at the hospital." To her relief, the trolley bell rung, and she spotted it approaching down the street.

Mr. Osborne's dark eyebrows furrowed. "I mean you no harm, Lady Virginia."

She offered him a polite smile. "Then you're welcome to

come to the hospital to which I'm assigned tomorrow. The 15$^{th}$ General. Perhaps at three?"

He hesitated. "At three then."

Ginger boarded the tram as soon as it stopped, eager to get away. When she looked back, Osborne had gone. She shivered and sat, the unease she'd carried since she left the train only increasing. If she'd attracted the commissioner's attention, she might have crossed too far a line this time.

## CHAPTER FOUR

Jack finished plucking a shard of glass from the back of Noah's arm, then set the bloodied tweezers down. "I think that's all of it."

"You're a terrible nurse," Noah said with a grimace, then dabbed the bleeding wounds with the edge of his robe.

"Yeah, well, you're spoiled." Jack cleaned the medical supplies in the dim light. After Noah had jumped, they'd gone on the run, finally taking shelter in a boarded-up school once operated by Catholic monks. The Turks had seized the building at the war's beginning, then abandoned it. Abdullah's men had given them a good chase, too. Noah didn't quite know how he hadn't broken both his legs, though he'd grabbed onto a clothesline that had slowed his fall.

Unable to return to Jack's rented room, they'd spent all day waiting for sunset. Jack had done his best to remove the glass from Noah's arms, but the circumstances had forced some smaller shards to wait until nightfall, when they could return to Jack's room and use instruments. The wounds were puffy and red now and considerably more painful.

The map had survived but was the worse for wear. Some ink had smudged in the rain. Nothing to be done about it now. There'd be no map if he hadn't jumped. And he'd be dead.

"We'll need another disguise before we leave." Jack's brow set in concentration. "I only have one woman's burqa."

"Two overly large women? We may as well send up a flare." The mental image made Noah chuckle.

"Good point."

Noah pinched a deep wound on his forearm together. He probably needed stitches. The memory of Ginger leaning over him, stitching a similar wound he'd received in the desert, came back to him. She'd insisted later he try to cover it to avoid a scar. Blood seeped between his fingers. Her skilled hands would be a relief here.

Anger at Stephen soon replaced the thought of her.

"Do you think Stephen has been in Jerusalem the whole time?" he asked out loud. If only he'd thought to take a shot at Fisher while in that damnable room. Lord Helton would have been furious—he wanted Fisher brought in alive and had specifically avoided assigning Noah to search for Fisher. He believed Noah wouldn't hesitate to kill him, given the opportunity.

"I doubt it." Jack put his first-aid kit in his bag. "But you never know. Unfortunately, he's spent the last few years becoming an 'expert' in this region. Between his contacts with locals and his allegiance with the Turks, he's enjoyed even more freedom moving around the Transjordan and Syria than either of us."

Stephen. An Orientalist. Noah's jaw set. How many times had Stephen bumbled through his Arabic, disrespecting the local sheiks when he'd traveled with Noah? He had little love for this region or its people. Exploiting it, to be sure. "But if Braddock had an oil concession with Ibn Saud and Stephen knew about it, wouldn't he have simply tried to take the concession for himself? Rather than tell Abdullah about it, that is."

"Maybe he doesn't have the contract. Lord Braddock didn't completely trust him, especially not at the end. He could have put those things somewhere more secure." Jack studied the equipment at the rickety desk in his room. Expensive transmitters and receivers. He'd been intercepting messages from submarines in the Mediterranean, working to decode them. The work Jack did had the potential to save thousands of lives and now he'd have to abandon it for some time in order to help Noah.

The risk of pulling Jack away from his assignment was something Lord Helton had known. It only proved how much the British government prioritized the search for oil in this region. Noah had heard rumors of oil seepages throughout the Arabian peninsula, but had Lord Braddock known something more? "That concession must have cost Braddock a fortune."

"William D'Arcy paid tens of thousands to the Persian government for his concession—and that was just for the right to dig for oil." Jack pulled a crate out from under his desk and set it on the chair. "Ibn Saud would be a fool to sell a concession for anything less. And we both know he's no fool."

"Braddock didn't have that sort of money, in the end." Noah shifted, the cot creaking below him. "Which makes me think Stephen must have helped fund that concession." Noah bent his arm, examining the long, angry scratches above his elbow. "It could even be why Braddock was so in debt to Stephen."

"Probably." Jack set equipment into the crate. A wry grin lit his face. "If that's the case, you know how Lord Braddock made a small fortune in the oil business? He started with a large one."

Noah chuckled at the terrible joke. Jack never missed an opportunity to inject humor into every type of situation.

Jack's expression sobered and he shrugged. "My guess is

Stephen's not an official part of that agreement between Braddock and the Saud and that makes him angry. But he also has some reason for letting the British government know about it."

"Have there been oil explorations that far south?" Noah unfolded the map Abdullah had given him and scanned the area around the Arabian peninsula. They'd taken shifts sleeping in the schoolhouse, but neither had slept well. His eyes burned around the rims. He'd have to push through without rest. Night was the safest time for them to move.

"Ever since T.E. Lawrence started dealing with the Husseins, Ibn Saud's lands and support haven't seemed too important to the Brits." Jack came to stand beside Noah, crossing his arms. He looked down at the map. "You know, Kirkuk is promised to the French after the war. Your country is going to want to know about oil there."

"I may go to Baghdad from here. Speak to Gertrude Bell directly. I wouldn't be surprised if we suddenly forget our promises to the French." Noah grimaced, knowing how it sounded.

Giving up oil meant giving up power. With navies and armies increasingly dependent on oil for their ships and vehicles, only those in charge of the oil supply would rise to the top.

Whoever controlled it at the end of this war would be the true winner.

Whoever controlled the oil controlled the world.

Jack shook his head. "Don't get me wrong. I'd still throw my weight in with your country if I had to do it again—but does anyone over in Cairo or London have any idea what the hell they're doing with this part of the world? The bureaucrats don't know a damned thing about these people."

"No, they don't." Noah cleared the acid from his throat. His conflict about the deceit simmered low in his gut. "Though I'm not sure what the best option is. The Ottomans are falling apart.

This area is likely to dissolve into a chaos of warring tribes clamoring over the same lands."

Jack smirked. "Face it. No one would give a damn about any of that if there wasn't a fortune to be made in oil out here. I'm not saying other governments are less guilty of this, but since when has the British government ever colonized an area that didn't give back more than its share of natural resources?"

Noah folded the map in front of him. Jack was right. This map was only further evidence—learning the exact details of all the known oil concessions had been such a priority to his superiors that they'd pulled him from his work on the offensive.

"What's your plan with Abdullah's claim about Lord Braddock?" Jack moved to the back of the room, where a small wardrobe stood. He opened the door to reveal an arsenal of rifles, pistols, and ammunition. He pulled a couple of canvas bags out and packed two rifles into them. Despite his calm demeanor, there was a sense of urgency in his movements.

"I don't know." Noah joined him in packing. The cuts and scratches on his arms throbbed, and his body felt as though he'd been beaten by a sack of rocks. *Just a few more hours.* Then he could sleep. "I may not tell Helton about it. I can't help but feel partially responsible for what happened to the Whitman women. My investigation into Braddock exposed them. And now they're destitute."

Jack bent, gathering a few rations and canteens. "*If* the concession can be found, *if* it ends up being a location that has oil. *If* we get out of this goddamn city. That's a lot of *ifs*." Then he said with a more pointed look, "But if Lord Helton finds out that you knew and withheld it from him—you're looking at trouble."

Noah pursed his lips. "But as of right now, the only people who know I know anything are you, Stephen, and Abdullah.

The chances of Helton learning of it are remote. And if I can help Ginger and her family—"

"It might make you feel less guilty?" Jack closed a bag and lifted it onto his shoulder with effort. He put it back down and took a few things out. "Because that's all it will do. Her family isn't ever going to accept or like you."

"I know." Lady Braddock's last interaction with him resurfaced. Women of her class didn't show their outrage vocally, but her fury with him had been clear. In her eyes, he'd ruined her daughter and brought scandal and shame to her family.

"Have you ever told Ginger who your mother was?" Jack regarded him with an unreadable expression. "Just curious."

Noah hadn't told Ginger much of anything about his past when it really came down to it. "We never had the time to discuss it."

They finished packing, and Noah lifted his bag. The strap dug into his shoulder. A large cut on his arm dripped with blood. Leaving a trail of blood wouldn't be helpful, but hopefully it would be minimal. Jack radiated tension. With the entire city under martial law, nervous troops everywhere, and a strict curfew, their chances of getting out of here were low.

Jack pulled out a bundle from the back of the wardrobe. "I'll take the burqa. You can use this wig and cover your face a bit. I'll make a better-looking woman than you, anyway."

The rain had ended as they moved out into the dead of night, leaving only the soft petrichor against the stone. A few scraggly bushes that dared to grow in the gaps between the stones of the walls dripped. Darkness enveloped the ancient city, and they moved among the shadows. Jack was more familiar with the safe streets of the Old City than Noah was.

Jack had a motorcar waiting for them on the opposite side of the city, but they'd need to get through the walls without being stopped. Between the guns they carried and the map, even the most minimal of searches would cause their immediate arrest. One of Jack's contacts near the wall was the best shot for getting across.

The plan had always been for Jack to help him leave the city but not under these circumstances. By now, Stephen had likely informed Abdullah that Karim Sayed did not exist and never had. They'd be looking for Noah and had all the information they could ever want about him from Stephen.

Stephen also had the advantage of knowing most safe houses and individuals that had helped Noah in the past. His work in Cairo Intelligence had given him years of access to information. Lord Helton had attempted to contact as many of their allies as possible after Stephen's betrayal, but some had already vanished. Whether they had escaped or been taken by the Turks, they didn't know.

Noah followed Jack closely. They traveled through the labyrinth of a bazaar, avoiding the places troops typically gathered at night. The souk's stalls were closed for the night, but mice and lizards crept from their resting places, scurrying past them. Within a few hours, the call of the muezzin would float through the narrow passages, and the scents of cooking and spices would fill the air. Church bells would peal, the city come to life. The sun would transform the buildings into serene hues of sand and peach with a sacredness clinging to it all.

When he and Jack had come here long ago, the city had fascinated them. At sunset, the walls that surrounded the Old City gleamed like burnished gold. For as long as Jerusalem had existed, there had been walls around it in some form. The Ottomans had built the walls that surrounded it now, both to restore the glory of the old walls and for protection.

Now, they presented an obstacle.

To exit the Old City, they'd need to go through a gate. Scaling the walls without being seen was impossible. Most were nearly forty feet high on the exterior. And exiting through a gate meant presenting forged paperwork to Turkish guards.

Jack's motorcar waited for them outside the Lion's Gate, in the Kidron Valley between the Old City wall and the Mount of Olives. Getting to the car was vital—they could get away further and faster with it than they'd do on foot.

Noah had never felt more exposed in his life.

Though Jack had said nothing, he must feel the pressure too, given the weapons he'd brought. Were they headed straight into the enemy's waiting arms?

Jack ducked suddenly, then crouched by a low wall. Noah came up beside him. "What is it?"

"Four Turkish soldiers. On patrol." Jack's dark eyes peered out from the slit in the burqa.

They started in the other direction, but the scent of cigarette smoke and several soldiers laughing around the corner stopped them. Sidling up to a wall, they slipped onto the ground, as footsteps came closer.

Noah slid the bags behind them, then kicked his legs out in front of him. Crumpling his body, he kept a firm grip on his gun, pretending to sleep as Jack assumed a beggar's pose, palms up, hands in front of his face.

The Turkish soldiers came closer. Peering through his eyelashes, Noah watched their booted feet as they strolled past Noah and Jack.

Then one of them stopped. Poking Noah with the barrel of his gun, the soldier mumbled to the men with him. Noah's finger tightened on the trigger of his gun and he slowed his breath, feeling his heart rate dropping as he forced a state of calm. Another soldier chuckled, then placed a cigarette in Jack's outstretched hands. They continued forward.

When the soldier's footsteps had faded, Jack sat up. He pocketed the cigarette. "We may need to consider the possibility that leaving the bags behind might get us through easier."

Noah gripped the strap of his bag. Going without weapons would make it easier to move and to flee and arouse less suspicion. But that left them what? Noah had seven rounds in his gun. Jack might have a few rounds in his. "Where should we leave the bags?"

Jack glanced over his shoulder. "It's too late to go back now. So it looks like right here's as good a place as any." They were near a church. Wrought-iron gates pierced the walls. Jack slung his bag from his shoulder, then dropped it on the other side of the gate as quietly as he could. Noah did the same, and they started forward once more, in the opposite direction from the soldiers on patrol.

A cat sprang from where it hid as they passed, startling them both. It yowled, baring its teeth, then ran off, its feet so light that it didn't make a sound. Jack swore. "Damn cat almost made me shit my pants."

"They always seem to know just when to jump from a shadow." Noah loosened his jaw. He'd been clenching it as they walked, and now it ached. The wig Jack had loaned him suffocated—and stank, too. A bead of sweat rolled down his temple, and he wiped it away.

They went down another alleyway, drawing closer to the Temple Mount and the *Qubbat al-Sakhrah*. The gold dome of the famed mosque gleamed in the faint moonlight. Only a short walk remained between them and the *Via Dolorosa*, the famous path representing the steps of Christ to Calvary. It would lead them to the Lion's Gate, which might be the hardest part of their trip.

As they passed another alley, Noah heard the soft clicking mechanism of a gun being cocked. Noah reached for his gun.

Stephen stepped forward from the shadows, pointing a gun

at him. "What a surprise. Even with that ridiculous wig, I knew you in an instant." His gaze flickered toward Jack. "And who might that hideous creature beside you be? Take the face covering off. Now."

Jack lowered it, then winked at Stephen with a slight pucker of his lips. "And here I thought you wanted to pay me for a good time."

Stephen scowled. "I might have known. Wherever Noah Benson is, his clown follows closely." He sniffed and stepped menacingly toward Noah. "You know, I could shoot you now. I've certainly dreamed of the possibility."

"Then why don't you?" Noah glowered at him. How many times had he had the same thought? What he would do to Stephen if he ever got his hands on him. How he'd make him suffer for what he'd put Ginger through. No quick and painless death.

It stood to reason that Stephen felt the same way. He wouldn't shoot Noah now if he could help it. Stephen was a schemer. He'd want to be much more creative in punishing Noah. Stephen gave an exaggerated sigh. "As it so happens, we're able to help one another. You'd like to leave the Old City—through the Lion's Gate, I presume? Someone or something waits near the Mount of Olives. You're a creature of habit, Benson."

Habits had served him well enough before. He just hadn't planned for someone who knew his habits, like Stephen, to be the one hunting for him.

*Help one another?* Stephen seemed to have something up his sleeve, and an uneasy feeling crept into Noah's already-taut shoulders.

"There's no way you'll make it out of here without my help. Not after Abdullah alerted the Turks to a British spy in Jerusalem. And two spies? Imagine the reward I might earn for myself." Stephen sniffed. "But that's not what I want. I want to get out of this stinking city. To surrender. Therefore, I'm going to help you leave. And you're going to help me get back into Cairo so I can turn myself over to the authorities there."

He had to be lying.

Noah and Jack exchanged glances. "You want to leave this stinking city to go to another stinking city?" Jack asked.

*What the hell is Stephen playing at?* Surrender was the last thing Noah expected Stephen would do.

Noah's eyes narrowed at him. "And what makes you so sure I'll take you all the way to Cairo? I might take advantage of your offer and then shoot you as soon as we're free. You know I wouldn't hesitate."

Stephen offered a practiced and patronizing smile. "Because I've already wired Lord Helton and informed him I'm surrendering myself to you. That you've promised to deliver me to him free from harm. So, really, you only have two options. Believe me or face the Turks. I can guarantee they won't be so merciful."

Was it possible? Stephen was such a skillful liar, his tells were difficult to distinguish. And he had everything in his favor. Noah had no way of asking Lord Helton.

Jack shifted beside Noah. "What's option three?"

Stephen rolled his eyes with a heavy sigh. "Option three is that I shoot you and deal only with Noah, just to spare me the stupidity of your commentary on the trip to Cairo. Now, will you or won't you accept my surrender?"

The sound of approaching footsteps made Noah lift his head. The Turks on patrol were approaching, though they were still thirty yards away.

Noah had to decide now. If they saw Stephen pointing a gun at them, there wouldn't be a choice. Gritting his teeth, he fought the temptation to punch the wall beside him. Whatever Stephen was planning, working with him would only put them further into his control. But they didn't have a choice. The Turks would execute them both.

He inhaled sharply through his nose. "We'll accept your surrender."

Stephen put his gun away, a satisfied gleam in his eye. "Good. Now let me escort you to the gate."

# CHAPTER FIVE

Peeling back a dressing on her patient, Ginger paused, blinking rapidly as she tried to focus. This was mindless work. *Peel the dressing, clean the wound, redress.* Over and over, day in, and day out. But the mundaneness gave her too much time to think. And she was more unnerved than ever since she'd returned to the hospital from her family's home the previous night.

For what seemed like the hundredth time, she wondered what Sir Reginald Wingate could want with her.

The sharp sting of antiseptic burned her nostrils as she poured it onto a fresh cloth strip.

She couldn't ignore the voice in her head. *Be alert.* Noah had told her not to ignore her instincts. She'd learned the hard way that her "feelings" about people could often be more accurate than she gave herself credit for. She'd loathed Stephen for years before he'd shown his true nature. No one else had agreed with her assessment of him, save for Noah.

If only she could send a message to Noah. Speak to him when she felt worried. But her promise to Lord Helton didn't expire until the war's end. Lord Helton had offered his protection for her family, but only if she stayed away from Noah. That wasn't something she took lightly. Stephen was still out there. Her father's role and position had accustomed her to a certain sense of security and connection, something that no longer existed here in Egypt without Lord Helton's help.

She tied off another strip of cloth. The patient beside her coughed. Elsewhere in the room, the sounds of murmurs, groans, and bed frames creaking echoed through the high ceilings. Her good friend Beatrice had once said she could set a clock to the rhythm of the noise in a hospital ward.

As she finished her dressing, the young private she'd been working on stirred. "Hello, Sister," he said, blinking bleary eyes.

"Good morning." She leaned down to inspect the wound. "How's your leg feeling this morning?"

"Much better now that you're tending to me." He grinned. "Let's say we leave this place and go and get married."

She laughed as she collected her supplies. "Tempting as it may be, I wouldn't be able to keep working here if I did. No married women in the Queen Alexandra's. That wouldn't be fair to all the other soldiers, would it?"

He grimaced. "To hell with fair. Fair went out the window when this war started."

*Well, that had gone sour.* It took little to remind the war-weary wounded of their troubles.

The soft tinkling of a bell broke into her thoughts. *Tea time.* Miss Fitzgibbon insisted on such things. Ginger sighed and finished with her patient. As she made her way toward the tea cart in the 'corner of the room, she caught sight of a fresh crop of wounded men being brought in by orderlies. She wiped her hands on her starched apron and stopped where Sister Helen Wagner stood watching, teacup in hand.

"Poor lad," Sister Wagner said, shaking her head at one man, whose stump of a leg was bandaged above the knee. The orderlies lifted him from the stretcher and moved him to the bed.

"Any idea what happened to him?" Ginger asked. A Voluntary Aid Detachment nurse handed her a teacup, and Ginger accepted it with a tight-lipped smile.

"Railcar accident. He was going between two cars when they bumped together. Leg got caught between them and sliced it clear off."

Ginger gasped. The Australian from the train? The chance that he'd ended up in the same hospital as her seemed so remote. He wouldn't be here too long. Most likely they'd brought him to rest for a few days before voyaging back to Australia, his service ended. "That's awful."

Sister Wagner sighed. "He's got a rough road ahead. There won't be any pension waiting for him at home. The army only awards pensions to soldiers whose wound came from the enemy."

*How horrible—and unfair.*

"Matron." Ginger directed her comment to Miss Fitzgibbon as the matron came over for tea. She nodded toward the 'other side of the room. "I'd like to cut my break short if you wouldn't mind and start with those new patients right away."

Miss Fitzgibbon frowned at her. Normally the volunteer nurses did the initial work of receiving the patients. They gave the tasks of cutting off bloodstained pajamas and washing the patients to less experienced nurses, whose skills weren't as expansive as Ginger's. If it came to it, she'd explain to the matron her previous contact with the Australian soldier. But given the lieutenant's warning of consequences, Ginger wanted to avoid talking about that ordeal, if possible.

At last, the older woman's expression softened. "Very well."

One minor victory. Ginger ignored the curious stares of the

other nurses and set to work. Going to the bed of the Australian, she introduced herself and lifted his sick card.

"Private Emerson?" She scanned the card. *Will he remember me?*

"That's right." His gaze didn't meet hers. He continued to stare across the room, toward the enormous windows on one side. A lock of red hair—a similar shade to her own—hung down across his forehead.

"And how are you today?" Ginger pulled the sheet back from the stump of his leg and worked on his dressings.

"How do you think?"

She tensed. Some men licked their wounds and kept going. Far more, especially the most injured, behaved like this. The officers encouraged the nurses to help keep the men's spirits up. But how could they laugh and joke around those who lost everything and knew it?

"Christmas is around the corner." She forced the words out. Situations like this reinforced her preference for assisting in surgery. She disliked the sound of her own voice when she attempted to be cheery amid sorrow. It all felt hollow.

Private Emerson laid his hand on hers. "Please." His bloodshot eyes closed. "No pretense."

"Would you prefer I not speak?"

"Unless you know any verse. Something to distract me."

"I have some poetry in my room." She didn't, but she could get a book from the local bookstore.

"Bonzer." He settled back on his pillow, eyes still closed.

She changed his dressings in silence. She wished she could think of more to say to him. He'd barely looked at her. "Where in Australia are you from?" she asked at last.

"Adelaide." He didn't open his eyes. "And I can bet you haven't heard of it."

"No, I haven't." She waited a beat before going on cautiously.

"I've worked with many Australian nurses. I'm surprised they didn't put you with them here." With the overflow from the battle, though, the English nurses had been treating whatever wounded came to them.

He didn't reply, but his Adam's apple rose and fell. He didn't want to talk. She wouldn't attempt it again. For now.

When she stood to leave, his eyes drifted to the window once more. He didn't seem to remember her at all.

"Would you like to see if I can get you closer to the window?" She didn't know why she was trying so hard with him. But his plea on the train haunted her. *"Save my leg."*

She couldn't have. Amputation had been the only option. But now he faced being discarded from service without a pension for his sacrifice. He'd made the mistake of injuring himself in their eyes.

Private Emerson blinked at her. "Can you?"

"I can try." She turned to go.

"Wait."

She turned back to him. He peered at her, searching her face. A flicker of familiarity glowed in his eyes and then went out. "Never mind. I thought I recognized you."

*Should I tell him?*

She couldn't.

Shaken, she approached an orderly. "Can you help me move a bed?"

He looked as though she'd sprouted a horn. "Move a bed?"

"Yes, that's right." She didn't want to make any of the other wounded men move. Squeezing another bed into the row by the window seemed the best solution.

"To where?" the orderly asked.

"Over by the window. I want to fit another bed into that row. And then I'll need some help to move the patient."

The orderly scratched his head. "I don't think I can do that."

She didn't have time to argue with him. She tilted her head. "I wasn't really asking."

His mouth opened, his face reddening. He shut his mouth once more and nodded.

"Good." She smiled congenially. Pulling rank wouldn't earn her any favors, but she didn't care about that right now. Too many other worrisome thoughts troubled her. "Now, if you please."

As she went back to work, she passed Private Emerson once more. He didn't smile or thank her.

*No pretense.* She mused on the concept as she moved from soldier to soldier. So much of her life was filled with pretense. The request, while simple, refreshed her. The only person in her life she didn't have to pretend around was Noah. And she never saw him.

Their time together had been so brief. So passionate. She barely knew him. Their likes and dislikes, family history, and interests had seemed so unimportant when they'd been together. Their love affair had surprised them both. And there were times over the summer when she'd wondered if she hadn't just magnified the entire experience in her mind.

Her father and Henry had tried to convince her that Noah wasn't the type to take a serious interest in a woman. That he'd been using her. Sometimes their words rang through her nightmares, reminding her of the risk she'd taken.

"There you are." Miss Fitzgibbon seemed to materialize beside her. "You have a guest waiting to speak to you in my office. A Mr. Peter Osborne, from the Foreign Office."

Ginger lifted her chin sharply. *Mr. Osborne is already here?* She'd been so busy, she'd barely noticed the passage of time. Pressure built at the base of her neck.

She removed her apron, then draped it over one arm as she followed Miss Fitzgibbon to her office. As they drew closer,

Ginger tried to relax her shoulders. This conversation could go wrong in several different ways.

Miss Fitzgibbon opened the door for her, and Mr. Osborne stood from his chair. "Thank you, Matron. I'll require a few minutes to discuss a private matter."

Miss Fitzgibbon's dark eyes were on Ginger. "Is that amenable to you, Sister Whitman?"

"Yes, of course." She appreciated the matron asking. Many matrons listened to the chain of command without question. That the matron had taken the time to inquire whether Ginger wanted to be left alone with Peter Osborne spoke of her excellent character.

The door shut and Osborne faced her. In the light of day and at closer proximity, he was younger than she'd imagined—perhaps in his late twenties. His jaw was strong, with a full but well-trimmed beard and moustache a similar dark blond color to his hair. He was handsome. The corners of his grey eyes had soft lines that crinkled with his smile. He removed his hat. "I hope you're more at ease today, Lady Virginia. I realized after I left you last night how very startling my appearance may have been."

"Mr. Osborne." Ginger clasped her hands together in front of her. "How can I help you?"

Osborne motioned toward the chair beside him. "Please. Do be seated."

She did, stiffly, feeling encroached upon with him still so close.

He moved around to the other side of the desk, inspected the matron's chair, then sat. With his eyes still on her, he pulled out a silver cigarette case and offered her a cigarette, which she declined.

Lighting a cigarette, he leaned back in his seat, his manner elegant. "Lady Virginia, it's come to Sir Reginald Wingate's attention that there's been some quite irregular behavior surrounding you."

This must be about the deserter from the train. She set her hands on the arms of the chair. "I can explain, Mr. Osborne. I had two patients at once, both with equally dire wounds. The deserter would have died regardless of orders..."

He gave her a quizzical look. "Yes?"

"Is this about the deserter?"

"No." He drew on his cigarette. Smoke trailed from his lips.

Sheepishly, she set her hands back on her lap. "Ah." Heat rose to her cheeks. "In that case, please proceed."

He gave her a patient smile. "I don't think I have to inform you of the surprising discovery we made of your involvement in several government affairs last spring. The matter with your father was a messy business, one I'm certain you'd rather forget."

Her throat tightened. Just how much did he know of what had happened with her father? Or her? Lord Helton had promised to keep the information sealed. "I didn't know my involvement was known, to be honest."

"It isn't. But I'm able to know what I'd like." Osborne tapped the ash from the tip of his cigarette. "But you impressed Sir Reginald. Both with your ingenuity, determination, and discretion. Which makes you an ideal candidate for another task of such care and importance."

Her lips parted. He was ... *offering her a job?*

She settled back in her seat, the tension in her gut dissolving as the realization dawned on her. "Mr. Osborne"—she tried to think straight—"I'm flattered, but what little help I gave to the government was haphazard at best. I've always felt I muddled the whole affair."

"The reports we've had from Lord Helton have struck quite a different note." Osborne raised an eyebrow.

Lord Helton. He'd promised to help her—but sing her praises? "Whatever job you may have, I sincerely doubt I am the best suited for it. And I have my duties as a nurse, which are my priority."

"Yet your term of service is about to expire."

He'd looked into that? "Yes, but—"

"We would compensate you well for your work, Lady Virginia." Osborne extinguished his cigarette against the case, then dusted the ash from it, depositing the butt in the rubbish bin.

How well compensated? She leaned forward with interest. Money wasn't something she had the luxury of turning down anymore.

"The matter at hand is delicate and, frankly, Sir Reginald and I believe you may be the best person for the job."

*Me?* What on earth could Lord Helton have said about her?

Ginger bit her lower lip. "Would it be dangerous?"

The chair groaned as Osborne straightened, replacing his cigarette case in his front pocket. "It could be. Your discretion would have to be absolute. That would be the single factor that would determine how dangerous it is."

"Can I inquire more as to the job?"

"Unfortunately, we can't reveal much more until you've agreed to do it. Given us your word. However, as I think of it, it may be of use to have you continue some sort of work in a hospital as a cover, as we don't wish for your work with us to be known. You wish to attend the London School of Medicine, I think?"

Now his words truly floored her. Only a handful of people knew about that. She'd told Matron Fitzgibbons and a few nurses. And her former fiancé, Dr. James Clark. Who had they been talking to? She felt exposed and shifted under the weight of Mr. Osborne's intelligent gaze.

"Yes, that's my wish."

"An expensive wish, I believe. Your family has recently lost its fortune." He cleared his throat. "However, I may arrange a scholarship for you. As well as safe passage home to England for your mother and sister in the spring. In the meantime, I believe we could find an adequate situation for you to continue your work in service for the troops that would not require an extension of your service as a nurse."

His words made her head spin. Everything he offered would ease the problems she'd been worried about. It seemed too good to be true.

*But what about Noah?*

As it was, she didn't know when she'd see him again. Their promises to each other wouldn't change if she were here or in London. But the thought of being further from him made her uneasy.

The cornflower-blue sky outside the window seemed so peaceful, unlike her. "May I have time to consider your offer?"

Mr. Osborne stood and gave her his card. "I'll be at this location for the next two days. Then I return to Cairo. I'd like to have the matter settled by then." He replaced his hat. "Good day, Lady Virginia."

The door clicked shut as he left. Ginger stared at the space he'd vacated. For the second time that day, she wished she could contact Noah, ask for his advice. He'd be able to help her decide. She really had no one to discuss the matter with.

She tugged at her bloodstained apron, her fingertips trembling. The decision before her had the potential to change so much—and she'd have to make it utterly alone.

## CHAPTER SIX

Noah stopped the motorcar, cursing at the fuel gauge. They'd have to walk. After coasting on fumes for two miles, the engine had sputtered its way into silence.

Stephen leaned forward from the back seat. "Your escape plan seems to be riddled with problems, Benson. Or had you planned a suicide mission?"

Jack sighed impatiently and exchanged a look with Noah. His meaning was clear enough. Despite Noah's complete loathing of Fisher, something more existed in Jack's dislike of him: an intolerance of his arrogance. Jack had once described Fisher as *"the most punch-able man I've ever met."*

Noah placed his hands on the steering wheel. *The plan.* The plan had never included stumbling across Stephen in Jerusalem. And ever since he had, Stephen's presence had complicated everything. He wouldn't dare take Stephen to Fahad and Nasira's home. And finding his way to Baghdad to speak to Gertrude Bell with Stephen in tow was also an impossibility.

He had to go to Cairo. But first he'd need to wire Lord

Helton—or, better yet, make a telephone call—and ask him what the hell Helton wanted him to do with Stephen.

If Stephen hadn't been a target of such importance, Noah wouldn't have thought twice about simply shooting him and leaving the burden of transporting him behind. But Stephen had valuable intelligence to offer—more so now that he'd spent the last five months working with the Germans and the Turks.

NOAH COULDN'T LET his feelings for Ginger, or his own personal hatred toward Fisher, impede what was best for the British. And yet, each time he had to choose the good of others, it became more difficult.

Their best bet to avoid the Turks was by boat to a larger naval vessel and then to Port Said or Alexandria. But who knew when and where they'd find a ship? Naval support had been ordered near Jaffa, just south of Jerusalem, to aid with the battle up the coast. But he couldn't very well row that way and simply hope for the best.

And they'd left most of their weapons and supplies in Jerusalem.

The sunrise bloomed, the red streaks across the sky like fingers of an angered sun that was displeased at being woken. A trek through the Judean desert had not been in any *plan*.

"We'll have to walk. Get camels in the next village." Noah's tone was curt as he shed the wig and dropped it onto the front seat. He wouldn't allow Stephen to bait him. The provocative gleam in Stephen's eyes showed he intended to be like a burr in his boots.

Jack had disposed of the burqa and fashioned a headdress for himself out of a handkerchief. "To Beersheba?"

"That seems the best option." Noah opened the car door and stepped onto the rough desert ground. The wheels had bumped and jostled as they'd gone off the road held by the Turks, which had slowed their journey. He set his hands on the top of the car and looked back. They'd passed Bethlehem a short time ago. Even from here, he could see the signs of a village in the distance.

Stephen climbed out behind him. "Seems ironic." His light-blond hair had grown white in the summer sun. "The last time I saw you was very near Beersheba." He gave Noah a piercing look. "Just how is Ginny?"

Noah's fingers curled into fists. It would take a miracle to prevent him from striking Stephen at some point in this journey. *Then again, you never promised to deliver him unharmed.*

Jack climbed out and removed a bag from the back seat. The only drinking water they had was in it. He still said nothing, uncharacteristically. No doubt Jack was waiting until they could speak without Stephen listening.

Noah turned toward Stephen, stared him down. "What's your plan, Fisher? Why return to Cairo now? You're likely to be executed for treason."

"Perhaps." In his German uniform, Stephen looked thinner than Noah remembered, his face gaunt.

Could it be possible that he'd grown tired of being on the run?

The thought left Noah as quickly as it'd come. Stephen would never simply give up. He did nothing without an ulterior motive.

The sharp sting of an insect bite distracted him and he jerked his arm up, knocking away a fly drawn by the scent of blood on his arms. When he'd been in the desert in early September, several of his travel companions had contracted sandfly fever. He didn't want to replicate their experience.

"Hand me a canteen." Noah went around to the other side and held out his hand to Jack, who obliged.

He poured some into his cupped hand, then rinsed the dried blood from his arms as best he could. After capping the canteen, he handed it to Jack. Jack looked at Stephen, who watched them from the car, then dragged Noah in the opposite direction.

When they'd moved several paces away, Jack said, "Are we really taking Fisher back with us?"

"I don't see what choice we have." Noah leveled his gaze at Stephen and then glanced back at Jack's skeptical expression. "He's kept his word thus far. I can't see why he'd help us leave Jerusalem and then not allow us to get back to Cairo."

"I can think of a bunch of reasons. Starting with the fact that he could lead us into some bigger trap." Jack yawned. "It doesn't help that I'm exhausted and my head is killing me because I haven't had a decent cup of coffee for over a day. But I'm serious, Noah. I'm just getting a terrible feeling about this."

"So am I." The morning's soft bluish light had replaced the bright colors of sunrise. "But I'm also uncertain where my personal feelings about the matter end and the wisest course of action should begin."

"Spoken like a true Brit." Jack handled the butt of his pistol that jutted out from the holster at his side. "The Yankee in me wants to smack some sense into you. We can't trust this guy. We *don't* trust him. And it feels like we made a deal with the devil."

Noah gave him an impatient look, rolling his head, his neck stiff. Jack was simply echoing his own fears, but he didn't know what other option he had. "What would you do differently?" His voice was more clipped than he intended it to be.

"Other than put a bullet in him and claim it was an accident" —the muscles in Jack's temples moved as he ground his teeth— "I have no idea."

"Gentlemen, it occurs to me to offer my services to you once more." Stephen ambled toward them. "The Turks haven't yet abandoned their posts, but I believe the British Army isn't far, correct?"

He was right. A division of soldiers had been ordered to take the road to Jerusalem via Hebron and Bethlehem, but they hadn't broken through the Turkish line yet. Not that Stephen knew the details of the British orders. But, at this point, neither did Noah. While he remained behind the line and cut off from his contacts, Noah's intelligence was three days old at best.

"And how do you propose to help us?" Noah's gaze followed a black bird in flight overhead. Despite the sun, the clouds that were gathering in the sky were thick, threatening rain later.

"Instead of you having me tied up, you might take the role of my prisoners. I could get us as far as Hebron and then through the line. No one would have any reason to suspect me. But they will suspect this." Stephen lifted his hands.

Jack laughed contemptuously. "I'm never letting you tie me up again, Fisher." Then he pointed toward the distant village. "I think we'll find help in the Ta'amira tribe. Even camels. No way in hell I'm heading straight from the frying pan to the flames with your hands free to throw logs on the fire."

Stephen's expression was remarkably void of contempt. He turned toward Noah. "And you?"

His implication was Jack and Noah were not of one mind. Stephen knew how to use division to manipulate. Noah tilted his chin, then offered an unflappable answer. "Jack's more of an expert in the tribes than I am. I trust him implicitly."

Stephen started toward the village. "My intention is to cooperate. You do as you choose."

\* \* \*

As a Bedouin tribesman helped outfit the camels they'd purchased, Noah searched the surrounding area for Jack. He'd gone to fill the canteens at the well, toward the center of the hill bearing tented dwellings. A few scraggly olive trees stood out from the brush. Camels lazed near a crumbling wall beside Noah. The tribesman watched Noah with a wary eye, hands resting on his rifle.

Nearby, Stephen sat on the ground, his legs in front of him, his uniform hat now in his bound hands. He thumbed the brim, gripping it.

"Noah—run!" Jack's shout came from the distance, followed by an unexpected crack of gunfire. Noah whirled around, looking for the source, and the Bedouin man crouched down by the camel nearest to him.

The silence that followed was even more deafening. Noah's pulse raced, his breath hard against the dust-covered stone. He pressed his forehead down, pulling his gun out. The cool metal rested against his cheek as he lifted it, looking once more over the ridge.

"Jack?" he called out.

A shot cracked right past him, ricocheting off the stone and sending a spray of pebbles and sand on his head and into his eyes. He blinked it out rapidly, rubbing his eyes with his free hand. Jack didn't answer.

Stephen was gone.

Swearing in a low growl, Noah attempted to move further back against the wall, but the slightest movement prompted another shot in his direction and more dust. His eardrums screamed as though a shrill bell was inside them. The earthy scents of the nearby camels and their dung seemed heightened.

Where the hell was Jack?

The Bedouin man was still hiding behind the camel. "Where did the German go?" Noah asked in Arabic.

The man didn't respond.

*God damn it all.* He never should have given Stephen even the slightest sense of his lack of command. Who was helping him?

Noah dropped to his stomach and crawled low to the ground. The earth was rough against his face, and the robe he wore cumbersome.

The soft creak of a leather boot sounded behind him, then a footstep.

Noah stiffened.

An intense ache, quick and blunt, jolted the back of his head. Then blackness enclosed him.

# CHAPTER SEVEN

Despite her shift being over, Ginger made her way to the patient ward at bedtime. She couldn't sleep. She had to give Mr. Osborne an answer by tomorrow, and she still didn't have one.

The ward's familiar calm at night was comforting. No matter how weary or troubled she felt, being surrounded by the wounded helped her see her worries from a different perspective.

She approached Private Emerson's bed. "I came to read to you." She sat beside him. "Would that be all right?"

He tore his gaze from the darkness outside the window. "I thought there might be a sea view from here. I heard rumors you could see it."

She smiled and dug in her bag. "You're in the wrong hospital for that. The San Stefano is right on the waterfront. We're a few miles from the Eastern Harbor. But the rooftop is quite nice. There's a lovely view."

"And how am I supposed to get up there, Sister?" Private Emerson glanced at the stump of his leg.

Ginger cringed. Her comment had been needlessly insensitive. She didn't respond, knowing the route up three flights of steps would never be possible for him during his time here. She set the book on her lap. "As for a book, will Homer do?"

Private Emerson shrugged apathetically. Sometimes, with the more emotionally distant patients like him, Ginger wondered if her efforts were more of an attempt to make herself feel better.

She read to him until Private Emerson put a hand out to stop her.

"I think that's all for now." His look was thoughtful. "You read well. Where did you say you were from?"

"Somerset. In England." She pulled the ribbon to her page, then closed it. "My family's home was called Penmore."

"Was called?" Private Emerson squinted. "Did something happen to it?"

She hesitated. She rarely discussed her home or family with patients, though some had commented that they could tell her breeding through her pronunciation. "My father passed away. His estate was entailed away to a distant cousin." Her hands tightened on the book. "I had a brother, but he died in the war." Her thumb ran over the gilded printing on the cover.

Private Emerson held her gaze. "I guess in the end we're all human. War and death don't discriminate between the rich and the poor. It doesn't matter how good you are. How evil. If you're in its path, you simply lose."

The whimpers of nearby patients, their breath, caught her attention. The humanity. All these broken men—they weren't like those in the malaria ward or other rooms. What they'd lost they couldn't recover.

Had they all just been powerless to their fates?

*Am I?*

"I'm sorry. I didn't mean to pry." Private Emerson's voice interrupted her thoughts.

She gave him a taut smile. "No, not at all. I suppose I've always just felt that I could have done more to keep my family from all the destruction."

"And I thought I was safer as a brakeman for the train than out on the battlefield." Private Emerson let out a frustrated snort. "And then an emergency stop going down a hill took my leg." He settled further back against his pillow. "I think you take too much on your shoulders, Sister Whitman. You're here because you care for others. That's not the mark of a person who isn't willing to sacrifice when called upon."

It wasn't the first time she'd heard the chastisement. The pressure around her heart didn't ease, but she felt strangely better at his words. "The truth is you probably were safer as a brakeman—and you're alive. That's more than many."

His lips curled bitterly. "Did you know I opted to work for the engineers because I was scared? Almost blew myself up during training."

She furrowed her brow. "How did that happen?"

"Erm"—Private Emerson shifted in his bed—"the hand bombs. They have a pin you pull at the top. But you can continue to hold them so long as you grip the lever on the side. The instructor wanted us to learn to hold down the lever, then pull out the pin—to show us that if that lever was down, we were safe. But I fumbled it. Let the lever go too soon."

If that was the case, how had he survived? "Don't the hand bombs explode right away, though?"

"No, there's a delay of a few seconds. That's what saved me. The instructor snatched it and threw it. But I went right from there and requested to go into the engineering corps after my training. Thought I could spend my days in the army leaving the infantry work to others. So, you see? I'm a coward, really."

Ginger smirked. "Now who's the one taking too much on his shoulders? The railway and the engineering corps have been the lifeline of the entire Palestine campaign."

He didn't respond, but his expression softened.

She laid the book on the bed. "I'll leave this in case you'd like to read it on your own when I'm not here. Thank you, Private. Good night."

She headed back to her room. Still no closer to a decision, the time she'd spent reading to Private Emerson had been a much-needed distraction. More than that, it had reminded her how very much her work gave to her.

\* \* \*

"Sister Whitman!" Miss Fitzgibbon's voice sounded distant.

Ginger held onto the arm of the jaundiced soldier she'd taken for a walk on the grassy hill across the street from the hospital's main entrance. She blinked in the harsh light, facing the hospital. Matron stood there, waving a handkerchief.

She glanced at her patient. "It looks like they may cut our outing short. Shall we head back?"

The serene blue cloudless sky felt like the wrong backdrop to the turmoil in her mind. The hospital, a group of three multi-story rectangular brick buildings with a flat roof, had once served as the Abbassia secondary school of the Egyptian government.

When they reached the front entrance, Miss Fitzgibbons came toward her. "Sister … there's an officer from the RAMC here to see you. A Captain Stowell."

"Captain Stowell?" She'd never heard of him.

"In my office. If you don't mind. Any more visitors there and I might have to start calling it your office." Matron harrumphed as she took the patient's arm. "I'll see your patient to an orderly and meet you there." She glanced at Ginger's apron. "Tidy yourself first."

Splatters of dried blood crusted the apron on the starched and ironed white cloth. She'd spent the morning changing the dressings on her patients. She chuckled at the difference between life at the front and life at the hospitals. If her matron from the clearing station had ever seen her "this dirty," she would have been impressed with how immaculate Ginger's apron was. In the desert, there was no escaping grime.

Once inside the hospital, her eyes adjusted to the relative dark inside the foyer. She removed the offending apron and started down the hallway.

The quick click of heels scurried toward her and then the matron was at her side. "I'm afraid it's a rather serious matter, Sister Whitman, and I must insist on staying with you."

*Serious matter?* Ginger's heart dropped. What could it be now?

They arrived at the matron's office together. The RAMC officer, an older gentleman of medium build with greying dark hair, stood. He offered Ginger a polite nod. "Is this the nurse?"

"Yes, Captain Stowell. May I present Sister Virginia Whitman?"

Captain Stowell held out an envelope to Ginger. "Sister Whitman, I regret to inform you that your service with the Queen Alexandra's Imperial Nursing Service is at an end."

Ginger gasped audibly. Her ears rang. *What?*

With a shaky hand, she lifted the envelope. She opened it and unfolded the message inside. Her thoughts were too unfocused to read.

Miss Fitzgibbon was at her side and clasped her free hand. "This is an outrage. Sister Whitman's character and skill as a nurse are impeccable."

"Unfortunately, Miss Whitman willfully defied the orders of

Major General Hodson and refused to treat a deserter." Captain Stowell's face was void of expression. "A lieutenant of the 4th Lighthouse Brigade took up a complaint against her. After looking at Sister Whitman's history of breaking with protocol, it was determined she was incapable of continued service for the Queen Alexandra's."

The letter in Ginger's hand fluttered toward the ground, gracefully floating as though it were a bubble. Her eyes stung with tears.

"Isn't there to be a hearing?" Miss Fitzgibbon asked.

"They deemed no hearing necessary. Sister Whitman's record is against her, I'm afraid. The decision is irreversible." Captain Stowell's voice sounded distant as Ginger gripped Miss Fitzgibbon's hand.

And this was how her service was to end? In disgrace. Because she'd chosen to treat Private Emerson.

She hardly heard Captain Stowell excuse himself. The matron offered a comforting hug, then left her alone, telling her she would be outside the door.

Ginger sat in the hard wooden chair across from the matron's desk, numb.

No matter what she did, she always seemed to invite this fate. Maybe it was time for her to accept that it didn't suit her to be a nurse anymore.

Maybe she was ready for something more.

She'd been praying for an answer to the offer Mr. Osborne had made her. She'd go find him. Accept it. Her hesitations seemed nonsensical now. Why wouldn't she take a job and a way to get her family home?

And when the war ended, she and Noah would be reunited.

Wiping the moisture from her lashes, she released a breath. Whatever job Mr. Osborne had for her couldn't be much worse than anything she'd undergone already. She just hoped Noah wouldn't be angry at her for putting herself in the way of danger.

When she left the office, Miss Fitzgibbon gave her a gentle look. "I'm terribly sorry, my dear. You're an excellent nurse. Whoever complained is a fool."

"Thank you, Matron." Ginger squeezed her hand. "I suppose I should go and gather my things."

"I'll make arrangements for your departure. Most likely tomorrow. I must take you off your shift, I'm afraid, but you're free to wander the hospital at your discretion. Or perhaps go on a walk or into town. It may do you good. In the meantime, that soldier you've been reading to—Emerson, is it? He's asking for you."

She would have normally felt more pleased to hear about Emerson. Maybe she was finally getting through to him. Despite it all, her heart thumped. She'd saved his life. Even if it had cost her dearly.

The sadness on her face must have showed as she reached Private Emerson's bed. He gave her a quizzical look. "I'm sorry if I disturbed you, Sister."

"Oh"—she smoothed her skirt—"no, it wasn't you. It's been a long day. Already. I'm sorry."

"I can lend an ear. Not much more than that."

She gave him the most genuine smile she could under the circumstances. "What can I help you with?"

"I just wanted to say good-bye."

His words startled her. "I …" No, of course he couldn't be referring to her dismissal. *Stop being such a ninny.* "Are you leaving?"

"I just got the word. They're sending me back to Blighty." He looked down at his hands. "And I know I haven't been the easiest patient. So I wanted to thank you."

"*Save my leg, Sister.*" Would he feel that way if he knew she'd taken his leg?

She'd also saved his life. She had to remind herself of facts like that as well. Why was she so hard on herself? "I'm happy for you. I hope home is a comfort to you."

"They keep telling me I should be happy to go home." He wrinkled his nose. "I'm going home half a man. And who knows if the home I left even exists anymore? So many have died."

Their eyes met. It was a sentiment she understood well. She lifted the copy of *The Odyssey* she had left at his bedside table the night before. "I want you to have this. To remember me. I doubt our paths will cross again."

He took it from her, focusing on the cover. "Do you think any of it is true?"

"The adventure of Odysseus?" She raised her brows at him.

"No, not that. I'm not the most learned, but I know that's all fairy tales." He jerked his chin up. "About his wife, Penelope. Do you think there are women like that? Who wait no matter what?" He stared at his hands.

"Is there supposed to be someone waiting for you?" In the moments she'd spent with him the last few days, they never spoke of that.

"Her name is Mary. I've loved her all my life. But who's going to want a cripple?"

Ginger stared at the book's spine. "Well, it wasn't just Penelope who wanted him back. Odysseus wanted to go back to her. And he had challenges to overcome. He had to convince himself to leave a goddess who promised him immortality, to begin with." She smiled gently. "It was no easy journey he took to get back to her. But even when he failed, he kept trying."

For the first time since she'd met him, Private Emerson's eyes filled with tears. He blinked them back and cleared his throat. "Thank you, Sister Whitman. You've been a good friend. And don't let anyone underestimate you. You're a cut above."

"It was an honor to have met you, Private." As she passed the foot of his bed, she stared at his sick card. Together with his health records, made in triplicate and stored in the secretary's office, the sick card would determine his health history as he traveled. It would condemn him to a life without a pension. All because he hadn't lost his leg to an enemy the British identified.

Discreetly, she grabbed the sick card and continued on her way. What was one more rule to be broken? She may not always be able to do much to help the people she cared about, but she'd be damned if she didn't keep trying. Even if she lost the things she'd worked for.

She'd return a new card later that night and find a way to alter those records when the cover of darkness would shield her —records that wouldn't keep Private Emerson from a pension.

## CHAPTER EIGHT

Noah awoke to the scorching afternoon sun bearing down on him, his head throbbing with a violent headache. He opened his eyes and found himself upside down, his body draped over something hard. His face was pressed up against a leather surface that his disoriented mind couldn't identify. His mouth tasted of dust, and his body ached. And he was moving.

He startled, jerking his head as he tried to sit. But someone had tied his torso down. And the thumping movement came from a camel beneath him. They had strapped him to it.

Up ahead was another camel with a rider wearing Bedouin robes. From the position he was in, it was impossible to see much of anything and blood had rushed to his head. Noah swore, then called out. "Who's there?"

The camels slowed, and the rider brought both low to dismount. Noah struggled to keep his eyes open, his lids heavy as the rider came toward him.

The face he recognized. *Stephen.*

Dread crept into him as Stephen approached. "You're

awake." Stephen crouched beside him and untied the rope that held him. To Noah's surprise, Stephen helped him from the camel.

Noah stumbled onto the hard ground, not caring that a rock dug into him as he sat. He felt light-headed and flecks swam in his vision, the pain in his head like a spike in his skull. He fingered the side of his head and found a large contusion crusted with dried blood. "What the hell happened?"

"A group of Turkish soldiers came into the Bedouin encampment. Whether the Bedouin informed them we were there or they happened to come by, I don't know." Stephen took out a canteen. He uncapped it and held it out to Noah.

*Jack's canteen.*

Noah licked his cracked lips. He turned the canteen over in his hands, but didn't take a sip. "Where's Jack?"

Stephen's eyes were cool. "When I last saw him, the Turks had him."

Noah struggled to get to his feet, but his footing evaded him and he collapsed on his hands and knees. With a heaving breath, he managed, "We have to go back." An earsplitting sound pulsed through his head.

"He's dead, Benson. They executed him as I escaped with you. You would be dead too if it weren't for me."

Stephen delivered the news without ceremony, without pity.

Noah's fingertips curled into the rough ground. *It can't be. Not Jack.*

"No." The word ripped from his mouth, fierce and full of venom. "No." He glared at Stephen. "You're lying."

Jack was a fighter. He would be the type to go down screaming in a blaze—not at the hands of a firing squad.

It wasn't possible.

"What could I possibly have to gain by lying about this?"

Stephen smirked. "We detest one another equally, Benson. I have no reason to spare your feelings."

*Why?* The sand shifted under Noah's fingers, his temples throbbing. "Because you know I won't go anywhere without him." Noah's thirst was overwhelming, his headache unbearable. He sat once more. "I'm going back for him, even if it's to retrieve his body."

"Retrieve his body? Don't be a fool. You think you'll be able to get anywhere near Jerusalem again? They're looking for you, Benson. And I've put everything on the line at this point. They'll be looking for me too. Even if he were alive, it would be suicide. But he's dead, I tell you." Stephen nodded toward the canteen. "Drink some water. Rest. We're nearly to Beersheba."

Noah leaned back against the camel, using its warm body to prop himself up. He allowed himself a sip of warm water, then another.

*Jack ...*

He couldn't trust anything that came out of Stephen's mouth.

But could Stephen be right? Could his closest friend be dead?

His mind wouldn't accept it. Wouldn't allow for it. Jack had been more of a brother to him than even his own brother. Noah didn't trust anyone the way he trusted Jack.

He slung back the canteen, downing more water, then wiped his mouth. Putting one foot up, then the other, he struggled to his feet. "I don't care if it's suicide. I'm going back for Jack."

Stephen pulled a pistol from his robes ... the one Fahad had given Noah. "I'm sorry, but I just can't allow it. I'm not going back for that carcass."

*Of course.*

"You won't shoot me. I'm your ticket to Cairo."

"Actually, we're out of Ottoman-held territory now. I could

easily go and surrender to the closest battalion, have them arrange my trip to Cairo. But, frankly, I don't want to have your death as another crime I'm responsible for. I have enough trouble facing me as it is." Stephen had no sympathy in his voice as he went on. "And Jack is dead. There's no point in either of us going back. You're injured and likely to die attempting it. They'll hold me responsible for your death, and then where will I be?"

Whatever Stephen was playing at, he was fully in control now. He showed a restraint Noah wouldn't have returned were the situation reversed.

"I want proof he's dead." Noah winced and touched the wound on his head. What had struck him? And who? "Did you do this?"

"I had to." Stephen tapped his foot. "You were calling attention to us. Reaching Darby was already a lost cause. He was surrounded."

Noah examined the tips of his fingers. A trace amount of fresh blood tinged his skin. What had Stephen hit him with? A rock?

Stephen's confession disconcerted him. He knew Stephen to be a liar, and yet, during their interactions in the last day, nearly everything he'd told Noah had seemed true, or at least partially so. Noah was certain he obscured or omitted things for his purposes.

But would he lie about Jack's death?

Stephen still trained the gun at him, his stance unwavering. The cracked lines of the dry earth beneath his feet were harsh, the sun relentless.

"I'm going after Jack." Noah stepped forward, toward the camel.

The pistol in Stephen's hands discharged, the earth beside Noah's feet sending up a spray of pebbles. Noah froze and swung his gaze toward Stephen. "I missed on purpose." Stephen's eyes were flat. "Next time I won't. Don't try my patience, Benson. I truly don't need one more reason to shoot you. Get up on that camel, please, and let's go to Beersheba. From there you can send a message to Lord Helton and find everything is just as I've said it was. You may even inquire as to Jack's death."

Noah didn't doubt he was lying about shooting him. His frustration had nowhere to go, his hands tightening into useless fists at his sides.

Then it occurred to him that Stephen must have searched him to take the pistol.

*The map.*

He searched the pouch inside his tunic for it. Relief relaxed his shoulders as he felt it there. A glance at Stephen showed him watching. He smirked. "You see? I didn't take your precious map. In fact, I'm more useful to you than any chit Abdullah could have given you." He motioned toward the camel with the barrel of his pistol. "But please. Get on the camel. Then we'll talk."

Noah couldn't will his feet forward. Leaving here meant giving up on Jack.

Jack, who would never give up on him and saved him more times than he could count.

Yet if he didn't, Stephen would likely kill him. Leave him here to become a feast for desert vultures. And then where would Jack be?

Stephen sighed. "I don't know what she sees in you, truly I don't."

Noah's heart gave a painful thump. More frustrating than not knowing one was being manipulated was knowing yet being powerless to prevent the manipulation. Stephen had mentioned Ginger to remind him of what Noah risked by being careless.

He climbed onto the camel slowly, pulling it upright. Stephen also mounted and then brought his camel to Noah's side. "You see, Benson? Just like the times of old. You and I riding two dromedaries across these deserts. I simply cannot wait to return to proper society once more."

Noah scoffed at him as they started forward. "In what world do you live, Fisher? If I'm taking you to Cairo, it's to have you executed for treason."

"Perhaps. You may find that the information I have to offer the British government is reason enough to keep me alive—perhaps even negotiate a pardon."

*A pardon?*

Stephen was from the world of the unbelievably rich and influential. Noah had spent half the war watching how the actions of some of the rich and influential could impact millions. "Because of Lord Braddock's oil concession with Ibn Saud?"

Stephen removed a package of Turkish cigarettes from his robe. He offered one to Noah, who shook his head. *A mistake.* His head ached too much to move it much.

"Among other things." Stephen pulled out a lighter and lit his cigarette, looking cool and collected as the camels pushed forward. "You are interested in that matter, aren't you? I'm certain Cairo Intelligence will be as well."

And once Cairo Intelligence knew of it, Ginger's family would probably lose the only possible way for them to find wealth again. "Is there actually a concession?"

Stephen shrugged. "I was there when both men signed it. I believe Captain Shakespear arranged the meeting."

The idea of Lord Braddock signing an oil concession with Ibn Saud seemed far-fetched. "But what were the terms?"

"Don't remember the particulars. Lord Braddock was interested in financing oil explorations to the area—hence my involvement. The man had all the ideas but none of the funding. I'm uncertain what came of it all. I didn't have the time to track everything the man did. But I would imagine he made some arrangement for the concession in his estate—wouldn't you think?" Stephen released a stream of smoke from his lips.

Noah's hands curved over the riser on the camel's saddle. He didn't know what to think of it all. That Lord Braddock would have been involved in oil dealings wasn't wholly surprising. He'd been desperate to restore his former fortune. But what had come of the concession?

He may have to call on Lady Braddock after all.

They crested a hill. In the hazy lines of the horizon, the advancing army of the British came into view. Had anyone other than Stephen been with him, Noah would have felt relief to see his countrymen. But, as it was, Jack's voice rang in his mind, about how they'd made a deal with the devil.

Noah glanced over his shoulder, in the direction he'd left Jack. And though there was nothing he could do, he whispered a plea for forgiveness.

# CHAPTER NINE

The Continental-Savoy Hotel in Cairo had been transformed. Like so many hotels and large buildings throughout Egypt, the British had requisitioned it for their use during the war. To Ginger, it seemed an odd location to house the Arab Bureau and other offices for the Cairo Intelligence Department.

Standing inside the main lounge, she took in the graceful arches of the high ceilings and polished marble floor. A luxury outfit meant for entertainment, not the grim business of war. How many times had Noah been in this building? Both her father and Henry had worked here as well.

She clasped her handbag in gloved hands. Her family had been surprised when she'd turned up the evening before at the house in Cairo. Seeing the shutters removed, sheets pulled from the furniture had taken her aback and left her unsettled. She had never expected to sleep there again. Her family had helped William find a few staff members already.

The oddest part of it all, though, was her lack of uniform. She had come to Egypt already a nurse. The only other time she'd spent so much time out of uniform was the spring before, when the ordeal with her father had occurred.

Mr. Osborne approached. "Lady Virginia." Osborne smiled pleasantly and shook her hand. "I'm so glad to see you. Shall we?"

She followed him down the hallway. He looked over his shoulder at her. "Did you have a pleasant journey from Alexandria?"

Ginger hurried to keep up with his brisk pace. "Yes, thank you."

He stopped at a door, rapped with the back of his knuckles, then opened it. A man inside rose from a desk—Lord Helton.

Ginger stepped back, chilled. Regardless of how he'd helped her family, the man unnerved her.

*What is he doing here?*

Lord Helton's hair had been silver from the time she'd met him, but something in his appearance looked older. His job in intelligence couldn't be a peaceful one.

"Ah, Lady Virginia. How good of you to join us." He didn't emerge from behind the desk, gesturing to the two chairs in front of it. "Do be seated."

As she settled herself in the chair, the door clicked shut and Osborne took the chair opposite her. Lord Helton studied her, then pulled out a file and set it squarely in front of him.

She'd never imagined working with Lord Helton—he seemed to detest her. He opened the file and sat, adjusting his spectacles. "And your family? I trust they are well?"

"As well as can be expected. They'd recently come back to Cairo with the new Lord Braddock, William Thorne." Politeness dictated that she should inquire about his daughter, Victoria, but Ginger didn't. She wasn't interested in Lord Helton's snobbish daughter, who had made clear her dislike for Ginger. Victoria resented Ginger for having won Noah's attentions.

"That's very interesting. I'll have to call." Lord Helton nodded toward Mr. Osborne, as though giving him the reins to the conversation.

Osborne leaned forward. "I've brought Lord Helton up to speed with what we discussed in Alexandria. While it's regrettable that you won't be able to work with the QAs anymore, we have found you a post assisting a female surgeon in a local hospital—a Dr. Jane Radford. I don't suppose you're acquainted with her?"

She stifled a chuckle. As though she'd be acquainted with every doctor. His comment was oddly sweet and endearing, though. "No, I can't say I am."

"She's a fine woman." Osborne handed her an envelope. "She's expecting you tomorrow. I don't know what your duties will be specifically, but it will serve as the reason you shall provide to anyone who inquires why you're in Cairo. Dr. Radford is well aware that you may need more flexibility to your schedule than others."

Ginger set the envelope in her lap. She tried to keep her knee from bouncing, but she could do nothing about the fluttery nerves in her stomach.

Osborne lifted a wooden case from the desk. "We're also issuing you a service revolver." He opened the case to reveal the weapon nestled inside. "You likely won't need to use this, but we'd like you to have it all the same."

She blinked at the gun. She'd sworn to herself she would never touch another gun again. Not after the last time. She tightly clasped the fingers of one hand in the other.

If she'd never picked up that gun, Henry would be alive.

*But Noah would be dead.*

The case clicked shut. "Thank you."

Osborne's facial features sobered. "Now, as to the finer details. I hate to reiterate the facts I mentioned to you in

Alexandria, but I feel I must. Whatever we discuss here cannot leave this room, you understand?"

Even though she had never wanted to become involved in the world of intelligence again, the jittery feeling in her legs betrayed her underlying excitement. "I understand."

Rising from his seat, Osborne stood and crossed the room for a water pitcher and two glasses. He placed one in front of Ginger and poured some water for her, then for himself. Taking a sip, he remained standing and said, "One of our officers had a brief romantic relationship with you last spring, yes? While he was on an assignment involving your father?"

Ginger shifted in her seat under the weight of Lord Helton's gaze. She couldn't deny it with Lord Helton here. Heat rose on her cheeks. What did Mr. Osborne want to know? "What of it, sir?"

"I'll come right to the point. I understand you have had no contact with Colonel Benson since that time, correct?" Osborne's grey eyes seemed to pierce her own, as though he could find the answer he sought there. She glanced away, feeling exposed.

She'd made a promise to stay away from Noah. And while Noah claimed he'd never agreed not to see her, he'd told her Lord Helton had done his best to prevent their meeting.

Noah's ring weighed heavily on her finger. Would they know he'd given it to her? She kept her face blank. "No, I haven't attempted to communicate with him." A lie of omission rather than an outright one would have to do.

"Very good." Osborne hesitated, then his voice softened, as though he hated to make her uncomfortable. "And do you intend to resume that relationship with Colonel Benson in the future?"

Lord Helton's look was disdainful. "Were you to resume a romantic relationship with Colonel Benson, you'd be not only violating our prior agreement but also putting your reputation into question. You and the colonel were scandalously linked in the papers. I doubt the matter has been forgotten."

"Yes, thank you, Lord Helton." Any guilt she felt for lying to him evaporated. "I hardly need the reminder. And I can assure you the colonel and I have nothing to do with each other."

Osborne grimaced. "Not to worry, Lady Virginia. I believe you. And while Lord Helton sings Colonel Benson's praises, I'm convinced of your innocence in the matter. Your reputation"— he gave Lord Helton a firm look—"is not at risk. I've investigated Colonel Benson and worry that he may not have the best interests of the British Empire at heart. But you're an entirely different matter to him."

*What?* She absorbed Osborne's words with an outward sense of calm that didn't match the confusion in her mind.

She didn't believe it.

Noah would never betray the British. A feeling of déjà vu washed over her, from when she'd been less than certain of Noah's loyalties.

But he'd proven himself beyond reasonable doubt. Why would Osborne think otherwise?

Lord Helton remained inscrutable in his expression but watched her closely.

Not commenting on the matter seemed wise. "I understand, Mr. Osborne."

Osborne cleared his throat. "Shall we go on, then? I don't want to keep you in suspense." He looked to Lord Helton.

Lord Helton leaned forward. "Lady Virginia, were you aware that your late father had obtained an oil concession from one of the local Arabian warlords?"

She raised her brows. Her father had spoken about oil and the importance it held to the motivation for the British

Empire's presence in this region. "An oil concession? What would that entail?"

"Typically, it's a contract between a landowner and an investor, giving permission to drill," Osborne said, amiably. "Both parties split the profits at a certain percentage. Unfortunately, the details about your father's concession are unknown, other than that Ibn Saud appears to have granted it. We can't find any record or paperwork for it."

She held back a laugh. His attempt to educate her about a concession was both charming and patronizing, as though she didn't understand that part of it. She'd been in Egypt long enough to hear the word *concession* used, both for digging archeological sites and for oil exploration. "I know what a concession is, Mr. Osborne. I wondered about the details of the concession in question. You need the paperwork?"

"Precisely," Osborne said. "Ibn Saud and your father would have come up with a written agreement as to the concession—what area it covered and the terms, both financial and legal. With the agreement, we may see about doing oil exploration. As it stands, without the paperwork, the concession does no one any good."

In a typically impatient fashion, Lord Helton sighed. "The details are unimportant. As your father most likely obtained the concession under the auspices of representing His Majesty's government, he was not under any authority to get one to add to his own personal wealth."

Annoyance made the muscles in her shoulders bunch. Lord Helton said it as a fact but how could he know? The government would assume her father had obtained the concession illegally. Knowing her father, he'd likely been looking for a way to recover the fortune he'd lost. "Isn't this a rather trivial thing for the government to waste their time with? Aren't there more consequential matters to tend to besides hunting down and seizing the property of a dead man?"

Osborne barked with laughter and then stilled it. He glanced at Lord Helton, as though to assure himself that his surprised reaction hadn't been inappropriate. Lord Helton didn't so much as twitch.

Sobering, Osborne said, "It's a complex issue, Lady Virginia. We must think of our interests beyond this war. And oil could very well determine the outcome of the war itself. Our enemies are exhausting their resources. Think of what it might mean if Germany or the Ottomans find a fresh supply of oil—it might change the tide of the war. You could have a hand in preventing that from happening by helping us."

She stared at him evenly. He implied it was her patriotic duty. "Has oil been found in Ibn Saud's lands?"

"We don't know. But it's likely the land shows promise. I doubt your father would have arranged for a concession otherwise." Lord Helton stood and faced the window in the office, staring out at the busy street. "And our enemies know of it. They also know of the concession paperwork and that the agreement is in question with the death of your father. They may attempt to see what they can do about obtaining their own concession."

"From Ibn Saud?" Ginger asked. She was finding it difficult to follow Lord Helton's logic—and not just because he was being vague. The geopolitics of the region were cloaked with intrigue and conflicts between the locals that went back for centuries.

Lord Helton continued to face away from her, as though it pained him to have to answer her questions. "The more likely course of action is that they would attempt to strengthen Ibn Rashid's forces against the Saud and obtain a concession from Rashid."

Ginger's gaze bore into the back of Lord Helton's head. Facing her as he spoke to her was the minimum courtesy. *As though I'm not worthy of such a conversation.* She'd made it a point to study and was determined to prove she understood him. "Of course. Because Ibn Rashid declared himself loyal to the Ottomans."

Osborne lifted a brow, clearly surprised she knew anything.

Ginger put on a pleasant smile. "These are interesting speculations, Lord Helton. But if there's no known oil in that region, and the concession is nowhere to be found, and even if it is found, the government intends to seize it—I don't know what this has to do with me. Why ask me to be involved at all?"

"We'd like you to find the concession if you can. If you are successful, we will bestow a ten percent private stake in the concession for your family." Osborne settled his weight against the back of his chair.

A ten percent stake? Ginger's jaw dropped. If the concession produced oil, that could mean untold wealth for her family. "I —" She frowned. "That's generous. Unless the concession wasn't obtained illegally. In which case it belongs to my family."

Osborne smiled easily. "Well, I'd say that's even more motivation to find the paperwork. If your father did nothing illegal, it would be in your family's best interest to prove it. You won't be able to do so without the agreement."

*He has a point.* "The logical first step would be to ask my mother about this."

"We have. She claims to know nothing of it." Lord Helton still didn't turn around from the window.

*Claims to.* His doubt was clear enough. When had they talked to her mother? "And you think I'll have more success?"

"Hopefully." Mr. Osborne looked apologetic at Lord Helton's rudeness. "Besides which, we're offering you significantly more motivation to learn what happened to the paperwork—and find it for us, if you can."

Ginger raised her chin. "You have men in your office dedicated to this sort of thing, don't you? Wouldn't it be easier to ask them?"

Osborne rubbed the bridge of his nose. "We've made little headway in discovering anything. And your father's most trusted associates seem to go mute when we approach them. We're hoping they might be more congenial to his daughter."

"You were also at home prior to your father's death. You might investigate his activities during those last days." Lord Helton's voice was flat.

"And if I'm unable to accomplish what you want? I may learn nothing about the concession—or be able to find the paperwork."

Lord Helton turned his profile. "Then you'll get a safe passage to England and a good day."

The man was awful. If he hadn't done so much to help her family in the spring, she'd be tempted to treat him with equal contempt. "Can you give me a starting point, at least? Surely you must know something more about the matter. Or send an envoy to Ibn Saud? He'd certainly know about it."

"Ibn Saud's Ikhwan army is currently at odds with Sherif Hussein, which makes our situation with him tenuous. He's also at war with Ibn Rashid. Sending a diplomatic mission to him right now could be a waste of men and extremely dangerous, especially when we need our best men in Palestine now." Lord Helton's tone was clipped, but at least he did her the favor of assuming she understood. Perhaps she'd proven she could keep up earlier.

Osborne's grey eyes were warmer. "To answer your other question—no, we know little. However, we have a name that you might find useful: Freddy Mortimer. Apparently, the man was connected to the concession. How, we don't know. And I would caution you that asking about him isn't likely to help. We've tried to find more about the man, without results. But it's a start, I suppose."

She had never heard the name before, but it was better than nothing. She was completely inadequate for this job.

Lord Helton rose from his seat. "We appreciate your willingness to help, Lady Virginia, and we'll apprise you with further information as we have it. Mr. Osborne will meet with you tomorrow at the hospital and give you any further instructions we might have."

His posture indicated the conversation was over. Ginger stood and gathered her things. "Mr. Osborne, give me a moment to speak to Lady Virginia."

Osborne's brow furrowed. He looked apologetically toward Ginger as he left the office, closing the door behind him.

Lord Helton clasped his hands behind his back. "I feel the need to make myself clear. Nothing has changed regarding my wishes with Colonel Benson. Hopefully, your emotional attachment has ended, but if not, let me remind you of your promises."

She sucked her cheeks in. Lord Helton wasn't the sort of man to trifle with. "Our arrangement wasn't that I'm not allowed to be in love with him, Lord Helton. It was that I would cease contact with him until the end of the war. I've done as you asked."

"I know what our arrangement was." Lord Helton's face was stern. "I also know what I've commanded of Colonel Benson. I can't keep the man from seeking you out, but I will not have you distracting him once again, is that clear? Unless you'd like the newspapers filled with the sordid crimes of your father."

Her jaw set. Lord Helton had protected her family from complete ruin by keeping her father's crimes concealed. As far as Ginger knew, only a handful of people were aware of her father's misdeeds.

"Are you suggesting that—even now—you'd be willing to allow my father's name to be besmirched and my family ruined simply to punish me?" Ginger stared at him, appalled.

"We had an arrangement, Lady Virginia. I can't help it if the true nature of your father's crimes sees the light of day. They deserved to be and I spared you from that as a reward for your service to our country. Don't forget that. And do remind Colonel Benson of the fact when he seeks you out again."

She stood unnaturally still, her spine rigid. He knew Noah had found her in Palestine. She didn't meet his gaze, afraid of what he'd see there. Would he be furious at her for breaking her promise?

He set both hands on the desk and leaned forward. "You are to keep your distance, understood? I don't care what means you employ to convince Colonel Benson that you are not available to him. Just do it."

Swallowing hard, she took her leave of Lord Helton, allowing Osborne to escort her back toward the entrance of the Savoy.

"I apologize about Lord Helton," Osborne said as they walked toward the lobby. "The man is an insufferable snob. But he's an excellent spymaster. Perhaps the two go hand in hand." A smile lit his eyes. "Fortunately for us, I'll be handling most of the work with you. Lord Helton is just overseeing occasionally. I'm very much looking forward to working with you, Lady Virginia."

Ginger said good-bye, then left him in the lobby. Thank goodness she'd be working with Osborne instead of Lord Helton.

Lord Helton's threats to release information about her father unnerved her. Even now, her family enjoyed relative acceptance in society, despite their lack of funds. But if her father's crimes were exposed, her family would never be admitted to polite society again.

Diving into the world her father had been so deeply involved in before his death worried her. She shivered.

Who knew what skeletons she might uncover?

# CHAPTER TEN

Ginger had just arrived home from her meeting at the Savoy and stood in the foyer of the Braddocks' home in Cairo, removing her hat. A servant had helped her inside, but it didn't appear anyone other than the servants were here.

Her eyes drifted to the closed door of her father's study. She had avoided it. The whole house felt rather haunted. She half-expected her father to come to the doorway, pipe in hand. Or Henry.

Their ghosts crept around this place, reminding her of their last minutes together and the shocking violence.

She swallowed, then crossed toward the staircase. Though her own bedroom held its own set of frightening memories, she would rather be in there. Especially when no one else was home.

Bounding up the stairs, she rushed to her room, then closed the door. She set her back to the wall, panting, the wooden box containing the pistol tucked under her arm, her hat in her hand. Her trunk remained at the foot of her bed, closed and unpacked, as she'd requested. She opened it and pushed some of her nursing uniforms to the side, then plunked the pistol case inside it.

Sitting on the floor, she set her elbow on the edge of the open trunk and covered her eyes with her hands. She'd thought she could come back here. That she was stronger now.

Her meeting had made her doubt that.

Looking down at her hand, she fingered Noah's ring. The questions it could raise worried her. She removed the ring, then placed it in a jewelry pouch.

Her finger felt strangely naked. Strange, given that she'd only worn it for a few weeks. She closed the trunk and stood. *Noah's at the front. He won't know you removed it.*

When her family had come to Cairo, they'd thrown themselves into society. Yet those friends and social circles had largely abandoned them this past year. Ginger's name had been tarnished so profoundly that even the boldest retraction couldn't restore it.

By coming to Cairo, she'd face taking part in society again. Dread filled her.

She went to the wardrobe in the room and pushed it open. It was empty, and the scent of warm cedar greeted her. After the spring, she'd sold almost all her frocks and jewelry. They had sold everything of value in the house to pay off some of her father's enormous debts.

Fortunately, the largest debt her father had owed was to Stephen and, though that debt remained unsettled, Stephen wouldn't return to demand repayment. The house and furniture alone had remained unsold, as there was a question as to its role in the estate. Her father's solicitor in Cairo had advised them that the new earl might have a say in the whole matter.

She didn't have a single thing she could wear to a ball—unless her mother had brought from Alexandria that dress she'd purchased for the dinner with William. Her wardrobe was severely limited, and what little she'd kept would serve for one or two outings before the gossipers in Cairo society took notice. They needed little encouragement to skewer her.

Perhaps Lucy would have something she could wear. They were nearly the same size, though Lucy had grown about an inch taller. Ginger's recent time on the front had also made her slenderer than her younger sister. Rations of tinned foods and bully beef seemed to have that effect on almost everyone.

Ginger left the room and headed toward Lucy's. Once inside, she was surprised at how quickly Lucy had accommodated herself. The décor was sparse but comfortable, as though Lucy had brought most of her things from Alexandria. Ginger went to her wardrobe and opened the doors. As she did, a hatbox, poorly situated inside, tumbled forward.

The lid of the box popped off, the contents spilling. Ginger leaned forward to collect the assortment of envelopes and postcards when familiar handwriting caught her attention.

The style was distinct, and she'd been the recipient of weekly letters from the sender for years.

*Stephen.*

A chill went through her. Ginger lifted the letter. It pulled free from a bundle—all from Stephen.

MY DARLING LUCY,
*I long to see you, feel your lips pressed to mine once more ...*

GINGER'S PULSE pounded in her ears. *A love letter?*

She skimmed it faster, feeling sick, light-headed. She could barely concentrate on the contents, her face flushing. *What on earth?* When had Stephen sent Lucy love letters? And why?

Stephen had claimed for years that Ginger was the object of his desires, and his obsession had been dangerous.

What could he possibly have been up to?

She scanned the letter for a date but found none. The absence of envelopes also stymied the satisfaction of her curiosity.

"I'll just be a minute ..." Lucy's voice came from just outside the door, then the door opened.

Ginger jerked her head up as Lucy froze in the doorway.

*Fantastic.*

Lucy's eyebrows drew together, then her eyes moved to the letter in Ginger's hands.

Ginger lowered the letter. Nothing could be done now. Lucy had caught her with the evidence.

Lucy stormed up to Ginger, hand outstretched. "What in God's name are you doing? Searching my things?" She snatched the letter, then her face paled.

"No, I came to see if I could borrow a dress, and the hatbox fell." Ginger tried to remain composed. "When did Stephen write this?"

"Don't you dare ask me questions. It's none of your concern." Lucy's dark eyes flashed. She gathered her letters, then replaced them. "Anyhow, it doesn't matter. It was a long time ago, and none of us have heard from him for months." Tears filled her eyes. "And I tried to call on Angelica yesterday and she wouldn't see me. I'm an outcast in society now."

Demanding an answer from Lucy would be fruitless. In Lucy's eyes, Ginger had violated her privacy about a secret matter. And she believed Ginger was to blame for their position, though Ginger and her mother had explained that losing the family fortune had to do with their father's debts. The scandal that had erupted between Ginger and Noah before her father's death had overshadowed everything.

Ginger put a hand on Lucy's shoulder. "Lucy, you aren't an outcast. We may not have the money we once did, but we still have a place in respectable society."

"Do we?" Lucy placed the hatbox back into her wardrobe, then shut the doors. "I'm not so sure. I can hardly expect to keep up with my friends, even though William has been so generous and paid for everything we've done."

Had it been only the week earlier, Ginger would have brushed Lucy's concerns to the side. But she'd need to return to society if she was to ask questions regarding her father's associates. And though their worries stemmed from different motivations, she felt the sting of being unprepared to fit into the world they'd once occupied.

She glanced at the closed wardrobe doors. "Lucy, what advances did Stephen make toward you?" Had she made a mistake by not disclosing everything about Stephen and her father to her family? Her mother had known some of it, but Lucy knew nothing of what Stephen really was.

Lucy's face grew cross once again. "Those letters were meant for me and me alone. And they're all I have."

*Had her sister been in love with Stephen?*

A nauseated feeling made her throat clench. Stephen was nearly ten years Lucy's senior. How could Ginger have been so unaware? The fierce tug of sisterly protection gripped Ginger. "Stephen is not the sort of man for you. Please trust me on this. I haven't always shared as much as I should have, perhaps, but he would have only brought you harm. Be glad those letters are all you have."

"I'll thank you not to lecture me on what sort of man is good for me. Not after you had that scandalous affair with Noah Benson. Everyone else may not know the truth, but I do. And then you ignore poor cousin William and won't even consider his attentions." Lucy's words were defensive and biting.

Ginger lifted her chin sharply. "If cousin William suits you, then you're free to encourage him yourself. You're right, I made a fool out of myself for love once. I have no interest in being the object of William's desires." How could she convince Lucy to trust her about Stephen? And William?

"You think it hasn't crossed my mind?" Lucy tugged her gloves off, then crossed the room to lay them on her vanity. "But I'm not the one who has caught his eye, am I? Speaking of which, he was inquiring if you could join us for dinner at Shepheard's."

Ginger regretted her own words. Lucy was only seventeen, after all. She wouldn't be eighteen for another two months. And while other women married at such a young age, Lucy had never had the chance to experience life as a young woman outside of the war. Encouraging her to marry William was hypocritical, especially when she'd learned the hard way what accepting the wrong marriage proposal could do. "I would be happy to. But I'll need a dress." Ginger offered a rueful smile. "Which is why I came in."

"You should have just waited to ask." Lucy sat at her vanity and unpinned her hair.

The hostility between them discouraged Ginger. She couldn't seem to find any way to relate to Lucy. The gap in their ages had always made it difficult. Henry had been the sibling she'd been closest to while Lucy was the baby watching them from a distance.

Ginger sighed. She didn't regret discovering the letters. She'd need to think of the best way to handle what she'd learned. But Lucy didn't need another reason to resent her. Ginger came up behind her. "May I?" She lifted a pin.

Lucy paused, hand in midair, then nodded. Ginger leaned down, searching for the remaining pins. "I don't have the same level of skill that Bahiti does, but I'm happy to help with your hair if you'd like. Not having a maid the last three years forced me to learn to do my hair."

Lucy smirked. "Yes, you're the domestic one now."

"Hardly." Ginger reached for the silver-handled brush on the vanity. "I can boil a kettle of water for tea. Open a tin. That's about it. I'd make a sorry housewife without a cook." She drew the brush through her sister's thick, dark hair.

"At least you can be a nurse. I have nothing to recommend me." Lucy rested her hands on her lap. "I'm not even as pretty as you are."

Ginger hugged Lucy from behind, settling her chin on Lucy's shoulder. Their eyes met in the mirror's reflection. "We're two sides of the same coin." Ginger searched their reflections. "Whitman women. Daughters of the Earl of Braddock. That's not nothing. You were raised in a way that gives you a great deal to recommend you. And you're much more beautiful than I."

The corners of Lucy's mouth tipped in a smile and she heaved a relenting sigh. "All right. I'll lend you a dress. You don't have to fib."

Ginger laughed, her heart warming.

They both dressed and readied themselves for dinner. When they'd finished, Ginger glanced in the mirror. Last spring, Lucy had refused to rid herself of a single outfit. Though it had frustrated Ginger, she was glad Lucy had been so stubborn. They'd never have the money for a dress like this now.

Down the stairs, William and her mother waited for them. A suave smile spread on William's lips as he saw Ginger with Lucy. "Cousin Virginia. I'm so happy Lucy could convince you to join us."

Ginger adjusted the tops of her long gloves. Lucy's fashion-forward sensibilities had a downside—Ginger had never been such a risk-taker with fashion. She felt quite bare, especially given how vastly different the elegant gown was from her uniform. "I'm happy to join you." The smile on her mother's face brightened.

*Not her too.*

How could she explain to her family that there was no hope of anything developing between her and William?

William had arranged for a driver. As Ginger climbed into the car, it occurred to her that William must have his own source of independent wealth. She knew nothing about his family or occupation. Perhaps a letter to her aunt or grandmother in England would be in order.

They started through the streets of Cairo and William turned from the front seat to look back at her. "It's been such an adventure here." He held on to his hat. "We went to the most remarkable souk today. It's a pity you couldn't join us. Your mother and Lucy had to teach me to haggle, which I enjoyed immensely. I can't say I knew the true value of anything, but I bought a replica of a sarcophagus I plan to take back to England. It's enormous."

Ginger laughed lightly. "A replica of a sarcophagus? What on earth are you planning to do with that?" She could picture the horrified expressions on the faces of the servants at Penmore. Where would he put it? The foyer?

"I'm not sure yet." William winked. "But I may tell my friends that it's real and contains a mummy. That would be a riot, wouldn't it?"

The scent of petrol filled Ginger's nose. As they approached the main road, the sights and sounds of Cairo gave her a strangely settled feeling, like home. Street peddlers and beggars moved in the shadows. Aromas of animals, dust, and cooking were strong. Carts and carriages passed by on the street, drawn by both camels and horses, and street dogs darted between them, nosing for scraps in the trash that lay along the sides of the roads. Yet all of it was wonderfully familiar.

"Cairo is exciting. Have you been to the museum yet?" Ginger smiled, thinking of her own enthusiasm for the antiquities of Egypt when her family had arrived. "I nearly wanted to trade my nurse's cape for a pith helmet after spending time amongst the mummies."

"We may go tomorrow. If you'd like to come. Your mother tells me you had a penchant for reading books about Ancient Egypt before the war. You'd be a useful guide." William gave her a hopeful look.

Ginger heard Lucy's audible sigh beside her. Thankfully, the noise from the crowded streets had likely made it impossible for William to hear. "Unfortunately, I'm starting my work at a new hospital tomorrow. It's a bit of a different assignment, one that will allow me to come home after work—I'll be working as an assistant for a female surgeon."

William nodded a few times. "Good. Very good. A female surgeon. That's marvelous."

"You think so?" Ginger furrowed her brow. She wasn't accustomed to men who were supportive of the notion of female physicians. Even the army hadn't known what to do with them.

"Oh, yes. There's nothing quite so admirable as the women seeking to improve the circumstances of their sex." William motioned toward her. "I think this war has proven how capable women are of assisting with roles such as those."

"Goodness," her mother said with a sparkle in her eye. "A man who supports Ginger's wild ideas. What a notion. We can't have two of you in the family."

Ginger gritted her teeth. Her mother would think of it as something that would Ginger look at William favorably. She needed to tell Mama about Noah and soon. Disappointing her would be best done quickly.

But William had done her the favor of making a relatively easy segue into the conversation about medical school. "As it so happens," Ginger said, her heart rate speeding, "I'm thinking of attending medical school myself. I'm preparing to send the inquiries to the London School of Medicine for Women soon."

Her mother and Lucy stared at her as though she'd gone mad. Her mother pressed her lips together, her face blanching. "Perhaps we should save that discussion for another time."

"I think it would suit you well." William's smile offered Ginger encouragement. "Given your work the last few years, I'm certain you'd be admitted."

Her mother's green-eyed gaze pierced Ginger as they drew closer to the bustling boulevard between Shepheard's and Ezbekieh Gardens. At this time of night, Shepheard's was heaving with life as officers and ladies came out for the evening.

The driver stopped, then exited the car to hold the door for them. Ginger wobbled on her heels, the pavement uneven, then thanked the driver. She blinked toward the bright lights of the terrace. The hotel terrace was as famous and popular among the officers and British colonial aristocracy as was the interior. The rails to the balcony of the terrace flanked both sides of the enormous staircase that led to the main entrance. Two large planters sat on each side of the staircase, and black iron-wrought railings decoratively edged the outer edge of the terrace. Dragoman guides, wearing long dark robes and tall red fez hats, were posted on each side of the giant arched main door. Ginger glided up the stairs, Lucy at her side.

"Admit it," Lucy said with an eager smile. "You missed this."

Ginger met her eyes, then grinned. "I missed this. There's something about the energy of Shepheard's that brings me back to happier days."

They were ushered inside and soon found themselves seated at a table for dinner. Lucy's eyes seemed to be anywhere but on the table as she searched for familiar faces. "Look," she said to her mother, "the Wescotts are here. And Lady Lovelace."

Names unfamiliar to Ginger. She exchanged a smile with William. "I'm afraid I won't be any help to you at all in Cairo society. I've spent most of my time with the nursing units."

William nodded toward the waiter as he offered them wine. "I'm glad to know I'm not the only one lost in the crowd. But I must ask you how you wish to be addressed—Lucy calls you Ginny, your mother Ginger, and I know your name is Virginia."

"Ginger." His question produced another smile. No one in her family took much time to consider what she wanted with her name. "My mother's family always called me Ginger, as a tease at first, because of my hair. But I grew to love it."

"Oh, look, Mama, it's—" Then Lucy stopped short, and her gaze shot to Ginger. She froze, then lowered her hand. "Never mind."

But Lucy's reaction had piqued Ginger's curiosity. She lifted her eyes in the direction Lucy had been looking.

Her heart nearly lurched to a stop.

On the other side of the room, Lord Helton was dining with his daughter, Victoria Everill. And seated with them was Noah.

## CHAPTER ELEVEN

Trying to converse with Victoria Everill when Ginger was only twenty yards away was distracting. Noah lifted his glass of water as Ginger's eyes met his. He didn't react—her family was watching her too closely for that—and forced himself to look away.

He'd noticed her the instant she'd come into the room. *Good God,* she looked beautiful. He'd only ever seen her dressed for a dinner like this once before and it had been here at Shepheard's. But what was she doing in Cairo?

Ginger wouldn't be happy to see him with Victoria. Though his false engagement to Victoria had been dissolved in the eyes of the public, his continued association with both Victoria and Lord Helton had provoked whispers. Whispers that neither Ginger nor her family would have heard, as they'd been removed to Alexandria.

The whispers he could explain to Ginger well enough.

What he'd have a harder time dealing with was the way Victoria continued to behave as though nothing had changed between them. His requests that she squash the rumors had been met by tepid shrugs. Then again, she'd made clear she didn't care how those rumors affected Ginger or him.

Sipping his wine, he forced his focus back toward Victoria, who was still speaking.

"... going back now would be madness—you must see that." Victoria dabbed her mouth with her serviette. "Give it a few days. Speak to the American. William Yale is his name, I believe. He may assist."

"I've met the fellow. I don't see what he could do about it. Or any other American. Jack wasn't there on behalf of the Americans."

"He's not there officially on the behalf of the British either," Lord Helton said pointedly. "Acknowledging that we sent him could bring us further problems."

Noah bristled and returned his glass to its place. His fury over Lord Helton's apathy at Jack's situation when he'd arrived in Cairo two days prior had barely waned. Jack had been risking life and limb to gather vital intelligence for Helton for the last couple of years. "Then we just leave him there? Fisher is lying. He had me over a barrel, but I'm not simply—"

Victoria reached across the table and put a cool hand on his. "Don't be hasty. I know how deep your friendship with Jack is, but you need to consider that he could be dead. You're able to keep a cool head in these situations. It won't do for you to be brash now."

Her touch was obviously possessive. He'd need to put Victoria in her place about this once and for all.

*Damned Shepheard's.* Of all the places he could have accepted the invitation to dinner, this was the most likely one where he'd encounter people he knew. Though he'd never cared much about who saw him, until he'd seen Ginger.

"I fear Colonel Benson has been distracted by Lady Virginia

Whitman." Lord Helton carved his steak as he spoke, not lifting his gaze.

*Of course he noticed.* Helton's eyes were as sharp as Noah's.

Victoria paled and discreetly appraised the room. "What on earth is she doing here?"

Noah offered a wry smile. "It appears she's here for dinner."

Victoria scowled. "Hilarious."

He returned to the topic they'd been discussing. "I need more than the bumbling ineptitude of diplomats and government aides to settle my fears about Jack. If you won't authorize my going back there, I'll do it on my own." Now he looked at Lord Helton. "Consequences be damned."

Lord Helton chewed slowly on his piece of steak, then swallowed. "Victoria is right, Benson. Rushing back there is likely to get you killed—or worse. You should know there are many things worse than death."

"Who is that with the Whitman women?" Victoria interrupted, staring more boldly now. She leaned forward, as though the change of posture would help her sight.

Noah raised a brow. Seeing Victoria this nonplussed was rare.

Noah caught the eye of Ginger's sister, who was clearly discussing him or Victoria. What was her name again? The man at the table he didn't recognize. He wore a crisp black evening jacket but lacked panache.

*Now you sound like Victoria.*

He detested this charade. Why shouldn't he go to the woman he loved? Being separated from her was challenge enough. He remembered her tears when he'd found her in the desert, the feel of her soft body in his arms.

And after what had happened with Jack, he wanted nothing more than to embrace her.

But she'd promised to stay away. And he doubted she was

ready to own up to her continued relationship with him to her family in the middle of Shepheard's.

Victoria rose from her seat. The jeweled combs in her dark hair sparkled in the chandeliers' light. "Well, if we're all going to sit here staring at them so shamelessly, we may as well go over there. I'd rather face this head-on."

Victoria's black satin gown swished as she headed toward the other table. Noah groaned inwardly. Lord Helton raised his eyes to the ceiling as if to show he had little control over her. "Victoria can't stand the thought of idle gossip about her."

Noah guffawed. Victoria reveled in idle gossip about her. When Lord Helton made clear that he had no intention of moving from his seat, Noah folded his serviette in his lap.

"Don't you dare go over there, you fool." Lord Helton sawed through his steak neatly. "You're well aware of the trouble it can cause you both."

Eyes peered in his direction. The Anglo-Cairo society was small enough that this encounter would be part of the night's entertainment. "You overstepped when you forced her into that ridiculous promise," he said through gritted teeth.

"Ridiculous, is it?" Lord Helton's gaze snapped toward him. "Since that woman entered your life, you've lost your ability to think clearly. You've defied me time and time again with her. I need not remind you that your duty is to your country, Benson. And I'm out of patience with you."

"I've bled for my country more than once." Noah's jaw set as his eyes flickered toward the exchange of pleasantries between Victoria and the Whitman women. Ginger didn't dare look his way.

She was a better actress than Helton had ever given her credit for.

"And you're still standing, aren't you?" Lord Helton stabbed a piece of steak with his fork, blood running onto the plate below it. "You think you can compare your sacrifice with those who have given their lives for this cause? Your country still needs you and the unique services you can provide."

Noah's appetite was fading fast. "This is one area of my life you have no right to control. The army can order me to do many things—but not to stay away from the woman I love."

Helton leaned closer. "Yes—but fornication, adultery ... those are all punishable acts." His eyes hardened like flint. "I'll do what it takes to rein you in, Benson. I'd advise you not to cross me."

Just what was he threatening?

Noah had been too careless. Allowed his love—and lust—to put both Ginger and himself in a compromising situation. And he'd given Helton the upper hand.

Before Noah could say anything more, Victoria returned to the table. Her face was flushed. "Was that entire scene really necessary?" Noah glowered at her.

"Quite necessary. Consider it my favor to you. You and that woman were infamously linked. Congeniality sends a powerful signal that there was nothing to the matter." Victoria sat, then dusted her hands on her serviette as though ridding herself of the grime of the moment. Her smile was eager. "And you'll never guess who's with them."

Noah settled his features to a purposefully bored look. "Do I care?"

"The Earl of Braddock. He's come to Cairo to see to the estate. But according to Lady Braddock, she's thrilled to have him join the family for the winter season. I think she's hoping for a new son-in-law. And he seems quite taken with Lady Virginia."

Resisting the urge to take another look at the man, Noah's shoulders tightened. Lady Braddock's hopes were natural, but they represented yet another way in which Noah would be measured and found wanting.

Lord Helton had nearly finished his dinner. Noah stared at his uneaten meal and frowned. This entire night was wrong. The colorful dresses of the ladies, the gaiety of laughter trilling through the air, the fuss of the Egyptian waiters over the British colonizers they increasingly felt betrayed by. And who could blame them? Ever since arriving back in Cairo, Noah had sensed the angry simmer on the streets that pulsed in the heart of the native Cairenes.

"You look positively triumphant, dearest." Lord Helton dabbed his mouth with his serviette.

"You should have seen Lady Virginia squirm." Victoria gave Noah a sharp look. "Promise me you'll keep away from her this time, Noah. She's no good for you."

Noah set his serviette on the table. "As I came to discuss the matter with Jack, I think I've had quite enough of the company for the evening." Standing, he bowed his head toward Lord Helton, then Victoria. "Good evening."

The shocked expression on Victoria's face was satisfaction enough. He headed for the exit without waiting for another word from either of them. After all, he'd never promised to stay away from Ginger, despite Lord Helton's demands. Victoria had no reason to assume his feelings had changed.

Suffocated as he made his way toward the lift, he stopped. Walking away from that dining room was torture, but not because of Victoria's actions. Now that he knew Ginger was so close, he needed to see her, to speak to her.

A grimmer thought occurred: he needed to tell her about Stephen's sudden reappearance in their lives. Before she heard about it from someone else.

He paced, then went directly to the concierge. "I need to give a note to a lady in that dining room."

# CHAPTER TWELVE

With dinner over, Ginger's family had entered the part of the evening that Ginger loathed the most—making social rounds. As people that Ginger had never met stopped to greet them, a dragoman slipped past Ginger. He paused, reaching toward the floor beside her. *"As-salaam alykum."* He offered her a slip of paper. "You dropped this, miss."

Ginger took the paper as he continued past. Unfolding the square, she read one word: *Ezbekieh.*

Her heart thumped.

*Noah.*

Since she'd seen him, she'd thought of little else. The dinner had dragged, and the snide comments her family had muttered about him only made it worse. Could he be inviting her to meet him in the famed Ezbekieh Gardens across the street?

She crumpled the paper, then pushed it into her handbag.

*Stay away from him.*

Her conscience nagged her. Lord Helton had been clear. Her family could be at risk if she went.

But Noah had to know he was being watched. He wouldn't

ask her to meet him if he didn't think it was safe. After all, Ezbekieh had sprawling paths amidst trees and shrubs, fountains and more—plenty of places to be out of sight.

Before she lost her nerve, Ginger stood. Lucy and her mother were wrapped up with introducing William. Ginger moved toward them. "Mama, if you'll excuse me—I think I'll hire a carriage and go home for the evening. I have an early start in the morning."

Her mother searched her gaze. Did she suspect Ginger would lie? She pressed a kiss to Ginger's cheek. "Be safe, darling."

Ginger gathered her shawl and her handbag. As she left the dining room, she glanced back at the table Lord Helton and Victoria had vacated nearly an hour before. Seeing Noah with Victoria had brought back memories of a darker time. She pushed those thoughts aside, feeling more sure-footed as she went. For now, her love for Noah had to hide in the shadows. Someday they would be free.

Outside, mild temperatures welcomed her, a warm breeze sending a tendril of her hair across her eyes. She smiled and hurried down the stairs, gripping the handrail. She waited for a motorcar to pass, then crossed the boulevard, the clopping of horse hooves behind her.

Walking into the gardens at Ezbekieh, Ginger studied the split in the path before her. If Noah wanted her here, she had to trust he would find her. The gardens were among the most beautiful in Cairo and faced Shepheard's. They also teemed with soldiers. The YMCA had set up a complex in the gardens to keep the soldiers occupied. The area included an open-air theater, skating rink, restaurant, cinema, and a swimming pool —and loads of other entertainment.

Both here and eight miles north in Zeitoun, the organization had worked tirelessly to give a wholesome alternative to the draw of the nearby Wazzir district of Cairo. Ginger wrinkled her nose. The epidemic of venereal diseases had been terrible among the soldiers. When the matron of the hospital where she'd worked wanted to give a nurse a punishment, it often meant an assignment to the VD wards.

Ginger inspected the landscape as she walked, greeting the couples she passed. It wasn't difficult for the young English women of Cairo to find suitors these days. She crossed a bridge over a stream, then took a winding pathway through lush tropical plants, tall palm trees, and spacious lawns.

Still no sign of Noah.

*Where was he?*

The note should have been more direct. She wished he'd given her some clue where to meet him.

Someone bumped past her, moving at a rapid speed. A flash of white gleamed in the moonlight—an Egyptian wearing the traditional loose-fitting *galabeyah* tunic. The wearer was a tall man with broad shoulders, who glanced back. He wore a turban, and a face veil covered his mouth and nose, leaving only a slit for his eyes. It had to be Noah.

She followed closely. The path wound at a curve to a more isolated area. It made sense he'd want to greet her out of the view of others, but she'd nearly lost sight of him.

A firm hand gripped her by the elbow and she stopped. Noah stood behind her, dressed in his uniform. Her joy at seeing him was replaced with fear. She looked uncertainly in the direction she'd been heading.

"Where are you going?" Noah's voice was clipped, his dark-blue gaze following hers.

"I-I thought I was following you." Her throat went dry. "Your note wasn't the clearest."

Noah's brows furrowed, then his hand slid up to her bicep, pulling her closer to his side. "What did the note say?"

"Ezbekieh." Now she felt foolish. *Was it possible he hadn't sent it?*

Noah shook his head slowly. "I gave the concierge a note to give to you. But it was lengthier." His fingertips had unbuttoned the holster of his sidearm.

"Then why are you here?" Ginger stepped back.

"Because I saw you leave. Naturally I was curious." Noah narrowed his gaze. "And now I'm even more curious. Wait here."

Ginger stayed behind while Noah moved forward, gun drawn. As he slipped out of view, Ginger held her breath. Whom had she been following?

More frightening still, who had replaced Noah's note?

Someone had intended to waylay her in the garden.

A muffled cry broke the stillness. The sound of a scuffle followed.

Despite Noah's instructions, Ginger rushed toward him. As she rounded the corner, Noah and the Egyptian came into view, caught in a struggle. Blood dripped down Noah's arm, pooling on the cuff of his jacket. "Noah!" A knife lay on the path between them.

Ginger stooped for the knife and grabbed it, then ran toward them both.

The Egyptian looked at her. In his distraction, Noah threw his fist at the man's nose. The Egyptian stumbled back, holding his face. Blood stained the face veil. Then the man turned and crashed through the hedges, fleeing.

Ginger ran to his side. "What on earth did he do to you?"

Noah winced, then replaced his sidearm. "As always, the company you keep is marvelous, *rohi*." The tear of endearment he'd chosen for her, meaning *my soulmate* in Arabic, made her heart settle, even as he removed the knife from her hand.

He wrapped the knife in a handkerchief and put it in the inside pocket of his jacket. "But thank you. Remind me in the future that you're more useful in battle than I give you credit for. You looked like a wild warrior come to murder. One would never suspect such an elegant woman of such fury."

She suppressed a laugh despite the gravity of the situation. Noah's sarcastic demeanor was among the things she loved about him. The path was littered with the debris and branches of the shrubbery that had been broken in the Egyptian's flight. "Are you going after him?"

"No, he's gone for now. And I'm not about to leave you after that." Noah's eyes clouded. "There was something familiar about the man, even with that face veil."

The hedge where the man had fled was still. The whole incident had been so fast, she'd hardly wrapped her mind around what could have been. Who would want to attack her?

She scanned the vicinity. "Lord Helton told me to stay away from you. Do you think he intercepted your note? He may have been angry you were trying to contact me."

The concern on his face was clear. "I'm not sure. That would make more sense if the man hadn't attacked me. I have a friend who may trace where the knife came from." His fingers were wet with blood. "Why don't we retire to somewhere more in the open?"

Her nervousness amplified. She shouldn't have come. The risk had been too great. "I-I don't think I should. Lord Helton knows you met me in Palestine. He was furious. Threatened my family and me."

Noah drew her closer to him. "Don't let him frighten you this way. He can threaten all he likes. He can't keep it up forever." His closeness was comforting, and she wanted to sink into his arms. "Should we return? I can keep my distance and watch you get back safely to Shepheard's."

She hesitated. Now that he was here, she wanted to tell him

of the business Lord Helton and Peter Osborne had pulled her into.

"Not before I've had a look at your arm." She unbuttoned his jacket, then pulled it down from his shoulders. "I saw little of the attacker's face. But I'm certain you broke his nose. That should be a clue if you search for him." His shirtsleeve was crimson and wet with blood, but the gash was close to his shoulder. She frowned, her fingers moving the clean tear in his sleeve where the knife had entered. She couldn't see much of the wound, but it was certainly deep.

"This needs to be sutured." She found a clean handkerchief in her handbag and pressed it against his wound. "How did the man manage this when you had a gun?"

"He sprang out of the bush at me. He nearly disarmed me." With his free hand, his fingers brushed her cheek as his palm cupped her face. He leaned down to her and pressed a kiss to her lips.

Her breath caught and she curled an arm around his neck, tilting her face to receive his kiss. She closed her eyes, her heart speeding at the touch of his lips. His lips were feather-light against hers, gentle, searching. As she returned his kiss, it deepened and his hand glided toward her waist, drawing her closer.

Ginger pulled away and searched his eyes. "Aren't you in pain?"

He shrugged noncommittally. "I'd rather do this than think of that right now."

She kissed him once more, then dragged her mouth from his. "Should I meet you back in your room? If you give me your room number, I can try to sneak—"

Noah lifted a brow.

The look he gave her only heightened her state of arousal. Her face flushed. "I meant—to suture your arm."

He chuckled, releasing her. "You carry medical supplies in your handbag?"

"Not this one. I'd have to go and get some first." She tugged at his hand. "And I refuse to just leave your arm untreated, if that's your next suggestion."

"Not that I don't want you in my room, but someone could see you going there. You're worried about eyes and ears here in Ezbekieh. This is nothing compared to Shepheard's. There's no way for you to go to my room without being seen." Noah surveyed the space. His eyes stopped at a stone bench under a palm, and he tilted his head toward it. "Shall we sit?"

"If you don't allow me to suture that cut, you must promise to go to the closest hospital and have it taken care of." She released the pressure she'd held on the wound with the handkerchief. The wound bled less now. She sat beside him on the bench.

"I promise." Noah laid his uniform jacket on his arm. "I've gone through more uniforms this year than ever before. I'll need to have the whole sleeve on this replaced." Noah settled his shoulders back, his jaw clenching reflexively.

His proximity helped put her fears about the Egyptian to one side. "We should talk for a few minutes. A great deal has happened since I last saw you."

A smile tugged at his lips. "I assumed. Considering you were in Cairo with your family ... not on leave, I suppose?"

"No, they dismissed me from duty." Ginger cringed, thinking of the awful lieutenant. "They gave me the choice between saving the life of a deserter they intended to execute later and that of a young man who needed an emergency amputation." She cleared her throat. "Actually, I spoke poorly. Not the choice. They commanded me to patch up the deserter. I *chose* not to."

Noah released an exasperated sigh. "When will the military learn that logic isn't the enemy?" He interlaced his fingers with hers. "Regardless of what they did, I'm quite proud of you. Noble Lady Virginia."

The only advantage of having followed that Egyptian is that he'd lured her to a place of relative privacy. Even if they were being watched, as the night grew later, they could converse more openly. No one could be close enough to listen to their low tones. Much as she wanted to tell him of Osborne and Lord Helton, she was curious about why he'd sent a note. "What did the note you intended for me say?"

Noah's features darkened. He turned his body toward her, his knees against hers. "Stephen Fisher is in Cairo. I brought him back after my last mission went horribly awry and Lord Helton has jailed him in a special facility while they question him. Even I don't know where it is."

Stephen … caught? The news brought her equal jolts of relief and fear. "Will they charge him for my father's death?"

"I'm not sure. His capture is a secret. Lord Helton doesn't want it to get out yet. His family has been raising hell back in England trying to learn what happened to him." Noah didn't deliver the news with any hint of satisfaction. "There's more, Ginger … He surrendered to me in Jerusalem. He claimed he no longer wanted to be with the Germans and would rather take his chances with the British. I think he feels he can negotiate, given what he knows."

*Stephen surrendered?* He'd been free. Why would he come back to Cairo, where he was being hunted? "The British government will cooperate with him? They must hold him accountable for his crimes."

"I don't know what he's up to, but I'm certain he's planning something. I …" His grip on her hand tightened. Ginger eyed him curiously. Whatever he was trying to say was clearly hard for him.

"What is it?" The flutter of nerves went through her stomach, the rich meal from Shepheard's no longer sitting well.

"I was with Jack in Jerusalem"—Noah's voice was strained—"when Stephen surrendered. We escaped and ended up in a tribal encampment outside of the city. Then we were attacked, and I lost consciousness. When I awoke, Stephen had tied me to a camel. He forced me at gunpoint to take him back to the British side. But Jack…" He swallowed. "Jack was left behind. Stephen claimed the Turks executed him."

She gripped his forearm to steady herself. "No, not Jack." Her eyes darted to Noah's face. Could he really be gone? She loved Noah's American friend nearly as much as Noah did. He'd been a loyal friend and the only one who'd taken the time to console her after she and Noah had parted last spring. Then he'd been sent off for intelligence work, and she hadn't heard from him since.

"I don't believe he's dead. Stephen had every reason to lie to me. If he hadn't pulled a gun on me, I would have gone back, and he knew it."

The idea of Noah heading back into the front lines of the Turkish occupation brought a sick feeling to her gut, but didn't surprise her. Noah would never leave Jack captured. "Are you planning to go back, then?"

Noah's pupils were large in the dark. "Yes."

She swallowed a lump in her throat. She'd known of the danger he faced, but not always so concretely. "When?"

"As soon as I can arrange it." Distant laughter sounded in the park. Perhaps patrons of the theater or the nearby opera house getting out from a picture show or production. "But I'm sure Stephen is playing some larger game. I can't tell you more because I don't know more. But you needed to know that he's returned, especially now that you're in Cairo."

She didn't want to think about Stephen being back.

But the attack in the garden tonight … She shivered. Could he have had something to do with it?

Ginger's eyes were drawn to his wound. Even though he could go to a hospital easily enough, she didn't want to send him off with a wound, not when it was her fault that he'd received it. "Are you certain you won't allow me to treat this? If you're planning on heading back to the front, the last thing you'll want is an infection."

"I'm certain I want you to treat it. But taking you back to my room after Victoria's little stunt would be foolish. All it would take is one person who recognizes you to do irreparable damage." Noah kissed her temple, his lips hovering above her skin so that his breath was warm against her. "Were it up to me, I wouldn't let you go back tonight, particularly not when your mother is threatening to marry you off."

Ginger rolled her eyes. "I've already told her it's not a possibility, but I think she's hoping she can prevail upon me."

"Is that why you've removed the ring I gave you?"

Noah was too astute not to notice a significant detail like that. She rubbed the bare spot on her finger. "I didn't want anyone asking questions, to be honest. My mother and Lucy won't be happy when I tell them we plan to marry." *Or Lord Helton.* "And my promise to Lord Helton to stay away from you—I know he's watching you. If he knows we spoke tonight it will just be one more instance to infuriate him."

"Leave him to me. I'll speak to him about the matter. Disabuse him of the notion that it's your fault." Noah curled his good arm around her, pressing her in against him.

"But your arm—"

"Leave the damned thing. I'll be fine." He set his chin on the top of her head. "At any rate, I suppose you're right about your family. Especially if your mother hopes a marriage to the new earl can settle the inheritance issues that arose when Henry died. Speaking of inheritance—did your father ever mention Ibn Saud?"

Her lips parted in surprise. What did Noah know of this?

She'd intended to tell him about Peter Osborne but hadn't expected for him to bring up the issue first. "Yes, but not for many years. He went on some sort of diplomatic mission to Hayil to meet Ibn Rashid and ended up staying with Ibn Saud instead. I don't know the details."

He had a thoughtful look in his eyes. "That's not surprising. Ibn Rashid and Ibn Saud are enemy leaders of different tribes in Arabia. Ibn Rashid declared his loyalty to the Ottomans early in the war."

She closed her eyes, relishing the warmth of his closeness, the comfort of his heartbeat against her ear. Certain she knew where he was going with this line of thought, she asked, "Does this have to do with the oil concession granted to my father?"

Silence ensued. Then, after a few beats, Noah nodded. "Who told you about it?"

"As it so happened, around the time they dismissed me from nursing, one of Sir Reginald Wingate's men approached me about a job. A delicate matter, he said—"

"Who?" Noah's voice was flat.

Naturally, he'd want to know. Chances were he even knew Osborne. "A man named Peter Osborne. Do you know him?"

"Osborne?" Noah's face scrunched as he considered the name. "I can't say I do."

"He offered me passage for my sister and mother out of Egypt when I'm through with the job he has for me. And to pay for my medical school. And a position working as the assistant to a female surgeon here in Cairo."

"It sounds as though he knew just how to bait you into the game." Noah flexed his arm, the only sign he'd given of the pain he must be in. "What was the job?"

She told him, a nervous feeling creeping up her spine as she spoke. Though there was no one around to listen, she couldn't help feeling watched. Especially after the incident with the Egyptian man.

Noah listened without a visible response. When she'd finished, his blue eyes scanned hers. "And you agreed to do it?"

Ginger grimaced. "Yes. They're offering me the opportunity to earn a ten percent stake if I help them find the concession. Otherwise, the British government intends to seize it in its entirety, on the grounds that my father got it illegally."

"I worried about that. In fact, when I first learned of it, I considered not telling my superiors at all about it. I didn't want the CID taking any more from your family. But as I had to bring Stephen along with me, it forced me to, in case Stephen shared the information with them."

Noah stared out at the gardens that surrounded them, his eyes unreadable. "Ginger, the world your father was involved in —it was dangerous. The men your father trusted were dangerous."

She bit her lip. He wasn't happy about it, as she'd suspected. "Are you angry with me?"

"No." He released a frustrated breath. "Just concerned."

His sentiment was heartwarming. She squinted. "Do you think my father hid the paperwork about the concession?"

"It wouldn't surprise me. And Stephen must have some goal in bringing the issue to light now. It can't be as a favor to your family, that much is certain."

Ginger settled back into the space she'd occupied against his chest. "I'll have to ask my mother if she knows anything. Lord Helton said they had, but that she'd been less than forthcoming."

"That was what I would suggest. But be careful how much you draw her into this. Your mother keeps her silence because she's aware of how dangerous your father's behavior was." Noah kissed the top of her head and then released her. He stood, holding his hand out for her. "Shall we go back? You can go on ahead, I'll keep watch."

As she stood, she smoothed out her dress. "Hopefully no harm has come to this dress—I had to borrow it from Lucy. I don't have any evening gowns left."

Noah gave her an approving glance. Something else lingered in his eyes, unreadable. "I didn't have the chance to tell you how beautiful you look, by the way."

The feel of his hand in hers had a way of making her pulse beat faster. "Well, thank you. You looked quite dashing yourself, though the blood hasn't done you any favors."

Noah set the jacket over his shoulders, slipping one arm into the sleeves at a time. "I'll go to have it sutured directly."

She didn't want to leave him.

They stood in silence, bathed by the moonlight, the palm fronds of the surrounding trees dancing in the wind. Speaking with Noah had allowed her to forget her fears for a few minutes. What would this evening have been like if Noah hadn't been keeping watch? Ginger shuddered. "Thank you for saving me, once again."

"I'm going to have a talk with the concierge. See what happened to my note."

She had a feeling she knew. Ginger clasped his hand tighter. "Lord Helton is once again demanding I keep my distance from you." She stopped, glancing at him. "He said I needed to do whatever it took to convince you to stay away."

Noah didn't respond, his thumb grazing the back of her hand softly. "Is that what you want? I'll wait for you as long as it takes, *rohi*. Even if it tortures me to keep my distance."

"I think it's what we have to do, isn't it?" Her heartbeat seemed to slow. Despite all of Lord Helton's threats, she couldn't make herself say what she didn't mean. "But it's not what I want." Her voice was barely audible.

His voice was equally low. "It's not what I want either."

She should return. She'd lingered long enough. "Make me a promise, at least?" She turned to face him as they walked away from the bench.

He smiled, his handsome features seeming to relax at the earnest way she looked up at him. "What's that?"

"Promise me you won't go after Jack without letting me say good-bye."

Noah kissed the back of her hand softly. "Then I should say good-bye now, *rohi*. But I promise to send word when I've gone."

## CHAPTER THIRTEEN

On al-Maghrabi Street, Noah inspected the bustling pavement packed with tables, cane-woven wooden chairs, and soldiers. Maison Groppi was a popular patisserie and deli with the troops, but Noah considered it a tourist trap, preferring to patronize some of the small cafés in Old Cairo.

He found who he was looking for, mostly because Captain Alastair Taylor refused to wear his uniform. Slender with lanky limbs, Alastair wore a tweed jacket with khaki trousers, a navy-blue bowtie, and his favored straw Panama hat over dark curly hair. He smoked a pipe as he sat reading his newspaper, fully absorbed.

Noah made his way to the table and sat. Alastair didn't look up. "Did you see the headlines today?" Alastair's voice was dry.

"Yes." Noah unbuttoned his military jacket, feeling more restricted in it since the young nurse from the clinic had applied a thick dressing over his shoulder. As though he needed that much padding on his arm. He had half a mind to remove the dressing while he sat there.

Alastair folded the newspaper, taking a pull of his pipe. He held the smoke in his mouth momentarily, then released it. "Damned fools. I always worried about the Russians." The streets crawled thick with carts and motorcars. "Mark my words, there will be riots today. Tea?"

"Coffee, preferably." The locals who worked at Groppi's weren't likely to be the best gauge of the feelings of the native population. They were too accustomed to the treatment of the colonials—and their patronage. But Noah agreed with Alastair. Since the Bolsheviks had overthrown the Russian government weeks earlier, he'd worried what might come of it politically. Now, a group of the Russian Communists had discovered the details of Sir Mark Sykes' ill-advised agreement with Georges Picot, the French diplomat. As the best of former allies turned enemies did, the Russians had turned around and published the details of the agreement in the newspapers.

The whole of the Arab policy seemed to flounder. A few seemed to understand it better than others—T. E. Lawrence and Gertrude Bell came to mind—but even they were short-sighted with their beliefs on what would be "best" for the locals. "Sykes was the damned fool if we're honest about it. Giving the French all of Syria. Major parts of the Transjordan. Worse still, divvying up the spoils of war when they haven't the foggiest how to handle the locals. As though they can simply throw the Shias and Sunnis together and make a nation of them." Noah cracked his knuckles, impatient and angry.

"Or any other of the warring tribes." Alastair motioned toward the waiter. "Bring my friend your best cup of *ahwa* and something delicious. Surprise him. He's not picky." Alastair wagged a finger. " ... except with his *ahwa*. Make it the best."

"I can't stay long." Noah's eyes followed the receding form of the waiter. He pulled out the knife he'd taken from the assailant at Ezbekieh the previous evening. After unwrapping it from the handkerchief, he handed it to Alastair. "Do you think you might find its owner?"

Alastair turned the knife over in his hands. "The blade is ordinary, though straight, which eliminates several local forges. But what a unique handle. Ivory, is it?"

"It looks like bone to me." Noah flicked away a fly that landed on the table. "The carvings are hieroglyphs, but crude. I believe they mean brotherhood of *burj Aleaqrab.*"

"Brotherhood of the scorpion? I believe you're right." A divot showed between Alastair's dark brows. "Interesting." He folded the knife in the handkerchief once again. "I shall endeavor to learn the origin and report back to you with the results. Now, about the other matter—"

The waiter had reappeared with steaming coffee and a pastry filled with Chantilly crème. Noah thanked him as he set it in front of him. He hadn't intended to eat but the smell of the coffee changed his mind. When he'd come to Egypt years before, the very first sip of the brew had made him abandon tea permanently.

Alastair leaned forward in his seat as the waiter left. "I have heard nothing definitive, but you're right—Darby wasn't killed at Ta'amira. My contact in Jerusalem saw him."

Noah sank back in his chair, bowing his head. "Thank God." His relief was mixed with guilt. He never should have left him. *Damn Fisher.*

"He has been captured, but as of the last sighting he was still alive and taken back to Jerusalem. But with the army at the gates of Jaffa, it's likely he'll have been taken on the road to Nablus."

"To Aleppo, you think?" Noah sipped the coffee. Any satisfaction he gained from knowing Jack was alive was replaced by worry. They would torture Jack. He had to leave to go back out there. Immediately.

"I'm not sure. Damascus is more likely. The retreating Turkish Army has better things to do than transport their prisoners. But, then again, Jack Darby isn't an ordinary prisoner." Alastair lifted his pipe once more.

"Try reminding Lord Helton of that fact." Noah bit into the pastry, which was cloyingly sweet. "His chief concern is to learn what secrets Fisher kept."

Alastair clamped the end of his pipe in his teeth. "He's in a position where that, unfortunately, makes sense. Do try to see the logic in it. Not that it gives me any pleasure in telling you that. I'm as worried about Jack as you are. And as soon as I have even the slightest information on where he is, I'll send word directly. But, until then, be cautious. It won't do any good for you to risk your life when he could be anywhere."

If anyone else had said it, Noah would have waved them off. But Alastair's contacts throughout the Arab world were unparalleled. Between that and the safe houses he operated, Alastair could do whatever he wanted in the eyes of the government. He considered his rank and title ceremonial. The War Office went to him when they needed information, but he did *not* work for them.

Noah sighed. "How's Khalib?"

Alastair's face lit up. "He's my best tutee. Hardly surprising. He already learned so much from you."

Smiling faintly, Noah felt relief in knowing Khalib was safe now. He'd rescued the orphaned Bedouin boy years earlier, and Khalib had repaid him with unwavering loyalty. Noah pulled out an envelope from his jacket pocket, which he handed to Alastair. "Here's the money for his quarterly expenses. Let me know if he needs anything, of course. I'm basing it off what we last discussed. Is he managing with the prosthesis?"

"Yes, though he's growing so fast he'll likely need another soon." Alastair set the envelope down without looking through it. "I know he'll be pleased to see you soon though. He misses you terribly."

Noah's guilt at having ever allowed the boy to accompany him on his dangerous missions in the field had never diminished. Khalib had paid too high a price—Stephen had tortured him and severed his hand. Noah would live with that regret for life.

"Tell him I will be by to see him as soon as I can." Noah finished his pastry with a few bites. "I have another favor to ask you, about someone else."

A gleam came to Alastair's eye. *"La belle femme?"*

Noah pursed his lips to keep the laughter at bay. Trust Alastair to have his own nickname for Ginger. "Fiancée, wife, love of my life that will send me to my deathbed." He motioned toward the knife. "With Fisher's return, there seem to be several odd things happening at once. I need someone to monitor her."

"What a romantic you've become." Alastair sniggered. "Just eyes? Or someone who can handle an attack?"

"The latter." He should probably tell Ginger that he planned to keep a guard on her, but it would defeat the purpose. If Alastair had a man for the job, that man would be nearly invisible. Ginger knowing might only draw awareness to him.

"I have just the man. We can go and speak to him after this. But it will be rather costly. How long?"

"Only for the next few weeks, I imagine." The tops of the acacia trees across the street stood still, giving Noah a rather ominous feeling. As though the city held its breath, waiting. The headlines from the morning were influencing his reactions. "I doubt Fisher will wait too long to strike. Not after that attack last night in Ezbekieh."

The sweet scent of pipe tobacco drifted from Alastair's side of the table. "Don't underestimate him, Noah. The man is capable of infinite patience if necessary."

"Not that I underestimate him. It's that he's already waited for a while to strike. Six months is long enough for him to put together a sound plan." Noah drained his coffee cup. "And he has more than enough friends here in Cairo. I should have left him for the vultures in the Judean Hills when I had a chance."

"You should have. But that's what makes you different from Fisher. You're a decent man with a conscience. He's a scoundrel without a moral bone in his body." Alastair winked. "Also, presumably, why *la belle femme* chose you instead of him."

Noah chuckled, then leaned back in his chair. "Should we move on from here?"

A crash boomed through the air. Then, the crackle of gunfire, distant. Both men looked up, then were on their feet. "Wazzir?" Alastair asked, taking out a few coins to settle the bill. He pressed them into the hands of the passing waiter.

This had to be about the headlines in the newspaper.

The infamous red-light district of Cairo would be the most likely place for conflict. It was also situated just a few blocks away.

More pops of gunfire. Noah listened intently. It did sound as though it came from Wazzir. A confrontation between the troops and the locals? "I think so."

Alastair sighed wearily. "You're going to want to go there, aren't you?"

"I work for the CID. Whether or not I'm on leave. If gunfire erupts in the city and I don't go and ask questions before witnesses make themselves scarce, the police will bungle the whole affair." Noah gave his friend a wry glance. "And you're coming with me. Wouldn't you rather have your own eyes on the scene?"

Alastair put his fingers over the bowl of his pipe and extinguished it. "Lead the way, *Se-Osiris*. It's a beautiful day for an adventure with bullets whizzing past my head."

## CHAPTER FOURTEEN

Dr. Jane Radford wasn't at all what Ginger had expected.

To begin with, she was only a few years older than Ginger. With auburn hair and an aquiline nose, she was rather pretty, though she had a look of skepticism that seemed to live permanently in her tall forehead.

Best of all, she was friendly.

"A woman in intelligence," Dr. Radford said, as they made their way through the hospital corridor. "I've heard of them but never met any."

"I could say the same about women surgeons." Ginger smoothed the starched white apron of her uniform. She'd removed the famous QA red cape and insignias, but in the absence of knowing what to wear, her uniform had seemed the best option. "I hope I dressed appropriately."

Dr. Radford smiled. "The RAMC hasn't known what to do with us women physicians either. Or our uniforms. We've been fighting battle after battle with them since this damned war began." Then she blushed. "Excuse me. You'll find I've unintentionally adopted some of the language of the troops."

Ginger laughed. "I did the same. Especially when I was out in the clearing stations. My mother nearly fainted upon hearing me when I came home for leave one time."

Giving a throaty appreciative murmur, Dr. Radford's hazel eyes glinted. "I like you already, Sister Whitman." She paused in front of a door and turned the knob to reveal her office. Ginger followed her inside.

"I asked Peter Osborne to give me your file. I must admit, I was intrigued by it. You may be the first nurse I've stumbled across that has sections of her file redacted." Dr. Radford sat at her desk and invited Ginger to take the seat opposite her. "As far as your credentials go, I'm impressed. And I'm rather looking forward to having a nurse working directly for me instead of another organization."

Until now, Ginger had given little thought to that opportunity. Working for Dr. Radford directly might give her a freedom she'd never experienced. And she appeared to be young, motivated, and possibly even a bit of a rebel.

"I'm excited for this also. Especially because I've dreamed of going to medical school myself and it's lovely to have someone I can speak to who's experienced it."

"It feels ages ago now." Dr. Radford rifled through some papers on her desk. "When I finished in 1912, I thought I'd have a small country clinic. I never expected the adventure I've been on."

"Yes, I can imagine." Dr. Radford had two framed portraits on her desk. One of an older couple Ginger assumed to be her parents. The other was of a soldier.

Dr. Radford followed Ginger's gaze. "My brother. Killed at the Marne." Her face sobered. "He's the reason I offered my services to the RAMC. He was so glad to take up arms and do his bit—didn't even make it out of the first month of the war." Her voice trembled. "When I think of the entire generation of men this war has cost us, it makes me want to scream. They could have been scientists, philosophers, poets, statesmen. All that might have been if not for the ambitions of men drunk on power who simply saw their soldiers as expendable."

Silence hung between them.

Ginger agreed with her, but she'd rarely met women so willing to speak their minds freely and honestly. In some ways she reminded Ginger of her friend from nursing for so many years, Beatrice Thornton. When Beatrice had sailed for France recently, Ginger hadn't expected to hear from her. Her letter of good-bye had brought tears to her eyes and made Ginger feel more alone than ever. The events of the previous spring had done irreparable damage to their friendship.

Dr. Radford cleared her throat and gave a feeble smile. "Pardon me. I have the tendency to get carried away."

"No, I agree wholeheartedly." Ginger sighed, settling back against her chair. "The situation in Egypt is no less complex. Are you familiar with the local politics?"

"Not very." Dr. Radford adjusted a pin in the tight chignon at the back of her head. "But, I've only recently arrived from Malta. Which was wonderful. I adored it there. But the hospitals are closing all over the island, and the army said they had need of me here, so here I am."

Before their conversation could continue, a knock sounded on the door. "Come in," Dr. Radford called.

The door opened and Mr. Osborne came inside. Ginger stood, and he waved her back down again. "No need, no need. I'm only dropping in to see how the morning is going."

Dr. Radford gave Osborne a beaming smile. "She's wonderful, just as you said she would be."

Osborne seemed to shift uncomfortably, his neck reddening.

He didn't meet Ginger's gaze. "Excellent. Remember, her schedule is to be as flexible as possible when necessary. And, Lady Virginia—" He halted, then glanced at Dr. Radford.

Dr. Radford looked between the two of them, then stood abruptly. "Why don't I give you a chance to speak in private?"

As the door clicked shut, Osborne rested his weight against the desk. Ginger sensed that he planned to bring up Noah. It would be better to be up front rather than appear to be concealing anything from him.

Ginger sat straighter. "I wanted to tell you I saw Colonel Benson last night, as it so happens. I assume he'll be returning to the front soon? If he's to be in Cairo, there's a chance our paths may cross from time to time. I didn't want you to think I'd been dishonest with you yesterday."

"Yes, Lord Helton mentioned the encounter." Osborne's grey eyes gave nothing away. "As it so happens, Colonel Benson has been granted some medical leave. He suffered a minor head injury while out at the front. But, between us, I think his motives are suspect." He clasped his hands, his brow furrowing. "How well do you know Colonel Benson?"

"Not very well." A pang of guilt went through her, but it couldn't be helped. "But we are friendly."

Osborne studied her and she shifted under the weight of his scrutiny. "It occurs to me, Lady Virginia, that Colonel Benson may be a superb source of information about that concession. His intelligence report made us aware of it. Lord Helton wouldn't want me to ask this of you but if you can speak to the colonel, see what you can find out about how he learned of it."

She held back an ironic laugh. He wanted her to question Noah? "He's not likely to share that information with me, Mr. Osborne."

"Isn't he? I'd heard he was quite taken with you—even to the point of sharing information he shouldn't have in the past."

Osborne gave her a pointed look. Ginger felt herself tense, but he offered a kind smile. "Come now, Lady Virginia. I know about your history with him. The man is in love with you. And while you claim to no longer share that interest, I think some encouragement on your part may do the trick should you want information on the concession."

Ginger's pulse increased. "But I told Lord Helton I would stay away from Colonel Benson, sir." *Just what was he suggesting?*

Osborne chuckled. "What you don't want Lord Helton to know, I won't share. We have a mutual goal: learn about the concession. My rules about the methods you use to find it are less particular. You work directly for me. And Lord Helton lets Colonel Benson get away with unscrupulous, possibly treasonous, behavior. Why not see if we can't take advantage of that?"

It wasn't the first time Osborne had implied that Noah was less than loyal to the Crown. "Frankly, Mr. Osborne, I'm surprised that you seem to distrust Colonel Benson."

Osborne's lips twisted below his moustache. "I know—his record seems impeccable on the surface. It's what's under that which concerns me. There's a group of men in the intelligence world who lately have grown more vocal with their criticisms of the British policies with our colonies. Colonel Benson is among them. And when I investigated him—"

Osborne stopped short, as though he realized she may not be the best person to entrust with his suspicions.

Osborne's eyes locked with hers. Only the ticking of a nearby clock on a shelf sounded. Then, he straightened. "Very well. For now, I'll come speak to you here in the mornings. This afternoon, I'll expect you'll need the time to acquaint yourself with the hospital. But you'll be free to go each day at noon from here, which should give you the time to attend to the matter we've hired you for. You can ring me at the Savoy if necessary.

Thank you for your cooperation with this. His Majesty's government is grateful for loyal citizens."

*As grateful as they were for the contributions of men like Noah?* Ginger frowned as he left her. The more she thought about it, the more absurd it seemed that he should have any concern about Noah's loyalty. Noah had sacrificed himself in so many ways throughout the years.

She lifted her head as Dr. Radford breezed back into the office. "Ready to begin the day?" The doctor gave her a bright smile. "I have a full schedule."

Ginger stood. She hadn't been away from nursing long enough to miss it, but now that she'd met Dr. Radford, she felt excited. "I'm ready."

They headed out of the office. "Has anyone ever trained you in anesthesia, Sister Whitman?"

"I wish it had been possible. I had studied it, but then the RAMC strictly forbade it for all English and Australian nurses. A few New Zealander nurses were able to proceed with studying and practicing it though."

Dr. Radford's eyes sparkled. "Strictly speaking, I don't think you're employed directly by the RAMC anymore, are you? Why don't we give you some materials to study?"

A thrill rose within her. Working with Dr. Radford might be her favorite assignment yet. If Ginger truly wanted to be a physician, this might be the start.

# CHAPTER FIFTEEN

*P*reparing to leave for the day, Ginger was keenly aware of her feet throbbing. She washed her hands for what felt like the fortieth time and removed her apron, then headed for the door. At least, unlike most of the other nurses, she could go home tonight.

The thought of a hot bath and warm dinner with servants tending to her wasn't unwelcome. She gathered the stacks of papers and booklets Dr. Radford had given her to study when she'd come by to check on Ginger.

Evening had fallen on Cairo. The scent of smoke came from close by as she stepped onto the pavement. The streets seemed thick with activity.

She looked for an unoccupied cab. Most the cabs that past appeared empty, but the drivers didn't stop at her hailing.

A motorcar approached and stopped beside her. Noah sat in the driver's seat. Ginger furrowed her brow at him, even though the sight of him made her heart skip. "What are you doing here?"

"Waiting for you." Noah got out and came around to her. He held the door for her. "I have been for over two hours. Get in."

*Two hours?* "This is the exact opposite of staying away from me. You're doing a marvelous job of persuading Lord Helton you're as in love with me as ever." Ginger rocked her head in disbelief. "I can't be seen with you, you know that."

"They can hang themselves for all I care. I *am* in love with you. But that's not why I'm here." He threw her a smile. "There are riots in several parts of the city. Some locals are refusing to accept the business of the British today. I wanted to make certain you'd get home safely."

"Riots?" Ginger searched the surrounding area. Is that why the city smelled of smoke? She didn't see any riots nearby, though.

"Yes. And given the tension between the locals and the British, I'm not taking any chances with you." His eyes flickered toward the entrance of the hospital. "I don't need Lord Helton's permission to assure your safety. And you're the only reason I stayed in Cairo this afternoon."

She shifted, taking a step back. Noah was making it impossible for her to keep her promise, and she should be angrier with him for it than she was. "You'll tell Lord Helton this was your doing? And that I protested?"

"I'll tell him I had to practically throw you over my shoulder." Noah's eyes glinted with humor.

The crack of a distant gunshot helped her decide. She climbed into the seat. "What's happened? Why are there riots?" she asked as Noah sat back behind the steering wheel again.

Noah pulled out onto the street. "We've finally shown our true colors. Some of the Egyptians are learning the extent to which we've been lying to the Arab world. The Russians released the details of the Sykes-Picot Agreement to the newspapers yesterday. Sir Mark Sykes took it upon himself to parse out the divisions of the Arab world between us and the French after the war."

"Assuming we win, of course." Ginger winced. Whatever the arrangement was, she doubted it was a good look for the British, especially after the contentious Balfour Declaration.

"Of course. Once again we've imposed ourselves on people that don't want to be governed by us or anyone else. And the Sykes agreement directly contradicts the promises that T. E. Lawrence has made to the Arabs who have been fighting for us under Sherif Hussein."

Noah scanned the street in front of him, then he turned, going another route. He drove with a confidence that made Ginger believe he could easily be dropped in any part of the city and find his way out of it.

No wonder Peter Osborne was worried. For an officer of Noah's rank to question the official British position on the Arab policies was radical, even though Ginger understood it and agreed with his perspective. The local Egyptian resentment toward the British was justified. They didn't want the Ottoman rule the British had "freed" them from when they'd declared them a protectorate at the start of the war, effectively ending the Ottoman authority over Egypt.

The British had then overthrown the pro-Ottoman government in Cairo, installing a puppet sultan who favored the British. She'd understood the rationale behind the British, even celebrated it. The Suez Canal was too important to the war effort to lose.

But the Egyptian nationalists had also been led to believe the British installment would be of short duration. What was more, the Egyptian Labor Corp, set up as a voluntary effort to recruit the locals into the war effort, had become compulsory in the interim. The locals resented being pressed into service. The peasants had lost crops of cotton and food to the requisition of the war, leaving them even more destitute.

And now they were learning the British had no intention of leaving at all. No wonder there were riots. Still, she frowned at Noah. Even though she knew the answer, she said in a casual tone, "Darling, have you been so vocal about your opinions of the British situation here in Egypt with others?"

Noah shrugged. "At times. Lord Helton and Victoria have certainly heard my complaints. And some of my friends. I refuse to be a silent, acquiescent party to their deception."

She removed her nurse's cap, unrolling her hair from the tight knot at the back of her head. Her scalp felt instantly freer, the tension in her head releasing. "Don't you think that could bring you problems?"

"Perhaps. But I've proven my loyalty in other ways. I won't apologize for believing that we're blundering in this part of the world. Our motivation for being here will soon out itself. The strategy was always about controlling the oil supply."

She frowned. Her father had claimed the Palestine campaign was about oil, but she'd questioned it. Now the idea of a concession made even more sense. Her father had many flaws but idiocy had not been among them—he'd been assigned to this region of the world with the Foreign Office because he was an expert in the Arab world.

Not for the first time, she wished she could ask her father about everything. It was a wasted hope—he never would have answered her questions. She touched Noah's shoulder. "Did you have your injury treated?"

"Yes, *rohi*. I promised I would." Noah sped, then turned sharply.

She didn't recognize their surroundings. "Where are you going?" He seemed to have taken her further from the European area of Cairo, and the streets were narrower and crowded.

A hint of a smile played at his lips. "I've spent the day trying to come up with the best possible solution of how to deal with Lord Helton's determination to keep us apart. And I think I finally came up with one."

"And that would be?"

An enigmatic gleam was in his eyes. He turned the car into an alleyway and parked.

"Where are we?" she asked as he opened the door for her.

"Old Cairo. We'll walk from here. There isn't a place to park the motorcar where I'd like to take you." There wasn't much room in the alley for him to hold the door and she had to brush past him to get by. As she did, he lifted her chin with his thumb and forefinger. Leaning lower, he kissed her, drawing her closer to him.

She melted into his kiss, feeling as though he'd cloaked her in a blanket of safety and consolation. It amazed her how he made her heart race despite the passage of time. She hadn't imagined what she felt for him. Their love was just as real as the intensity and passion of his kiss. When she pulled away breathless, she searched his gaze. "Isn't Old Cairo a dangerous place to be if there are riots?"

"We shouldn't run into any trouble here. But you ought to change out of that uniform."

"I brought nothing else." She shifted her handbag. "I planned to go home and change there."

"Let's get you some different clothes, then." He reached into the back of the motorcar and pulled out a package in brown paper. He tucked it under his arm, interlaced his fingers with hers, and tugged her down the alleyway. At the warmth of his hand against hers, she felt her face flush. Their relationship had never been one of careless strolls, holding hands.

"What about the motorcar?" She'd left the books Dr. Radford had given her inside it.

"This alley is directly behind the house of an old friend of mine. He'll keep watch over it—he knows to expect it. It's his motorcar."

He had a ready answer for everything. Noah's ability to seem collected and prepared was one of his strongest attributes. She always felt like a harried mess beside him.

They moved into a busy market. In these areas of Cairo, the native Cairenes kept wildly different hours than in the European quarters. The days started later, and the shops remained open until after midnight.

But in their uniforms, they stood out. "How do you know where you're going all the time?"

"Good sense of direction." The smile he gave her was charming. They stopped in front of a café, and a man greeted Noah enthusiastically in rapid Arabic. Noah handed Ginger the package. "If you'll follow the man, he's going to let you use a room beside the kitchen to change."

The paper crinkled as she took it from him. Raising a brow, she asked, "What are we doing here?"

Pointing toward the café, he offered a devious expression. "Don't worry, I'll tell you what I have in mind. After you've changed."

She followed the café owner past tables, further inside. The smell of spices and wood smoke grew stronger as she drew closer to the kitchen. Her stomach growled in response. She had eaten nothing since tea earlier that afternoon. This seemed like the sort of place Noah would frequent though.

And he must, considering that he knew the owner well enough for the man to let her borrow a room. The room was a storage closet with a single electric bulb hanging down in the center. Despite Noah being near, she wedged the back of a chair under the doorknob, to be certain she'd be left alone.

She unwrapped the package, revealing a smoky blue silk gown

—not quite European but not traditional Egyptian either. The bodice hugged the curves of her breasts, the neckline a deep-V embroidered with beads. From there, it flared to a full, long skirt. A pair of sandals and a light-blue head scarf were also in the package.

Whatever Noah had planned, he wanted her well-dressed for it. Forbidden as it was to be with him, a thrill of excitement curled within her.

After she'd dressed, she did her best to fold her uniform neatly into the package and tie it up. Her flame-red hair wreathed her face as she arranged the veil. Without a mirror, she didn't know how she looked, but she hoped she'd done well enough.

She left the storeroom and passed back out to the street. Hugging her uniform to her chest, she searched for Noah. She didn't see him, but the street was dark, streetlamps throwing light onto the surroundings. A pigeon near one table of the café cooed and flapped its wings, boldly coming closer to her, despite the time of night. It tilted its head toward her, beady black eyes fixed on her package.

"Oh, be off," she told it. "I don't have any food for you."

A low whistle caught her attention. Noah approached from the shadows across the street. He gave her an admiring look as he stopped in front of her. "You look beautiful."

She laughed, enjoying his compliments. He'd never been so overtly flirtatious or so jovial in his attentions toward her. "I thought you'd abandoned me," she teased.

He pulled her into his arms and kissed her, as though there weren't dozens of other people around to see. People who would probably disapprove of their public displays of affection. But Noah didn't seem to care. He seemed ... happy. Releasing her, he stepped back, a warm smile still in his eyes. "You ready?"

"Ready for what?" Why on earth was he being so cryptic?

He slipped his hands into hers. "To get married."

*Married?* She stared at him, her jaw dropping. A thousand thoughts assailed her. She didn't know whether to fling her arms around his neck with joy or punch him for being a tease. "Today? Are you serious?"

He kissed the back of her knuckles. "Completely." He kept his gaze locked to hers. "I know it isn't the wedding we talked about, but I refuse to allow anyone to threaten you. Including Lord Helton. This will be the last time someone will threaten you and you can't come to me."

She wanted to melt at his words. She hadn't paid attention before, but he wore his dress uniform. Her eyes filled with tears of relief, of knowing she had his protection to rely on. The fears of Lord Helton's threats against her family had been gnawing on her. "But what about my promise to him? He says he'll ruin my family."

He took the package containing her uniform and held it under one arm. Holding her hand with his free one, he tugged her down the pavement. "To hell with that promise."

His hand tightened. "I won't have you being blackmailed and bribed to stay away from me. We don't have to tell anyone but Lord Helton about our marriage. For now. We can meet in secret so that you can worry less about your family. As it is, I can't promise you a life together right now. I'll be sent away on an assignment soon enough. But at least we'll be married and no one will ever be able to separate us."

Her mind raced. "But won't Lord Helton be furious?" Much as she wanted to marry him, she didn't follow his logic. How would marrying help solve things?

She wrinkled her nose at a dead mouse under the window of a shop they passed. They crossed a busy street, and she blinked up in surprise as they approached a familiar wall of banded red and white Roman masonry. "Is this the Fortress of Babylon?" she asked.

Noah nodded as they passed through an arch. "There's a Coptic church here where the priest has agreed to marry us." He cleared his throat, stopping under a row of hedges. "I'm going to tell Lord Helton that if he continues to threaten my wife, I'm requesting a transfer. He doesn't want that to happen." His eyes darkened. "And this way, if something happens to me, at least you'd have some pension."

Ginger fought a wave of fear. "How utterly romantic. Please don't talk like that." Her throat tightened. She could hardly imagine the many dangers he had yet to face. "Marriage with a backdrop of riots seems graceless."

He held her hands. "Love is the only remedy to death and destruction—the only thing that reminds us what we have to live for." Noah kissed her, pushing a tendril of hair from her face with a gentle touch. "You taught me that, *rohi*. I would rather live one day amid war as your husband than a thousand years of peace without your love. So marry me. Here. And later, if your family wishes it. I'll marry twenty times so long as you're the one standing with me."

She wanted to marry him. More than anything. But what would her mother say? She searched his gaze. "But don't we have to go to the consulate?"

"We'll do that later when we're able to have our marriage be in the open. Today, I'll settle for marrying you in the church. I can keep the paperwork until you're ready to share it."

He seemed to have thought the whole thing through more than she gave him credit for. "But—"

"I'm not taking no for an answer." He rubbed his thumb over the back of her hand. "And you'll find that when I'm determined to get what I want, I do."

Had he concocted this scheme today? Her excitement grew.

"Oh, I never doubted that." She leaned forward and kissed him. "You're mad. This is mad. And I love you."

"Then you'll do it?" Church bells tolled and they both looked up at the path, past the ruins of the old fort. The famous churches of St. George and the Hanging Church were around the corner.

She cocked an eyebrow at him. The bells continued to echo against the stone walls, the warm winter breeze enveloping them both. "It didn't seem like you were asking my permission."

"Always. It doesn't count if you don't say yes."

Her heart felt strangely light. "Then, yes."

He squeezed her hand. "Good."

As he led her away from the more famous ruins in the fort, she tried to wrap her mind around Noah's proposal.

*What if we haven't thought this through enough?* She didn't know how she would break the news to her mother. Especially now that her mother seemed so interested in setting her up with William.

She doubled her steps to keep up with Noah's stride. He looked striking in his uniform, and it was the way she always thought of him. This wasn't the way she'd ever pictured her wedding—racing hand in hand with him down the narrow streets of Coptic Cairo while protests broke out over the city.

"Which church are you taking me to?" She peered around as they headed into an ancient pathway between buildings.

"The Church of St. Barbara. It's not like the other churches here in the fort. The exterior is unassuming, but it's one of my favorites."

"A Catholic church?" She'd never even set foot in one before. "My father may roll over in his grave."

Noah gave her a rueful expression. "Unfortunately, the church won't consider our marriage valid unless I'm married by a Catholic priest. And since we're currently neglecting the validity of our marriage through the government, we may as well have it through the church."

"You're Catholic?" She shouldn't be surprised. He was Irish, after all. But it was among the many things she probably ought to have known about him before she'd agreed to marry him.

This would do nothing to warm her mother to him. She bit her lip. Well, it wouldn't be the first scandal she'd faced. She hadn't planned on a return to society life at any rate. Would the priest mind she was Anglican?

Noah continued to lead the way through the narrow streets. It only felt as though they'd walked a block when Noah slowed in front of a nondescript building. She surveyed a small sign on the exterior. She couldn't read Arabic. "This is the church? It seems so hidden."

"And yet," Noah held open the wooden door, "it's lovely inside." As they entered, her heart pounded.

Noah led her through the back of the church, which appeared to have only one sanctuary. "Wait here," he told her. "I have to find the priest."

She frowned. "And if he says no?"

"He won't. I've already arranged it."

Her eyes drifted toward the altar as he left. The church was distinctly beautiful, though small. A few rows of carved wooden benches sat in front of the altar, marble columns flanking them. The architecture was warm, distinctly Coptic.

She avoided the gaze of the saint depicted in an icon near to where she stood. Catholics believed firmly in the need for confession, and she'd committed so many sins, especially in the past year. What atonement was required of her?

"That's St. Barbara." Noah's voice came from behind her, and she startled. He wrapped his arms around her waist, pulling her to rest against him as they stared at the icon together. "The scene depicted is when her father locked her in a tower for refusing to marry any of the young, wealthy aristocrats he preferred for her."

This time she looked at the serene expression of the saint more closely. The story was one she could relate to. She relaxed into Noah's arms, her worries dissolving. "Did she end up marrying a mysterious soldier at night instead?"

Before Noah could answer, they were interrupted by the shuffling sound of footsteps. An elderly priest in vestments approached them. He bowed his head at Ginger and she curtsied.

"Shall we begin?" the priest asked in broken English. He pointed them down the aisle, toward the altar.

Just like that? No organ, no bridesmaids. Flowers or family.

*Just Noah.*

It was perfect. Just as it should be.

Noah took his place beside her and removed his hat. The priest began the ceremony. As the words poured from his lips, she held back a smile. She'd never thought that her wedding would take place in a language she didn't understand. Let alone in a Catholic church.

She met Noah's eyes. "I don't understand a thing, you know," she muttered to him.

Noah leaned toward her and whispered, "It's Coptic. The closest language there is to that of the Ancient Egyptians. But the only words that matter are the ones we say to each other."

His words produced a shiver. The ancient language of the people of this land—a land she loved and felt forever tied to. Now more than ever.

As it came time for them to say their vows, the priest resumed his English. Noah clasped her hands as she said, "I, Virginia, take thee Noah, to be my wedded husband …"

Goosebumps rose on her arms as she continued. Noah's eyes didn't move from hers, and the sound of the words faded into the furthest recesses of her mind. When Noah spoke, she barely heard him. He'd whispered these words to her when he'd been fading in the desert. There was no difference between what he'd said then and now. Except that there was a witness.

Her heart and soul already belonged to him.

When Noah finished his vows, the priest held out his hand for a ring to bless it.

The corners of his mouth curved in a smile and he reached into his pocket. "Since you've absconded with my mother's ring, I had to come up with one of my own." The ring in the palm of his hand was a simple delicate gold band, with the ankh symbol part of the design. The ankh was sideways, the bottom of it melting away into the band.

Tears misted in her eyes. "I love it, Noah."

She stared at the ring, their hands together. "With this ring, I thee wed. In the name of the Father, and of the Son, and of the Holy Spirit." Noah's voice was clear as he slipped it onto her finger.

Her mind went back to Lord Helton's threats. She couldn't bear the thought of losing Noah. Not now. Not ever.

## CHAPTER SIXTEEN

The sharp knocking at the door of Noah's room in Shepheard's came while he slept. He awoke abruptly, disoriented, reaching for the gun he kept beside his pillow. The soft feel of sheets over his body brought him back to the present, and he stood. He pulled a pair of trousers on, then made his way to the door.

Lord Helton stood there. He didn't wait for an invitation to enter and pushed past, his booted footsteps thumping against the floor.

Noah closed the door, then turned on a lamp. He blinked as his eyes adjusted to the light, reading the tension of Lord Helton's posture. *Damn.* Had he learned of Noah's marriage to Ginger already? At least Noah had had the sense not to bring her back to his room, however much he'd wanted to. "What—"

"They've taken her." Lord Helton faced him. A look of wild desperation had filled his eyes.

Noah reached for his jacket. His shoulder ached where he'd been cut the night before, the sutures feeling restrictive. "Who?"

"Victoria. They've kidnapped her. During the riots. I didn't realize she was missing for some time. I thought she was out at a late dinner." Lord Helton paced, going toward the window of the room. He glanced out, then pulled the drapery tighter.

Victoria? Kidnapped? Noah felt a reflexive surge of ire. "Do you know who took her?" He buttoned his jacket, his fingers feeling steadier now.

"A group of Egyptian nationalists calling themselves the Brotherhood of the Scorpion."

A spark of disbelief simmered to the surface of Noah's sleep-addled mind. The Aleaqrab? The same group whose assailant had attacked Ginger. "How did you learn of it?"

"They delivered a note an hour ago. Along with a message in her writing confirming the veracity of their words." Lord Helton pulled a folded paper from his pocket, his hand shaking. "They tied it to a brick and threw the note through a window of my home."

If the Aleaqrab had attacked Ginger and then kidnapped Victoria, it was no coincidence. Both acts appeared to have deliberate targets that would affect both him and Lord Helton.

Noah took the note from him. It was written in Arabic.

*Your daughter is safe. We will contact you to negotiate her release. Go to the authorities and she dies.*

*Brotherhood of the Scorpion.*

"They have made no demands." He furrowed his brow at Lord Helton.

"I'm aware. I think they simply intended to inform me." Lord Helton approached Noah, his frame sagging.

Lord Helton's gaze swept the room before he found the desk and chair. He sat, his expression haunted. "You care for Victoria. Maybe not the way she'd hoped, but you've always treated her with respect. And you're the only one I would trust with this. You read the note yourself. If I go to the police or the government, they'll kill her. I won't wait to find out what they want.

Please, Benson. I know you intended to go and find Jack on your leave. But find Victoria for me, please."

Noah didn't like the idea of Victoria being in the hands of anyone who might consider themselves the enemy of the British. Noah smoothed his bedsheets then sat. "Unofficially?"

"It would be a personal favor to me. I can't afford for Victoria's reputation to be compromised, let alone my position. I wouldn't want anyone to know even if they hadn't threatened her life. A spymaster with such an exposed vulnerability—I may as well hang up the entire operation and go back to England." Lord Helton removed a handkerchief and wiped his nose. For once, he looked truly terrified. "And my daughter, in the hands of such men …" He blinked away the fear that flashed in his eyes. "I'll pay you handsomely for it."

"I don't need you to pay me." Noah considered Lord Helton's words. He'd intended to inform Helton about his marriage to Ginger the next time he saw him, but right now wasn't the time. Helton's offer gave him some leverage, though. *What if I can use this to defuse his fury?*

"I'll need Alastair's help." Noah sucked in a breath, torn by what this meant. If he could find Victoria quickly, that would be one thing. But it would keep him from going after Jack. He raked his fingers through his hair and then winced, his fingertips stumbling on the scabs from the injury Stephen had given him.

He looked back at Lord Helton. "Where's Fisher?"

"Surely you're not suggesting he's involved?"

Noah gave him a skeptical look. "That's precisely what I'm suggesting. A group of nationalists targeted Victoria and kidnapped her? Why? To what end?" He grabbed his gun and holster, then strapped them to his hip. "Can you take me to him?"

Lord Helton rubbed his thin, precisely trimmed beard. Then

he stood. "Yes. We'll go directly. Does this mean you'll help me find her?"

Choosing between his friends was something Noah detested, particularly when one of those friends was Jack. But Victoria's kidnapping was new, and she could be in more immediate danger. Had Jack survived this long, the Turks may not be in a hurry to kill him.

The thought of either of them in enemy hands sent chills down his spine. "I'll help. But in return, you'll release Ginger Whitman from her promise to you."

Helton's eyes shifted to his with faint surprise. "If that's what you require."

"It is." Then, seeing Lord Helton's broken look, Noah added in a softer tone, "I'll do everything I can to find her, I promise."

Noah finished dressing, and the two men left Shepheard's. Lord Helton's car waited outside, the driver keeping the engine running. As he climbed into the back, Noah thought of the Egyptian in Ezbekieh. What could the motive be to take both Ginger and Victoria? To kill them?

The thought flooded him with furious adrenaline. Stephen had to be behind this.

The only thing they had in common was Noah. Both women could be used to manipulate and hurt him—and now Lord Helton. Much as he couldn't give Victoria what she wanted, he cared about her deeply. And he'd seen more than once what a group of men could do to a woman they kidnapped, especially a beautiful one like Victoria.

Nearby palms were dark silhouettes in the night, inky black giants that loomed over them. The car wove them through the streets of Cairo more quickly than it ever could have done during the day. The city rested—it was nearly three in the morning. Yet, even with the night, the air felt rife with brewing conflict. If he could, he would send Ginger home with her family. This wasn't the time to be in Cairo.

With the state of the world, it didn't seem like the time to be anywhere.

Some of the tension in his shoulders released, thinking of the evening he'd spent with Ginger. After their marriage ceremony, they'd gone back to the café, where Noah's friend had prepared them a small feast. Noah had relished the intimacy. Then he'd been forced to return her home. Spending the night together would have to wait for now. But eating a meal with Ginger wasn't something he took for granted. Their time together had always been so limited, especially with simple moments.

Whatever Lord Helton's reasons for involving Ginger in the intelligence world, he loathed the thought of it. She was smart and capable. She'd already proven herself capable of rising to the challenge. The more they seemed to confront danger together, the braver she became. And if she hadn't been the woman he loved, he would have been the first to recommend her.

But with each passing day he grew more convinced that Stephen had something elaborate planned. First Jack, now Victoria. The odds of these events coinciding with Stephen's return seemed impossible.

Alastair had warned him not to underestimate Stephen. That wasn't the problem. Noah knew too well Stephen was capable of anything. But Stephen's plan seemed too disjointed for Noah's mind to make sense of it all. He was missing something important. Some piece of the puzzle that might not be clear until it was too late.

As the motorcar sped from the heart of Cairo, Noah recognized the well-beaten path toward Giza from his younger days. Rarely did he find the occasion to go to the most famous location in all Egypt—the site of the Sphinx and the Great Pyramid—except for military business.

The pyramids themselves soon came into view, standing like sentinels in the cold moonlight. They continued past them, past the famed Mena Hotel that now served as a hospital for the Australians, past the encampments of troops.

At last they arrived at a lonely building of crumbling stone that barely seemed well-maintained enough to be habitable, let alone house a prisoner as important as Stephen. The motorcar stopped beside it. From their perch near the entrance, two guards lifted their heads, hands on their rifles.

Lord Helton led the way and the guards saluted him, clearing the way on sight. Just inside the entrance, another four guards were in a room just off the main door. One of them came to greet Lord Helton.

"We need to see Fisher. Right now." Lord Helton gave no sign to the guard of his distress. The guard nodded.

*Just how many prisoners are housed here?* Noah hadn't been here before, which seemed odd. But six heavily armed guards—those he could see—for one man made it appear this place might be for the prisoners the CID didn't want interfered with.

They passed through a dark corridor, the sound of sand and dirt crunching against the floor. The guard used a torch. Given the location of the place, it wasn't likely to have electricity.

At last they reached a doorway, and the guard pulled out a set of keys. He opened a trapdoor inset in the door, only large enough for a man to get a hand through, and shone the light in. "Fisher. You have guests."

Then he unlocked the door.

The smell of human refuse and decay wafted past as the door opened, a smell so pungent that Noah lifted his curled forefinger against his nostrils. Lord Helton strode in front of

Noah, taking the torch from the guard. "You may go," Lord Helton said.

As the guard retreated, Lord Helton focused the beam of the light onto the floor. Stephen lay on a filthy rattan mat, dressed in a *galabeyah*, shackles on his hands and feet. The cell was cramped, and the only other object inside was a stone pit in the corner no bigger than the circumference of a bowl, which acted as a privy.

No wonder the stench was so strong.

A window, high off the ground and the size of a gun slot, was the only view to the outside world.

The hair on his face had grown into the smattering of a beard, and his hair appeared greasy and unkempt. His eyes squinted toward them, then he struggled to stand. "M-my dear … fellows." Stephen coughed. "C-come to mock me?"

As poor as the conditions were, Stephen didn't appear to be injured. Perhaps he'd been shoved around—certainly not the torture Jack was likely enduring.

At the thought of his friend, Noah's fists tightened. He approached Stephen and grabbed him by the shirtfront. Noah jerked him to his bare feet, then pushed him against the wall. Stephen did little to resist, because he hadn't been expecting it or because he was too weak.

"What do you know of the Brotherhood of the Scorpion?" Noah demanded.

Stephen drew a shaky breath. Then, the slightest of smiles tipped at his mouth, but his eyes lolled back, his face pale. "So … much … might. There's little you can do to me now."

Lord Helton set a hand on Noah's shoulder. Noah stepped back, his fingertips tingling. No torment would be sufficient. In the past, Noah had told himself he wanted Stephen to suffer. Now that he was powerless to do anything about it, the truth was he simply wanted Stephen dead.

Lord Helton took a case from his breast pocket, then offered a cigarette to Stephen. Stephen nodded and Lord Helton placed it in his lips, then struck a match and lit it.

The burning scent of the extinguished match was a relief, helping mask the smell of refuse, although a temporary one. Stephen drew in a deep breath, his features relaxing visibly, the lines of dirt around his eyes and forehead smoothing. "You see, Benson? Lord Helton knows c-c-civility. Not th-that … you know much about manners. You fool others well enough." Stephen took a drag from his cigarette, and it shook between his fingers with such force as to be almost pitiable. "Y-you'll never be anything other than a bastard w-without breeding. Or culture."

"Do not mistake my gesture for congeniality, Fisher." Lord Helton's voice was raw. "Egyptian nationalists have taken my daughter. I haven't the patience for your games this evening. Do you know anything about the Brotherhood of the Scorpion?"

Despite Stephen's inability to repeat the information to anyone, Noah didn't like how much Lord Helton had given away. Noah had hoped to put Stephen in a position where he could find out for himself if Stephen knew about Victoria's kidnapping.

Stephen clamped the cigarette in his teeth. Then, with effort, he lifted his hands to his mouth. The shackles had worn sores on his wrists. He held the cigarette between his thumb and forefinger. "The Aleaqrab." He gestured faintly. "Amongst themselves."

"Do you know their leader?" Noah asked.

Stephen's lips curled. "It'll take more than a cigarette for me t-to tell you."

Noah's fist landed squarely in Stephen's gut and he doubled over in pain, dropping his cigarette on the floor. Noah jerked him upright. "Is that motivating enough for you?"

Coughing, Stephen stooped down and lifted the cigarette he'd dropped. He rubbed the dirt from the moist end of it and replaced it in his mouth in a desperate movement. When his eyes lifted to meet Noah's, he didn't conceal his contempt. His coughing continued. "A ... a ... glass of water?"

"If it were up to me, I'd give you nothing but the parting gift of a noose." Noah glowered down at him, knowing his rage was spiraling. Lord Helton had kept him out of Stephen's handling for this reason. Stephen had done too much to him and Jack's capture was merely the latest foul act that had extinguished the last bit of decency Noah could muster with the man. "Victoria's kidnapping has your stench all over it."

Stephen's face flickered, a trace of fear in his features. He sat, wearily, back to the wall. "And how am I to have accomplished such a feat from this ... this *place*?" He spoke the last word as though it were a bitter poison.

"You could have ordered it before you surrendered." Noah stepped back, curling his hand into a fist that he flexed. His wrist ached from punching Stephen.

Stephen's gaze flicked toward Lord Helton. "I could have ... but I didn't. I hoped to come here and offer everything I've learned while working for the enemy for—r-redemption. To keep my head from a noose. Perhaps I would have been better off with the Germans. I'll find no justice in you."

"What's just? For Lord Braddock and his son to be rotting in their graves while you smoke Turkish cigarettes in Jerusalem?" Noah narrowed his gaze. "For Ginger to have your initials permanently carved into her skin?" His feet stayed firmly planted, despite the memory motivating him to thrash Stephen once again. "Or Jack to be in a prisoner of war camp?"

Stephen's eyes flashed. *The bastard knows we have caught him lying about Jack.*

Lord Helton tensed beside Noah as though expecting Noah

to attack once again. Steeling himself to stay calm, Noah stepped further back. When he spoke, his voice felt steadier. "You want to show you deserve a chance at breathing air that doesn't smell like shit? Start by telling us about the Aleaqrab."

Stephen stared at the burning end of his cigarette. "Khaled Al-Mashat. The leader. The group is young, motivated, and armed. They're furious about the Egyptian conscription and the oppression of the British." He flicked ash toward the ground. "I don't know what motivation they could have to take Victoria, but I doubt they'll treat her kindly."

The name was a start. Alastair could do wonders with a name. "Do you know how to find them?" Lord Helton asked.

"They're very secretive. The group would only meet with me if I agreed to wear a sack over my head."

"How did you meet with them?" Noah asked.

"I was given a place to wait in Old Cairo, and then I was taken to Al-Mashat. They blindfolded and bound me and placed me in a cart. That's all I know." Stephen gave him an icy look.

If Alastair were here, he would have been more skilled at learning what else Stephen knew. But Alastair was an expert in that—and Noah wasn't. The information gave him a place to start, even if Noah didn't believe Stephen's denial of involvement. He nodded toward Lord Helton. "We can leave now."

The two men started for the door. Behind them, Stephen's shackles clinked and scraped. Noah turned to see Stephen struggle to his feet. In the fading beam of the torchlight, Stephen's eyes were like the slits of a cat.

Stephen's voice was a raspy whisper. "I-I'm going to take everything away from you, Benson. Soon."

## CHAPTER SEVENTEEN

Ginger found her mother in the garden in the morning, pruning a rosebush. At home in England, her mother's roses had been prize-winning, but Ginger had always suspected the gardener's touch had brought about the awards. Egypt had proved that suspicion wrong. Her mother had tended to the roses in her garden in Cairo with loving attention, often rising early, like this morning, to work before the sun was full in the sky.

Since she'd been out of the Cairo house for so many months, her mother had probably been aghast at the state of her plants.

Ginger watched her from the verandah, her heart a mixture of nervous anticipation, unbridled excitement, and fear. She'd woken feeling as though she was floating on a cloud. Marrying the man she loved had been the best decision she could have made.

But her marriage meant more secrets and lies to her family.

At the same time, she wasn't ready to tell them yet.

Her mother pushed a veil of mosquito netting away from her hat and removed it, revealing her own red hair glistening in the soft light of the golden morning. As she tilted her face toward the sun, she spotted Ginger and her lips turned up in a smile. "You startled me." She removed her dirt-covered gloves and came toward Ginger, holding them in her palm. "Leaving for the hospital already?"

"In the next half hour." Ginger smoothed her hand over her apron.

"They kept you out late last night." Her mother continued past her and set her gloves on a rattan table on the verandah. "Or was it the colonel?"

Ginger's face flushed. She'd told Noah to leave her in the back of the house, for fear her mother might spot him dropping her off. And he had—but then he'd kissed her. And a few kisses later, they'd had to drag themselves away from each other regretfully. "Mama…"

Her mother wrinkled her straight nose and placed her pruning shears beside the gloves. "Come now, don't lie to me. It's unbecoming."

Ginger lifted her chin, determined to act with as much grace as she could. But it was better to be direct with her mother. "How did you know?"

"I saw your display of affection toward each other. And now I understand why you've been keeping poor William at a distance." Her mother didn't look her way, giving a gracious smile to a servant who came outside with tea. She must have ordered it earlier.

When the servant had retired from the area, she turned toward Ginger, her face unreadable. "I thought you'd put that affair to rest last May."

"Mama, you don't know him—"

"Nor do I care to. The man is an unscrupulous debaucher. He nearly destroyed your reputation. And it still hasn't recovered. He'll bring you nothing but ruin."

Ginger wished her mother's voice held the anger that she knew she must be feeling. Instead, she spoke in a manner that was detached and unemotional, as though they were discussing the weather.

Ginger wrestled with telling her mother the whole truth but she held her tongue. "We're going to marry, Mama. We love each other—that never stopped."

Her mother sat and poured herself a cup of tea. "Well, make it stop. Before you finish destroying what's left of this family. You know the difference between having emotions and acting on them." Her calm broke as she lifted her tea to her lips, her fingers quivering. She steadied her hand, replacing the cup on the saucer. "I don't know what you're thinking. But I know that when that man appeared in our lives, our entire family was devastated. Whatever hand he had in your father and brother's deaths..." She swallowed hard.

Ginger's chest compressed and she struggled to breathe. Her mother thought Noah was to blame for her father and Henry's deaths? Then a worse thought occurred: *what will Mother think of me if she ever learns the truth about how Henry died?*

Would her mother ever forgive her?

Ginger lived daily with the reality of what she'd done. Especially now, being in this house, haunted by the memories of what she had been so powerless to stop. Though her father and brother were ultimately to blame, she'd participated in the destruction of her family.

Finding her voice at last, Ginger said, "Stephen Fisher killed Papa, I told you that. He's the only one to blame. And he's the reason our family came to ruin." She cleared her throat and then added in a softer voice, "And now he's returned."

Her mother flinched. "What do you mean?"

"He's been captured and he's back in Cairo. And he's told the authorities about the concession Father supposedly obtained from Ibn Saud." Ginger set her shoulders back. "Noah told me last night."

"Damn." Her mother's voice was a breathless whisper. She rarely swore. Her mother set both hands on the edge of the table, gripping it so firmly that her knuckles turned white. She sat rigid in her chair. "No wonder they were asking me about it."

Her reaction proved to be exactly what Ginger had feared the most. "Does that mean the concession exists?"

Her mother's face paled. "Your father told me not to speak of it. He feared the government would try to take it from him after they'd learned of his crimes. He said it could be quite valuable after the war and wanted me to sell it to provide for our family rather than wait for the exploration, which could take decades."

"The government *does* intend to seize it." Ginger approached her, then sat and took her hand comfortingly. "Noah said if I help them locate the papers about the concession, they'll allow us to have ten percent. Otherwise, they plan to seize it in its entirety."

"He didn't obtain it illegally!" Her mother had a desperate edge to her voice. Then, as though realizing her composure had slipped, she drew a deep breath. "What are you going to do?"

"To begin with, I thought I'd ask you."

"I'm uncertain what happened to it. It's missing. Mr. Brandeis couldn't find any paperwork about it in his files. Your father entrusted everything to him."

"Father's solicitor in Cairo?" *How can something so important go missing?* Ginger's disappointment stung.

Her mother gave a furtive glance back toward the house. "After your father's death, I paid Mr. Brandeis a visit to ask him about it and the rest of the estate. The paperwork about the concession had vanished. And with it, any claim we have. Only your father could have induced Mr. Brandeis to turn over something so valuable. But Brandeis claimed he never gave it to your father."

However modest a lead, it might help. She'd have to speak to Mr. Brandeis. "Do you have his address here in Cairo?"

Concern showed in her mother's eyes. "Will you try to find the concession?"

"I must. There's no choice, really. If it isn't found and if I don't help, we'll be left with nothing." She didn't want to tell her mother just how far she'd involved herself with the matter—leaving it as a casual hint would be best for now. "Do you think it's possible Father tried to hide the concession in the days before his death?"

"Of course it's possible. Your father was mad with worry." Her mother raised her gaze to Ginger's. "But the world your father was a part of was also what led to his downfall. We know that better than anyone. Please do be careful how deeply you dig. I might have some of his old files and his datebook. The CID took most of it, but I hid some things that might have been incriminating."

*Incriminating of her mother?* Ginger didn't want to know anything that she might want to forget later. "Can you give me what you have?"

Her mother's gaze faltered. "I'll see. In the meantime, you would do well to remember that your obligation to your family is foremost. Any of the servants could have seen you last night. I won't hesitate to tell Colonel Benson to keep his hands off you if I see him again."

Ginger cringed with embarrassment. "Mother—"

"No, absolutely not—no argument from you. I can't pretend not to be disappointed to find you right back to the behavior that tore us apart. I thought you had learned your lesson." Her mother eyed the wedding ring on Ginger's hand. She sniffed. "I suppose he gave you that?"

Ginger tugged it between the fingers of her right hand. She threw her shoulders back. "He loves me, Mama. I can't save our family through marriage to William, I'm sorry. Not when I love Noah."

"You hardly know anything about the man!" Her mother's voice was a frustrated growl this time. She settled her expression, then said, "Who is his mother? His father? Where was he born? For goodness' sake, Ginger—I married for love *and* money, and look where it got me. Having to rely on the money my mother can divert toward me, ashamed, and isolated. Marry a kind man. That will get you much further in the end."

"Noah is a kind man—"

Her mother sipped her tea then frowned. A gnat floated on the top of it. She sighed and removed it. "A man that's willing to allow your name to be ruined is not a kind man. Your Colonel Benson may be many things, including handsome, but you should remember that he's made a career in the military by being an accomplished liar." Frowning, her mother poured her tea into the dirt beside the verandah.

Ginger held her tongue. The truth was, on that point, she couldn't argue.

* * *

"Did you look over some of the study materials I gave you?" Dr. Radford glanced from her work on the patient in surgery toward Ginger. She'd excised a gangrenous piece of flesh while Ginger irrigated the wound with Dakin's solution.

"Briefly." Ginger dabbed the surrounding skin with gauze. She'd hardly been able to sleep after she'd arrived home, too happy after her evening with Noah. In the end, Dr. Radford's books had been the only thing that had helped her settle her mind. "I read one volume through once, which isn't usually enough for me when I'm studying anything. But it was quite interesting."

Dr. Radford gave her a pleased look. "If you can prepare, I'll give you the first round of exams in a few days. See if you qualify to be trained in anesthesia."

Ginger drew her hand back from the wound, and Dr. Radford continued her work. "I'm uncertain I'm going to be a nurse for much longer. I hope to return to England in a few months and study as you did," Ginger said.

Dr. Radford raised an eyebrow. "I have to admit, I was hoping to keep you to myself for longer than that." After a few beats, she added, "But I'm happy to help you in any way I can."

Ginger swallowed, thinking of her mother's anger when she'd learned of her continued relationship with Noah. How would she respond when Ginger told her the plans for medical school? She'd made light of Ginger's wishes when it had come to William. "Nothing is settled yet."

Dr. Radford was silent for a few minutes, her brow furrowed in concentration. When she pulled away for Ginger to irrigate the wound once again, she glanced up. "Well, approval isn't ever going to come with this job. The world isn't ready for female physicians. Not even if we keep the progress we've made during the war. Perhaps someday. For now, there are many challenges and very little gratitude for our trouble."

Her words were without ceremony and hit Ginger in the gut. Feeling chastened, Ginger asked, "What are some difficulties you've faced?"

Dr. Radford inspected her work. "I think we removed all the necrotic flesh. Let's dress it for now, with instructions to irrigate every three hours." She straightened as Ginger set to work with the dressing.

"The difficulties I've faced? To begin with, my mother wept when I told her. She's immensely proud of me now, but it wasn't always that way. Then the RAMC refused to accept our help at the war's start. When they finally did, they sent us to Malta but refused us the uniform of the RAMC doctors. We aren't given a rank or status. I've had men working under me refuse my orders and deride my position. And don't forget men consider me unmarriageable because of my work. The list goes on." Dr. Radford stood beside Ginger. "You work with efficiency, Sister Whitman."

"Thank you, Doctor." Ginger continued her work, aware of Dr. Radford's close gaze. Though she'd done dressings thousands of times before, she felt an uptick of nerves in her back. She wanted to impress Dr. Radford in a way that she hadn't with some of the male doctors she'd worked with.

When they finished, Ginger headed toward the nurses' lavatory to change out of her uniform. The morning had passed faster than Ginger had expected. There was something strange about simply walking out of the hospital at the end of her shift, especially with an entire afternoon ahead of her.

She'd spent so long as a nurse that it had felt natural to slip back into that world. But she wasn't a part of it, not really. She missed the camaraderie of the QAs and the other nurses. The closeness of the work with the patients. Right now, it felt very much as though she had one foot out the door.

The address her mother had given her for Mr. Brandeis was a short walk from the hospital. Ginger set off on foot. A walk would do her good and help clear some nagging, troubling thoughts.

The passing carriages and cabs reminded her of how Noah had shown up the night before. Hopefully the protests that had broken out the day before had been quelled. The local government had little tolerance for anti-British demonstrations. But she was more wary of the people she passed on the street. The anger of the locals was taut like a violin string ready to break.

She hurried, passing the shops emblazoned with English and Arabic signs. There were many among the Egyptian community that had welcomed the British, especially after centuries of Ottoman oppression. How would the peoples of the British colonies—especially the Moslem ones—respond to the British policies of late? In Palestine, there had been an equal number of troops from far-flung places such as India.

The surroundings were familiar, though Ginger rarely walked alone on the streets of Cairo. At last, she saw the small sign posted above a doorway: *Jacob Brandeis, Esq.*

A bell on the door jingled as she opened it.

Mr. Brandeis received her within a minute of her arrival. A stout man, he mopped a bead of sweat from his forehead despite the circulating air from a large fan in the room. "Lady Virginia." He held a seat for her. "I'm so pleased to see you. Are you well? Still serving as a nurse?"

"I am. Both well and serving as a nurse." She tucked her feet to the side, resting her hands on her lap. "I'm sorry to drop in on you so unexpectedly, but thank you for taking the time to see me."

Mr. Brandeis' face was amicable. "It's always a pleasure to see you. The Whitman family is always welcome here. How is your mother?"

"Newly in Cairo once more. My father's heir has come to town, and my mother and Lucy have been showing him the sights."

"That's wonderful. Your mother left a gaping hole in our small community when she left." Mr. Brandeis sat in front of a large desk cluttered with papers, ledgers, and files. He nudged a few of them to the side to make a space for his hands, which he clasped and set on the desk. "How can I help you?"

Should she come right out and ask about the concession? "I had some questions about an issue regarding my father's estate."

Mr. Brandeis pulled out a leather file and set his hands on it. He gave her an abrupt placid smile. "Unfortunately, I'm uncertain I have the information you're seeking. I reviewed everything with your mother. The entailment and estate were to be settled by your father's man in London. The only parts of your father's estate I handled were his properties here in Egypt and the one in Malta, which I believe your mother shuttered until his debts could be settled."

*Malta?* Ginger blinked. She'd never heard of her father having any property in Malta. And the use of the word *properties* intrigued her. The only property she knew her father had purchased was the house in Cairo. Were there others?

And her mother clearly knew about it all. Why hadn't she mentioned them? What other secrets did her mother keep? She hesitated. Caution would be wise. Mr. Brandeis may not be so willing to share information if he thought Ginger knew nothing about it. "Then you do not know of a concession?"

The smile Mr. Brandeis gave her was enigmatic. "To dig? Not at all. But I didn't realize your father was of the archeological bent. I can look over his papers once again, see if I missed something."

*He was lying.*

She ducked her chin. What was he playing at? Perhaps he thought she couldn't know much about the matter and could deflect it by implying the concession would be for archeology—she imagined most, if not all, the concessions that were obtained in Egypt were for that purpose. "No, you're quite right. My father loathed mummies and 'all that nonsense.'" Ginger gave him a sharp look. "But he didn't loathe oil—and that's the concession I'm referring to. The one he negotiated with Ibn Saud. I must admit I'm surprised at your confusion. My mother said you'd handled the matter."

A streak of crimson crept up Mr. Brandeis' thick neck, and

he coughed. "Yes, well—" He reached for a glass of water and slurped it.

"Come now, Mr. Brandeis, I'm not angry. I'm certain my father directed you not to speak of the matter." Ginger gave him a smooth, sweet smile.

"Yes, of course, of course." Mr. Brandeis still appeared as though he had swallowed something excruciatingly bitter. He attempted to regain his composure. "Yes, that's absolutely correct."

Feeling as though she'd gained the upper hand in the conversation, Ginger leveled her shoulders. Now was the time to ask for the information she wanted—he would be less likely to lie to her while he was flustered. "Mr. Brandeis, it's my understanding that Freddy Mortimer may have been involved with the concession."

Mr. Brandeis blanched. He stood abruptly and gathered his papers. "I'm so sorry, Lady Virginia, but I completely forgot a meeting I must attend this afternoon."

His reaction wasn't entirely surprising, given his attempt to lie to her. But she had to press him further. Clearly he knew something about Freddy Mortimer. And because the concession was missing, perhaps Mortimer was involved. She tried a bold guess. "Mr. Brandeis, did you give the paperwork about the concession to Mr. Mortimer?"

He made another feeble attempt at an excuse, then sank back into his chair, mopping his brow. Now his face looked pained. "Please, Lady Virginia, you must understand. He came with a letter from your father. And because he was so well connected to your father and Lady Hendricks, I had no reason to doubt him. He was supposed to return with a document detailing the precise location of the concession paperwork." His upper lip had broken out into a sweat too.

*The paperwork had been stolen, then.*

A sinking feeling went through Ginger. How on earth was she supposed to track it? Had Mortimer been a thief? A con artist? "Then I suppose it's fruitless to ask where Mortimer is now?"

"I don't know, I haven't seen him for several months." Mr. Brandeis gave her a pitiful look. "I swear I wouldn't have given a thing of such value to him if—"

Ginger cut him down with a look. "Do you have the letter Mortimer presented you? From my father?"

Mr. Brandeis reddened further. He opened the file in front of him. With a trembling hand, he removed an envelope with a broken seal and handed it to her.

Ginger frowned. The seal she recognized immediately. Her father had used a signet ring with the family crest to seal his letters. Her heart sank further. The handwriting was undoubtedly her father's. And he did direct Mr. Brandeis to give the paperwork to Freddy Mortimer, freeing Mr. Brandeis of responsibility.

"You're entirely correct, Mr. Brandeis. This was from my father." She folded it and returned it to him. "Do you remember what Mortimer looked like?"

Relief filled Mr. Brandeis' expression. He replaced the letter, his countenance clearing. "He was a tall man. Thin. Reddish hair—but not like yours. More auburn. A bit of a dandy."

*That could be anyone.*

Ginger rose. "Thank you for your time, Mr. Brandeis. That's a promising start. You said he was connected to Lady Hendricks?" She didn't know who that was, but from the way he had said it, she imagined her mother or Lucy might know.

Mr. Brandeis gave her a hesitant smile, as though delighted she hadn't raked him over the coals. "Yes, yes. He dined with her at Shepheard's frequently."

Ginger wanted to groan. Another person to question—and this time, one that didn't know her. She glanced at the ledgers on Mr. Brandeis' desk, thinking of all he had shared. Then, impulsively, she asked, "Would you mind writing the addresses for my father's properties out for me? My mother wanted to have them handy."

"Of course." Mr. Brandeis opened the file and flipped through a few pages. He pulled out a fountain pen and a fresh sheet of paper, then copied quickly.

She took the paper from him and folded it. "Thank you so much. I appreciate you receiving me."

"Happy to be of service." The solicitor started toward the door.

She thanked him and left, tucking the paper Mr. Brandeis had given her into her handbag. She hailed a calishe and climbed in. As the driver took her toward her house, she pulled the list out. Four properties in Egypt were listed, along with the one in Malta.

Why had her father obtained so much property? And how? He couldn't have had the money for this.

But, then again, he'd borrowed a great deal of money from Stephen. He must have used Stephen's money for these properties. Were they still in her father's name? Her mother might know.

She shuddered. The plain fact was that Stephen likely knew more about her father than she'd ever known. She hadn't been admitted to her father's inner circle. And Stephen had been as close to her father as Henry had been, since Stephen had been Henry's best friend.

Stephen would be an excellent source of information about the concession but she'd rather get nothing from it than to ever speak to him again.

She replaced the list of properties in her handbag. One property was in Old Cairo. She frowned. Why would her father have another property here?

She would have to ask her mother about all of this. But her mother's silence made Ginger wonder if she could trust her mother as much as she once had. After all, her mother had been informed of her father's activities, to some extent. A heavy feeling rested on Ginger's shoulders.

Flies swarmed on the horse attached to the calishe, and she watched the tawny tail swish. A dirty, scrawny thing, she felt sorry for the poor animal. She sat further back against the seat of the calishe, frustrated by the day. She'd hoped Mr. Brandeis could provide a simple answer, but this seemed more complicated than ever.

Then again, if any of this had been easy, the CID wouldn't have likely felt the need to ask for her help.

She needed to find Freddy Mortimer.

## CHAPTER EIGHTEEN

Deep within the heart of the Khan-el-Khalili, Noah had picked up a shadow.

He'd noticed the man following him when he'd dropped into a stall to grill one of his contacts about the Aleaqrab. When Noah had left, he'd purposely gone past a stall covered with beautiful ornate oil lamps of hand-blown glass.

Sure enough, the man was in the reflections of the lamps, about twenty feet behind him. A darker Egyptian, it appeared, with a trim black beard and a *taqiyah* skullcap.

How long had the man been behind him? He wasn't in uniform.

If he'd been followed from Shepheard's to here, it meant one thing: whoever was following him knew his habits.

The idea added to Noah's frustration that he hadn't gotten the answers he'd hoped from the Khan.

Every time he'd mentioned the Aleaqrab, he was met with blank stares or fear. Those who knew about the organization weren't speaking about it, no matter what Noah offered.

The man following him might be a lead.

Noah sped up, heading for a narrow lane. The man following him had some skill—Noah trusted he could keep up—and Noah rounded the corner into a darker alley with a blind turn. He waited just past the turn, back to the wall.

Within moments, the man was upon him. The man realized, seconds too late, that he'd been caught. Noah grabbed him by the front of his robe and shoved him hard against the stone wall of the alley. The man scrambled to get away, but Noah held him with an unrelenting grip, his sidearm at the ready.

"Who sent you?" Noah kept his voice to a low growl.

The man eyed the gun in Noah's hands, his breath foul. He gave Noah a pleading expression. He babbled in rapid Arabic about being at Noah's service and *baksheesh*.

Noah tilted his head. He preferred to get the man somewhere less visible. As it was, anyone might see the confrontation as they passed the alley. "Walk," he said in Arabic. He released the man and motioned toward the alley, keeping the gun level with his back.

"Who hired you?" Noah asked.

"An Englishman," the man said, his shudders lessening.

"I want a name."

The man hesitated then said, "Osborne. He said his name was Osborne."

*Osborne?*

That was the fellow who had hired Ginger.

Noah slowed. He had never met Osborne. Why would someone within the Foreign Office send an Egyptian to follow Noah?

Questioning the man was likely to be a waste of time and he was already weary of the task. "Go." Noah shoved the man forward. "And don't let me catch you following me again."

The man gave a sniveling apology before running down the alley. Noah watched him disappear. He'd barely slept, and his head throbbed with the exhaustion. A strong cup of coffee would help—his progress had been less than promising anyway.

Hopefully Alastair had had more luck. He'd dropped in on his friend in Old Cairo after leaving Lord Helton. If anyone could find more information on the Aleaqrab or Khaled Al-Mashat, it would be Alastair.

He wound his way out of the Khan, stopping only for some coffee and a late breakfast. Then he headed toward the Savoy-Continental. Whatever reason Peter Osborne had for sending a man behind him, Noah was determined to learn of it.

He breezed into the Savoy still in his disguise. He strode toward Lord Helton's office and let himself in without a knock.

Lord Helton was at his desk. He raised a brow as Noah sank into a chair. Setting his pen down, Helton's thin lips twitched. "Do you have news?"

"No. I don't suppose they'd sent you any further communications?" The paper in front of Lord Helton was in Arabic. One of Helton's many assets was his thorough fluency in the language. But he'd been in Egypt for nearly thirty years. He'd even married an Egyptian woman, though she'd died in childbirth with Victoria.

That Lord Helton had never married again was one of the few manners in which his gentler side was apparent. But Noah doubted many people knew the story of his wife. Noah had only learned it through his friendship with Victoria.

Lord Helton shook his head, paling. "Alastair?" More than likely Helton struggled to restrain the emotion he'd showed the night before.

"Alastair will send word when he knows something. I spent the morning combing through my contacts at the Khan. I'm leaving Old Cairo to Alastair—his network there is more extensive." Noah leaned lazily against the chair's arm, feeling more tired than ever now that he'd sat. "An Egyptian followed me. Sent by Peter Osborne at the Foreign Office."

"Osborne?" Lord Helton's eyebrows drew together quizzically. "Why would he send a man to follow you?"

Noah kept his face blank. This was the sort of information Lord Helton ought to have heard before Noah brought it to him. *Is he simply playing dumb?* "I intend to find out. Is his office here at the Savoy?"

"I don't believe so. But"—Lord Helton checked his pocket watch—"in a few hours he'll be at the polo match the Ladies of the Missionary Society are hosting in Ezbekieh. It's a charity match to raise money for the Red Cross, and they've recruited some officers to play." He folded his hands. "For that matter, I need to send my regrets. I was set to play in the match, and I'm not feeling up to it given the circumstances." He gave Noah a sharp look. "Would you care to take my place?"

Noah rubbed the back of his neck. He hadn't played polo in over a year and was completely out of practice. Lord Helton was one of those men who regularly played in the Gezirah Club. "I'm not certain they'll view me as a suitable replacement but if Osborne is there, it might be worth my while."

"He'll be there. He's on the other team." Lord Helton wrote an address on a slip of paper. "This is the headquarters for the Ladies of the Missionary Society. Please give them my regrets."

Noah took the address from Lord Helton and stood. As he turned to go, Lord Helton said, "Peter Osborne thinks you're responsible for the crimes that Lord Braddock committed last spring. He's been digging, trying to find out the truth about the information I concealed on behalf of your lover."

Noah recognized Lord Helton's purposeful dig at Ginger for what it was: an attempt to draw blood where he could. This might the best time to tell Lord Helton about the marriage, have the matter done with before Helton found out another way.

But if Peter Osborne dug too deeply, Ginger's family could be at risk. They'd be ousted from society.

Noah met Lord Helton's eyes. "Which crimes, precisely?" Why had he played dumb about the man following Noah, then?

"All of them. He's very concerned about the smuggling ring and the underground network with the extremist nationalists though. He believes both to be currently active."

"And are they?"

"They've changed leadership, to be sure." A haggard expression crossed Lord Helton's face. "We captured who we could, and Fisher is cooperating and giving us names we've needed all along. But it's too late for some of it. Trails have long since gone cold. Men have vanished."

"Are you at risk from Osborne's search?"

Lord Helton lifted his pen. "We'll see. I concealed more than I should have." He nodded toward the door. "You'd do well to remember that when you're around the Whitman woman."

Lord Helton's words weighed heavily on Noah. He knew what Helton had risked. When he'd chosen to spare Ginger and her family from Lord Braddock's crimes being known, Helton had put himself in a position where his own job could be scrutinized.

But how had Osborne learned of any of it?

"It would be highly coincidental for Peter Osborne to dig into Braddock's crimes at the same time as Stephen's return, wouldn't it?" Noah remained fixed in front Lord Helton's desk.

Lord Helton's gaze was analytical. "What are you suggesting?"

"I'm suggesting Peter Osborne has had his information from the only other person who knew the extent of Braddock's crimes: Fisher himself." Noah set his hands on Lord Helton's desk and leaned toward him, an energized buzz in his arms. "Think of it. Who else could have given him the threads with which to search? Fisher was certainly forthcoming about Lord Braddock's concession—but why? What could he possibly have to gain from making so much of this information available?"

"Are you asking me or simply musing upon the possibilities?" The breath that Lord Helton drew was exasperated. "I've told you before and I'll repeat it. You're too emotionally involved with this whole affair. You can't be a part of this investigation any longer. You've lost complete objectivity with Fisher."

"It's my emotional involvement that kept me searching for a trace of the Aleaqrab from midnight until now," Noah remarked dryly. "I need to question Fisher. With Alastair's help. You know Alastair has the means—"

"Alastair's methods will not be acceptable for a man of Fisher's social status." Lord Helton tapped his pen against the desk. "Trust me to do my job, Benson. Fisher is no longer your concern. And neither is the Whitman woman. Don't force me to say more on the subject."

Noah came to a fully upright position. "So long as I'm breathing, Ginger Whitman will always be my concern. She's my wife not my lover, for the record. And if you threaten her again, not only will I stop my search for Victoria, but I'll also request an immediate transfer to France. Fortunately, I know French and German just as well as Arabic. Don't forget it." Then Noah left Lord Helton's office, before he said anything he might regret.

## CHAPTER NINETEEN

"You'll never guess what's waiting for you in your bedroom!" Lucy's voice was bubbly as Ginger came through the entrance to her house. Lucy sailed down the stairs as Ginger removed her hat and gloves. "Thank goodness you're home so early—let's go."

Ginger greeted the butler, who closed the front door behind her. She hurried behind Lucy, who was already on her way back up the stairs. She joined Lucy in the doorway of her room. On the bed was a large swath of opened packages revealing neatly arranged dresses, skirts, blouses, shoes, and hats.

Jaw dropping, Ginger approached the bed. "Is this all for me?" Lucy nodded eagerly. Ginger touched the fabric of a dress Lucy had laid out on the bed. Had her mother done this?

As ready-made outfits, they weren't of the same caliber as the custom-tailored clothing Ginger had worn for most of her life before the war—but they were beautiful and stylish. More stylish than anything she currently owned.

She bit her lip, surveying everything Lucy had taken out. It didn't surprise her that Lucy would have gone through it. Had she helped select it? "Where did this come from?" It must have cost a small fortune.

Lucy gave her a look of surprise. "Well, William, of course. Who else could afford all this?"

Of course. But the news produced a discomforting feeling in her gut. She didn't want to owe William anything else, especially now that she was married. And Noah wouldn't likely be thrilled with the idea. "Where is William?" She should probably thank him for his troubles.

"Getting ready for the charity polo match at Ezbekieh this afternoon. You should join us."

"Should I?" Ginger smirked. She couldn't think of a ready reason not to. "I suppose I can't say I have nothing to wear."

"Try this one." Lucy thrust a light-blue tea party dress at her. "You'll look so pretty in this."

Lucy's eagerness only confirmed that she'd chosen the outfits. Ginger bit her lip and walked behind the dressing screen in the room with the dress in hand. "Lucy, is there a reason you worry so much about the way I look?"

"To begin with, it's a waste of your beauty for you to be constantly stuck in nursing uniforms and plain dresses." Lucy's voice carried over the dressing screen as Ginger disrobed.

"And ...?" Ginger hung her skirt over the dressing screen.

"And what?"

"You said 'to begin with.' What's the rest of it?"

Lucy cleared her throat. "Oh, I don't know. I suppose I've just missed you. I always thought we'd do these things together someday."

"Gush over frocks?" Ginger poked her head out and smiled at Lucy as she stepped into the dress.

"And go out in society together." Lucy moved to the other side of the bed and leaned against it.

Ginger buttoned what she could, then came out from around the screen. "Can you help me finish?"

Lucy beamed then came over to help. "You look just as pretty in this as I thought you would."

Ginger couldn't remember the last time Lucy had been so affectionate. Was she up to something? Rather than voice her suspicions, she thanked her, then changed the subject. "Speaking of society, do you know of a Lady Hendricks?"

Lucy guffawed. "Of course I know her. Everyone knows her. She's unpleasant, but filthy rich, so she's invited to everything. She'll be at the charity polo match. She's quite philanthropic."

Ginger smoothed her hands over the front of her dress, glancing in the mirror. Lucy was right. The color contrasted nicely with her hair and skin tone. "Do you think you can introduce me to Lady Hendricks if I go with you?"

"I can—or Mama. She knows her better than I do." Lucy wrinkled her nose. "And I'd rather avoid Lady Hendricks if I can. Be careful around her. She's likely not to have forgotten the scandal involving you and Colonel Benson. She remembers everything."

Just what Ginger needed. As though finding out about Freddy Mortimer wasn't difficult enough. She grasped the wedding band on her finger.

The drive to Ezbekieh didn't take long, as the Braddock home was close to the European quarter of Cairo where the most popular places like Shepheard's, the Opera House, and the gardens were located. As Ginger made her way to the polo field, she felt out of place despite her new outfit.

Did she really fit in anywhere anymore?

Not in the intelligence world, not as a nurse.

Not with her family.

She drew closer and the sounds of pony hooves from the game thudded against the hard earth. A few women stared at her. She didn't recognize them. The men and women observing the match from lawn chairs were grouped within the cliques of their ilk.

"Mama, you won't mind if we steal William to sit with our friends rather than yours?" Lucy said, shielding her eyes as she scanned the crowd for familiar faces.

Her mother gave William an encouraging smile. "No, of course not. I'm certain William has better things to do than listen to the gossip of old women like me."

"Francine!" Lucy called out. Lucy's friend stood from her seat, waving from a few feet away.

As Lucy hurried over toward her and the other young women in the party, Ginger exchanged a glance with William. "I'm certain Lucy's introduced you to half of Cairo at this point."

William smirked. "If I'm honest, I don't remember even two names. It's all been a bit of a blur." He held his palm out, indicating that Ginger should lead the way. "Lucy has more energy than I."

"She's certainly an enthusiastic socialite." Ginger smiled, clasping her handbag in her fingertips.

"And I take it you're less enthusiastic?" William quirked a brow.

A breeze ruffled Ginger's skirt, a welcome break from the heat of the late-afternoon sun. "I don't think it takes too much to be less enthusiastic than Lucy. She's quite young." She regretted the words immediately. Lucy wanted to be taken seriously and probably by William. Painting her as a young girl in front of William would only cause problems later.

Lucy had already seated herself beside two young women Ginger didn't recognize, along with a few officers. "Come and meet my friends. Francine and Katherine Platt, my sister Virginia. But we all call her ..." Lucy stopped, with a look to Ginger, "Ginger."

*That was unusual.* Lucy had never cared one whit what Ginger preferred. Maybe she'd been paying attention when William had asked the question the other night.

Francine and Katherine offered pleasant, identical smiles and Ginger blinked. They were clearly twins. They introduced the officers with them. Ginger took one of the open seats near them on the lawn, and William sat between her and Lucy. "Ready to watch the match?" Ginger asked Lucy, leaning forward so she could see past William.

Lucy laughed. "Oh, you know me. I don't know a thing about polo, but I love the refreshments." Since her family had returned to Cairo, Lucy practically glowed. She was back in her element.

As Lucy turned back toward her friends, William's eyes drifted over Ginger. "You look lovely, by the way. Is that from your new wardrobe?"

She fidgeted with her handbag. Not only had he spent that much money on her but he'd likely felt some level of encouragement to do so.

"Yes, thank you." She gave him a faint smile. "I'm so grateful—"

The sound of the ponies drew closer, drowning out her words. Ginger looked up at the players on the field, the sunlight bright in her eyes.

Then one man on horseback came into view. Noah.

What was he doing here?

Fate would have it he would be playing. After all, he was a skilled horseman and athletic. Any team of officers that met on this field would gladly snatch him up.

He hadn't noticed her yet and she bit her lip, staring at him. In the golden light of the sun with sweat soaking the shirt that clung to his muscles, he reminded her of a tanned, dark-haired ...

She stopped her train of thought, then blushed.

Lucy watched her.

She looked away, then down at her lap. With her wedding ring there, their secret felt shared.

As alluring as he was, she couldn't be the only one attracted to him. Jealousy snaked around her mind. *He's mine now though.*

Lucy arched a brow. "Enjoying the view?"

"Aren't we all?" one of Lucy's friends chirped from her seat. She and her sister giggled.

Ginger pressed the cool side of her fingers to her cheek, wishing she'd brought a fan. "It's warmer than I expected it to be."

William gave an affable smile. "Isn't this so splendid? When I think of the weather back home in England, it seems like I've come on a proper holiday."

Lucy snickered at William's obliviousness. Of course, Noah wasn't the only comely man out there, but he stood out. It wasn't the first time Ginger had seen women fawn over him. He had a magnetism, combined with an utter lack of interest in the attention given him, that made him irresistible.

*Stupid, stupid Ginger.* She had to do a better job of hiding her attraction to her husband.

The thought almost made her melt right there.

A smattering of applause broke into her thoughts as one team scored. "Do you know what chukka this is?" Ginger asked Lucy's friend, who was closest to her. She didn't know how Lucy could tell the sisters apart.

"The second," the officer beside her replied.

William accepted a tall Pimm's Cup from a man serving refreshments, then took one for Ginger. "Here, I'm certain you're eager to unwind after your long day of work."

"Ginny is a nurse," Lucy told her friends. "She's recently come to Cairo from Alexandria to work at a hospital here."

As they murmured congenial responses, Ginger handled the

cold glass. Cucumber and orange floated near the top, along with mint. She sipped it, sneaking a glance back at the field. Had Noah seen her?

"Are you a polo enthusiast?" William asked.

"It's a fine sport." The truth was she'd rarely paid attention to a match. Not that Henry and Stephen hadn't dragged her to their fair share of games during the London Season when she was younger. But back then she'd had her own friends to keep her distracted. "You?"

"One of my favorites. That is ... before." William's eyes drifted to his sling. "I was quite the polo player. Won several tournaments with the boys in my club. But that's what we all did back then. Play games, spend the days in careless exhilaration. Those were the days, weren't they?"

Ginger's lips tightened. Something about the way William had said it made her wonder. Not that she didn't imagine he couldn't have been an athlete. But the way he spoke could be considered braggadocious. Yet William didn't appear to have that quality. Not really.

Taking another sip of her drink, she glanced at Lucy. She'd better get on with the reason she'd come. "Is Lady Hendricks here?"

"Yes, I think she's over with Mother, in fact. You should ask her for an introduction." Lucy's facial expression made it clear that she didn't intend to accompany Ginger.

Ginger excused herself from the party and continued down the field. She paused as the polo players came closer. Then she startled. It appeared Mr. Osborne was on the team opposing Noah. She hadn't expected that. Hopefully he wouldn't think she was wasting time by being here.

When she reached the older women, her mother introduced her to the group. Ginger recognized some of them but she focused her attention on Lady Hendricks.

Lady Olivia Hendricks was far younger than Ginger had expected.

In fact, she appeared to be closer to Ginger's age than her mother's. Her presence with the older, married women spoke of her wealth and marriage status, but the black arm band on her left arm told a different story, perhaps. She was in mourning. For her husband?

Lady Hendricks' chestnut-brown hair was well-coiffed under her hat, a birdcage veil partially shading her eyes. She was stylish but somewhat plain. She gave Ginger a warm smile that disarmed her. She didn't at all seem to be the frosty woman Lucy had suggested she might be. "Lady Virginia, what a pleasure. I've always wondered when I might meet you."

"Likewise, Lady Hendricks. My sister has spoken highly of your devotion to aiding the troops." Ginger positioned herself closer to her.

"Yes, well, we must all do what we can. But I don't have to tell you that, do I?" An insect settled itself on Lady Hendricks' sleeve, and she swatted it away. She motioned toward the empty chair beside her. "Please, be seated. I fear my dear Stewart has wandered off."

Stewart? Ginger felt sheepish inquiring about to whom she referred. Lady Hendricks assumed she knew who Stewart was.

"I'm so impressed with you and your admirable service," Lady Hendricks said as Ginger sat beside her. "Such marvelous bravery you've shown, going to the front lines. I hear you're newly returned to work in the hospitals in Cairo. How are you finding them?"

"Now that we're a few years into the war, they're all well-staffed and equipped. They were in a dreadful state when the war began." Ginger's eyes flitted to the field as the sounds of hooves came closer. *Don't let Noah distract you.* His proximity made her feel comforted though.

"Is there anything you need more of? I'm happy to order items from England and have them shipped." Lady Hendricks sipped her drink. "I hear the Gypos working in the hospitals are such terrible thieves. One nurse told me horror stories of how they must lock everything away when they're on duty, or it will get filched."

Ginger winced at the racial epithet for the native Egyptians. Some nurses used it too, and it always produced a sour feeling in Ginger's stomach. She gave a tight-lipped smile. "Thievery in times of war is quite common, even amongst the troops—as the boys say, 'There is only one thief in the army. Everyone else is simply trying to recover what he's lost.'" The men used more vulgar terms, but she didn't dare use them with Lady Hendricks.

"Indeed? How amusing." Lady Hendricks lifted her brows, but the glimmer in her eye showed she didn't appreciate Ginger's subtle implication that the natives weren't the only ones to blame for thievery. Her gaze wandered past Ginger, a hint of distraction in it.

There was that superiority Lucy had referenced. Ginger ought to give her sister more credit. On more than one occasion Lucy had proved herself to be insightful. Sensing she was on the verge of losing Lady Hendricks' attention, Ginger cleared her throat. "By the way, Lady Hendricks, I understand we share an acquaintance. Freddy Mortimer."

Lady Hendricks' hand jerked in her lap, spilling her drink. "Oh!" She looked down at the liquid pooling on her lap and stood, trying to brush it off before the tawny fabric absorbed it.

*What an odd reaction.*

Ginger stood and reached for a handkerchief. "Here, let me help." Ginger held out the handkerchief. A manservant hurried over with a serviette.

When Lady Hendricks lifted her eyes to Ginger, they blazed. Her lips twisted, a vein throbbing in her temple. She said nothing, then her gaze moved across the field. "Ah, it appears Stewart may need me after all. Excuse me, Lady Virginia." Without another word, Lady Hendricks hurried away.

What on earth?

Lady Hendricks' reaction was more than unusual. She'd been flustered and angry. But why would she react that way to Freddy Mortimer's name? Mr. Brandeis had said they often dined together at Shepheard's.

Her mother was involved in a conversation, so Ginger ducked away. Hopefully her mother hadn't noticed the exchange. She didn't want to be the source of further embarrassment. She returned to Lucy and William, never so glad to sit with Lucy in her life.

The hint of a smile flashed across Lucy's mouth. "How did it go?"

"Don't ask." Ginger shook her head. "She's as awful as you said."

Lucy gave her a knowing look. "One day you'll learn I know what I'm talking about."

"Who are you ladies discussing?" William shifted between them. Their speaking across him was likely making him uncomfortable.

"Oh, never mind." Lucy laughed and scooted him from his seat, switching with him. She leaned closer to Ginger and lowered her voice. "But I'm curious … what did you say to make her run away from you as though you'd invoked a mummy's curse?"

Ginger's lips curled with laughter at Lucy's accurate depiction of Lady Hendricks' flight. But if Lucy had noticed it all the way from here, it was likely other people had noticed also. "I mentioned Freddy Mortimer to her."

Lucy's eyes widened. "No, you didn't."

"Why?" Ginger asked. She bit her lip, feeling unusually out of her depth.

Lucy looked around and then whispered, "Freddy Mortimer was Lady Hendricks' lover. Until her husband came back injured from the war and put a stop to it, that is."

*Lover?* Ginger's mouth opened in surprise. "And this was a known fact?"

"Well …" Lucy eyeballed her friends. "Rumored, of course. But all anyone had to do was take one look at them to know. Quite scandalous, of course, but the woman can get away with practically anything, given her fortune. No one would dare cross or insult her."

Unless they unknowingly committed the faux paus, as Ginger had. Just what she needed.

But it also made Lady Hendricks her best option to learn more about Freddy Mortimer. "You don't know where Mr. Mortimer lives, do you?"

"He had a room at Shepheard's. I'll ask Francine if she knows." Giving Ginger a curious look, Lucy added, "Why?"

Ginger hesitated. Much as she wanted to confide in Lucy, it was better if her sister didn't know about the concession. Even the slightest wrong word might lead Ginger down a terrible rabbit hole of trying to explain—and lie—about their father's behavior. What Lucy didn't know was better at this point and would keep her safer.

"A nursing friend of mine from Alexandria asked me to give him a letter when I got to Cairo. She hadn't been able to have it delivered to him successfully."

Lucy seemed to accept the explanation. Before she could say anything more, though, William looked over at them. "Come now, I simply must know what you're discussing."

Lucy gave him a bright smile. "Oh, did you ask Ginger about what I mentioned?" Lucy and her friends looked at Ginger.

Settling some stray hairs under her hat, Ginger said, "Did he ask me what?"

"If you want to go Sphinxing with him." Lucy exchanged smiles with hidden meaning to her friends.

Ginger lifted an eyebrow. Sphinxing was a popular term for going to visit the Sphinx, though most of the nurses she'd known who went that way usually did it with an officer or two as an escort. It also was frequently a site for romance, as many of the trips were done in the moonlight.

Instead of bristling at her sister's teasing, Ginger opted to pretend she didn't understand. She gave William a regretful look. "I'm sorry to have to disappoint. But perhaps Lucy or my mother would go Sphinxing with you? Lucy, maybe even your friends would like to go."

Lucy and her friends erupted into another round of giggles. William exchanged a puzzled look with Ginger. "I'm afraid I don't understand the joke."

Ginger eyed the empty glasses beside Lucy. Then she offered, "It must be the Pimm's."

William chuckled. "Quite right." He sipped his drink. "Nothing like a good gin in the afternoon. Can I get you a tea sandwich, Ginger?"

As Ginger sat under the sun, sipping her own drink and eating sandwiches, she found herself unexpectedly unwinding. Lucy was in a jovial mood, and her friends, though vapid, were companionable and amiable. And despite her conversation with William lacking any depth, she enjoyed his company.

Not to mention *the view*, as Lucy had put it.

With only eight men on the field, it was entirely possible for her to watch Noah unreservedly. Maybe it was the alcohol in her own drink, but she didn't think she'd ever enjoyed watching a man on horseback swinging a mallet so much.

She'd like to go Sphinxing with Noah.

As the game ended, she had absolutely no idea as to the score.

Then, Noah started across the field. He brought the dark bay pony to a trot, then dismounted. His gaze locked with hers, and he brought the reins back over the pony's neck. Leading the pony toward her, he stopped only a few feet away.

Ginger didn't dare look away, despite the murmurs she heard around her. "Lord Braddock." Noah gave a polite smile to William, then gave his full attention to Ginger. "Lady Virginia." He wiped some of the sweat from his brow, and Ginger wobbled up from her seat.

*How many Pimm's Cups have I had?*

"You played polo well." Her voice sounded raspy. "I didn't know you played. Do you play often?"

Her comment elicited one of Noah's rare smiles. "Occasionally. In this case, the men from the CID were short a player, and I agreed to step in."

Then she noticed a small stain of blood near his shoulder. She came closer. Perhaps it was the alcohol, but she couldn't will herself to care about being seen with Noah right now. "Oh, dear, Colonel Benson, you appear to be injured." When she was close enough to him so only he could hear, she said, "I think you may have popped your sutures."

He didn't bother to look at his shoulder, as though completely unbothered. "You look beautiful."

She wanted to kiss him but she couldn't do it with people watching. "Thank you." She dared not tell him that William had bought it for her.

Noah glanced over to the group she'd been sitting with. "Can I steal you from your party? I must return the pony. Walk with me."

Ginger excused herself from William and Lucy. William

studied Noah intently then replaced the look with a blank expression.

As they left together, Ginger steadied herself on Noah's forearm. "I hate we can only steal a few minutes together. I shouldn't have let you leave me at home last night. I should have insisted we have a proper wedding night."

"It was better you didn't." Noah adjusted his handle on the reins.

"When can I see you? I want—" She broke off, a shy feeling crept through her. Was it wrong to tell her new husband she wanted to be intimate with him?

His eyes held hers, giving her reassurance, and he smiled. "I want to also." Noah looked back toward the spectators on the field.

They'd walked sufficiently far enough away from the onlookers that they were in no danger of being overheard. He brought the pony to a stop and turned toward her. "Ginger, I want you to go home. To England."

She furrowed her brow. "What? Why?"

"Someone has kidnapped Victoria Everill. The same group who sent an attacker after you in Ezbekieh." Noah's voice was just a shade above a whisper. "No one can know of it, so please don't speak of it."

Ginger gasped, then quivers ran down her spine. Is that why she'd been followed at Ezbekieh? And Victoria … gooseflesh pebbled on her skin.

Ginger searched his face. She had no love for Victoria, but the news was horrifying. What would happen to her? More to the point, how was Noah? Victoria had always been a source of jealousy for her. "Are you—"

"Worried for her? Yes." Noah's eyes reflected the cornflower blue of the sky. "The group that took her claim to be Egyptian nationalists, but I'm convinced Stephen has something to do with this. And it's driving me mad that I don't know what he's up to. I can't be sure you're safe, and whatever Stephen is playing at is dangerous."

"But he's in prison, isn't he?" Ginger had consoled herself with the fact. That Noah thought Stephen continued to be a threat made her pulse tick faster.

"He is." Noah brushed her jawline with a light graze of his fingertips, clearly unconcerned with who might see him. "But I don't trust him. Which is why I want you to leave Egypt with your family if you can. If I felt I could keep you safer by my side, I wouldn't ask, but I don't. With Jack and Victoria both captured, it's more important than ever."

"Noah ..." Ginger closed her eyes, relishing in his touch. Her skin tingled. Her heart thumped painfully. "I'm not leaving you. Not again."

Noah pursed his lips. "You frustrate me no end."

She laughed lightly. "And you do the same. But I need to learn about that concession paperwork anyway." She pulled open her handbag. "I went to see my father's solicitor today in Cairo. And he told me that my father had several properties I knew nothing about."

She unfolded the list of addresses, then handed it to him. "Look. Do you think it may be worth investigating what my father left there?"

Noah studied the paper. "It may be. I don't know if the government knows about these."

Was that even possible? She should have asked Mr. Brandeis, who was likely to know the details of the sales. "He apparently entrusted the concession to a man named Freddy Mortimer on behalf of my father. Apparently, Mr. Mortimer was supposed to take the concession to a safer location and bring back the details of it for my mother. But he never returned."

Noah's eyebrows rose in surprise. "That doesn't sound promising for Mr. Mortimer."

"Odd, isn't it?" Ginger pursed her lips. "Do you think he's dead?"

"It seems likely. I'll try to find out what I can." Noah looked lost in thought. "And you won't leave?"

"No, my love. You think Stephen is involved with all this, don't you?"

"Only Stephen knew of the concession." Noah handed her back the paper, which she replaced in her handbag. "I think he's baiting you somehow, Ginger."

"He's baiting both of us." Ginger sighed and looked back to the crowd. "I should rejoin my party. Before my mother becomes infuriated over this."

A warm light shone his eyes. "In the meantime, I'll do my best to go on waiting until I can tell the world you're my wife. Though there's something I appreciate about sharing the secret with you."

Noah's face sobered. "Lord Helton has asked me to help find Victoria. I spent the better part of the day trying to learn more about the group of men who have claimed responsibility for her kidnapping. You may not see me much in the next few days—but, hopefully, Victoria will be safely returned to us as soon as possible."

*Returned to us.* Gauche as it may be, she felt a stab of jealousy. Noah's friendship with that woman would never be something she'd understand. She *wanted* him to find Victoria. Just not care about her. "What about Jack? I thought you were going after him."

Noah released a guttural sigh. "Don't remind me. I'll leave as soon as I find Victoria. Hopefully finding her will help soften Lord Helton's anger toward us. He agreed to release you of your promise to him if I helped."

She smiled, her relief palpable. "Thank goodness." That had gone better than expected.

"And one more thing." Noah tore his gaze from the field. "Be careful with Peter Osborne. I have my doubts about him. He sent a man to follow me today." Before she could tell him about Osborne's less than savory comments about him, he bowed his head more formally. "I should go."

Noah continued across the field, soon becoming a silhouette in the blazing sun. She squinted, shading her eyes, then looked back toward the other players.

Osborne had sent a man to follow Noah? An unsettled feeling crept into her lungs, burning the oxygen there. Just what had she gotten herself involved in?

# CHAPTER TWENTY

"Of all the places I'd never thought I'd see you set foot, the Turf Club ranks up at the top." Alastair smiled as Noah sat across from him at a table in the lounge. A chess game lay in front of Alastair, ready for players. Noah settled in his seat, then moved a white pawn forward.

Noah scanned the interior of the exclusive men-only club. Alastair exaggerated: Noah had been in here before. One could hardly try to be effectual in the world of intelligence and politics in Cairo without entering the Turf Club. Noah suspected Alastair kept his membership for the same reason. But Noah did loathe it, especially as the war had gone on.

"The epicenter of misogynistic British imperialism?" Noah raised a brow. "We put a club a few blocks from Opera Square, then bar entrance to any locals, no matter their status. No wonder they hate us."

Alastair chuckled, sipping his tea. He pushed a pawn forward. "How was the polo match yesterday?"

"Uneventful." Seeing Ginger had been a highlight, but his shoulder was sorer. "Though, I have more reason than ever to believe Stephen Fisher is planning something." Noah studied the chess board. Alastair had pushed his lowly pawn into a position to be taken by his own. But today Noah didn't feel like forcing his mind into studying his opponent. He did that enough in everyday life. He took Alastair's pawn with his own.

Alastair leaned back in his leather chair. "That's hardly news. I have two pieces of information for you." He moved his knight out, his eyes guarded.

Noah held a smile back. He knew better than to try to win a game of chess with either Alastair or Jack. The two of them understood the mechanics of the game in a way Noah's mind couldn't fathom. Knowing he was being baited, he moved his own knight forward to protect his pawn. He asked a passing waiter for coffee, then turned his attention back to Alastair. "The Aleaqrab?"

"Fisher was right. They're highly secretive. But not too secretive for me." A ghost of a smile spread on Alastair's lips. "One of my contacts told me of a meeting they're having tonight. To recruit. This is the password to get in." Alastair slid an envelope across the table. "They're meeting in the basement of Café Riche." He patted a canvas rucksack beside his chair. "I have clothes for you here, no big disguise. You'll be in close quarters, and I don't know what they'll put you through for recruitment." Alastair moved his queen to threaten Noah's pawn once again.

The lead about the Aleaqrab was significant. Noah hadn't been able to pick up any other trace of them, even among his most trusted contacts. But that they had yet to contact Lord Helton with further news was even more worrisome. Helton was half-mad with worry. Noah had never seen him like this. This morning the man had greeted him in his dressing gown, unshaven, with insomnia written on every crease of his face.

Noah took the envelope and tucked it into the breast pocket

of his uniform. "What's the second piece of information?" He moved his bishop across the board to protect the threatened pawn.

"Just an interesting tidbit. Your camel bone knife—the one your assailant at Ezbekieh had?" As Alastair moved his queen to threaten both Noah's bishop and king, his lips twitched.

Noah blinked up from the game. Whatever he did now, Alastair would be likely to win quickly. He moved his bishop to protect the king. "What of it?" He'd forgotten about the damned knife.

Alastair waved at a passing acquaintance, then took one of Noah's pawns with his queen. "I traced it to a merchant in the Khan. He claims he sold that knife to an English gentleman. He was quite proud of the fact."

Noah moved his bishop out and tilted his head with surprise at Alastair's words.

The news was more than an interesting tidbit. While the merchant could be lying, Noah doubted it. Culturally, many of the Egyptian merchants enjoyed their boasting, but Alastair was known among the native population. Few would dare to lie to his face. "How did the knife get from an English gentleman to the Aleaqrab?" Noah asked.

Alastair gave him a sharp look, then moved his own bishop out. "How indeed?"

*Fisher.* Noah frowned. Stephen had been out of Egypt for over six months. The timing didn't seem likely. "Could Fisher have bought the knife while he was still in Cairo?" He looked at the game in front of him, then nearly groaned at the trap Alastair had set for him. Only a handful of moves and another humiliating loss would be his. Alastair's eyes reflected as much.

"The merchant claims he sold it only a month ago." A pensive look came to Alastair's eyes as he took another of

Noah's pieces. "You know I'm going to win in the next move, don't you?"

Noah took one of Alastair's pieces then knocked his own king over. "One of these days I'll take the time to read that book on chess you bought me. If you'd like to play checkers, you might find my skills are much better."

Alastair huffed, moving his queen into checkmate. "Don't take the fun out of the game, old boy. Checkmate." He set the board up once again as the waiter brought Noah's coffee. "You'd better get Darby sooner rather than later. I haven't had a decent game of chess since he left."

"As soon as I have Victoria back, I'm leaving." The delay in going to get Jack weighed on him heavily. Noah ducked his chin. "Speaking of information, I have two more people to inquire about. Peter Osborne, who works for the Foreign Office, and Freddy Mortimer. The latter is connected to the Braddock concession and Ginger needs to find him."

Alastair pulled a notebook from his breast pocket and scribbled the names with a pencil. He glanced over the edge of the book. "And the Osborne fellow?"

"He's apparently investigating me for Lord Braddock's crimes." Noah's lips twisted. He'd tried to confront Osborne three times the previous afternoon, both before and after the polo game. Somehow the man had skillfully avoided him.

He might have to pay a visit to the Foreign Office.

Alastair slipped the notebook back into his pocket and nodded toward the chess board. "Shall we play another round?"

"I suppose. Though I've never been inclined to do anything where I'm certain to lose." Noah rolled his shoulders.

The laugh Alastair released was loud. "Truer words have never been spoken, my friend. At least you're aware of it."

\* \* \*

THE SUN HAD long set when Noah approached Midan Suliman Pasha, but the streets near the square still bustled with activity. Turning his attention to Café Riche, Noah waited as a tram passed, its whistle merrily ringing in the air. This part of Cairo attracted tourists, who called it "the Paris on the Nile" because of the buildings artfully arranged along six streets radiating out from a traffic circle. Elegant and French neoclassical in style, the restaurants and shops here were a favorite among the Anglo-Cairo community.

He approached the dark wood-trimmed glass doors of Café Riche. The café was packed.

He'd donned a simple cotton *galabeyah* tunic and a muted *keffiyeh* headpiece, along with a wig. But with this many people still out at night, the risk of being seen and recognized seemed high. He wished his disguise could have been better.

Still, he made his way inside and headed toward the door that led to the basement, keeping his gaze down. When he reached the door, he gave a tap.

The door opened, and a man with thin wire-rimmed glasses peered at him. *"As-salaam alykum."* Noah bent his head, the fabric of his *keffiyeh* grazing his cheek. He gave the greeting Alastair had instructed him to use.

He was admitted into a passageway that led to stairs. The man at the door directed him to move on. In the basement, he found a room guarded by two men with rifles, and inside two dozen men were gathered. They didn't all sit together. Some stood, while others lounged on floor pillows. The room was dimly lit but adequate. In the corner was a large printing press.

Noah hung back near the door. Instinctually, he didn't like the look of the place. If the only exit was the door he'd come through, the danger in being here increased exponentially. He preferred a place with multiple points of entry.

He scanned the room, then found a few more doors. Exits?

Who knew where they led.

He recognized some faces of the leaders of the nationalist movements the British had labeled as extreme, the ones now calling for the overthrow of the British. These were the men who encouraged resistance and riots.

Unlike the way the upper crust of Anglo-Cairo society liked to characterize these men, they were not peasants. Some were lawyers and writers. Others were members of distinguished families in Egypt. Men whose ardent sense of nationalism had bloomed under the likes of Mustafa Kamel and other nationalists who had come before the war. What they lacked, more than anything, was a leader to unite them.

Noah lifted his gaze at the sound of approaching footsteps. A tall man emerged from one of the other doors, hunched over. He straightened once inside.

"Al-Mashat," one man said to the newcomer with a welcoming voice. "We were thinking you wouldn't come."

*Khaled Al-Mashat?* That was the name Stephen had given Noah as the leader of the Aleaqrab. Noah peered at him closer, then stiffened.

No wonder Alastair hadn't been able to find him.

Though he'd been called Al-Mashat, that wasn't his name. Noah knew him in an instant: Khaled El-Masry. The son of one of the most distinguished generals from the Mahdist war in Egypt in the late 1880s.

And Noah's uncle.

Would Masry recognize him? The last time he'd seen his uncle, he'd thrown Noah from his doorstep and spat in his face. Noah had come to Egypt to learn about the family he'd never met. The few things Noah's mother had told him, he'd kept close to his heart, repeating names and phrases. But the aunt that had raised him—his father's sister—had done her best to encourage him to forget it.

*"Tell no one your mother was Egyptian. They'll hate you for it."*

Noah's brother didn't have the same interest in knowing. He'd been five when their parents died. Neal couldn't remember their mother. Didn't retain any of the Arabic she'd taught them as children.

But Noah had. He'd studied it in secret. Learned to read and write it. His aunt and uncle had a servant who spoke it. He'd taught Noah what he could, along with Farsi. Noah had soaked up every word thrown at him. And when his aunt had discovered it, she sent him to learn the languages "that mattered"—German, French, Spanish, and Italian.

But his longing to learn more of his roots had continued. And as an ignorant boy who thought he was a man, he'd set out to Egypt to find his family.

As the men in the basement discussed the Sykes-Picot Agreement, Noah edged closer to the door he'd come from. If Masry recognized him, he'd need to flee.

However, the chances of that happening were remote. After all, it'd been ten years. And they'd only met that once. Noah resembled his father—but who knew how well Masry had known him. His aunt had claimed he sometimes looked like his mother, but Noah had only one picture to compare himself to.

"The British have no intention of leaving us to govern ourselves…" Masry spoke in Arabic. Noah focused his thoughts away from the glowing embers of the past. Their discussion needed his full attention. Victoria's life could depend on it.

"They lied to Sherif Hussein. They lied to us. We all saw it coming," another man said. Murmurs broke out among the group.

Masry put both his hands out. "They ridicule us…"

The men vocalized their agreement.

"… call us weak and spineless…"

The murmurs grew louder. Noah shifted so that his face was

further in shadow. The air in the basement was stale, dry. Body odor and breath permeated the room, and it had grown unexpectedly hot.

" … conscript our men, steal from our farmers. Steal the treasures of our people. We are not given the right to our own newspapers. They are no better than the Turks they replaced."

The rhetoric went on for some time. Despite speaking of methods of raising funds to arm their cause, no mention of something as obvious as a ransom arose.

Though, perhaps, if they held Victoria, they wouldn't want to tell everyone of it. There was a risk in doing so.

As the meeting wound to a conclusion, Masry said, "We have need for volunteers for an opportunity—one that has recently presented itself to us. We have little time to waste."

Noah leaned forward with interest. Could this have to do with Victoria?

Either way, getting closer to the inner ranks of Masry's organization could be beneficial. The more they trusted him, the more likely it was he could learn where they were keeping her. Noah stepped forward to volunteer as Masry's gaze swept the room.

Then his eyes landed on Noah. His gaze narrowed.

Noah's heart slammed hard against his ribs. He'd developed the skill of slowing his heart rate to have better accuracy when firing a pistol. Right now, the tricks he used evaded him.

Masry waved him forward. "Newcomer?"

The tight cords of Noah's neck released. Masry didn't appear to recognize him.

"We will put you to the test. Come."

*Test?* Any relief he felt at Masry's apparent lack of recognition faded. He'd spent enough time with men like this to know that tests of loyalty could be violent. Masry put a hand on Noah's shoulder, leading him back out the door through which he'd come in. Three more men came with them. They eyed each other with suspicion.

"What is your name?" Masry asked.

"Karim Sayed," Noah said. Despite the alias having been compromised with Abdullah and Stephen, it was also one of his better ones in Egypt. The chance of Masry knowing what had happened to Karim Sayed in Jerusalem also seemed slim.

The area outside the door was dark, but they reached another doorway, which opened to reveal a tunnel. Noah gave an impressed look. "I didn't know there were tunnels to Café Riche," he said.

Masry smiled. He had straight white teeth. If Noah was honest, he could see a flash of resemblance to himself in the man, a fact that brought him no pride. "These lands once belonged to a palace. Then again, there are undiscovered tunnels all over Egypt, no?"

A couple of inches over six feet, Noah hunched as he walked, the ceiling of the tunnel at his height. Noah smirked, noticing that Masry had to do the same. Noah's father had been tall, but apparently he'd received that attribute from both sides of his lineage.

"Do you have any experience with weapons, Karim?" Masry asked.

"Some."

"Good, that is useful. We need soldiers. You look like a soldier." Masry said nothing more for some time. Their footsteps and quiet breathing were the only sounds. Calmer now, Noah felt disoriented in the tunnel, not knowing where he was heading. Let alone for what purpose.

Minutes later they stopped before a ladder. They took turns climbing it, to what appeared to be a drain cover, which was pushed back. As Noah climbed out, a dog slinked past him. Noah gave it berth, wanting to avoid the fleas that clung to it.

He turned, blinking in the moon's light, trying to see where he was.

A boulevard flanked by trees was on the opposite side of a traffic circle across from where they stood, which was a vacant lot. They were in Ismailia Square. The CID would be fascinated to know about this tunnel.

He dusted his hands from the climb up the ladder, wishing for his boots instead of sandals. His feet weren't as tanned as his arms and face, but the disguise Alastair had given him included sandals. He only hoped Masry wouldn't notice his feet.

Masry directed them to an awaiting motorcar. He gestured Noah to climb into the back seat, while one man who'd accompanied them took the driver's seat. Then they were off, driving through the streets of the city.

Releasing a tense breath, Noah inhaled another and it was filled with the scent of petrol and cigarette smoke. He was one of the few men he knew who didn't care for cigarettes, but he accepted one from Masry. He'd learned to smoke as part of his work. He'd learned to do many things he didn't care to do. As the acrid taste filled his mouth and throat, he ground his teeth.

Whatever Masry expected of him would be just another thing he'd do for his job. Nothing more.

The drive was a short one, past the fish market of the Clot Bey end of Wagh El Birket Street—infamous for its association with prostitution. The squalor of Clot Bey filled the car, the scents of rotting fish and refuse mixing with the petrol of the engine in a nauseating combination. They passed through the district, the tires rumbling down the street that came alive this time of night. When the driver stopped, they'd come closer toward the Ezbekieh end of the street, and the motorcar idled behind the back of the El Dorado, an Egyptian singing and dancing club.

Noah leaned back in the seat, peering out. "In a few minutes, a man will come from the back door," Masry instructed them all, pointing with a squint. "And when he does, we'd like to teach him a lesson on manners."

"What type of lesson?" one man asked.

Noah stared at the back door to the El Dorado, willing it not to open. He wasn't in the mood for assaulting someone this evening, let alone to humor the appetites of his uncle. Since they'd parked behind the building, they were relatively isolated from the view of the main street. No one lurked back here but rats and insects.

Masry shrugged his thick shoulders. "I leave that up to you. But the message must be clear. Fail me and the *fellahin* will find your body in the Nile tomorrow. There is no use for men who waste my time."

Noah stared at the backs of his knuckles, rotating his wrist. After he'd punched Stephen, he'd been forced to ice it. The polo match hadn't helped. "What has the man done?"

"He defiled an Egyptian singer. He claimed he paid her but she was no prostitute. The police turned a blind eye because she was Egyptian. She died giving birth to his bastard."

The meaning of Masry's words was clear. Whoever this man was, he was not an Egyptian. He was probably white and British.

Noah's suspicions were confirmed by the opening of the back door. A British officer in uniform exited into the dim light of the alley.

Masry gave the men a nod. They stepped out into the filth and refuse that lined the streets in the Wazzir. Noah avoided the puddles, the stench stinging his nose.

The British officer who'd come out of the El Dorado lit a cigarette, then turned to walk down the alley, away from them. Noah's feet felt heavy as he pushed himself forward, toward the man. If he'd done what Masry suggested, he deserved a beating

—or far worse. But not from these men. They were likely to kill him.

Still, he felt Masry's eyes on him. The penalty for failure was his own death. His pulse throbbed in his neck. He could try to run. But if he left now, he risked the best opportunity he had to learn about Victoria.

Stay, and he'd have to participate in the assault of a fellow British officer. One whose guilt hadn't been proven.

He couldn't stop them from hurting the man. Not now. But could he help him in the long run?

They prowled behind the man. Separating himself from the other men, Noah closed the gap, reaching him first. Noah wrapped his arm around the man's throat with a speed and efficiency that allowed him access to the man's sidearm with his free hand. The officer's body went rigid against him as he put both hands up to grab Noah's arm.

"Pretend to be unconsciousness quickly. I'll help you if I can," he whispered in the man's ear.

Then the other men were at his side, and he couldn't risk saying more.

Noah increased the pressure on the man's throat and he gasped, sputtering. At last, the British officer found a weapon—the heel of his boot against Noah's bare toes. A flash of pain traveled up Noah's foot. Releasing him, Noah darted to the man's side.

With a swipe of his leg, Noah knocked the man's legs out from under him. The officer tumbled back, landing on the stones of the alleyway with a sickening thud. Dazed, the officer blinked, tilting his head against the stones. Noah loomed over him, willing him to pretend he was unconscious.

*Damn it.*

Noah's jaw clenched as the officer stared up at him in fear, then wide-eyed recognition. All Noah could hear was his pulse pounding at his eardrums. Harold Young.

*Please don't say my name.*

Harold had worked with Noah for two years at the CID. An awkward, nervous man—but no older than twenty-two.

He knew what Noah looked like in local street clothes, wig or not.

Could he have done what Masry accused him of?

Noah didn't know him well enough for that. Not that it mattered now.

Masry's men took advantage of Young being on the ground and began their own attack, kicking and beating him as he moaned.

Masry stood off to the side, watching him intently. If Noah backed away now, Masry would think him weak. Maybe even kill him.

He tried to think. Of how Victoria needed him.

Of how to help Young.

Masry lifted his hand. The other men stopped and Masry stepped forward, toward Young, who lay shaking and groaning with pain. Blood dripped from his mouth, and his face was disfigured with bruises. He pressed his arms into his stomach, his legs curling in.

Masry leaned down and said in accented but perfect English, "We remember the woman you defiled. We remember everything your people have done to us." He spat on Young's face, then stood. Sniffing, he nodded to the men. "Finish it."

Noah could only pray that Young would survive long enough for him to take him to the hospital later. Maybe if he left Young unconscious, quickly, it might be enough that the others would stop their attack before they killed him.

Noah unleashed a savage punch.

## CHAPTER TWENTY-ONE

"Shall we go to the picture show? The new Charlie Chaplin picture is at the theater—*Easy Street*, I think it's called. They have a late showing tonight." Lucy had stopped in Ginger's doorway, dressed to the nines for dinner. No doubt her mother and William were going also, as it wouldn't have been appropriate for Lucy to go alone.

Ginger glanced up from her bed, where she'd spread the books on anesthesia. She stretched her neck, rubbing the back of it with light fingertips. She hadn't realized what an awkward position she'd been sitting in. She checked the clock on the mantel. Nine o'clock. Quite a normal time for dinner and dancing, perhaps even picture shows.

But not for nurses who had anesthesia exams to take in the morning. "I'm sorry. I promised Dr. Radford I'd take an exam tomorrow. To see if I qualify to be trained in anesthesia."

Lucy gave her a pensive look. She shut the door, then came into the room. "You really aren't interested at all in poor William, are you?"

Ginger straightened. She shook her head ruefully. "No, I'm not."

"It's because of Colonel Benson, isn't it?" Lucy gave her a shrewd glance. "Don't deny it. I've seen the way you look at him. When the man was playing polo, you spent the whole match practically fanning yourself."

Despite her best effort, Ginger snickered. She covered her mouth, a blush heating her cheeks. To her credit, Lucy laughed. "You see," Lucy said. "I knew it. The man is devastatingly handsome, whatever his other qualities might be."

This could be an opportunity to smooth whatever rough edges Lucy had in her memories of Noah. "His other qualities," Ginger said, standing, "are quite wonderful."

Lucy sighed and sat on the stool in front of the vanity, facing Ginger. "Yes, I know. You love him. You told me as much before." She wrinkled her nose. "I don't know what being in love is, if I'm honest. I thought once—" She broke off abruptly, then looked down at her gloved hand.

*Had Lucy thought she loved Stephen?* Given the letters Ginger had found, she couldn't imagine Lucy meant anyone else. And it explained a great deal—such as why Lucy had always been so insistent on her friendship with Angelica.

She didn't want to ruin whatever fragile truce Lucy offered by coming in here. They'd never been adult women together. Ginger wasn't even sure she'd ever considered Lucy an adult. She rested her hip against the bedpost. "It took me a long time to know what being in love was," Ginger said, her voice quiet. "I thought I was in love with James Clark, simply because he seemed compatible."

Lucy rolled her eyes. "I knew you didn't love him. But I suppose I never thought you cared much about being in love. That's the sort of silly, fanciful thing you always left to me. You

—you were books and politics and ... all that." Lucy gestured to the papers spread on Ginger's bedspread.

"I wasn't always so studious." Ginger quirked a brow at her. "You make me sound like a bore."

"You are a bore." Lucy laughed. "In fact, I don't know that I've ever had so much fun sitting next to you as I did during that polo match. It was oddly comforting to see you light up the way you did while watching the colonel. He brings out a side in you I'm not sure I know too well. Makes you quite human."

"You missed the part of my life when I wasn't quite such a bore, but you were barely out of the nursery at that point." In all her exchanges with Lucy recently, Ginger had never really felt the need to pry into the depths of Lucy's personality, to ask her about her own worldview, until now. They were sisters but could they also be friends—despite the age gap between them? Ginger had always thought Lucy too different from her for that. "But I suppose the war has made me more serious than I used to be."

"More than serious." Lucy's lament was filled less with her usual drama and more with a reflection of her growing maturity. "It wouldn't do you harm to enjoy yourself occasionally. I can't pretend to have seen what you've seen, Ginny, but do you really want it to control your outlook on life and rob you of joy?"

Ginger considered her words, sitting on the edge of the bed. How long had it been since she'd thought about simply enjoying herself? The other sisters she'd worked with weren't all like her, were they? She remembered equally as much laughter and gossip from her time among them as she did the difficult times. "Once when I was working in Alexandria, a ship came in from Gallipoli—carrying a load of frozen human feet."

Lucy twisted her face in disgust. "That's horrifying."

"It was." Ginger shrugged, running her hand against the

coverlet. "And, it wasn't. My mind had to disconnect at some point, I think. I'm not sure anyone who's seen what I've seen can come out of this war unchanged."

Lucy stood and marched over to Ginger. Slipping her arms around her neck, she embraced her.

Ginger hesitated, then returned her embrace. She couldn't think of the last time she'd hugged her sister. But her family seldom hugged one another. Some of her mother's relatives—her Aunt Madeline, who was the warmest person Ginger knew—was fond of hugs. But no one else. Lucy stepped back, her face bright. "If I haven't told you before, I admire what you've done. And I know how hard you worked to help Mama and me over the last few months. But don't let it all change you. I want you to be happy too. Even if it's with that colonel."

Where was this coming from? Ginger stared at her, stunned. Lucy seemed changed over the last couple of weeks. She seemed content.

"Mother doesn't approve of the colonel," Ginger said. Confiding in Lucy was oddly comforting, but she did so tentatively. Telling Lucy anything like this had always felt too risky before. "She saw Noah kiss me. Lectured me the next morning, telling me how much pain I've caused her."

"Mama is still mourning Father and Henry. I don't think she can bear the thought of losing you to the man that almost ruined the family. Give her time." Lucy played with a simple gold chain around her neck.

Ginger hated that Lucy saw Noah that way. "Or that I won't marry the man who is offering us a lifeboat."

"That too." Lucy straightened, smoothing out her skirt. "But I suppose that's what younger sisters are for. To learn from the mistakes of their older sisters and remedy accordingly."

Ginger gave Lucy a surprised look. Was Lucy interested in

William? "Does that mean you're going to consider William as a beau?"

Lucy gave a girlish smile. "I suppose. I could do worse. And then I'll outrank you. I'll be a countess and you just an officer's wife." Lucy lifted her eyebrows in mock wickedness. "Really, I should thank you."

"I don't want you to marry him if you don't want to."

"I like him. Honestly. He's not the sort of man I would have picked for myself, but what do I know of men? Though, I may not have much to do with the decision. He still seems quite taken with you." Lucy gave a twist of her lips. "So if you do plan to marry the colonel, I wish you'd just say so and let William know."

Lucy left the room, and Ginger felt an unexpected peace as she sat back down to her papers. She rang for tea, leafing through her books but no longer able to concentrate. She hadn't thought that William's coming here would be anything to cause her family this much hope.

If Lucy married William, they didn't need her so much, did they?

She untied her hair from its knot, running her fingers through the long strands. Her scalp hurt from wearing her hair with so many pins. Tumbling it over her shoulders, she lay back on the bed, folding an open book over her chest. The encounter with Lucy had dissolved her tension. She closed her eyes, listening to the soft tick of the clock, like a heartbeat.

When she woke, a hand covered her mouth. She stifled a scream, blinking in the garish electric light. Noah's face hovered close to hers.

She sat bolt upright, the book tumbling onto her lap. Noah leaned against the bedpost. "My bride covered with books—what a tempting scene," Noah said. A slight slur filled his speech. His eyes were unusually bright. Even from here she could sense the alcohol seeping from his skin.

Ginger scrambled up, tucking her legs underneath her as she gathered her hair over her shoulder. "You scared me half to death. What are you doing here?" She scrubbed her eyes, still trying to adjust. "You're drunk. And dressed like that, you're fortunate I didn't scream."

Noah wore an Egyptian *galabeyah* tunic. He stepped, swayed, then sat on the bed. "I found myself in need of the gentle ministrations that only your gentle breasts could provide."

Her jaw dropped open. "Noah!" He'd never been so bold.

He chuckled. "I meant hands." His face was worn with exhaustion. He closed his eyes.

"Somehow I doubt that. But, speaking of hands, what on earth did you do to yours?" She climbed across the bed toward him, taking his hand in hers. The backs of his knuckles were bruised, bloody, and swollen.

Keeping one eye shut, Noah squinted at her. "I beat a man to a bloody pulp. On behalf of the Egyptian nationalist extremists I've recently joined." With a fumbling gesture, he lifted the sleeve of his left arm to reveal something even more frightening—the mark of a scorpion, on his forearm just above his wrist. The way his skin was burned and red, it looked as though he'd been branded with a hot iron.

She gasped, then reached for it. He'd need medical attention. The nationalists? "What happened?" She inspected the mark, touching the inflamed skin near the burn gently. He'd carry that mark for life.

"I suppose I passed the test. They gave me the finest of their wine, then had me bite down on a leather strap while they branded me." Noah closed his eyes once again.

"Who did you have to beat?" From the look of Noah's hands,

whoever had been on the receiving end of the blows couldn't be doing well.

"An English officer, one I know, actually. They said he violated an Egyptian dancer and escaped justice. I'm attempting to console myself with what I did to him by hoping that's true. He's in hospital now. I went back later and collected him—left him on the front steps myself."

She covered her mouth, feeling ill. She shouldn't have asked if she didn't want to know. "Noah—why?"

"To gain the leader's trust. And avoid being killed." He swallowed, his jaw clenching as though he didn't want to remember it. "They have Victoria. I've spent the day trying to find her—and all of this ... for not a single clue."

"And you had to beat a British officer?" Ginger could barely process his words. "Can't you be arrested for that?"

"I can. But I'm praying if it comes to it I can redeem myself with Young, if he remembers. I knocked him unconscious so that they'd stop their attack and they did. Young won't know about that, of course ..." Noah trailed off and closed his eyes. "I did whatever I could to help him. My ability to help was limited."

The anguish on his face was palpable. He'd placed himself in a horrible position. She felt a bitter simmer of resentment within her at the idea he'd endangered himself so much for just *the chance* of learning more about Victoria. However desperate he was to find her, there should have been another way.

"You couldn't have tried to gain the leader's trust another way? Noah, you were reckless. Beating one of your fellow officers—it's unconscionable." She regretted the words immediately, seeing the effect they had on his expression.

"Once I'd volunteered for the task, they said they'd kill me if I didn't." He stared at her dully. "Why do you think I've been drinking?"

She tried to think clearly. He'd come to her, distressed. Perhaps it wasn't the time to scold him right now. She was his wife, after all. Not that she knew how a wife should react to this. But he needed her clearly enough.

Coming closer, she tugged on Noah's shirt. "Sit up. Remove the tunic. I'm treating you."

A smile curved at the edge of his full lips. "You don't need my tunic off to treat my hands and forearm, do you?"

Laughter escaped her, her cheeks warming. "I wanted to check on your shoulder. See if it's healing well."

Noah sat, pulling at the tunic. Under it, he wore white baggy *sirwal* trousers. Even in his current state, she felt the pull toward him, the magnetic draw that made her core seem to turn to liquid. Noah smiled as she knelt on the bed beside him. He cupped her face in his hands before she could even glance at his shoulder. He lowered his lips to hers.

She returned his kiss, relishing the way his touch made tingles spread sensuously through her body. *He is a remarkably gifted kisser*, she decided, not that it seemed that unusual for him. Noah didn't seem to do anything truly badly. She pulled away from him and draped her arm over his shoulder. "Do you think I'm a bore?"

He laughed and gave her a look that made it clear he'd rather continue kissing her. "Why on earth would I think that?"

She rose and crossed the room toward her door and locked it, then turned back around. The sight of him reclining on her bed brought her more happiness than she probably deserved, considering what her mother would say if she knew Noah was here. But if she was being honest, the thrill of having him to herself for the first time since she'd come to Cairo was intoxicating.

Especially now that they were married.

She crossed her arms. "You didn't answer my question."

Noah sat, the taut muscles of his torso rippling as he did. In the shadowy light provided only by the lamp at her bedside, the scars on his shoulder and chest from where he'd been shot in the spring were more visible. She tried not to react to either of her observations, though her body betrayed her. He held a hand toward her. "Come here, and I'll show exactly how interesting I find you."

"I know you well enough to know that you're quite skilled at changing the subject when you're trying to evade my questions." She went over to her trunk and pulled the lid open. Her medical kit was near the top. Finding a bottle of iodine, a bandage, and an ointment, she glanced at him.

An amused look played in the bleariness of his eyes. "Yes, darling, you're quite boring. You jump headfirst into the intelligence world every time my back is turned, don't question running at an assailant when necessary, and you're one of the few women I feel I can speak with plainly about political intrigue."

She sat beside him and lifted his left hand, then poured iodine on his burn. Noah sucked a breath in through his teeth as it stung. "You'll need to change the bandage on this twice a day and layer the ointment thickly."

Noah smirked. "The man who branded me told me to rub lemon and salt into it a few times a day, let it re-scab several times."

She winced, shaking her head. "I won't say his methods aren't useful if you want a deep brand." She wrapped his arm. "But they also increase your chance of infection." She finished the bandage and put her materials down.

Noah slid his free hand around her waist, tracing his fingers down the small of her back, then smoothing his palm over her curves. She twitched, catching her breath with anticipation, then lifted her eyes to his. "You're determined to distract me, aren't you?" she said.

"You're determined to take care of me. I'm simply arguing with the methods you're employing." Noah's lips nuzzled her neck. "When you're this close to me, lips parted with concentration, your scent driving me mad, it suddenly makes me very jealous of all the men you spend your days with. How many marriage proposals have you fended off?"

Given his state of inebriation, Noah's tongue was looser than usual, and she grinned. He *would be* a chatty drunk. Alcohol had a way of bringing out the side an individual normally restrained.

She kissed his jaw, then caught his earlobe in her lips and gave it a teasing tug. "I'm not finished examining you yet," she whispered in his ear, attempting to draw back.

He groaned, his hands like steel around her waist. "Of all the ways I've been tortured, this may be the cruelest. I come to you in need, heart devastated—" He winced as she peeled his hand from her hip and then cleaned the cuts on his knuckles.

She raised a wry brow at him. "How is it you're devastated?"

He blinked at the backs of his hands. "Nearly beating a man to death with your bare hands is …" Then he trailed off, closing his eyes. Pain etched his face but not from his physical wounds.

The darkness into which he'd taken his soul had to be a consuming. Ginger had seen the near euphoria of men relishing in the kills they'd made during battle.

*Kill or be killed.*

But it was more than that. The adrenaline that pulsed through them was their bodies' way of surviving and rationalizing the darkness.

And Noah seemed all too aware of that fact.

That he'd taken such a risk for Victoria made her throat clench. She pushed the thought away.

She held his face, kissing his closed lids. His breath faltered at the touch of her lips. The response of his body to hers had always aroused her. When she dropped her lips to his this time, she made no attempt to pull away quickly.

Her lips parted over his and her tongue dipped against his, teasingly, then coaxing. Ginger slid her arms around his neck, caught in the wild, passionate kiss she'd been dreaming of sharing with him since she'd first arrived in Cairo.

Noah's hands slid over her thighs and pushed up her skirts, his hands moving more boldly now. "Noah," she whispered hotly as her senses got the better of her, "my family could be home at any minute. My sister has to walk by my door to get to hers. And the"—she gasped as his roving hands slid firmly around her backside—"the servants."

Making love in her family's home seemed horribly risky. That knowledge both frightened and roused her. "We can be quiet," Noah murmured against the curve of her neck.

She gave a shattered tremble as his fingers dipped lower. Her medical kit was still open on the bed beside them, her books all over the mattress. He paused, then turned her around so that her back was to his chest, his arm wrapped against her hips. His trousers were thin, his need for her pushing hard against her.

"Noah!" She kept her voice to a low hiss as he tossed her onto the bed with a heave. Her back and head hit books, and she grunted. "Ouch!"

"Did I hurt you?" Noah's eyes held a lust-filled gleam as he stalked her onto the bed.

She pulled the books out and shoved them to the side. "No, but the books did." As he pushed them all away, she shuddered at the thuds they made on the rug below the bed. She gave him a gaping look. "That's quiet?"

"Call it my enthusiasm to be at your side." Noah's hands resumed their roving, but he gave her a frustrated look. "How is it you still have so many articles of clothing on? Wasn't there a dressing gown in the clothing I had sent here?"

*He'd sent the clothing?* "You? I thought—"

"You thought what?" His dark brows furrowed.

She clamped her lips shut, then gave him a pretty smile. "Nothing at all. I meant to thank you for it."

Noah gave her an impatient look. "You thought that buffoonish cousin of yours gave them to you, didn't you? He's certainly been eager to return the Whitman women to their former lifestyles."

She gave him a sheepish look. "I had no idea you'd spend that amount of money on me—"

Now he laughed, coming closer until he deftly unbuttoned her blouse. "What you mean to say is that you didn't think I had the money to buy my wife clothing." He gave her a crooked drunken smile, then quickly finished the job of disrobing her. His gaze swept her admiringly. "God, you're beautiful. Each time I see you like this, it's a shock to my senses."

Then he swept her onto her back, grasping her. The veil of mosquito netting over the open canopy of the bed gave the ceiling a gauzy look. She blinked at him dazedly, aware of the gooseflesh that had broken out across her skin and the hardening of her nipples. As the strength of his arms pressed around her, his weight nearly crushed her for the briefest moment, then she gasped as he joined their bodies together intimately.

He tasted of alcohol, and the brine of his sweat lingered on her lips as he moaned softly, "God, *rohi*. I love you."

And maybe because Lucy had called her a bore, but also because she loved him, she lay back and enjoyed the moment, Noah's drunken murmurs of her beauty and his lack of restraint in telling her—exactly—what he thought.

## CHAPTER TWENTY-TWO

Ginger hadn't expected to feel so much guilt for spending the night with Noah after they were married—but her guilt had little to do with their behavior. Or with how much she'd enjoyed the previous night. Noah had slept in her arms for a few hours, then woken her to make love again before he'd left under the cloak of darkness.

He'd likely wanted to drown out his thoughts when the alcohol had worn off.

But standing in front of Captain Harold Young at the operating table in the hospital, she understood Noah's behavior better. Dr. Radford had pulled her into the surgery as soon as Ginger had arrived that morning. She hadn't even had the opportunity to do her daily debrief with Peter Osborne. She hoped he wouldn't be annoyed at having to wait.

Ginger felt sick. Captain Young's face was disfigured, his jaw and nose broken in several places. Dr. Radford had commented that he'd been lucky his attacker hadn't blinded him. His face, swollen and hideously puffy, didn't reflect the story that Noah had relayed to her—that he'd tried to save Young from being killed. And no one knew Noah had taken him to the hospital either. How on earth could Noah be exonerated from participating in this?

One of Young's arms had also been broken, and he'd suffered several cracked ribs. They'd reset the bone in his broken arm, and Dr. Radford was examining her work when he stirred from the anesthesia.

Ginger wiped the spittle from his torn lips, not wanting to see his broken teeth. *How could Noah do this?*

How could Noah do this and then spend the night in her arms?

She felt the taint of his crime on her skin.

This couldn't be legal, no matter what Lord Helton had authorized him to do to find Victoria. She'd seen Noah kill before. And her brain had rationalized it because they'd been enemy soldiers, men who would kill her or him. Who were trying to kill them.

This felt different.

And yet Noah had claimed the nationalists would have killed him if he hadn't.

Captain Young's eyes were too swollen to open, but his lips moved.

Dr. Radford looked up sharply. "What's that?"

Both women leaned closer to Captain Young. His words were a raspy gurgle. *"Bennn ... sonnn ..."*

Panic welled in Ginger's throat. Young remembered.

Dr. Radford gave her a querying look. "Did you understand him?"

*Lie.*

She had to. She couldn't very well tell Dr. Radford the truth. The doctor may not know who Noah was, but she could repeat his name to the authorities.

Ginger gulped down a breath, trying to think of a response.

"No, it was a mumble."

But Young wasn't done attempting to communicate. *"Bennnnsonnn ..."* The word sounded malformed coming from his swollen lips.

This time Dr. Radford understood. "Benthon?" She repeated the word as Young had pronounced it. Dr. Radford exchanged a look with Ginger and grabbed a notepad. She scribbled the word down. "Is this a name—no, don't speak. Just give one nod if you can."

Young nodded.

Fear crawled down Ginger's back like a hundred baby spiders breaking free from the base of her neck. Young slipped out of consciousness again shortly after, but the damage was already done.

As the women left the operating theater, Dr. Radford stared at the name she'd written. "Poor man. I can't imagine how much pain he must be in. I told you how an orderly found him on the steps of the hospital last night? Simply awful."

"Quite. It's a frightening time to be in Cairo." Ginger's throat was thick, and she swallowed a few times to clear it. "Did you still want me to do that test today?" She didn't deserve it, given the circumstances.

"Oh, yes." Dr. Radford's face brightened, and she gave Ginger an eager smile. "I would. And, in fact, I thought it might be nice to go for tea together afterward. I know I've been pushing you quite hard, but it's only because I see so much potential in you, Sister Whitman."

Normally, Ginger would have felt pleased with the compliment. Dr. Radford didn't seem like the type of woman who gave them lightly. "Thank you." She had to gasp the words out. "You're welcome to call me Ginger, if you'd like."

"Only if you call me Jane." She stopped in front of the door to her office, where she knew Peter Osborne waited. "I'd like us to be friends, Sis—Ginger. I know I'm a bit brash."

The offer of friendship overwhelmed Ginger in a way she couldn't quite understand. She'd been desperately needing a friend since Beatrice had left, and her sisterly moment with Lucy the night before had only furthered that need. But would Jane Radford hate her if she knew the activities Ginger was involved in?

She gave a wordless nod, smiling. Jane opened the door to her office, and Peter Osborne rose from his chair. "Mr. Osborne." Jane breezed into her office, dashing to gather a few files from her desk. "I apologize for keeping Sister Whitman occupied this morning. We had an emergency that needed to be tended to first thing."

Osborne removed his hat. "No trouble at all, Doctor." He stood beside his chair, indicating that he wouldn't continue speaking with Ginger until Dr. Radford had left.

Jane held the files in her hand. "I'll be right down the hall, Sister Whitman. You can take the test directly after this."

"Test?" Osborne asked as Jane shut the door.

Ginger settled into the chair across from him. "Yes, a test to see if I can qualify to be trained in administering anesthesia." She folded her hands in her lap. "I'm sorry to say, Mr. Osborne, I don't have any news to share. I have made little progress on finding Mr. Mortimer since the polo match." She'd been forced to tell him about the debacle with Lady Hendricks the day before. "I'm hoping Lady Hendricks will accept my offer to go to tea, but she hasn't responded to my note yet. Other than that, I was terribly busy studying last night."

Osborne cocked a brow at her. "Even when Colonel Benson snuck into your house near midnight?"

She froze. *They are watching me.* She tried not to squirm under his gaze. "Goodness, that's quite an accusation." She drew a shallow breath that did nothing to relieve the light-headedness she felt.

"He wasn't seen leaving until almost four in the morning." Osborne leaned toward her, calm but clearly unrelenting in his accusation. He knew he'd caught her in a lie.

Ginger blinked at him, then scrambled to her feet. "I don't see how that has anything to do with you, sir."

Osborne caught her by the wrist, his grip strong. "Lady Virginia, you forget yourself. You swore an oath not only to me but to your country. I must insist on the truth from you."

"You'll release my hand." Damn, but she wished she had the pistol he'd given her. Even though he offered no direct threat, she'd let herself get too comfortable around him, too trusting that he presented no harm.

"Then you'll explain why you felt it necessary to lie to me. Colonel Benson visited your bedroom, yes?" His grey eyes were unflinchingly cold.

Osborne released her wrist and she rubbed it. She should take him to task for it. But the situation with Captain Young clouded her thoughts. She could tell Osborne about her marriage, but she'd previously told him she wasn't close to Noah.

"You told me to make myself available to Colonel Benson to find out what he knew of the concession, and I did. I didn't think that required me giving you any details that would only bring my reputation harm. I've told you the truth—"

"That you didn't see him?"

She glared at him. "That he told me nothing of relevance to you. Unless you'd like to hear his declarations of love for me."

"Maybe I would." Osborne crossed his arms. "I'd certainly prefer that to your lies." He stared down his nose at her. "We followed Colonel Benson to a nationalist meeting last evening.

He disappeared after that, only to reappear—much to our surprise—outside your home."

She gathered her shredded dignity from the floorboards. "I have nothing more to say about my interactions with Colonel Benson last night."

Osborne gave her a disdainful look. "Don't forget who you work for, Lady Virginia. Benson has been stalking me lately, trying to corner me. I don't know what it is you told him, but I fear I was wrong in confiding anything to you. Get back to work."

Her face burned as she left the office. She was utterly humiliated. Angry with Noah for putting her in such a compromising situation. He had been careless in his drunkenness. She was furious with herself for allowing it.

She'd known the CID watched her closely.

How foolish could she be?

Her expression must have reflected her distress as she opened the door to the office. Across the hall, Jane straightened, then gave her a concerned look.

Before Jane could say anything, Osborne came out behind her. "Excuse me, ladies." He tipped his hat at Jane. "Good day."

"Oh, Mr. Osborne, one question. The soldier who was brought in last night was attacked. He mentioned a name after surgery." Jane held out her note. "Benthon. Should I go to Cairo police or speak to the army? I'm not sure if the procedure is different here compared to the way we handled this sort of thing in Malta."

*Oh, God, no.* Ginger felt the blood drain from her face.

Osborne's eyes swiveled to Ginger's face, and he took the note from Jane. "Benthon?" Despite the lisp Jane had given the name, Osborne was too bright not to be suspicious. This time he didn't bother to request a private audience. "Nothing to tell me, Lady Virginia?" The rebuke in his voice was acidic.

"I forgot about this," Ginger's voice was an aching whisper, but she held herself with whatever last shred of pride she could.

Osborne gave Jane a pleasant smile. "Take me to the soldier. I'll handle the situation myself."

*Damn him, damn him, damn him.*

Ginger remained fixed in place as Jane and Osborne's footsteps retreated down the hallway. She crumpled against the doorway to Jane's office, bracing herself against the frame. She struggled to breathe, and tears stung her eyes. She wouldn't cry, not here.

The worst part was that she didn't even know which of them she was most angry with—Osborne or Noah.

At the sound of footsteps approaching once more, Ginger straightened. Her cheeks still flamed as Jane came to her side.

The surgeon appeared to see through her attempt at disguising her emotions. Jane bit her lower lip, then checked her wristwatch. The radium-painted dials glowed in the dark hallway. "Why don't you take the test tomorrow? It's been a trying morning."

Truthfully, Ginger had no desire to take a test. She was too distracted. "I'm afraid I'm not quite myself at the moment."

"I can see that." Jane glanced down the hall. "I hope you don't find it terribly intrusive of me to ask, but Mr. Osborne didn't mistreat you, did he? I know how men in positions of authority can be, even pleasant ones like Mr. Osborne."

Ginger was tempted to trust her with her struggles. But she hardly knew Jane. There was no telling how well she knew Osborne either. "Mr. Osborne was harsh, but, no, he didn't mistreat me." She gave Jane a curious look. "How is it you and Mr. Osborne are acquainted?"

"He was my patient." Jane lowered her voice. "This past summer. He was quite emaciated when he was in the hospital, the poor man."

"Your patient?" Ginger lifted a brow. Osborne was the picture of health. A bit on the thin side, perhaps, but she wouldn't have imagined him being emaciated. "What was he in the hospital for?"

"He had been a prisoner of war after Kut—spent over a year in a POW camp and was finally released in a prisoner exchange late in the spring after the fall of Baghdad." Jane folded her hands together. "He's quite admirable, given what he's been through. The poor men who were abandoned at the siege of Kut were left starving. Mr. Osborne told me that the Indian men he commanded had to break the rules of their religion and eat horse meat to survive."

Ginger had followed the atrocities of Kut the year before. The events that had unfolded there had been horrific and absolutely humiliating for the British. She felt a twinge of guilt. She never would have imagined Osborne as having gone through such an ordeal. Because of his current position, she'd imagined him as one of the more fortunate men during the war—the ones serving behind desks. But perhaps he'd earned the current position due to his previous trials.

Whatever Osborne's story was, Noah was right to be concerned about him.

# CHAPTER TWENTY-THREE

Allowing the noise of the city to drown out his thoughts, Noah focused on the children scurrying through the streets of Cairo. They spoke in broken English to the European soldiers or residents who passed , offering services for *baksheesh*. A beggar blinked numbly into the crowded street from his perch in front of a hotel. His body was swathed in rags, a stump of an arm exposed to the sun.

Noah gave the beggar money, then climbed on the arriving tram. The act of charity did little to ease his guilt. His night had been filled with fitful dreams and Harold Young had been in them.

When he arrived at Lord Helton's, the butler showed him into the sitting room.

Lord Helton descended a few minutes later. He'd shaved, at least, and was dressed. But he still looked as though he hadn't slept well. "I found the Aleaqrab leader." Noah rubbed his bruised knuckles, his fingers curving over the bumps. "But I have heard nothing about Victoria yet."

Helton pulled a note from his breast pocket and held it out

to Noah. "They've sent another message. They want arms and munitions. They've specified what and where. They say they want it delivered tonight to the address listed."

Noah read the message. It had been written in English, though there were grammatical mistakes. "They make no mention of releasing her."

"They must release her if I make this exchange." Lord Helton's eyes were wild behind his spectacles.

*He can't be serious.* "You're going to give them weapons?"

"Of course I am. They have my daughter, not my dog. They sent another note from her." Lord Helton thrust it into his hands.

Noah recognized Victoria's familiar script. *"Please give them what they want."* A troubling feeling knotted his stomach. "Neither note makes a promise of her release. You can't give a group of men intending revolution the weapons with which to do it."

"I can worry about that later, once she's safe at home." Lord Helton paced, then sat. He rang for his butler, who appeared within moments. "Fetch Jahi for me." As the butler left, Helton turned back to Noah. "I'll need you to get the arms for me."

Noah raised his brows. "How's that?"

"I'll send a letter. Tell them you need them to blow up a bridge. Something of that nature."

"And when the arms disappear and no bridge is destroyed?" Noah sat stiffly. The weapons themselves weren't difficult to obtain—no one would question a message from Lord Helton. But if the matter was investigated, they both could be held responsible. "We should go to a higher authority. You and I both have friends in the CID who would be discreet. I can go to—"

"And risk my daughter's life? I trusted you, Benson. How dare you even suggest such a thing?"

"Because stealing weapons is more reasonable? There's little guarantee that I won't be seen. And someone has been following me once again." His eyes bored into Helton's.

The corners of Lord Helton's mouth twitched. "I told you Osborne—"

"Told me what?" Noah cocked his head to the side. "No matter how much I've tried to confront Osborne, he's able to evade me. You know what he's doing. You have the power to put an end to it. Now tell me exactly what the man is after. And why."

Lord Helton swore under his breath. "Sir Reginald Wingate received troubling news about you, regarding your parentage. Given that you've publicly expressed your sympathies for the nationalists, he was duly concerned. I told him and Osborne they had nothing to worry about, but they wanted to keep you under watch." Lord Helton shot him a narrow gaze of frustration. "Summary enough for you?"

"Not particularly." Lord Helton's account and lack of specificity was a half-hearted attempt at getting through the specifics to placate him, and Noah knew it. "Why did you see fit to engage Ginger in the services of the CID?"

"We need to find that concession. We know Lady Braddock is most likely hiding information. Virginia seemed like the easiest route to learning the truth." Lord Helton's mouth thinned. "I'm certain she would prefer to keep her mother out of prison if it comes to it. What's the harm of having her involved? We offered her more than a generous compensation and that was only because of my intervention."

Noah gave Lord Helton a skeptical look. "Need to find it? To what end? If it is lost, what difference does it make? You know Ibn Saud is likely to strike a new deal if the timing is right. Why the sudden need to seize the property of a dead man? Unless you see some personal gain in it."

"How dare you question my integrity? You think I'm not

angry with Lady Virginia for blatantly disregarding her promise to me? I have been more than patient with her. And you."

Noah stepped closer to him, using his height to his advantage. "Unless you'd like to find someone else to supply the Aleaqrab with their requested weapons."

Lord Helton's lips were pallid. "This is precisely the problem with that woman. Before her, you questioned nothing I asked of you. My daughter's life isn't a bargaining chip, Benson."

"You'll shut down this investigation on me. Don't tell me you don't have the means." Noah straightened, knowing he had the upper hand. Helton would do anything for his daughter—including suggest that Noah steal a cache of weapons and hand them to British enemies. "After all, what you want from me is treason. You may have other lackeys, but none who could obtain what you need for the purposes you need them. And keep your secrets. Which you know I will."

Before Helton could respond, the door to the sitting room opened. Jahi, Lord Helton's trusted Egyptian servant, strolled into the room, his red tarboosh on his head. He gave a bow to Lord Helton, then startled at Noah.

Jahi wore an ugly bruise on his face, dark circles surrounding his eyes. A cracked scab was exposed on the bridge of his nose.

Noah's pulse mellowed, and his eyes hardened. Jahi had broken his nose recently.

*The Egyptian attacker in Ezbekieh would show similar signs of injury.*

Noah barely heard Lord Helton as he spoke. "Jahi will accompany you to the depot to get the weapons. Work with him on the coordination. My suggestion would be to take a lorry."

Noah snapped his gaze back to Lord Helton. "And my terms?"

Lord Helton gave a weary wave of his hand. "Yes, yes. Whatever you wish. I have more important things to worry about than Osborne's ridiculous investigation."

"I want whatever information you have on Osborne. His files. Everything."

Annoyance spread on Lord Helton's face. "Don't overplay your hand, Benson. I could always give you another assignment immediately. Restrict your ability to go and save Darby."

*Bastard.* Noah set his jaw and cocked his head. "His files?"

"As you wish." Lord Helton moved to leave the room.

"There's one more thing," Noah said. Jahi had brought a feeling of uncertainty to what was happening.

Lord Helton stopped. His heels clicked together as he turned to face Noah. "What's that?"

"I can't deliver the arms for you. There's too much of a risk the Aleaqrab would recognize me. I can get the weapons from the army." He studied the list. "With this amount, I'll need to borrow a lorry. And register what I'm taking from the munition dump. I'll be responsible for them." At the voice of caution in his mind, he asked, "What if the army investigates this? They'll be suspicious that all these weapons disappeared."

"I can smooth it over. Tell them I sent you on a secret mission. You've taken weapons dozens of times before for such purposes."

"But never just outright stolen them. And never so many. Anytime I've taken weapons in the past, their purpose has been accounted for in an official report." Noah's eyes narrowed. "What you're asking of me could be considered treason if something goes awry with the delivery. You know the army would never approve of you taking the weapons and turning them over to our enemies."

"Good God, man, what would you have me do? They have a knife to my throat. I'd rather ask for forgiveness later than ask for permission, which you're right, they would refuse. And then where would I be? They've likely already defiled her. Would you like to see her dead?"

Noah swallowed the tight lump in his throat. *No.* The thought of Victoria being killed made him sick. "I'll obtain the weapons, then meet with Jahi. Then Jahi can drive them to the rendezvous point. I can follow at a distance on horseback, see the arms collected. If Victoria is at the exchange, I will be there to help her, should anything arise."

"You make the plans, Benson. I trust you." Then Helton left, shutting the door behind him.

Jahi stood beside the door, hands neatly folded in front of him.

Noah approached him. When he was close, Noah grabbed a fistful of his robes and pushed him against the door. He peeled back the sleeve of Jahi's left arm, revealing a scorpion brand. Unlike Noah's, it was long scarred over. "It was you, wasn't it?"

Jahi responded by slipping a knife from his pocket. The sharp blade separated their torsos, the tip scraping against Noah's collar. He gave a slow twist to his head, his eyes flat.

Releasing Jahi from his grasp, Noah stepped back, furious with himself. He'd showed his cards too soon. Jahi wouldn't be easily intimidated.

"Who are you working for?" Noah asked. Jahi being involved with the Aleaqrab was believable and he had access to Victoria. He would have known where she was. How to kidnap her.

Jahi didn't answer, his eyes dark. When he sprang forward, Noah grabbed the side of a chair, then lifted it and blocked Jahi's body with it. The chair snapped over Jahi's head, a splintering crack in the air.

Jahi tumbled onto the floorboards, the tarboosh rolling into the wall. The knife clattered across the wooden slats of the floor.

A few seconds later, Lord Helton threw the door open.

"What the devil—?" He froze at the sight of a dazed and groaning Jahi on the floor.

Noah released what remained of the chair from his hands, and it fell with a crash. "I think we have the key to finding Victoria." Squatting, Noah showed Lord Helton the brand on Jahi's arm. "He's with the Aleaqrab. He tried to attack Ginger in Ezbekieh after she arrived in Cairo. I thought the attacker looked familiar, but he was disguised."

Lord Helton's face darkened. "Where's my daughter, Jahi?"

Jahi muttered in an undiscernible voice then spat at Noah. The spittle landed on Noah's cheek and slid onto the floor. "Step aside, Benson." Lord Helton encroached upon both men.

Noah wiped his face with a handkerchief and stood, stepping back. A spark of fear ignited in Jahi's eyes. Like Noah, he'd seen Helton question an enemy before. Lord Helton's affectations of a gentleman who didn't dirty his own hands were effective. But it was pretense—he wasn't a man to be underestimated.

"Where is she?" The question was spoken so quietly that Noah barely heard it over his own breathing. His pulse was still quick from the confrontation with Jahi, and he inhaled deeply to still it. He was more nervous than he'd realized, probably from the hope that Victoria could be soon found.

"I don't know." Jahi reached for his tarboosh, and Lord Helton crushed his fingers under the toes of his boot.

Jahi cried out as Lord Helton leaned down. "I'm going to kill you, Jahi. But only you can choose how merciful and dignified a death you will have."

"I-I don't know w-where they've t-taken her." Jahi gasped as Helton put more weight on his hand. "I sw-swear it."

"Did you take her?" Lord Helton pushed the heel of his boot up against the fleshy part of Jahi's palm. Then Helton slid his heel down so that he pinched Jahi's skin between his heel and the floor.

Sweat had broken out across Jahi's forehead. "He ... he ordered it."

Lord Helton eased the pressure, and Jahi snatched his hand back and cradled it. "Who ordered it?"

Jahi's shoulders fell in a defeated slump. Noah's fingers curled with anticipation. Jahi didn't look up, his eyes closing. "Stephen Fisher."

## CHAPTER TWENTY-FOUR

The lorry bounced on the unpaved road, and Noah squinted in the darkness. In the seat beside him, Jahi squirmed, his hands and feet bound. Sweat shone on his forehead, and a bruise darkened the side of his face from where Noah had struck him with the chair earlier in the day.

Lord Helton was to meet them at a crossroads up ahead. Without Jahi to depend on to make the delivery alone, Lord Helton had been forced to drive the lorry from the meeting place north to Zeitoun, where they were to leave the arms.

Noah would then follow at a distance on horseback, to watch the arms be collected.

Passing the hamlet of impoverished huts that were near the crossroads, Noah pulled the lorry over. Jahi gave a pitiful whimper. He knew he'd been fortunate to spend the afternoon with Noah, getting the weapons. Lord Helton had gone to question Fisher. That had given Jahi a momentary respite from what lay before him. But Noah would have to turn him over to Helton now—who wasn't likely to be in a merciful mood after dealing with Fisher.

Noah was relieved that Lord Helton hadn't demanded he participate in Jahi's questioning. The spring before, Jahi had been tasked with the unfortunate job of delivering Ginger to Fisher. Though Lord Helton had commanded it, Noah still hadn't forgotten Jahi's role in the matter. If Ginger hadn't escaped...

Noah's jaw set angrily.

That betrayal had changed everything for him. Helton had delivered Ginger to Stephen without an ounce of concern of how it might affect her or Noah. Lord Helton had said earlier today that Noah's loyalty to him wasn't what it had once been. And that was why.

Helton had proven that everything and everyone was expendable as long as his objectives were achieved. Except Victoria—which was why Stephen must have targeted her. Noah's eyes flicked toward the back of the lorry.

He should have refused to get the arms for Lord Helton to give to the nationalists. Gone to his friends in the CID, Lord Helton's instructions be damned. Now it was Noah's name on the register. He was responsible for these weapons, even if Lord Helton had given the order. If the army investigated why a lorry of weapons went missing, they'd know Noah had taken them.

The knot in his stomach tightened further.

He'd told himself he could worry later about the fallout from giving arms to the enemy. But what if something happened in the meantime?

Still, the thought of Victoria in the hands of those men made him go cold. He hadn't allowed himself to think of the worst of the possibilities. While they'd pretended to be engaged, it had been easy to lose himself to the ruse. Victoria wasn't like other women and she hadn't been afraid to express what she felt for him.

Jack had told him it was foolish to let her think something

might develop from their flirtations, but Noah had cared for her. He'd just never been in love with her.

A flash of movement caught his attention. Lord Helton approached on horseback. He looked a far cry from the proper English gentleman now, dressed in casual clothing and sandals, with an accompanying brown fedora on his head.

Lord Helton brought the brown stallion to a trot, then stopped. Noah opened the door to the lorry as Lord Helton dismounted. He handed Noah the reins. "And Fisher?" Noah asked, raising a brow.

"I've dealt with him." Lord Helton's eyes were guarded. "Did you have any trouble?"

Noah slipped his foot into the stirrup, then hoisted himself onto the horse. "No, sir. Not that I expected any. It's all there." He checked the glowing dial of his wristwatch. "Have you planned anything if they don't bring her?"

"I plan to call on Masry's law office tomorrow if they don't bring her to me today. Put him on short notice before I go to the authorities." Lord Helton's eyes glittered in the moonlight. "You've done good work, Benson. I owe you more than you know." His voice was raw with emotion.

It was the closest to a compliment Helton would come. Words failed Noah as silence engulfed them. Noah snapped the reins, spurring the horse forward. He took it to a canter and circled around behind the lorry.

The door to the lorry slammed shut. Noah watched as the lorry pulled back onto the road, the wheels spinning dust into the air. He could follow the vehicle from the dust trail alone.

He stayed at a distance, thankful for the night ride. The smooth rhythm of the horse in the desert sands was a preferable form of transportation anyway. Something about traveling in the golden surrounds of desert and dusty ground at night felt freeing to his soul. The encampments of the

Australian and New Zealand forces were tented silhouettes in the distance.

Men who were tired and ready to go on with their lives back at home.

And here he was providing arms to their enemies.

His throat thickened, and he swallowed the guilt.

When he'd been younger, he'd been more naïve, more convinced of the blacks and the whites of morality.

Like the night that surrounded him, so much of that had turned to shades of grey.

He stayed back as the lorry rolled to a stop, then pulled a pair of binoculars from his bag. He turned the dial, focusing on the lorry, then scanned the surrounding area. Lord Helton emerged from the vehicle and stood in front of it, but Jahi didn't.

Within minutes, a wagon pulled by two horses approached. Four men climbed down from the wagon. Masry wasn't among them. They were too far for Noah to hear the exchange but he didn't see Victoria anywhere.

Lord Helton removed a torch from the lorry, then shone it into the cab, toward Jahi. Was he attempting to use him as an exchange for Victoria? If so, Noah doubted the move would be effective. Jahi's position was likely to be only important to the Aleaqrab while he'd been undercover. Now that Lord Helton had found him out, he would cease to be useful to them.

The exchange between Lord Helton and the men appeared to be calm. Noah swatted a horse fly circling near his head. The fly moved toward the beast beneath him instead, and its ears flicked. The men began to unload the weapons from the back of the lorry and carry them to the wagon.

A man from the Aleaqrab went to the front of the wagon. Without an ounce of gentility, he yanked a bedraggled figure from the seat of the wagon. Noah's heart lurched.

*Victoria.*

She was bareheaded, wearing a skirt and blouse that appeared ragged and unkempt. Her long dark hair was loose, streaming over her shoulders. And her hands were bound. The man who'd brought her down held her at gunpoint.

The sound of horses' hooves caught his attention.

Noah scanned the horizon, the sound preceding any visible movement.

Then he saw it: a patrol of five British soldiers heading toward the lorry and the wagon. *Of all the rotten luck.* Lord Helton and the Aleaqrab hadn't noticed them yet.

Noah swore, his pulse speeding as he spurred the horse into action. The horse tore off across the open plain, and Noah pushed the horse harder, bringing it to a full gallop. The Aleaqrab would likely think Lord Helton had betrayed them.

Gunfire crackled, splitting the cool Egyptian night.

The shots appeared to have been warnings—from the British troops—but they were met by return fire from the nationalists. British troops were about to find Lord Helton in the middle of a dubious exchange.

Noah tried to keep his eyes on Victoria, but they'd already started to whisk her away, pushing her back onto the wagon. The nationalists abandoned their work, taking only what they'd loaded as they continued to exchange gunfire with the British troops.

When Noah was still twenty feet away, one of them pointed a gun toward Helton. A gunshot ripped the air, and Lord Helton tumbled toward the ground. Victoria screamed and tore away from the man holding her, diving toward her father.

Noah reached the lorry, then jumped from the horse. "Victoria!"

She lifted her head, dazed, searching for him. Her dark eyes found his, and she gave a cry. Bullets whizzed past them, bouncing from the side of the lorry. The British troops would be upon them within a minute or less.

Lord Helton was still alive, groaning in pain, though Noah couldn't tell from his vantage point where he'd been shot. "Go!" Helton pushed Victoria forward, toward Noah. She crossed the space toward him as two of the nationalists reached Helton. With Victoria further away, the men grabbed Helton and hauled him to his feet. They dragged him toward the wagon, then threw him onto the back as they climbed in and took off.

Noah caught Victoria in his arms. She shook as he guided her to the horse. "Get on," he said. Through the open door to the lorry, Noah caught a glance of Jahi. He lay slumped against the window, dead. A bullet hole punctured the window beside him, a spiderweb of bloodied cracked glass around it.

There wasn't time to spare. Some troops chased after the nationalists. With the nationalists continuing to engage with the troops, Noah and Victoria would likely be shot before they could explain themselves.

Noah climbed up behind Victoria and reared the horse, then took off into the desert, galloping away from the gunfire, away from the lorry. He pushed the horse even faster than he had before and was thankful that Lord Helton had been the one to provide the stallion. The horse was likely faster than anything the ANZAC soldiers rode, even with the extra weight of Victoria on it.

But the horse would also tire faster. Thankfully, the patrol appeared to have trained their attention on the wagon. He continued at a gallop for another few minutes, then slowed the horse as they approached the hamlet where he'd met Lord Helton.

The villagers seemed shut up in their huts for the night. All that greeted them was a few beggars and howling dogs. Noah brought the horse to a trot. Victoria was breathing hard, her body trembling.

As he stopped, Victoria drew her legs up on one side of the horse, then turned her body into his. She slid her arms around his neck, sobbing, tears streaking her face as she trembled. Aware of the curious gaze of villagers who had opened their doors a crack to stare at them, Noah pushed the horse further forward, swallowing hard as he held her firmly with one arm.

"You're safe now." The pressure in his chest was unusually tight. His relief at her being with him was strong, but overpowered by the thoughts that buzzed through his mind. The lorry would be recovered by the British. It wouldn't take long for them to learn who had taken the vehicle.

And then what?

Lord Helton was now the one missing. This situation was beyond him now. He had to go to the CID, on the offensive.

"Noah—oh, Noah." She covered her eyes with her fingertips. "My father! You must go after him."

Tears spilled onto his shirtfront, then Victoria drew back. Holding his neck, she leaned toward him and kissed him, her lips soft and warm and salty with her tears.

Ginger's face flashed in his mind, and he pulled away. Her hands remained on his neck and she ducked her chin, her jaw tightening. "Did you see where they shot him?" Noah's voice was soft. He didn't want to remind her of what had just unfolded. But, for all he knew, Lord Helton could die from his injuries.

"I don't know. I didn't have time to see." Victoria cleared her throat, then pushed the hair from her face and tucked it behind her ear.

"I promise you, wherever he is—I'm certain he's glad it's him that's there rather than you." Noah pushed aside his guilt. She'd been a friend to him at the worst of times, and, despite her feelings for him, she deserved his comfort and friendship now. "Let's get you back to Cairo."

Victoria shook her head. "I don't want to go home. I can't go back there. I don't want to be alone, Noah."

Her fears weren't unfounded. Jahi had probably taken her from her home. And who knew what she'd been through since then. Noah swallowed the lump in his throat. "You won't be alone."

## CHAPTER TWENTY-FIVE

After the events of the day before, with Peter Osborne's fury at her for lying and Harold Young's injuries, it seemed a fitting day to be in church asking forgiveness for her own sins. *If God doesn't strike you down with a bolt of lightning.*

She couldn't remember the last time she'd gone to a Sunday church service with her family. Then again, she hadn't lived at home for ages. With the nurses, church attendance and prayer were a requirement of the profession. The nurses were to be an example of godly behavior. Shining white visions of purity. The unspoken truth was that, while the nurses were closely watched, no one could monitor them all. More than one sister had been found "compromised."

As the last strain of the closing hymn wound to a close, the organ a dissonant sound in the lofty ceilings, Ginger glanced down the pew to her family. Her mother had been particularly pleased with Ginger's company for the service. With each little reminder of how far she had drifted from the fold, Ginger's guilt toward her family increased.

She turned, then startled. Mr. Osborne was near the back of

the church. He nodded briefly at her, then turned and walked away, down the aisle.

Was he expecting to speak to her today? She had made no progress on Lady Hendricks anyway. Dr. Radford had given her the day and future Sundays off, something Osborne had to be aware of if he was here.

"Should we get tea at Groppi's? If we hurry we can get a seat in the garden," Lucy said as they climbed down the front steps of All Saints Church.

Ginger nearly groaned. The service had been crowded, the need for a new Anglican church more clear than ever. The last time she'd been here, the back of the church hadn't been so populated with standing worshippers. But with the influx of troops there simply wasn't room anymore. She knew a good majority of the congregation now would head to places like Groppi for more tightly-packed chaos.

William looked around, shading his eyes with his hand as he squinted. "And where's that from here?"

"Not far." Lucy pointed the way for William. "We're awfully close to everything that matters around Cairo. If you go just down this street you'll find Ezbekieh and Shepheard's."

Ginger arched a brow at her sister. She acted as though they still had a fortune awaiting them. "Really, Lucy, you make being a snob entirely effortless." *Everything that matters.* She cringed at the thought. This area of Cairo was thoroughly dedicated to the British, it was true. With the wide, cleaner streets, European architecture, imported trees, manicured gardens, there were places where Cairo seemed to disappear altogether. Across the Nile on Gezira Island, the Gezira Club offered landscapes that looked like home.

Meanwhile, the precolonial native quarters suffered from poor sanitation, cramped living spaces, and dark areas of crime. Ginger understood why the British stayed away. But as the war had progressed, the segregation had bothered her more, particularly when confronted by the reality that a great deal of locals saw them as invaders.

"Dearest, I believe there's a man waiting to speak to you." Her mother broke her train of thought.

At the end of the pavement, Osborne waited, hands behind his back. Did her mother know him? It was a possibility, given that they'd talked to her about the concession. Unless Lord Helton had handled that himself.

Her mother gave her a questioning look.

"Ah, yes—it's my friend, Mr. Osborne. Go ahead to Groppi's. I'll follow along." Without waiting for a response, Ginger went toward him. She didn't need to look back to know her family would be curious.

She played with the button on the wrist of her gloves as she approached him. "Mr. Osborne. What a surprise." Her family climbed into the car William had hired. She refocused on Mr. Osborne. "I didn't expect we'd need to speak today."

"My apologies. I tried to visit you at your home, and your butler informed me the family was here." Osborne removed his hat, a bead of perspiration on his brow. He mopped it with a handkerchief. "We always need to speak. Every morning, Lady Virginia."

*Every morning?* It seemed excessive. She rued the interruption that he'd given to an otherwise pleasant morning. "Why don't you walk with me? My family is on their way to Groppi's, and I told them I'd join them there. We can talk along the way." She didn't want to be seen standing outside of All Saints speaking with Osborne. Uneasiness came over her.

"As you wish." Osborne replaced his hat and extended his hand. "After you."

They started down the pavement. A bird chattered noisily in the tree overhead, and Ginger searched for it. European and native quarter—she loved Cairo. She and Lucy had that in common.

"Before I begin, I should mention that Lord Helton is quite unwell and has taken leave. The case has been assigned directly to me now, without his further involvement."

Unwell? She pressed her lips together tightly. Could this be because of Victoria? Something else might have happened. "Is it his health?"

"I'm not at liberty to divulge other details. Given Lord Helton's involvement with uncovering the concession, Sir Reginald at first believed that he would be an asset to the investigation. But Lord Helton has other pressing matters to attend to. From now on, should you need to speak to anyone about this matter, please direct yourself to me alone."

His words did little to settle the nerves that made her head ache with tension. Despite her dislike of Lord Helton, she trusted him much more than Mr. Osborne. In a tight voice, she said, "Thank you for letting me know."

"Have you made any further progress?"

"No, unfortunately not. But I intend to search my home later this afternoon when my family is out."

"The information you've provided me so far has been less than helpful." Osborne's face reddened further.

Ginger did her best to keep her composure. "I'm sorry that's been the case, but I'm doing what I can. You didn't assign me a time limit as far as I'm aware, what's the sudden urgency?"

"I just need to be certain you're giving this assignment your attention." Osborne gave her a cutting gaze. He clearly didn't trust her anymore. He sniffed, looking out toward the crowded street. "You're rather busy with personal matters, especially those involving Colonel Benson."

Her jaw clenched with irritation. Each time Noah entered their conversation, Osborne appeared to become more aggressive. On the stoop of a jewelry shop, a cat lazed in the sun. As they passed, it gave them a yowling hiss. Flecks of moisture showed on his shirt, and he frowned at the perspiration.

Perhaps his urgency came from a different source. One that she'd paid less attention to. He *wanted* to prove himself. As a newcomer to the Foreign Office, he'd probably wanted to show his skill. She frowned, feeling as though she should have listened to the voice of caution in her head in Alexandria when he'd approached her.

He was a young, intelligent officer. Likely wanting to make his mark. He'd probably been too curious, investigated what had befallen Lord Braddock a bit too deeply.

She blinked at him, a defensive feeling rising in her. Not just toward Noah but toward her family. What had he discovered? "I don't know what the official documents said, but the situation with my father was a complex one. Regardless of the activities he may have been involved in, he died in service to his country and protecting me."

"As you say, a complex situation exists with your father. I'm certain his name has been besmirched though. Something I'm sure you'd very much like for me to prove."

Ginger's stomach soured. Osborne was on the wrong hunt. "Mr. Osborne, if you'd like to understand what happened with my father, I suggest you investigate Stephen Fisher. Colonel Benson is not to blame."

His lips pursed, an angry bulge in the veins near his temples. "Colonel Benson is a menace. You saw what he did to Captain Young. He's ruthless. And he has no genuine regard for His Majesty's government. Do you have any idea what a coldhearted savage he is? Just ask him—ask him about his ruthlessness at Kut."

She kept her face blank. *At Kut?* That was where Osborne had become a prisoner of war. Noah had never told her about being there, but then, they'd barely discussed most of his work in the past. She was right. He'd targeted Noah for something personal.

"Has Colonel Benson done something to you?" Ginger felt chilled.

Whatever Osborne had intended by the statement, it was clear from his furtive survey of the pavement that he'd revealed more than he'd intended. "Let me remind you, Lady Virginia, I'm your superior. You don't ask me questions—it's the other way around."

She felt choked. How could she have been so misguided about Osborne's character? "And if I no longer want to participate?"

"But you will. Because I'm certain you're not the only one who has a vested interest in learning of the concession." He gave a meaningful glance toward Groppi's. "And I doubt very much your mother and sister would like to learn that the reason they're in such a terrible financial state is because you killed your own brother to protect Colonel Benson."

*He knows?* She stepped back, horrified. Besides Noah, only one other person knew the truth of her brother's death: Lord Helton. She'd never spoken of it to Jack or Beatrice, who had been close by when it happened. But Lord Helton had demanded the truth. Bile crept up her esophagus, and she prayed her reaction wouldn't show in her eyes, though her fear was palpable.

"Are you threatening me, Mr. Osborne?" The day no longer felt hopeful, the red sun beating on the back of her neck despite her hat. Her pulse pounded.

"Treason and sedition are very serious charges, Lady Virginia. If I have but even the slightest suspicion you're helping Benson, I'll have no other choice." Osborne stepped back, a congenial smile returning to his face. "But it won't come to that. Because we've come to an arrangement. I have a much bigger fish to catch. You'll find I can be an extremely understanding man when necessary."

She gaped at him, unsure how to respond. He'd gone from appearing like a stuttering, incompetent neophyte to someone who terrified her in a matter of seconds.

Mr. Osborne checked his watch. "I'll see you tomorrow morning. Be punctual." With a tip of his hat, he started the other way.

Thoroughly chilled, Ginger watched him go. Her hands trembled. How could she have been so fooled by his character? She'd thought him agreeable. Even pleasant.

She rushed down the pavement, desperate to put space between herself and Osborne.

A protective feeling came over her as Groppi's came into view. Ginger was determined to keep her family safe from men like Osborne, who wouldn't hesitate to use a deep secret to manipulate her.

Well, she wasn't about to let him. She'd tell her family the truth herself, if it came to it.

But how on earth would she ever be able to admit she'd killed Henry? They would hate her for it.

Her worries must have showed on her face when she arrived at the table in the garden of Groppi's. William stood, alarmed. "My dear Cousin Ginger—are you well?"

"Quite well, thank you." Her face had a habit of turning a bit too bright red when she was distressed or embarrassed, one downside of being a redhead. She sat, fanning herself with her gloved hand. "The walk was a bit more strenuous than I expected." She lifted the glass of water at her place setting, thankful that it was there.

"Who was the beau?" Lucy looked up from her tea with

interest. A warm breeze brought the fresh scent of baked bread, cardamom, honey, and other savory spices.

While she'd told her mother about the situation with the concession, Lucy didn't need to know anything about the matters that plagued their family from the past. It would only put her in danger. "Peter Osborne, with the Foreign Office. But he's just a casual acquaintance. Just inviting me for a picnic with some of the other nurses."

"A picnic for the nurses?" William gave an amused look. "War life in Cairo is much more adventurous than at home. Camel rides in the Sahara, the pyramids by moonlight, plus all the delightful places we saw in Alexandria. And nurses and officers everywhere at these sights."

Ginger drew a calming breath and sipped the cool water again. "Many of the nurses and soldiers who have been ordered here never would have been able to travel to places like these in their lifetimes, let alone have the access that they do. Besides"—she set her glass down with a bit more force than she intended—"we all need some distraction from the horrors faced daily."

William sobered. "Quite right. I apologize. I didn't mean to suggest the war has been pleasant here."

She shouldn't have displaced her anger onto William, but she couldn't help it. She was still seething from her conversation with Osborne.

"Well, I for one would love to go back to England." Lucy slathered cream on a scone. A dry smudge of crumbs beaded on her lips.

"If I might ask, why didn't you return earlier?" William directed his question to her mother. He shifted in his seat, and his knee bumped against Ginger's.

Ginger said nothing. His knee brushed against hers again and her breath stilled. Was he being flirtatious?

She shifted her leg back, to leave more space between them.

Her mother's lips pressed together as she considered William's question. She lifted the porcelain teacup in front of her. "When Edmund was first ordered to Egypt, officers and diplomats were encouraged to bring their wives and families. Soon there was an influx of wives here, which made for quite the social scene—but then the disastrous campaign at the Dardanelles began and the practice was outlawed, in part because of the many troops stationed here. But those of us who were already here were forbidden to leave."

"Because of the danger to passenger liners after *Lusitania*?" William asked with interest.

"In part. The navy has enough trouble keeping their vessels and hospital ships safe, let alone passenger liners." Her mother gave him a taut smile, her gaze traveling to the street vendors who passed in front of Groppi's.

"Oh, William, dearest," her mother said, "there's a vendor over there with head scarves. Can you and Lucy pick one out for me? I'd like to have one for our trip to Gezira this afternoon."

"Of course, Lady Braddock." William scrambled to his feet, setting his serviette down.

"You're going to Gezira Island?" Ginger hadn't heard of her family's plans, and she felt oddly disappointed. Not only to not have been included but because she would have enjoyed going with them on the outing. She ran her fingers along the soft folds of the serviette in her lap.

"Isn't it marvelous? All the best neighborhoods are in Gezira." Lucy beamed at William. "And then tomorrow we have dinner at the palace." She took his arm as they left the table together.

Maybe William really was growing on her younger sister.

"Dinner at the palace?" Ginger raised a brow. Only a few weeks down in Cairo, William was already settling in well.

"You're invited too, of course. The new sultan issued an invitation for all society members weeks ago. I didn't think at the time you would be available." Her mother's face sobered. She looked Ginger directly in the eye. "What happened with that man who was following you?"

Her mother's astuteness was unsurprising to her by now. Ginger poured herself a cup of tea, and the steam rose toward her face. "I work for Mr. Osborne." The aromatic scent of the tea leaves comforted her. "He's not the nicest man."

"Work for him ... how?"

Ginger kept her gaze down, knowing her mother wouldn't like the answer. "In intelligence. Trying to find the concession. That's why I came to Cairo."

"Oh, Ginger." Her mother bit her lip. "You know what we went through with your father."

"Only too well, Mama, and unfortunately, that's why they approached me."

Her mother paled. "Have you made any progress on the matter?"

Ginger lowered her voice, aware of the proximity of neighboring café patrons. "Not much. I stopped in to see Mr. Brandeis. He told me of the various properties father had throughout Egypt and in Malta?"

Her mother looked anxiously out toward the street, as though to make certain William and Lucy were still occupied. "The properties are in your name. Brandeis thought it best for us to wait to sell them until William had arrived and we'd settled the estate completely."

"But why in Malta?" Ginger's eyes wandered through the sea of uniforms present at Groppi's. How often had she come here with other QAs, like Beatrice? She missed those simpler times.

"Your father helped round up the Egyptian nationalists that were exiled and imprisoned on Malta after the beginning of the war. He was in Malta so often, he ended up purchasing a home to stay in."

"Father helped to round up the nationalists?" She hadn't ever heard him speak of it. Once again she felt as though he had hidden so much from her. How well had she really known her father?

"He rather disliked the task." Her mother wrinkled her nose. "But your father disliked many things he was assigned to do over the years." She shook her head, clearing the memories away like cobwebs in her mind. "At any rate, I take it Mr. Brandeis was of no more use to you than he was to me?"

Ginger hesitated. She didn't know how much to tell her mother but her mother might help smooth things over with Lady Hendricks. "Actually, I learned a few more details. Apparently, Father gave the concession to a Freddy Mortimer. Mortimer was to take the concession to a safe location and then bring back information about where he'd taken it. He never returned."

Her mother's eyes widened. "That's why Lady Hendricks gave you the cold shoulder."

"Then you know about him? Lucy told me later about the rumors—"

"Tell me you have said nothing to Lucy." Her mother's hand shot out toward Ginger.

"Of course not. I made up an excuse about why I needed to speak to Lady Hendricks." The waiter arrived, carrying a plate of sandwiches, which he set on the table. Ginger watched him leave. "Do you remember Mr. Mortimer? Mr. Brandeis said Father knew him well."

"Unfortunately, your father never introduced us." Her mother's lips hinted at a smile. "I heard he was quite handsome. Given his reputation with Lady Hendricks, I think Edmund wasn't eager for me to meet him."

"Well, that's where my inquiries ended. Lady Hendricks won't accept my invitations or apologies or return my notes." Ginger sighed and selected a sandwich from the tray. "I'm not sure where to go from here."

"Oddly enough, Lady Hendricks didn't answer my note yesterday either. I suppose she thought I was attempting a meeting on your behalf."

The cheerful sounds of people chatting and laughing, spoons clinking against porcelain, felt incongruous to Ginger's conversation with her mother.

Her mother glanced over Ginger's head, toward the street. "William and Lucy are on their way back. We'll have to discuss this further when we return from Gezira."

Lucy arrived and held a light-blue scarf toward her mother. "I bought this for you." Then she turned and handed Ginger a beautifully embroidered cream scarf. "And this is from William for you."

Ginger took the scarf. Much as she was touched by the gesture, it was just one more thing she owed him. "This is beautiful. Thank you, William."

"My pleasure. I only wish you were going to Gezira with us." William held Ginger's gaze. She'd avoided him recently. A part of her felt remorse. She didn't want to hurt him.

Ginger folded the scarf and placed it in her handbag.

"And look what William bought me." Lucy lifted a third headscarf, a long navy-blue one. It seemed Lucy was enjoying spending William's money on herself.

The thought provoked the question about William's background once again. "What did you do in Kent, William? Before the war. I feel I haven't had the time to ask you too much about yourself."

"I worked in banking." His answer was vague, though perhaps he intended it that way.

"I was always terrible with numbers," Ginger admitted as she fingered a sandwich. "Though I enjoyed literature. Do you read?" Inadvertently, she'd asked the question while thinking of Noah. She remembered Victoria describing Noah as a bookworm.

"Occasionally. I enjoy a good novel on a cold winter night." William leaned back in his seat, the caning on the seat creaking as it stretched under his weight. "Though, I think I could accustom myself to these Egyptian winters. They're rather more enjoyable than deep drifts of snow and shivering until you can't feel your toes."

"Snow," Lucy said the word reverently. "I miss it. And that first beautiful day in the spring—" She gave Ginger a knowing glance. "Ginny always used to call it her favorite day of the year."

Ginger shared a wistful smile with her sister. "That's true. There's nothing quite like that first warm day, when the birds have returned, and the skies have turned blue once again. And the green grass is so perfect for a horse ride ..." Ginger blushed and bit into her sandwich.

"You enjoy the natural world, then?" A breeze teased the hair near his ears.

Ginger swallowed her bite. "I do."

As Lucy told William about all their favorite outdoor places back home at Penmore, Ginger felt a mixture of nostalgia and wistful regret. When they'd left home at the beginning of the war, she'd never imagined she wouldn't return. Now the chances of her ever seeing Penmore outside of a passing visit were remote. She would never live there again.

Neither would her family. Unless Lucy married William. While that remained a possibility, she still felt guilt at the thought of Lucy being forced to marry someone just to save the family fortune.

A troubling thought struck her. At least she had a life with Noah to look forward to. For her family, the future had the potential to be much bleaker.

She sat back in her chair, sipping her tea, determined to enjoy this time. With her family going to Gezira Island for the afternoon, it left her some freedom in her schedule. Shepheard's was around the corner. Noah might be there.

She was going to pay him a visit. No matter who saw her.

## CHAPTER TWENTY-SIX

Under her gloved hand, Ginger's knock on the wooden door to Noah's room at Shepheard's sounded dull and soft. Within a few seconds, footsteps approached. Noah stood there. He blinked at her, surprise registering on his face. Then he stepped out into the hall, closing the door behind him. "Ginger. What are you doing here?"

Her brows drew together in puzzlement. Why did she get the feeling he wasn't pleased to see her? "I was at Groppi's and —" She glanced down the hallway. No one was in sight. "Can I come in?"

Noah's expression was wary. "Why don't I get my jacket and join you outside instead? In the garden?" He wore his uniform trousers and shirt but was missing his hat and jacket and was barefooted.

She reached past him for the knob. "I'd prefer the privacy of your room—" She turned it, pushing the door open behind him.

The room was shrouded in darkness, but movement came from the bed. A form rolled to the side as though stirred from sleep.

A woman.

Ginger's heart slammed against her ribs, her gaze flying back to Noah's. Frozen with shock, she stayed rooted in place, scanning his eyes.

*He has a woman in his bed.*

Feeling sick, Ginger stumbled back. She covered her mouth with her hand. "Oh my God."

Noah grabbed the doorknob and pulled the door shut, pushing them both back out into the hall. His hand encircled her wrist. Ginger's eyes darted down the hall, feeling like a caged animal who couldn't cry out without attracting unwanted attention. She yanked her hand back, but he didn't release it. "Let me go."

Reluctantly, he let her wrist go. She gave it an exaggerated rub, then turned and stalked down the hall, tears burning her eyes.

Noah caught up with her. "Stop and listen to me." His voice was low, as discreet as possible, but anxious. "Please. It's not what you're thinking. It's Victoria—"

"I don't want to hear it." She didn't slow. *How could I be so foolish?* Victoria, of all women! Noah knew the insecurities Victoria roused in her. "You were clearly trying to hide her presence from me." She reached the lift.

"I wasn't trying to hide her presence—"

*The hell he wasn't.* "Then why did you want to go to the garden?"

Noah held her by the shoulders, facing her toward him. "Because I was trying to let her rest."

"And your bedroom was a perfect place for that, wasn't it?" She gave him a cutting look. "Wasn't it just recently you told me you didn't want me suturing your shoulder in your room because of how it might look to others if we were seen? I suppose that didn't matter with her, did it? The risk is only worth it with her?"

An angry scowl flinched across his features. His shoulders lowered with a frustrated breath. "I rescued Victoria last night. The exchange resulted in Lord Helton being taken by her kidnappers. She could probably use a nurse or doctor to tend to her. I don't know what they did to her, but I didn't want to ask either. She was terrified of going back to her home and being alone."

A hundred thoughts assailed her at once. Her lips parted with shock. Lord Helton had been captured? No wonder Osborne had said he was indisposed. Noah had been out doing something incredibly dangerous the previous night, and she hadn't had a clue.

What if Noah had been killed? How would she have learned of it?

And … *Victoria*. The cool, emotionally detached woman that she'd practiced being both growing up and in nursing prevailed. "Is she injured?" she managed, crossing her arms. "I am a nurse, after all. You might have thought to tell me from the beginning and let me see to her."

Noah scanned her face, his dark-blue gaze hesitant. "I'm not sure you're the right woman for the job. She's been through an ordeal, Ginger—I don't want to add to it the sting of any humiliation she might feel around you. Especially given your initial reaction."

Ginger clenched her jaw, and her anger and hurt came tumbling back to the surface. "You're a married man now, Noah. You can't just take women back to your room and expect your wife to be happy about it."

"I didn't want to bring her here, but it was the best option, given the circumstances. She needed my help, Ginger. I brought her in discreetly. I've already sent for my friend who runs a safe house, to see if he can help her."

It wasn't just about Victoria being here. He'd put her in a horrible position with Peter Osborne by coming to her house. And then there was Captain Young.

"Do you have any idea what I've been through the last few days? Not only did I have to tend to Captain Young—who, by the way, remembered your involvement in his attack and spoke to Peter Osborne about it—but Osborne also informed me you were seen going into my home in the middle of the night." Her breath came in short, frustrated bursts.

Noah's expression was unreadable, but his shoulders slumped. "What does Osborne know? I'm hoping to go to the CID and tell one of my superiors about everything with Lord Helton as soon as Victoria leaves."

"I don't know. I'm not certain what Young told him." Her irritation grew. He hadn't even responded about the potential damage he'd done to her reputation. And Osborne's claims about Noah today bothered her in a way she knew they wouldn't if she hadn't found Victoria in his room.

What if she'd allowed her feelings for him to cloud the truth? He'd showed a side of moral greyness the last few days that worried her. She'd married him hastily. Had she made a mistake? *Don't be ridiculous, Ginger.*

In a shaky voice, she said, "Tell me about Kut. What you did there."

He looked at her enigmatically, his face hardening. "Kut?"

She set her hands on her hips. "Convince me you're the man I think you are and not the ruthless one I keep hearing about."

His lips twisted with displeasure. "You know nothing about Kut, no matter who has poisoned you with tales about it. Osborne?" He jerked his chin up. "And you're choosing to believe Osborne, without even asking me."

Disappointment gutted her. There must be some truth to what Osborne had said. How would Noah have known what she was referring to otherwise? "I'm asking you now, aren't I?"

The lift arrived and the operator pulled the gate back, the sound of metal scraping against the floor. "Please don't get on." Noah's eyes searched hers. "You know me." He sucked in a breath and looked back toward his room. "You need to believe me."

A quizzical expression filled the lift operator's face as he waited for her to climb on.

She started forward. Noah slipped his hand in hers. "Please, Ginger."

She looked over her shoulder at him. His explanation was reasonable. But she didn't want to be reasonable right now.

*Not yet.*

And he still hadn't bothered to address so many questions.

"You won't answer me, will you?" she asked, ever aware of the impatient look from the lift operator.

"I won't talk about Kut here." A spark flickered in Noah's gaze. "Or Victoria. She needs help and compassion, not your wounded ego."

"Ego?" Ginger's voice was loud enough that the lift operator flinched. He swung the gate closed, and the lift departed without her.

She wished she could leave too.

She glared at Noah. "Your choice to bring her here was unacceptable. This has nothing to do with my pride."

Noah gave a contemptuous, humorless chuckle. "Doesn't it? I told you the truth and that's still not good enough. Bringing her here was an error in judgement, perhaps, but I felt I had no choice. I can't change that Victoria was linked to me in the past, no more than I can that she has *unrequited* feelings for me. The only thing I can see keeping your anger alive now is your pride." He turned to go.

She was tempted to take the wedding ring off her finger and throw it at him.

Not that it was that simple now.

Unable to summon the right words, she started down the hallway, in the direction of the staircase.

*Her* pride?

She whirled back around, stalking toward him. "How dare you question my pride? Don't you remember what I sacrificed, what I lost, for you?"

She regretted the words the instant she spoke them. They hung in the air between them like a glass of water teetering on its side, about to fall onto the floor with a crash.

Noah stepped back, his gaze growing cool. He put a hand above his heart, as though the words had found their impact there. Raising his chin, he stared at her. "That's what this is about, isn't it? You'll never be able to look at me without thinking of what you lost. And you can't forgive yourself for it."

Her throat grew tighter, her hands in loose fists. Stubborn tears stung her eyes. At once she wanted to go to him, apologize, kiss him. When she'd almost lost him, when she'd spent months wondering if he'd survived, she'd never questioned what she'd done.

A tear found its way down her cheek, and she dashed it away with her gloved fingertip. "Find Dr. Jane Radford at the hospital where I work. She's an excellent physician, something I'm not. At this rate I probably never will be. But if you call and ask for her to come here and help with Victoria, she will. Tell her I sent you."

She rushed down the hall toward the stairs, her heart aching with emotions she didn't fully understand.

This time he didn't follow.

She loved Noah. She'd loved him almost from the start. Why was she so angry with him?

As she exited from the stairwell, she found her way through the lobby of Shepheard's, then out the door to the terrace. The bright afternoon was just as she'd left it, but the sun and cheerful surroundings did nothing for her heavy heart.

The terrace was thick with British patrons at the tables, much like Groppi's had been. And in the corner on one side of the terrace sat Lady Hendricks. Alone.

Ginger's fingers curled into fists.

Social convention be damned. Lady Hendricks fully intended to ignore Ginger from here on out anyway.

Ginger strode toward the table, her every step bolstered by her fury and indignation from leaving Noah upstairs. Her emotional state wasn't the best one to approach an important conversation. She had little choice.

She pulled out the empty chair beside Lady Hendricks and sat, gracefully, just as though she was supposed to be there.

Lady Hendricks startled, her gaze ripped from the street down below and settling on Ginger. "Lady Virginia," she said, working to remove the surprise from her features.

"Good afternoon, Lady Hendricks. I'm sorry to join you uninvited, but I really must insist on speaking to you." Ginger kept her voice low. The chance of being overheard at Shepheard's was high. "I'm searching for Freddy Mortimer, and you—"

"Don't you dare mention that name again." Lady Hendricks gave her a derisive look, then furrowed her brow. "Why? Did you have an entanglement with him? I've heard all about the sordid reputation of the eldest Braddock daughter."

Ginger leaned back in her seat and smirked. "And I've heard all about your entanglement with Mr. Mortimer. Unlike other women in society, I'm not impressed with your money, Lady Hendricks."

Lady Hendricks blanched, looking shocked that someone might speak to her in such a manner.

Ginger softened her expression. "But neither do I care about your personal affairs. Nor do I judge you for them. I've been serving the troops from the beginning of this war and we're all weary, aren't we? You're not the first lonely wife left at home by a husband who she's probably spent more time waiting for than married to. The letters I read to some of the injured soldiers told a whole other side of this war that's unspoken. The war at home is no less a struggle."

The horn of a motorcar drew Lady Hendricks' gaze away briefly. When she looked back, she'd composed herself. "That's where you're wrong about me," she said tersely. "I don't love Stewart. I never did. I married for comfort, which I have in spades. It also gives me the ability to not have to deal with the likes of people like you. At my word alone, I could see that you, your sister, and your mother are completely excluded from the events of the winter season." She leaned forward, over her teacup. "That's why I married Stewart. Because I enjoy being able to do what I want, however I want, to whomever I want."

Ginger had thought her a plain woman before, now she saw her as truly ugly. Her visage seemed to take on the blackness of her heart. How could she possibly prevail upon someone so cruel and with so little regard for the feelings of others? "My mother and sister have nothing to do with this, Lady Hendricks. But if you see fit to drive us away, so be it. It so happens that Freddy Mortimer stole something of great value to my family. You can hardly do more to us than he's already done."

"Freddy isn't a thief," Lady Hendricks said in a flat tone. Her quick defense gave away something more though. She still had feelings for him.

"Then he'll have to prove it for himself." Ginger dropped her voice another degree. She only had this one gamble, this one lead. If she cowered now, she would get nowhere. "And you'll find me to be just as unscrupulous as my reputation. I won't stop until I find Mr. Mortimer. I will continue my search, regardless of the damage I do to you in trying to find him. I fully intend to direct my next line of questions to your husband."

Lady Hendricks stared at her, blinking. Then her shoulders shrank, a defeated expression on her face. "I haven't seen or heard from Freddy in months." She fidgeted with the serviette in her lap. Then she added, "You know, you aren't the first to come asking questions about Freddy recently. I had government officials at my door months ago. What is it you think Freddy stole?"

*Months ago?*

Ginger stared back at her. But Noah had just brought news of the concession recently. Why would government officials have been asking about Freddy Mortimer months earlier? "The deed to a property my father left to me," Ginger said smoothly. That was as close to the truth as she was willing to admit. She scrutinized Lady Hendricks. "Did you say months ago?"

Lady Hendricks still looked wary but she sipped her tea. "Yes, they came in August. By then I hadn't seen Freddy for a few months, though. I escorted them to his room here in Shepheard's, but there was no trace of him."

Why would they have been asking about Freddy in August? Ginger had assumed that when Osborne had told her they'd tried to find out about him, it had been recently.

Unless they'd known about the concession before Noah found out about it.

"Is there anything about Mr. Mortimer that you didn't tell them? Anything that might help me find him?" Ginger released a slow, long breath and lifted her chin. "I can't expect you to understand my situation, Lady Hendricks, but we're not altogether that dissimilar. I had to sacrifice a life with the man I loved to better my family. And now I'm the only one that can help them try to recover what Mr. Mortimer took from us. Please. My mother counts you among her friends. Will you help me?"

She prayed her lie about Noah would be believable. Lady Hendricks certainly knew about him. Confirming that the rumors about them had been true might help to give her some sense of regained status between them.

Lady Hendricks was silent for what felt like a full minute. Then she set her teacup down with trembling fingers, the cup clattering.

She stared at the amber liquid inside. "His real name was Paul Hanover. Mortimer was just a pseudonym. As far as I know, he never shared that information with anyone else." Her eyes brimmed with tears. "And he claimed he loved me."

*A pseudonym?*

Ginger's heart beat faster with an excited pulse. This was something she might work with. "Thank you," Ginger said simply. Then she stood and left Lady Hendricks still staring at her tea.

## CHAPTER TWENTY-SEVEN

Noah waited outside the door to his hotel room as the doctor finished her examination of Victoria. He checked his pocket watch. Alastair was late in coming but would hopefully be here soon. Much as Victoria might want to stay with Noah, she couldn't. Especially not after his argument with Ginger. Alastair could provide Victoria both safety and anonymity in one of his safe houses.

And the sooner she left, the sooner he could try to find help at the CID. This had gone on long enough without involving a higher authority.

The door to the room opened, and Dr. Radford exited. She wore a serious expression. "She's resting. She'll need a good deal of rest, I imagine. But, I think she's fine staying out of the hospital."

He doubted that Dr. Radford would reveal anything intimate, but he wondered what Victoria had been through at the hands of the Aleaqrab. "Is there anything else I can do for her?"

"No, but she was asking for you. I'm certain she needs the comfort of a friend after her ordeal." Dr. Radford turned to go, then stopped. Fingering her black physician's case, she searched his face, her brow knitting. "Colonel Benson, I can't help but wonder, but are you acquainted with Captain Harold Young?"

"I am." Looking her in the eye grew more difficult.

"In that case I'm not sure I'm comfortable leaving Lady Victoria with you." Dr. Radford's lips set to a line.

What was the woman proposing? To stay and be a personal escort? "Dr. Radford, I work with Captain Young at the CID."

"I have the feeling you're aware of the precise incident I'm referring to. I've turned the matter over to the authorities, you know."

"I won't hurt Lady Victoria. But if you're concerned for her welfare, you're certainly welcome to ask her if she's comfortable staying with me." Noah's tone was a bit more biting than he'd intended.

Dr. Radford squared her shoulders. "I already have." Begrudgingly, she added, "She says there's no one in Egypt she trusts more than you."

Noah's lips curled with the irony of Victoria's statement of loyalty. His own wife was less convinced of his goodness. He had no desire to deny the matter with Young and had worried what would happen if Young accused him.

Lord Helton being in the hands of the Aleaqrab complicated his situation, though. Without Lord Helton to speak for him when an accusation came through, he'd have to explain the situation without giving a complete picture.

"If it helps—" Noah cleared his throat—"I brought Captain Young to the hospital the other night. Did my best to stop him from being killed by his attackers. I'm uncertain what Young remembers, but if I hadn't been there he would likely be dead."

Dr. Radford flinched. "It's not up to me to decide what happened. Even if your role was as noble as you claim, there are still gaps to the story, such as why you felt the need to leave him there telling no one what happened to him." Still, his explanation appeared to have mollified her somewhat. "You do understand I'll have to report this conversation?"

Noah leaned against the door frame. "When? I'm having Lady Victoria moved later this evening to a safer location."

"Most likely tomorrow morning." Dr. Radford sighed, a tired expression on her youthful-looking face. "Good evening, Colonel."

At least she was giving him some time to prepare.

As Dr. Radford left, Noah slipped back into the bedroom. The curtains were still drawn, the light in the room dim. With sunset approaching in a few hours, there wasn't much point in drawing them now.

Victoria sat on the bed, wearing the shirt he'd lent her. He poured a glass of water, then brought it to her side. She accepted it, offering him a grateful smile. A cut on the corner of her mouth and a shadowed bruise on her cheek told him she'd been struck in the face.

"Alastair should come soon," Noah said, sitting on the foot of the bed.

She sipped the water, averting her gaze. She knew what that meant. "It'll be good to see him."

"I told him to bring a burqa. You can wear it to go down through the lobby without being recognized."

"I'd rather stay with you." Victoria's dark eyes were red-rimmed, a rare moment of vulnerability for her. "Please don't send me away."

The air in the room felt stale and Noah wished he could open the window, allow some cooler air in. "Alastair is better at this sort of thing that I am. And you can trust him."

She placed the water on the bedside table. "And my father? Are you going after him?"

Finding Lord Helton was crucial—almost more for his own

sake than hers.

Noah scooted closer and took her hand. "I'll do what I can. I promise. I made some inroads with the organization that took you while I was searching for you. I'll go to the place they took me. See what I can learn." He squeezed her hand gently. "It may help me if there are any details you can give me, about where you were being held. What you remember."

If Jahi hadn't been killed, his help could have been invaluable. Noah wished he'd taken the time to interrogate the man more.

Victoria turned her face away. Her fingers curled against his. At last, she whispered, "I have little to tell you. They kept a sack over my head when they grabbed me and I didn't see where they took me. I think they kept me in a cellar—but it felt like a tomb."

"Who did you see while there?"

She shuddered. "There was one man …" Her lips pressed together, white. She appeared troubled.

He didn't push her further. The ordeal was too fresh. "If you remember anything, have Alastair send me a message. I won't be at Shepheard's after tomorrow morning. It's become a bit too dangerous for me."

"Where are you going?" Alarm registered on her face.

"I don't know." Even if he did, he wouldn't tell her. Much as he wanted to help Lord Helton, someone else from the CID would be better for this. And Jack was still out there. He'd wasted enough time before going after Jack already. Victoria was safe now.

Victoria lowered herself back onto the bed, her dark hair over her shoulders. She rolled on one side and wiped her cheek. "Please be careful. I can't bear the thought of losing you."

Noah stood and went to the chair where he'd spent the night. He removed the pillow and placed it back on the foot of the bed, lost in thought. This wasn't the time to have the conversation with her again about Ginger. She was raw and hurt.

Victoria's thoughts went there anyway, it seemed. "When she went missing in the desert, you chased down her captors, killed them all."

Irritation tingled down his arms, which he flexed, but the truth was she wasn't completely wrong. He'd done things to hunt for and recover Ginger that had been sheer madness. "I was trying to find you."

Silence followed. Then she said in a hollow, bitter voice, "I know. Just like you're trying to find Jack. But you're much more averse to the risks now, I suppose."

Noah blinked at her curled-up form. Her words were dizzying.

*God Almighty.* He couldn't do right by anyone, could he?

And yet ... Victoria wasn't wrong. He'd taken the time for a damned polo match while she'd been missing. Alastair had urged him to be cautious in going back for Jack, but when hadn't Alastair urged caution? Alastair was caution. He lived in a house without a front door and shrouded himself in secrets and spies and information. Noah knew all this, and yet he hadn't gone back for Jack—and that was before Victoria had been taken.

Because he had someone to live for. To be cautious for.

At least he'd thought he did.

He pulled a wooden case out from under the bed and set it on the desk in the room, then removed the materials he needed to clean his rifles. He laid out a cloth over the desk, then grabbed two rifles from the corner of the room. Who knew when he would have time for anything this methodical in the next few days? The trouble with desert warfare was that keeping one's guns clean was nearly impossible—sand seemed to get everywhere.

His gaze darted toward Victoria, who studied him. "You heard her come here, didn't you?" he said at last.

"Yes." Victoria propped her hands under her cheek. "I suppose that means she's no longer keeping her promise to my father to stay away from you."

Noah pulled the bolt back and cleaned the chamber with a rag. "Your father recruited her ... didn't you know? To find her father's concession. So he can then take it."

Victoria shook her head. "Had he asked my opinion, I would have told him—"

"That's irrelevant." Noah used a dry brush to sweep the barrel, then covered the end of the rifle with a condom—a trick Jack had taught him to keep out the dirt and sand. He kept his expression even. "At any rate, she wasn't reporting directly to your father anyway."

"Why on earth would anyone be so deluded as to believe she's equipped to learn anything?" Annoyance flashed in Victoria's face, and she pushed one bare leg out from under the covers. She tossed the covers aside and moved to the vacant chair beside the desk. "And I suppose she's been keeping you occupied doing her work for her."

Noah didn't answer.

He *had* been occupied. Busy trying to find Victoria. Busy trying to keep Ginger happy. Busy trying to learn what the hell Fisher was up to.

He'd been *kept* occupied.

He sat bolt upright.

"You're right." Noah raked his fingers across his scalp, wanting to tug at his hair in frustration.

Someone had wanted to keep him occupied. Occupied and here in Cairo.

It had to be Fisher.

"Why would Fisher want me in Cairo?" he asked aloud, focusing on the bullets littering the cloth.

Victoria was tense, alert. He could tell she knew he'd thought of something and believed it better not to interrupt his train of thought.

His plan had been to go back for Jack. And he would have. "Jack must know something. Or have something. Something they want to keep from me." He threw down the rag, his head snapping upright. "I have to go back for him."

Alarm crossed her features. "What about my father?"

*Lord Helton be damned.* But he couldn't say that to her. Heat rose on his neck. "I'll need to go to the CID and make them aware of what's been going on with the Aleaqrab."

"But you said they threatened to kill me if anyone else was involved. Wouldn't they do the same to him?" Victoria bristled. She grabbed his forearm, right over the spot where Masry's men had branded him. He grimaced and did his best not to display the raw pain shooting through his arm. "Please, Noah, you promised. Not even five minutes ago. I'm begging you—wait until they try to contact me. Please."

"I stayed to help your father because of how highly I regard you, Victoria. Don't ask me to put yet another obstacle in front of going after Jack." Noah grabbed a long canvas rucksack and packed it, adrenaline pumping through his veins. He needed to pay Stephen a visit. See what he could learn from him—and this time Lord Helton wouldn't be there to restrain him.

Victoria stood, crossing her arms. "If she asked you to help her, you would do it." Her dark eyes flashed.

Noah lifted his chin sharply. "You're right, I probably would. Which is apparently what Stephen has been counting on. My weakness with her. That I love her like no other."

She flinched. "Have you even told her who you really are or

anything about your background? You think that won't be an issue for her because you're both blind with infatuation, but I know women like her and people like her family. They will always look at you like you're less. Never accept you as one of them. And no matter what she says to you about wanting to leave her family behind, you know she'll always be a part of them."

She came closer to him and placed a hand on his chest. "You and I ... we're the same. We have Egypt in our blood. She doesn't understand this land or its customs."

Noah closed his eyes, his heart tightening at the hurt in her voice. "Victoria..."

She threw her arms around his neck, tears on her cheeks. "She doesn't love you the way I do. She never has. She's selfish—and, and—I heard her. She blames you for her brother's death! Please, Noah ... even if you don't love me, help my father ..." She dissolved into tears, her shoulders shaking, her words no longer coherent.

He'd never seen her lacking so much aplomb. She was always graceful, always composed.

He gathered her in his arms, holding her tightly as she wept. She'd probably be humiliated by this later, knowing her. After she'd calmed, he returned her to the bed and let her rest quietly while he packed the few belongings he wanted to take. His stomach felt sour, remembering how he and Jack had packed those bags in Jerusalem, only to have to abandon them on the street.

He'd been abandoning too much lately.

Alastair came for Victoria an hour later, and they parted without further incident. *Thank goodness.*

But Victoria's pleas echoed in his mind. What if the Aleaqrab *did* kill Helton because he went to the CID?

For all he knew, Helton could be dead. He may even have been shot.

One last visit to Masry might be a safer option before going to the CID.

Noah glanced at his reflection as he changed into the outfit he'd worn to the Aleaqrab meeting. Since Masry had Lord Helton, he'd have to continue to be Karim Sayed. At least his work in getting closer to the organization hadn't been entirely a waste.

Once darkness had fallen and the dining rush was over, Noah left Shepheard's and took the tram to Old Cairo. Much as he wanted to throttle Stephen Fisher, at least he had the assurance that he wasn't going anywhere for a while. Masry might be a faster way of finding Lord Helton.

He found the squalid row of buildings within one of the poorest areas in the historic part of the city. Masry himself might have been wealthy, but he didn't appear to want to bring his organization close to his home. After darting into an alleyway, Noah found the doorway. How he'd found his way back here without trouble was amazing, he'd been drunk and in blinding pain when he'd stumbled out of here the other night.

He tapped on the door and waited.

When the door opened a crack, he pulled down his sleeve, flashing the brand on his forearm. The door opened fully, and the man behind it gave him a nod. At least Noah would no longer have difficulty being admitted.

Noah's eyes drifted over the decrepit interior of the home, little more than a hovel. In this section of Old Cairo, families of fifteen people sometimes squeezed into one or two rooms. "Is Al-Mashat here?"

The man pointed back to a room off the ground floor. In the affluent homes of Old Cairo—like the one where Masry lived—the room would be called the *qa'a* and was used to receive only male guests. Despite the lack of space here, Masry was a man of ritual. He likely kept some of his customs.

The disconnect was poignant. The men of the Aleaqrab had to know of Masry's wealth because of his motorcar. Did they only know him as Al-Mashat? Or was the name just given to those who were new to protect Masry and his family?

Noah was admitted into the room. Five men were inside, including Masry, seated at a round table. Masry looked up at him with surprise, then rose. "Karim." He greeted him warmly. The air was thick and laden with tobacco smoke, sweetly pungent.

Noah bowed his head. *"As-salaam alykum.* I want to be of service to you."

"Our eager new recruit." Masry grasped his forearm for a firm shake, then invited him to the table. "Come and join us, my friend. When we last saw you, I worried we might find you asleep on the street later." Masry laughed, and Noah avoided looking him in the eye. Despite the success he'd had in avoiding Masry's recognition, Noah worried Masry would suddenly realize who he was.

The men gathered around the table looked as though they were enjoying a late-night tea, *shai,* and smoking on the *shisha* water pipe on the table, not potentially planning a revolt.

He pushed his *galabeyah* back and sat at a rickety chair. The men at the table eyed him. Noah recognized only one of them: a large, thick man who had been the one to hold the hot iron to his arm. Masry introduced Noah and told them about the "problem" Noah had taken care of a few nights earlier.

Noah shifted in his seat. He didn't enjoy being the center of attention under any circumstances, but this was particularly nerve-racking. No matter how many times he spent embedded with a group of militants or enemy soldiers, he preferred to keep a low profile, saying little that might arouse any sort of suspicion.

His silence seemed to benefit him. Within minutes, the men resumed their discussion.

"This plan … it's madness," one man said. He glared at the man smoking. "Anyone might find the device before the time is right."

"Our German friend said the device was safely delivered," the smoker answered.

Masry scowled at Noah with a quick, cutting look. Noah understood why. He hadn't done enough to prove himself yet, despite the other night. If Madry was smart, he wouldn't share information with a newcomer so liberally.

Masry lifted his tea. "I'm not worried about it being found. It will only be hidden one day. I will be in attendance. See to the detonation myself."

The fog of smoke in the room seemed to thicken, and Noah blinked, tensing, as the noise in the room became sharper to his ears.

*They've planted a bomb somewhere.* Adrenaline coiled through him.

He had to find out where and stop it.

Masry gave the others a stern look. "That's enough." He looked straight at Noah. "Karim. I assume you have some reason for joining us tonight?"

Noah tried to think clearly. He couldn't ask them to continue speaking of the bomb without appearing too curious. He'd have to wait for the topic to come up again later. Bide his time.

In the meantime, perhaps he could learn more about what he'd come here for. He had to hope they had heard about Jahi's death. "I was told one of our brothers, Jahi Gamal, was killed last night. Is it true?"

Five blank faces stared at him.

"Jahi?" Masry's thick brows furrowed, a flicker of anger in his face. "That lying dog. He's dead? How did you hear it?"

Noah's breath strained. Masry's response concerned him.

His mouth went dry as he struggled for an answer. He gave a confused look. "I've heard whispers on the streets."

Masry set both hands on the table, his face hardening as he rose to his feet. "Jahi is a traitor. He works for the English—and hasn't been seen in weeks. How do you know him? Did he send you here to spy on us?"

*Damn it all.*

Could Masry be telling the truth?

If Jahi hadn't been working for the Aleaqrab, it was possible the Aleaqrab wasn't involved with Victoria and Lord Helton's kidnapping at all—that Stephen had just wanted Noah to think they were.

It easily explained why Noah hadn't heard Victoria mentioned while among his uncle's men. He'd been on a fool's errand.

Noah could imagine the smirk in Stephen's eyes.

Enough was enough. He would go and interrogate Stephen himself. Before he went to the CID. This time, no one would be able to stop him.

Noah sagged back in his chair. The other men in the room shifted warily. He could be in danger if he didn't proceed with caution. "I heard it from Mohammed Hassan from El-Cid," Noah said. "I swear it. Jahi didn't send me."

He may as well be saying he heard it from a man named John Smith at Piccadilly Circus. Too unspecific to be caught in a lie.

And Masry knew it.

His voice was flat. "Is that so? You did good work the other night, Karim. It's the only reason you're still alive. But if you're a friend to Jahi Gamal, you're no friend to us. I suggest you don't show yourself here again."

# CHAPTER TWENTY-EIGHT

Standing in front of the door to her father's study, Ginger placed a trembling hand on the doorknob. The last time she'd been in this room her father had been alive. She couldn't remember the exact words they'd exchanged. But the betrayal and disappointment in her father's eyes—that had been branded to her soul.

She pulled the shawl tighter around her shoulders. She'd waited until everyone had gone to bed, not wanting to explain herself. Her head boiled with angry pressure, conflicted by her own rational thought and the emotions she'd done her best to control. She should go to Noah, apologize for her lack of compassion for Victoria, for her refusal to be civil.

Of course she didn't believe Osborne's claims about him.

Whatever had happened at Kut, Noah wasn't perfect. But he was honorable. He wouldn't betray the British the way Henry or her father had. No matter how disillusioned he might be.

She swallowed her fears and pushed open the heavy door.

Nighttime wasn't the best for this.

*Ghosts don't exist.*

Yet, she could feel her father here. The smell of his pipe tobacco. The creak of his shoes.

She closed the door, pressed her back against it, and shut her eyes. Her accelerated heart rate told her she *was* afraid. But not of ghosts, not real ones, anyway.

Just the ones she couldn't rid herself of: the memories of her father and Henry.

A few quick steps took her over to a lamp. She pulled off the sheet covering it and turned it on. The yellow glow of the bulb chased away some of the fearsome shadows.

Her mother clearly hadn't wanted to sort through her own ghosts—the study was still closed. No doubt coming here was painful in a way Ginger couldn't understand. Her mother had been forced to watch her father's demise but couldn't stop it.

That her mother had managed her knowledge of his affairs with such graceful silence and savvy only spoke to her intelligence. And the nature of her parents' relationship. Not all husbands troubled themselves with telling their wives about their business dealings. The more Ginger learned of her mother, the more she admired her.

Ginger moved toward the large mahogany desk, which was still shrouded. She uncovered it and bundled the sheet into the chair behind it. Her mother had told her the CID had taken some of her father's belongings. What if she couldn't find anything here?

She brushed her fingers along the grooves of the desk. How often had her father sat here, making notes in ledgers, his head buried in books? At home, his study in Penmore had been used for more personal matters. But in Egypt he'd done the lion's share of work here. She'd missed most of it, of course. Her work as a nurse had kept her in the hospitals or on the front.

She'd missed the last three years of her father's life. Henry's too.

A quick search revealed empty drawers, just as her mother had suggested. The CID had taken everything. A fountain pen rolled in the top drawer as it opened, smacking against the side. She sighed. Other than a few bits and bobs of junk, nothing else seemed to be inside the desk.

She sank into the chair, her back against the bundled sheet. What had she expected? To simply open the desk and find valuable information right there?

It would have been too easy.

Ginger closed her eyes once again, listening to the stillness of the room. While her father was alive, the butler would have taken care to wind the grandfather clock. She missed the familiar rhythm of its *tick-tock*, counting the seconds of life. Its life had been extinguished like her father's.

She stared at the desk. Her father loved his secrets. He wouldn't have hidden the paperwork for the concession, otherwise. Wouldn't have succeeded in his misdeeds as long as he had.

He wouldn't have left information about Paul Hanover anywhere that was easy to find, even if Paul used an alias.

Ginger leaned forward, then pulled the top drawer of the desk open once again. Back home in Penmore, her father had a secret compartment in his desk. She'd found it while exploring his desk as a child and received quite the scolding for it.

Running her fingertips along the sides of the drawer, she felt for anything unusual but found only the smooth grain of the wood.

She flattened her hands, ran them along the surface. Toward the back, she felt the slightest groove, barely big enough for two fingertips to fit in. She dipped her pointer and middle fingers into the groove and pushed them forward, toward the back of the drawer.

The bottom of the drawer slid open a crack, revealing a compartment underneath.

She was right.

A smile curved at her lips as she pushed it open further.

A flash of gold caught her eye. The compartment was lined with velvet, with thin wires embedded into the velvet to hold various objects in place. A pair of gold-hinged Egyptian cuff bracelets was tied down with the wire, the hinge open to accommodate the narrow space of the compartment. Ginger untied one of them, lifting it with wonder. Her lips parted. Hieroglyphs were inscribed on the inside of the bracelet, the outside encrusted with lapis lazuli.

If she'd ever needed proof her father was involved with smuggling, this was it.

A matching Egyptian broad collar necklace was carefully tied down beside the bracelets.

These objects were invaluable.

*And most likely stolen.*

A black leather book lay behind them. She placed the cuff bracelet on the desktop, then lifted the book. Flipping it open, she found her father's neat script. An address book.

Her heart thudded as she flipped through it.

*Paul Hanover.*

And an address listed for him in Giza.

She covered her mouth, a bubble of victorious joy rising within her.

The doorknob jingled.

Ginger held back a cry and slid the drawer shut, still holding the book. As the door opened, she noticed the bracelet still on the desktop. She palmed it as William opened the door.

"Ginger." His gaze swept over her. "I didn't expect to find you in here."

She tightened her shawl over her dressing gown. "I …"

Taking the bracelet and the address book, she came around from behind the desk. "I was thinking of my father. Wanted to spend some time in the space he used to inhabit."

William slipped inside, closing the door. "I can only imagine how difficult it is to have lost him." He came closer. "I was hoping to have some time to speak with you about it one day. But you seem to slip in and out of the house before I even see you."

"Oh—" She felt her face flush. "That's the difficulty of my schedule, I suppose. Nurses keep odd hours."

William shifted his weight onto his back foot, his head tilting as he considered her words. "That's good. I worried I might have chased you away."

"No, of course not." Her palm broke into a sweat against the objects there. She had no desire to explain them or herself to William, however likeable he was. He looked different tonight. His left arm wasn't in a sling and hung by his side instead. In his striped pajamas, he could have passed for one of the many patients she tended to in the hospital.

They stood in silence, then Ginger nodded. "I should go to bed." She hurried past him.

William reached out toward her. "Oh, Ginger—"

She sidestepped to avoid his hand and bumped into a chair near him. As her foot snagged on the fabric of a sheet draped over the chair, it entangled, and she tripped.

With catlike reflexes, William leapt forward, both arms outstretched. He caught her, keeping her from tumbling onto the floorboards.

Ginger froze, his face inches from hers.

Her eyes scanned his, then widened as she sprang away from him.

He'd caught her with both hands. Her jaw dropped and she stared at his left arm. He rubbed the back of his neck. "I—"

"You're not a cripple." Her words were a whisper.

William's face reddened and his head hung in shame. "No."

"But …" Disappointment crashed into her lungs and stole her words. "But why? Why would you lie?"

William sank into the chair she'd tripped on. "I wasn't—" He didn't meet her gaze. "I was never in the service. I'm a fraud."

On another day, she might have been able to handle his lies with more grace, but tonight her eyes stung with angry tears. "Why, William? Why would you lie to us?"

He paled, then swallowed. "I have a heart murmur. Since I was a boy. I tried to sign up for the service. It was my dream to serve my country. But they rejected me. Instead, I was handed white feathers for my cowardice. So many I could practically make wings."

Ginger thought of the many soldiers she'd known who lied about medical conditions or their age to serve. Either William was an honest man or he actually deserved those feathers for being a coward. And, right now, she didn't think of him as honest. "So you lied about your service? And the uniform?"

"The uniform belonged to a friend of mine who died. He was the pilot at the Battle of Aubers. Shot down. Killed." William flinched. "But when I heard I was to be the new Earl of Braddock, it occurred to me: how could a coward hold such a rank? So I pretended when I arrived at Penmore. And, from there, I didn't know how to stop the lie."

She didn't know how to respond. What if there was even more?

She crossed her arms. "What of the other things you've bragged about?"

His voice dropped by degrees. "Those were to impress you. Once I told your family about being a pilot, something seemed to change in the way they viewed me. Even you. The other lies came more easily afterward." He pulled at his collar. "I heard about the doctor you were engaged to." He cleared his throat. "I'm good at numbers. Nothing to interest a brave and intelligent woman like you."

"William." Ginger struggled to find sympathy for him. He'd lied repeatedly. So easily. "You didn't impress me when you bragged." Letting out a sigh, she went on, "That didn't seem to quite fit the parts of you that were impressive, like the kindness and generosity with which you've handled my family's situation."

William gave her an astonished, sheepish look. "Forgive me, Ginger. I'm so sorry. I never meant to lie to you. Well—I meant to, but what I mean is—I didn't intend for it to get this far."

"Then what exactly did you intend? To feign an injury for the rest of your life?" She couldn't make sense of how he'd believed he could continue such a lie.

"No. I simply thought one day my arm could show improvement." William sucked an audible breath through his teeth. "I didn't think it through. I was foolish and ashamed of my inability to contribute my service to my country. Going to Penmore felt like a fresh start." His mouth turned in a scornful smile. "I suppose now I'm even more foolish and ashamed."

Despite her best efforts, Ginger pitied him. How could she not? He wasn't the first man she'd met who'd been emasculated by his inability to serve in the war. But his lies hurt in a strange way. Her fingers tightened on the cool metal of the bracelet. She had hoped William was trustworthy. "I can't say I'm not disappointed, William."

He ducked his chin, his gaze downcast. "Will you forgive me, cousin?"

Ginger's heart throbbed. His apology seemed sincere. Mostly she felt annoyed at the ridiculous of it all. "I'll have to think about what you've told me. But no more lies, please. My family has faced their fair share of them these last few months."

She felt like a hypocrite saying it. "And I suggest you tell my mother and sister the truth. It would certainly be much easier to experience some adventures while here in Egypt if you can use both arms freely."

William extended a hand to her. Hesitantly, Ginger took it and William gave hers a warm squeeze. "I promise, Ginger. I won't lie. And I'll make this up to you and your family."

Ginger removed her hand from his, stiffly. She wanted to believe him. Wanted to hope that the good man she'd thought she'd recognized in him was real. But she didn't know what to believe anymore.

* * *

Ginger headed toward Jane Radford's office, tension creeping into her bunched shoulders. She'd been looking for the doctor all morning, but without success. She couldn't help feeling that Jane was avoiding her. Which made it particularly awkward given that Ginger had been wanting to ask to leave early for the day.

After she'd found Paul Hanover's address at Giza the previous night, she'd lain awake thinking about the possibilities. Even her dreams had been convoluted imaginings of a trip out to Giza.

Jane answered the door to her office when she knocked. She allowed Ginger in. "I'm sorry to assign you away from me this morning, I had some …" Jane trailed off and gave her a half-hearted, tense smile. "Apologies. Did you need something?"

Ginger furrowed her brows. Jane's instant apology spoke of guilt, but why would she be guilty? "Yes, actually. I thought of something that might be useful to Mr. Osborne, but it needs to be done as soon as possible. I wanted to request the rest of the morning off to see to it."

"Of course, whatever you need." Jane wrapped her hands over her elbows, her arms drawn in as though she hugged herself. "Ginger … I …" She looked down at the Oriental rug that lined her office, as though troubled. "I met Colonel Benson yesterday."

A knot formed in Ginger's throat. *Oh.* She should have expected this.

Jane's eyes lifted. "I realized right away that Captain Young had spoken his name. It's so obvious, really." She gave Ginger a cool look. "And you knew, didn't you? You knew who Captain Young meant?"

Ginger rolled her shoulders back and they creaked in response, so tense from bunching them. "I knew." She wanted to tell Jane the whole truth. But who knew if Jane could be trusted? "Colonel Benson and I had a brief romance in the spring."

Nodding, Jane went to her desk and gathered an open file. "I suppose I invited the possibility for mischief into the hospital when Peter Osborne approached me about allowing you to work for me." Shutting the file, she frowned. "But I'm increasingly unsettled about it all. I'm uncertain what your newfound profession asks, but I'm a physician first. My greatest interest is the welfare of my patients. The politics of war are secondary to me."

Being lectured by Jane Radford was something Ginger hadn't expected. And if it had been a year ago, she might have felt more chastened. But her last sentence made Ginger bristle. "It's easy to pretend we're neutral when we sit behind the lines, watching the carnage come in. But we aren't." Ginger twisted her mouth. "The politics of war find us anyway. They found me last spring in an enemy soldier who I knew would die if I handed him over. Then in a deserter who I allowed to die so I could save another man instead."

Ginger steeled her gaze. "I had doctors at the casualty

clearing station order me to allow men to die when I knew I could save them. I watched Irish and Indian soldiers receive unfair treatment. Nurses who offered lifesaving care were reprimanded or expelled from the service for simple things like walking late at night with a man or allowing a kiss." Ginger laughed sardonically. "And couldn't we all use the relief of romance right now?" She stepped toward Jane. "Look at yourself, unable to even use the rank that's rightfully yours. All of it is politics. Men in a room somewhere making decisions that affect the rest of us. We're all just pawns."

Jane blinked. Hugging the file she'd gathered, she said, "You sound as though you're at a crossroads. But I think you'll need to decide soon."

"Decide what?" Ginger asked. Irritation bubbled in her throat, choking her. She'd wanted so badly to be friends with Jane. That chance seemed to slip away now.

"What it is you're fighting for."

# CHAPTER TWENTY-NINE

*A* hawk screamed overhead, and Noah squinted into the crystalline sky. The sun had reached the highest point, but here the heat never lost its intensity during the day. The unforgiving surroundings, the barren Sahara Desert with its golden glow and smooth curving dunes, felt especially ominous today. Nothing moved near here. He tasted the sand on his lips.

Noah closed the door to the motorcar he'd borrowed from Alastair. He squinted, shielding his eyes as he looked toward the building where Lord Helton had brought him to visit Stephen before. In the daytime it appeared even more abandoned than it had at night.

No guards greeted him.

A flush of adrenaline tingled through his body as he came closer. He pulled out his revolver and held it in both hands.

"Hello?" His voice fell into the emptiness of the void around him.

The door to the place was open a crack.

Noah's heart thudded as he edged the door open. No one. Not a footstep. Not a shuffle.

Just the sound of his own breath.

No one had followed him here. He'd been keeping an eye out for a shadow since he'd left Cairo anyway.

He hesitated, then slipped into the building. Where guards had sat before, there was only dust.

He followed the hallway toward the cell where Stephen had been kept. He could practically visualize him there, chains around his hands and feet.

But the cell was empty. The only trace that anyone had been here recently was the refuse pit, which stank even worse than before.

Where was Fisher?

Lord Helton had said he'd dealt with him. Noah hadn't had time to ask for details.

A small square of paper lay in the center of the cell. Noah approached it with caution, his senses alert. He lifted the paper and unfolded it. One line, handwritten in a bold and elegant hand: *"They will never believe you."*

Noah crumpled the paper in his fist.

Whatever game Fisher was playing, he was winning.

*He's five steps ahead of me.*

He should have killed Fisher in Jerusalem when Jack suggested it.

Outside the cell, Noah found a staircase, then followed it to the flat roof. A buzzard flapped its wings as Noah stepped out and startled, jumping back.

He chided himself. The buzzard flapped again, then rasped a hiss, guarding a dead rat in its claw.

Finding his way back outside, he stared at the building.

He needed to think like Stephen.

But how?

Noah tore his hat from his head, then threw it onto the

passenger seat of the motorcar. Even though no one was near him, he felt hunted.

The serene breeze of the desert swept past him.

Nothing about what had happened was coincidence.

Fisher must have known that his uncle was the head of the Aleaqrab. How he'd learned of Noah's connection to El-Masry, he didn't know. But it couldn't be a coincidence that was the organization Stephen had sent Noah to investigate.

Neither was the timing of Ginger's involvement with the CID.

Whoever Peter Osborne was, he was no friend to Noah.

Osborne was proof that Noah wasn't the only one being toyed with. Ginger was being threatened too. And who knew who else…

He froze, his blood running cold.

What was it one of Masry's friends had said the previous night?

*"Our German friend said the device was safely delivered."*

*German friend.*

Stephen?

Just because Masry may not have kidnapped Helton and Victoria, it didn't mean that he wasn't involved with Stephen somehow.

And Masry was planning an attack.

Noah drove at a furious pace toward Cairo. Fortunately, Alastair had the money and means to buy a fast motorcar, which felt especially helpful as he passed the soldiers and tourists who bumped along the roads of Giza in their carriages and slower cars. They appeared carefree and bound for adventure.

How long it had been since Noah had thought of this land as an exciting place filled with the mysteries of the ancient world.

Victoria was right. Egypt was in his blood. But he'd spent the better part of a decade in this country as an Englishman. He looked like his Irish father, but that part of his life had also been lost when his parents died. His aunt, who had married an Englishman, had taken him out of Ireland and done her best to stamp the Irish out.

Now, both the worlds he'd come from were at odds with the British government, simmering nationalist movements growing to a boil point.

As he was at odds with himself.

He'd become quite good at this temporary job. But he was aware of how finite it would be.

*Enough.* He didn't have time to waste on sentimentality. Musing about a future that might not exist was also pointless.

When he reached Old Cairo, he'd been able to still his mind to a steady blank, one thing he appreciated about driving a car or riding a horse. He pulled into the alleyway behind Alastair's house and parked.

Alastair answered the door immediately, which spoke to his constant awareness of company. He raised a brow. "And?"

"And ..." Noah slipped inside the doorway. He stood in the dark foyer of Alastair's house, his eyes adjusting to the relative darkness.

The foyer, one that led to a selection of doors. Alastair loved to cloak everything he did in secrecy, including any sort of visual hint where one was going. Noah knew from visiting so many times where most of the doors led, but not all. "Fisher is gone. There's no trace of him."

Alastair paled. "Did someone help him escape?"

"I saw no signs of struggle. No blood. The guards were gone, the entire place emptied. And this." Noah handed him the note he'd found in Stephen's cell.

Alastair's eyes shifted as he scanned the note. His lips pursed. "Follow me. I have something to tell you."

When they reached the top of the staircase, Alastair allowed Noah past him once again before he shut the door. From here, the house appeared to be perfectly normal and elegantly decorated, with high ceilings in the hallway that led to a beautiful carved wood staircase. But if one was invited to Alastair's home, and few ever were, they'd find no front entrance.

Alastair saw him to the parlor, ordering tea from a servant along the way. As Noah settled into a chair, he unbuttoned the top button of his jacket. Alastair sat across from him, then offered Noah a cigarette.

Noah declined, a growing feeling of worry rising. Alastair seemed unsettled. "Has something else happened?"

"The man I had following Osborne for you—" Alastair removed a cigarette but didn't light it. "He followed Osborne to the hospital. Shortly thereafter, I intercepted a wire. Captain Young is dead, Noah."

Noah sank his head into one palm. Young had never been a friend of his, but he hadn't wanted him to die either. And Young could help exonerate him. Had he told Osborne? Noah's jaw clenched. "Osborne must be behind it. He wants to see me punished."

If Osborne had gone to the extreme of killing Young, then he was dangerous. And potentially the enemy.

Alastair tapped his cigarette against the arm of his chair. "That was my thought. I have found out little about him. On the surface he appears admirable. He was a POW after Kut for a year, released in June after a prisoner exchange. He even has a few medals."

Kut? That must be why Ginger had mentioned it. Noah thought back on the disastrous siege. He'd been a part of a group the government had sent to negotiate with the Turkish commander, General Pasha. They'd offered Pasha a bribe of a million pounds for the release of the troops, which had humiliatingly failed. Could Osborne know Noah had been involved? But even if he did, he couldn't hold Noah personally responsible for the failure of that mission. Or any of the other events in Kut.

The soft sound of footsteps intruded on his thoughts. He lifted his head, expecting to see the servant returning with tea. Instead, Victoria came into the room. "I thought it might be you. Any news on my father?"

Noah and Alastair both stood at her presence. She sat on the sofa nearest to Alastair. "No," Noah said, sitting once more. "In fact, it seems I'm further than before in my search. The Aleaqrab doesn't appear to have your father at all and I think they may not have even been involved in your kidnapping. And Stephen has vanished."

Victoria's expression was blank. "Then who do you think is involved?"

Alastair watched her closely, his gaze analytical. "You might be the best clue we have about that, dear girl. Have you been doing those memory exercises I taught you?"

Victoria's lips curled. "No, Alastair, and I'm not interested in reliving the experience just at the moment." She drew a sharp breath, her eyes meeting Noah's. "What do you have planned?"

"I don't know." Noah leaned back against the chair. "But I think it's high time we tell the CID what's been happening. I keep putting it off and it's reckless. We can't continue to fight Stephen alone. He's winning. We need help."

Victoria's face flushed. "But, Noah, you know what they said. My father's life could be at risk."

"As is mine," Noah snapped, irritated with her emotional response. Any guilt he might have felt at hurting her was mitigated by the fact that he was quickly running out of options. "I can't do this alone. What's more, the Aleaqrab is planning an attack and soon. One man last night mentioned a device that had been planted at a location. El-Masry responded it would only be there for a day. And I'm not sure where they mean or when."

Victoria exchanged a glance with Alastair. "The sultan's dinner?"

Alastair gave her a grave look. "That could be a good possibility."

Noah straightened, alert. "What dinner?"

Victoria smoothed her skirt. "Sultan Fuad is hosting a large gathering at Abdin Palace tonight. I had planned on inviting you to come as my guest, but—" She broke off abruptly. A shadow crossed her face. "The who's who of Anglo Cairo will be there."

They were right. The dinner would be a perfect place to plan an attack. "Are the upper-class Cairenes invited as well?" That would determine whether Masry would be there.

"I don't see why not," Victoria said with a shrug. She seemed to have regained some of her typical cool composure over the course of the day.

Noah leapt to his feet. "Then I need to go to the dinner. When does it start?"

Alastair crossed the room. He opened a secretary on a desk and retrieved an invitation. "I sent my regrets …" He thumbed the envelope open.

*Of course.* Alastair loathed events like that.

Alastair checked his pocket watch, then looked at Noah. "In two hours."

"That doesn't leave us much time," Noah said. Would Victoria be able to face society for something like this?

He didn't have to ask. Victoria held his gaze. "I can take you as my guest. Knowing Alastair, he can outfit me well enough with what he has here."

Alastair gave a smug smile. "Of course." He kept disguises and clothes for every occasion and size. And had a knack for knowing what would fit. It was part of the reason Noah had tasked him with obtaining a trousseau for Ginger.

"Are you certain?" Noah came closer to her. "I know you may not be ready—"

"I'll be fine, Noah." Victoria smiled tautly. "If no one even knows I was missing, I won't have to face their pitying looks. Besides which, if that Masry man you've mentioned is there and he plans to detonate a bomb, all those people could be at risk. My duty comes before my feelings."

*Duty before feelings.* If one motto described Victoria and her father well, that was it. She wasn't wrong though. "Alastair, I will need you to come out of your cave for this. Even if you've already given your regrets. Go to the CID. Or even those bumbling fools at the Cairo police. Gather a few people you can trust."

Alastair gave him a mock salute. "Aye, aye, Colonel."

"Just remember, no one is to do anything until I confirm Masry is present. This must be kept completely under wraps. If we're wrong about this being the time and place and someone is indiscreet, Masry may hear of it and change his mind about attacking now and bide his time. Then we won't have any lead at all about when he might strike."

"Couldn't we just arrest Masry? That might be the easiest course of action," Victoria said with a frown.

"You know how these organizations work, someone else would just take up his role. And then where would we be? Besides which, we have nothing to charge him with yet." If his uncle had more devious plans, arresting him on a charge that wouldn't be likely to result in jail time might not be wise either. They needed more intelligence on him.

The dinner at the palace tonight seemed like a promising lead. But he couldn't shake the nagging voice that told him he was missing something. Something that could doom him.

# CHAPTER THIRTY

Giza was alive with tourists, no matter the season. But now that winter had arrived, the area was particularly crowded. Eager faces of nurses leaned out of carts, veils flapping in the wind. And there was a sea of khaki uniforms everywhere too—soldiers didn't come to Cairo without checking off a visit to the famous pyramids.

Ginger remembered her first visit to the Great Pyramid. Even now it still took her breath away. The stones used to build the monuments were enormous. The first time she'd come, she'd stared at them in amazement, unable to comprehend how they'd been moved in ancient times.

As the driver of her hired carriage pulled to a stop, Ginger looked at the long line of motorcars, carriages, and other forms of transportation gathered near the pyramids.

The address for Paul Hanover was located just past the Khedive Abbas Bridge on the banks of the Nile. But when Ginger had called there, servants directed her to the Pyramid of Menkaure, the smallest of the three Queen's pyramids fronting the Great Pyramid.

Ginger paid the driver of the carriage and stepped out onto the open area of the desert, in front of the pyramids. Besides the tourists and dragoman guides, the area also boasted a few tents for archeologists on digs. One was set up near the Pyramid of Menkaure.

Ginger approached it hesitantly. She adjusted the hat she wore, squinting at the tent. As she did, a woman strode from the tent, wearing trousers and a simple cotton blouse. She was young, not much older than Ginger, and her long blonde hair was tied back with a ribbon.

"Excuse me." Ginger stepped toward her to get her attention. She shaded her eyes. "I'm looking for Paul Hanover."

The woman stopped and gave Ginger a puzzled look. Then she raised one eyebrow. "You and me both, lady," she said, her American accent strong. She continued past Ginger, heading toward an area of excavation near the base of the pyramid.

Ginger's jaw dropped. She couldn't remember the last time anyone had talked to her like that.

*But ...* it also meant the woman had heard of him. Ginger followed behind her. "Sorry, do you know Mr. Hanover?"

The woman looked over her shoulder at Ginger, studying her. Her mouth twisted. "Let me guess. He owes you money?"

"No." Ginger laughed. The woman's exasperated expression made it clear she wasn't overly enthusiastic about Mr. Hanover.

The woman cocked her head. "Got you pregnant?"

"I beg your pardon!" Who was this woman?

She shrugged unapologetically. "Well, that's why the last two women came around asking about him." She sighed and rolled her sleeves, exposing well-tanned, freckled skin. "I'll tell you the same thing I told them. I haven't seen him since May. And good riddance too. He can stay wherever the hell he went. Because if he shows up here again, I'll kill him."

With that, the woman lifted a Fedora that hung down her back and placed it on her head. She turned to go.

"Wait!" Ginger hardly could get the words out, still flabbergasted. The news that the woman didn't know where Paul Hanover was hardly registered compared to the way she'd delivered it. "Who are you?"

The woman turned and laughed. Then she held out her hand for a shake. "Sarah Hanover. I'm Paul's wife."

Ginger stared at her proffered hand, stunned. *His wife?*

Paul Hanover was quite a liar, wasn't he? Sarah didn't seem fazed by the idea that her husband was a philanderer though. Did she not care or was she simply beleaguered?

Sarah dropped her hand to her side, then smiled. "And you are?"

Her mind raced to catch up. "Lady Virginia Whitman. I—my father was acquainted with your husband."

Something in Sarah's demeanor shifted, her eyes more distrusting. "What was your father's name?"

"Edmund Whitman, Earl of Braddock."

A hint of recognition showed in Sarah's face. She straightened, then blinked. Looking back at the tent where Ginger had originally found her, Sarah hesitated. "Why don't we go back over to my tent? It's not a hell of a lot more private, but something is better than nothing."

Ginger followed her. Sarah was a strange woman, to be sure, but her behavior also had an unburdened freedom to it that Ginger found intriguing. She dressed like a man and talked like a man and, from her appearance, she appeared to be an archeologist working in the field like a man.

Inside the tent the air was cooler, and a rug on the sand provided a place to sit along with two folding chairs made of wood frames with leather slings. "Can I get you tea?" Sarah peeked out the opening of the tent. "I can have my man get some. I'm sorry, I'm not really set up to host. I don't entertain a lot of society ladies here." Sarah scratched an exposed area of skin at the base of her throat, leaving a red mark.

"No, thank you." Ginger inspected the area as Sarah sat in a chair. "And this is perfect, thank you." She took the chair opposite her. "You haven't seen your husband since May? And you haven't tried to learn where he is since then?"

"Don't know. Don't care." Sarah uncapped a canteen and swigged. "We came out here seven years ago for a life of adventure. No plans. I would have followed him to the great unknown." She gave a tight-lipped smile. "That didn't work out quite the way I expected."

Ginger should have expected the disappointment welling within her. For once, she'd felt like she might finally be moving in the right direction. She'd found the answer to the clue Osborne had given her, and once again she'd hit another obstacle. She struggled for words. "Then I suppose you don't know where your husband went in May?"

Sarah replaced the cap on her canteen. Her eyes were lively. "I didn't say that, did I? In fact, I know what you're looking for."

Could it be possible? Ginger sat straighter. "I'm sorry—I thought—"

"Lady Whitman—is that right? I never quite know how you Brits handle those titles." Laughing lightly, Sarah leaned forward.

"Please. Call me Ginger."

Sarah smiled, displaying straight white teeth. "I know what you probably think of me. Paul was a terrible husband. He would come back here, drunk and begging for forgiveness, but he never once lied to me. He'd tell me every damn thing he did, whether I wanted to know about it or not. And, believe me, after a while I hated him for it."

With a sigh, Sarah continued, "So, yes. I know about the oil company. And I know where he was heading when he left—to Malta."

*Malta?* Ginger's lips parted.

Her father had a house in Malta.

*It must be.*

"What do you mean 'the oil company'?"

"The Arab Anglo Oil Company, of course." Sarah gave her a doubtful expression. "I thought—" She broke off, then tilted her head. "You don't know?"

"I barely know about the concession," Ginger admitted, feeling foolish.

Sarah chewed on her lower lip as though she wondered what she should tell Ginger. "Paul met your father in 1911 in England. He'd gone there to speak to the British Museum about some archeological …"

She shook her head. "Never mind, it's not important. At any rate, your father learned Paul was a geologist. And he asked him about his opinion on which parts of Arabia showed the most promise for oil exploration. Together they negotiated a concession with Ibn Saud and formed the Arab Anglo Oil Company. Your father had a majority share as he invested most of the funds. Twenty thousand pounds, I believe. Paul was given a five percent share of the company, and Ibn Saud retained twenty percent of future royalties."

The news was shocking.

It also meant the government had no business trying to take her father's company and concession. Her father must have spent every penny he had on the concession.

Her heart fell.

*This is how her father lost his fortune.*

Why hadn't her father attempted to do anything with the concession and the oil company? "Then why is the company not on record? Did Mr. Hanover ever do oil exploration?"

Sarah shifted. "Well, that's the problem. Your father didn't want to formalize the company in his own name. He asked Paul to register it in America. He'd been following the way the British government had handled the Persians and Mr. D'Arcy's concession, and he was worried, especially once the war began. Ibn Saud also asked him for another twenty thousand pounds in the concession to begin the oil exploration, which your father needed to get from an investor."

*An investor like Stephen Fisher.* The pieces were coming together.

Ginger could no longer remain seated, her nerves were firing in a way that made her want to go for a brisk walk. "Mrs. Hanover, do you think you could come back with me to Cairo and make an official statement about what you've just told me?"

Sarah combed her fingers through her hair, then pushed it over one shoulder. "I can do that if it helps you. But I'm guessing it won't help unless you find Paul, will it?"

"No, you're right." Some of the hopeful feeling fizzled. "Without your husband, my family has nothing. My father entrusted your husband with the concession documents before my father's untimely death last May. Then your husband was never seen again."

"More than likely he left them on the island of Malta. It makes sense that he would have hidden them there." Sarah's tough exterior faded, her expression faltering. "Before he left, Paul told me he wanted a divorce. He had a woman in Cairo—the affair had been going on for some time. When the woman tried to end it, he, uh"—she swallowed hard—"he told me he realized she was the one he really loved." Sarah moistened her dry lips, then met Ginger's eyes. "Her name is Olivia Hendricks. He's probably with her. But if he is, he's using the name Freddy Mortimer."

Ginger's heart squeezed. That was why Sarah hadn't gone to

look for her husband. She hated Paul Hanover for it. And Lady Hendricks of all people? Sarah was a thousand times prettier and more pleasant.

"Mrs. Hanover—"

"Please, call me Sarah."

"—Lady Hendricks is the one who told me your husband's real name. I was looking for Freddy Mortimer in Cairo and found her. She hasn't seen him in months."

Sarah's face registered sadness as she blinked slowly. "Paul was worried about going to Malta. I'd never seen him like that." She released a slow breath. "Let me tell my team we're shutting down for the day. And then I can drive you back to Cairo."

A gust of wind rustled the sides of the tent and Ginger gave Sarah a hard stare. Osborne's behavior had been more than suspicious lately. Did she really trust Osborne anymore? "On second thought, why don't we keep the information about Malta to ourselves for now? We can tell the government officials in charge of this investigation you simply don't know what happened to your husband. If my father obtained that concession before the war, there's no reason to let the government think they deserve a part of it."

A smile tipped Sarah's lips. "I like the way you think."

\* \* \*

Osborne looked up from his notes as Sarah finished speaking. He tapped the end of his pencil against the book and frowned.

Ginger checked the time. She'd told her mother the evening before that she'd accompany them to the dinner at the palace this evening, but the afternoon was creeping along, and she hadn't been home since. Would they leave without her?

Beside her, Sarah shifted, then exchanged a look with

Ginger. She cleared her throat. "Is there anything else you need, Mr. Osborne?"

"Not now. You'll likely need to make a statement before a judge about all this." He set his pencil down and folded his hands together. "Unfortunately, Mrs. Hanover, I'm in the position of informing you that your husband perished."

*Paul Hanover was dead?*

A crushing feeling overcame Ginger. Her family would never benefit from the concession, then. She felt instant guilt at her own disappointment—her frustration stemmed only from Paul Hanover's inability to help her. Sarah had cared about the man.

*Why didn't Osborne tell me I was searching for a dead man?*

Sarah blanched and Ginger offered a comforting hand for Sarah to hold. Tense silence hung between them as Sarah sat frozen for several seconds. At last, she gave one tiny nod. "How did it happen?"

"We don't know. His body was found in the streets of Cairo in October, with only the scantest of identification. He had a card in his pocket and it bore the name Freddy Mortimer, along with that of Edmund Braddock and the Arab Anglo Oil Corporation. We searched for weeks to find more information on him, but to no avail." Osborne pulled another file from his desk. "This is the information we gathered from the coroner."

What were the chances of Mortimer carrying the precise information that they needed on his dead body? *Astronomical.* This didn't make sense.

Sarah looked pale as she opened the file. The report had been typed, and the date on the cover letter was clear enough: October 23, 1917.

That was two months after Lady Hendricks said the government officials had come asking about Freddy Mortimer. Ginger's expression didn't change, but her heart rate did.

*Something is wrong.*

She clasped the fingers of one hand tightly in the other. The government officials—Osborne, she assumed—had known about Freddy Mortimer at least in August. Assuming the report from the coroner was correct, he'd turned up dead in October.

Where had Paul Hanover been for those two months?

"Lady Virginia?" Osborne's voice cut into her thoughts.

She lifted her chin. "Yes, sir?"

His grey eyes glittered. "As I was saying, I suppose you've done what you could do. I must admit, I'm pleased with your progress. I think our business together is most likely at an end, though. We can continue to see if we can find any indication of what Mr. Hanover was up to." He stood and reached out his hand for the file from Sarah.

Relief filled her lungs. *Thank goodness.*

Sarah clearly hadn't finished with the file, but she closed it. A flash of confusion crossed her face as she handed it back. Osborne took it back with a polite smile. "Thank you for your time, Mrs. Hanover. I'll be certain to contact both of you ladies in the next few days."

Ginger stood. Since Osborne was summarily ending her work, she should ask about how to proceed. But there wasn't any need. She doubted Osborne had any intention of keeping his promises to her.

As she and Sarah left the office together, Sarah was quiet, clearly lost in thought. The street outside the Continental-Savoy buzzed with the life of a late afternoon, the day sweltering. "Can I give you a ride back to your house?" Sarah asked, going toward her motorcar.

"Yes, please, but—" Ginger glanced back toward the entrance to the Savoy. She climbed into the passenger seat and shut the door. "Before you go back to Giza, I'd like it if we talked to someone else. Would you mind terribly if we stopped by Shepheard's first?"

Shepheard's was only minutes away, but Noah didn't answer the door to his room. Frustrated, Ginger went to the front desk to leave a note for him.

"I'm sorry, my lady, but Colonel Benson checked out of his room this morning," the clerk said before turning away.

Ginger made her way out of Shepheard's, a growing feeling of frustration and worry mounting within her.

How was she supposed to reach Noah when she didn't know where to find him?

"You look deep in thought," Sarah commented as they sat in the car once again.

"Mr. Osborne worries me." Ginger directed Sarah forward as she pulled the motorcar onto the street. She was still impressed by the ease with which Sarah handled the car. Then again, women were driving ambulances in France these days too.

"Why's that?" Sarah asked above the roar of the engine.

"Because"—Ginger put her hand on her head to hold her hat down as a sudden gust of wind nearly blew it off—"Lady Hendricks said that the government came to question her about Freddy in August. The timing Osborne is mentioning with your husband's death seems strange."

"Death is too soft of a term. Paul was murdered." Sarah's voice was dry. "He didn't just 'turn up' dead. Someone left him to be found. And I sincerely doubt he carried a card with his pseudonym and your father's name on it. It's completely illogical. Does the man think we're idiots because we're women?"

Ginger had thought the same thing, but she was surprised Sarah was astute enough to voice it. The two women met each other's gaze, and despite everything, Ginger couldn't help but laugh. "Probably," she said, shaking her head. "Most men do, don't they?"

Sarah rolled her eyes. "If I had a nickel for every time people assumed Paul was the archeologist out of the two of us, I wouldn't need investors." She shook her head. "A card with your father's name ... ridiculous." She gave Ginger a thoughtful look. "But what does that mean, then? How did they know Paul was connected to the concession and your father?"

"There are only a handful of people who know of the concession, that we know of. What if one of those people started looking for the paperwork as soon as my father was killed?" Ginger mused aloud, unsure if Sarah even heard her. Stephen had to have told someone about the concession, well before Noah had learned of it. It was the only thing that made sense.

"What do you think we should do?" Sarah asked.

"I'm not sure." Ginger's annoyance at not being able to contact Noah was a reminder of how quickly she'd let herself be spoiled by his presence the last few days. She'd spent most of their relationship without the means to contact him. And Lord Helton couldn't help her now.

As Sarah pulled up to Ginger's home, Ginger hesitated to see her go. "I would ask you to come in, but I have a dinner at the palace to get ready for."

Sarah smirked. "You rich people say things like that as though it's a normal everyday event. I have a less interesting evening ahead of me—watching the sun set over the Nile. Somehow mine seems a bit more appealing."

Ginger couldn't agree more. The idea of going to hobnob with society was tedious. "Thank you, Sarah. I'm going to speak to someone I trust about the matter. Then I'll call upon you again."

As Sarah drove off, a plume of exhaust drifted from the

tailpipe. Ginger was left standing on the pavement, doused in the fuel's stench. She'd left this morning with such high hopes—that she'd finally be on her way to finding Paul Hanover and the concession paperwork, finally able to help her family.

But she'd just hit another obstacle.

What could Paul Hanover have done with the papers before he'd died?

Sarah's words seeped through her memory. *Paul was murdered.*

A grim feeling pressed on her. If Sarah was right, whoever had murdered Paul must not have been able to get the papers from him. Would that person have started his own search?

Ginger shuddered, thinking of how Osborne had reacted. Osborne—who seemed to hate Noah.

What if the person who had known about and murdered Paul Hanover was the same person who had tasked her to find the papers?

Noah had warned her to be cautious with Osborne.

Where was Noah?

# CHAPTER THIRTY-ONE

A red carpet had been rolled out to receive the guests at Abdin Palace. Ginger paused as she exited the carriage they'd come in. Built in the newer, European section of the city, the grand palace was a long stately building in front of Abdin Square. The enormous arched main doors were open as guests filtered inside.

Only two years earlier, Ginger and some fellow nurses had come here for the installation of the new sultan of Egypt. The pomp and circumstance had been a bright, festive occasion. Hard to believe the man had already died since then. He'd been kind to the nurses in Egypt, inviting them on several occasions to dinners and parties, both here and Alexandria.

William stepped out of the carriage to join Lucy, Ginger, and her mother. Ginger eyed his left arm, no longer in a sling. He must have told her family something but Ginger hadn't been there for it. In typical fashion for her family, they pretended nothing had happened.

"You look lovely tonight, Ginger." William sidled up to her.

He offered his arm. "Would you give me the honor of escorting you in?"

Ginger gave Lucy an uneasy glance. If Lucy truly had formed an attachment to William, Ginger didn't want her sister to feel bad.

Snubbing William's proffered arm would be an affront, though. Especially after the previous night's interaction. She gave him a taut smile. "It would be my pleasure."

She took William's arm and they made their way in, her family following. Whatever Lucy thought about William escorting Ginger, her facial expression didn't reveal. Then again, there was an excited gleam in Lucy's eyes as she took in the palace.

And with good reason. The cavernous marble staircase practically sparkled from the jewels of the women crowding it. Expansive, stately, and expensive, the five-hundred-room palace was the pinnacle of Khedivate Egypt. This sort of affair was exactly what Lucy had been dreaming of since they'd left England.

They reached the bottom of the staircase, and Ginger removed her arm from William's. Adjusting the tops of her long gloves, she tried to settle the flutter of nerves in her stomach. She shouldn't have come tonight. She needed to find Noah and tell him what she'd learned about Paul Hanover and her suspicions about Osborne.

Her time helping the CID felt like an utter sham. She'd been useful, but had it been because she was viewed as truly capable? Or had she been a mere pawn? And why did Osborne no longer want her involved?

Once they'd settled into the gathering, Ginger hung off to the side of the opulent stateroom with her family. The room glittered with majestic grandeur, both in décor and the dress of the guests, but relaxing into a jovial mood wasn't easy.

She accepted a glass of champagne from a servant listening to her mother and Lucy exchange greetings with some of their friends.

"You look about as ill at ease as I feel," William whispered to her. Then, a bit more loudly, he said, "It might be nice to have some fresh air before the dinner starts. It's warm in here. Would you like to come with me, Cousin Ginger?"

A familiar figure across the room caught her attention.

*Victoria?*

She was the last person Ginger had expected to see, given her recent ordeal. Ginger's fingers tightened on the stem of her glass. Whatever the woman had been through, she didn't seem to suffer as much as Noah had suggested the day before. In fact, she was smiling and laughing with some of her friends.

Lucy caught the direction of her stare. They'd tiptoed carefully around the topic of Victoria and the social losses that Lucy attributed to Ginger in the last few weeks. Ginger hadn't even really heard Lucy carry on about Angelica Fisher, as though Lucy was slowly growing more comfortable in society without an older, more experienced socialite to cling to.

"Ginger?" Her mother's voice broke into her thoughts. She gestured toward William expectantly. "I think William asked you something."

Ginger blinked, trying to remember what William had asked. *Oh, yes, go outside.* Her brows furrowed as she looked from her mother to William. They had only been in the stateroom for about ten minutes. What was the urgent need? "We've just arrived—"

"Ginger, go with William." Her mother gave her a stern look.

What was her mother playing at?

Lucy looked suddenly somber.

Ginger gave Lucy a sweet smile. "Lucy, would you like to come with us?"

Lucy lifted her gaze sharply. Her dark eyes seemed unusually bright. "I don't think that would be the best idea."

*Oh, no ...*

William cleared his throat. "Actually, Ginger, I really must speak to you. Forgive me if I wasn't clearer. It's regarding something that came up in our last discussion."

Ginger groaned inwardly. And he couldn't have done this at the house? Still, maybe something had come up in his confession to her family. She sipped her champagne. "In that case, to outside it is."

Ginger gave her mother a parting, questioning glance and made her way toward the back of the room with William. They proceeded out to a well-lit courtyard, then down a set of stairs onto the dusty path lit with flaming torches staked into the ground at intervals.

The grounds were lacking in gardens. Irritation tickled the back of her throat, and she'd been grinding her teeth while they walked. After downing a few more swallows of champagne, she discarded the empty glass to a passing servant.

They didn't appear to be the only guests who had come outside from the overly-crowded stateroom. Several ladies and gentlemen gathered in small groups, smoking or conversing together.

"I see you've regained full usage of your arm," Ginger said.

William bowed his head. "You can't know how much I regret lying to you, dear cousin. To all of you. I spoke with Lucy and your mother about it first thing this morning and made my apologies."

The moon was nearly full, illuminating the surrounding area. A few tall palms in the courtyard stood silhouetted against the inky sky awash with stars. She thought of her wedding to Noah, the warmth of the Egyptian night.

She shouldn't have come into the courtyard with William.

"Impersonating a serviceman is disgraceful, William. But pretending to be a cripple? After the work that I've done as a nurse, that's a little harder for me to forgive. You don't know what these men have suffered." Ginger bristled, realizing she was more frustrated with his deception than she'd had time to think about.

William stopped, clasping his hands behind his back. He ensured they were sufficiently alone, and asked, "Then you don't forgive me?"

She sighed with a bit too much exasperation. "It's not about forgiveness. I can forgive you easily enough. But if you lied about something like that, how do I know what else you'll lie about?"

William reached for her hands and took them in his own. "Allow me to make my apologies another way, then. Do me the honor of being my wife."

*He can't be serious.* "William!" She pulled her hands away, her own wedding ring seeming to weigh more noticeably than before.

"I want to assure you—I discussed it all thoroughly with your mother. I know your love for the medical world has your heart, but, I can promise you, I would take no issue with you continuing your studies if you wanted to in England. I must admit, I had the impression that you were in love with someone else, until your mother disabused me of the notion. And I can't tell you how much relief that brought me."

William reached for her, a hopeful smile hinting at his lips.

*My mother did what?*

Before she could answer, a servant carrying a tray of champagne glasses came waltzing by. He thrust the tray between them. *"Marhaba."*

The servant lifted his head, meeting her gaze. His dark-blue eyes fringed with long dark lashes scrutinized her. Her heart gave a jolt. *Noah!*

Why was he disguised like a servant? A scruffy beard hung low on his chest.

She swallowed hard, her tongue seeming to stick to the roof of her mouth.

A range of emotions clawed its way through her. Anger, irritation, relief ... and something else she couldn't quite name.

"Your presence is requested, my lady," Noah said before handing William the tray of champagne glasses. He put his hand on Ginger's elbow. "If you'll permit me."

William drew his head back, his lips parting. "My dear fellow—"

"Oh, William, dear, we will have to continue discussing this later. I'm certain it must be urgent. Please lead the way, sir," Ginger said, her cheeks flaming. As they hurried through the courtyard, she didn't look back at William. "You could have found a more appropriate way of interrupting," she hissed.

"Yes, I feel terrible. 'Dear' William looked like he was in the middle of something important." Noah didn't slow, making it nearly impossible for Ginger to keep up with him without tripping.

"Will you slow down? I'm not upset that you whisked me away, but what on earth are you doing here?" And where was he leading her? Not back to the party. He went back into the palace through one of the servants' entrances on the ground floor. A few servants exiting there gave Ginger an odd look, but no one dared to say anything.

Noah diverted her down the dimly lit corridor, a maze of closed doors. He opened one, then pulled her inside it.

As he closed the door, she attempted to catch her breath. They appeared to be in some sort of butler's pantry, but the only light revealing the space came from a small window on the far side of the room. "What are you doing?"

Noah's fingers tightened around her elbow. "I might ask you the same."

"I'm attending a party, for goodness' sake."

He lifted a wry brow. "I meant strolling in the moonlight with your cousin. But yes, I was surprised to find you here. You need to leave at once."

She bit her lower lip. "William had just proposed to me when you interrupted, actually." Would he be jealous? He hadn't seemed to be bothered by William's presence too much.

Noah smirked. "Then I see my timing was perfect." He raised his hand to her chin, tilting it up toward him with his fingertip. "I can't say that I blame him. You look ravishing tonight." He dipped a kiss to her lips, and she startled at the feel of his theatrical whiskers against her skin.

Then, relaxing into his kiss, she almost forgot what they were doing there. She'd never understood the allure of kissing until she'd fallen in love with Noah.

Tears misted Ginger's eyes, overwhelmed by the strength of her feelings toward him. "I'm sorry for leaving you the way I did yesterday." She'd known she would see him again, but the last few hours of not knowing *how* had frustrated her in a way it hadn't before. She flung her arms around his neck, her pulse speeding. "I'm so sorry." She buried her face against him.

Noah's lips were warm against the soft curve of her neck, his arms closing tightly around her waist. "It's already forgotten, *rohi*. I'm sorry too. And we'll speak more of it later. But you need to leave. Immediately. You can't be here tonight."

"Why?" She pulled back, surprised at the force of his words. "I need to speak to you. I found Freddy Mortimer ... or, at least, the man who used that pseudonym ... and then reported to Mr. Osborne."

Noah took her hand as though to delay them another moment. "You're quite good at this sort of thing. They knew what they were doing when they targeted you."

His words made her heart squeeze with worry. "Targeted me?"

"I think Osborne may very well be working for Stephen."

*Working for Stephen?* She shivered. He echoed her own conclusions about Osborne. "What do you mean?"

"Captain Young is dead. He died this afternoon."

His words registered with the sourness of spoilt milk.

*Dead? God Almighty.*

Ginger cleared the thickness at the back of her throat and gripped his forearm to steady herself. "No … it's not possible. He had serious injuries, to be sure, but nothing that would kill him."

"I'd asked my friend Alastair to put a man to follow him. The man saw Peter Osborne enter the hospital this afternoon. Shortly thereafter, Young died."

Ginger's fingers curled against the soft skin of his arm. "You think he murdered him? But why?"

"Maybe Young remembers what I did for him well enough. His word could condemn me, but also exonerate me. It's quite a different thing to charge a man with murder compared to assault."

Her eyes widened toward him. "You mean, he wants to arrest you for Young's murder?"

"I'm sure of it. I don't know when, but I'm certain he intends to strike soon. But"—he released a tense breath and set his hands on her shoulders—"there's more. I went this morning to question Stephen at the prison where Lord Helton had been holding him. It's entirely possible Lord Helton had him moved, but … Ginger, he wasn't there. No one was."

This time his words made her feel physically ill. "You mean

Stephen might be loose in Cairo?"

"I don't know." Noah held her close, his hands at her waist. "But whatever his plan is, I've been too slow to react to it. You said yourself that Peter Osborne knows I've been at nationalist meetings, and now he has me for the murder of a British officer in the CID, and God knows what else. As Jack would say, he's got the drop on us. And I can't risk hiding right now. An extreme nationalist group is planning an attack, and I need to help stop it."

*An attack?* She gave him a curious look. "What are they planning?"

"I believe they planted a bomb here and plan to detonate it tonight." Noah set his hands on her shoulders, giving her a serious look. "Which is why you need to leave. It's too dangerous for you to be here."

"A bomb?" she repeated, choking on the word. Her head spun.

Noah was right. Whatever game was being played, she felt like a marionette clumsily reacting, too slowly, to the direction of a master puppeteer. But what better place for the nationalists to plan an attack than Abdin Palace?

"I must get my family. Find some excuse for us to leave." Her chest felt constricted. "But what about all those people upstairs? Shouldn't someone warn them also?"

"We won't be certain that the bomb is here until we see the leader of the organization in attendance. He plans to detonate the device himself."

Ginger gripped his wrist. "Why would he be invited?"

"He's a Cairene from a prominent family." Noah's jaw tightened as he ground his teeth visibly. "Victoria is upstairs keeping a lookout for him. My friend Alastair is bringing help from the CID or police. Hopefully they'll arrive soon. Unfortunately, we didn't have time for a larger plan."

The news that more people were on their way was a relief. Whatever ill feelings Ginger harbored toward Victoria, she had to give the woman credit—Victoria was dedicated. Ginger lowered her voice by degrees, even though it was unlikely anyone was listening. "Noah, if there is a bomb at the palace and you don't catch this man, everyone here is at risk. What about telling the guards?"

"Because we don't know who is involved. For all we know the guards could be in on it. It's likely they had help to sneak the device in." Noah pulled a rucksack out from under what appeared to be a desk. He took his dress uniform from it and disrobed.

He went on, "I've been searching the building for the last hour. The servant's uniform helped me move around unnoticed. But I'm no closer to finding any signs of a device than I was when I started. Now that most of the guests should have arrived, I'm going upstairs to see if the man in question is here."

As Noah changed into his uniform, Ginger watched him with concern. What if the nationalist detonated a bomb before Noah could stop him? His life was at risk. The last part of the process was removing his theatrical beard, which appeared to be attached with some form of adhesive tape.

Within minutes, he was every bit the British officer. He folded the servant's uniform and placed it on the desk. "I'll escort you upstairs, and then we'll have to part."

"I need to know that you're safe after this." Ginger's fingers closed around his. "If my house is being watched, it's too dangerous for you to come to me, but can we meet somewhere? I called on you at Shepheard's earlier this evening, and they said you'd checked out."

Noah brushed a soft kiss to her lips. "Yes …" He paused, his eyes dark with thought. "My friend Alastair Taylor runs a safe house in Old Cairo." He pulled a small notepad out from his jacket and scribbled down the address with a pencil. "Go here after you've taken your family home. I'll meet you there tonight."

What would it mean if he didn't appear? "How will I know if I'm at the right house?"

"Khalib lives there. I'm certain he'll be happy to see you." He gave her a charming smile. "Shall we?"

She drew a sharp breath at his words but took his arm. *Khalib?* She hadn't seen the boy since the previous spring, when she'd very nearly sent him to his death by giving him a message for Noah. He'd lost a hand to Stephen's savagery as a result. What if the child blamed her for it?

They left the room and made their way back out the servants' exit. "I'm not sure what I'm supposed to tell my family." The thought of William made her cringe. She'd completely ignored his proposal.

"With Stephen up to his tricks, it may be time to consider telling them as much of the truth as you feel comfortable sharing." Noah's hand dipped to the small of her back as they reached the entrance to the crowded stateroom. He lowered his voice. "One day, we'll have to attend one of these events, and I'll actually be able to steal a dance with you."

Despite her anxiousness, she threw him a smile. "And you want to dance with me?"

"Always." Noah's pace slowed. "Though right now may not be the best time. Your sister is stalking in this direction with a murderous look on her face."

Ginger didn't know how he'd spotted Lucy so quickly. Lucy's face was red as she stopped a few feet from them. "I should have known you'd be with him," she muttered through clenched teeth.

"Good evening, Lady Laura," Noah said with a slight bow.

"It's Lucy." Lucy's eyes flashed.

Ginger resisted the urge to poke Noah for getting her name wrong. *The scoundrel.* He'd done it on purpose. "Is it?" His lips twitched with the faintest of laughter, then he stepped back, melting into the crowd.

Astounding how little time he'd spent with Lucy and yet he knew exactly how to agitate her. "What were you doing with him?" Lucy asked, gripping Ginger's arm. "Mama is furious with you, and you've completely humiliated William and ..." Her eyes misted.

*And you.* Ginger's heart ached for her. Lucy's hopes for William, her thoughts that perhaps he might take an interest in her—all dashed. Ginger touched Lucy's elbow. "Lucy, I'm sorry."

A bitter twist played at Lucy's lips. "Yes, well, why would he look at me when you were right there?" Lucy's voice quivered as though she wanted desperately to be blasé but couldn't manage the poise. "And there you were. Running around again with that man. Unable to stay away, no matter what William offers our family. Because you have the luxury ..." The words choked in her throat.

Turning, Lucy fled from the room.

Ginger rushed after her. She couldn't afford for Lucy to get lost in this throng. She was losing precious time. She needed to find her family and get them out of here. Ginger reached the staircase, cursing her elegant shoes, which weren't the easiest for chasing her sister. Lucy was several steps ahead of her.

Ginger set her hand on the rail, dashing down the stairs when Lucy reached the ground level. At the bottom of the staircase, Lucy gave a little cry. Then, she covered her mouth, before she flung her arms around the neck of the man standing near the bottom step.

*Stephen.*

The world around Ginger seemed to grind to a screeching, exaggerated halt. She gripped the rail, her knees buckling. Then

Stephen lifted his light-blue eyes to hers, his head tilting to the side as his arms enclosed Lucy.

The hair on the back of Ginger's neck stood on end.

He was dressed in white tie, his gaunt face clean-shaven.

As though he was a guest.

Ginger's heart slammed into her chest, then took off at a pulse that made her dizzy. Though it had long since healed, the scar above her heart burned at the memory of the last time she'd seen him in the desert.

She hesitated, wanting to run back and yell for Noah.

But she couldn't leave Lucy with him. Not even for a second.

Stephen held her gaze, unblinking, as she took the last steps down toward him, her legs feeling heavy. She needed a gun. A knife. *Anything.*

She needed to get him away from Lucy.

Ginger reached Lucy as she released Stephen from the tight embrace. Grabbing Lucy's arm, Ginger hauled her back toward her. "Ginny, look." Lucy wiped a few tears from her cheeks. "It's Stephen. He's back. At long last."

Not telling Lucy the truth about Stephen had been reckless. Ginger gave Stephen a contemptuous look, not caring who overheard her or what confusion she might cause Lucy. "Stay the hell away from my sister."

Lucy gasped. "Ginny! That's no way to greet an old friend."

A few passersby gave them a look, too polite to intervene but curious at the obvious display of Ginger's contempt for Stephen.

"*Darling.* I've missed that fire in your soul." Mockery seeped through Stephen's voice, contempt on his cracked lips. He couldn't hide his recent imprisonment entirely, no matter how well-dressed or clean he was now.

*But why was he free?*

His presence here showed an utter lack of concern at his status as a fugitive criminal.

Ginger positioned herself between Stephen and Lucy. "She might not know what you are, but, believe me, I will tell her. I see now I should have done it a long time ago. I know exactly what you are, you bastard. So stay away."

"Have you gone mad?" Lucy's hands clenched into tight fists.

Ginger stared her down over her shoulder with an unmistakable, hard look. "Go back upstairs and find Mother and William. Tell them we need to leave now." She prayed, for once, Lucy would cooperate. She didn't want to reveal Stephen's murder of their father right here but she would if it made Lucy listen to her.

Lucy's eyes searched hers, wide with confusion. "But it's Stephen—"

"And I'm telling you, he's not the man you think. Now go. I'm more than willing to make a scandalous, embarrassing scene that people will gossip about for weeks if you don't." Ginger didn't have to read her mind to understand her heartbreak. Whatever hopes Lucy had harbored for William had likely been destroyed today, either when William had talked to her family or just moments ago. And now, here Ginger was trying to cryptically inform her that the other man who had caught her childish fancy was a villain.

Anger burned in Lucy's eyes, unlike anything Ginger had seen before.

Whatever progress they'd made, the fractional advancement of their relationship into friendship teetered in the balance.

*She thinks I'm doing this on purpose.*

"You ruin everything." Lucy managed after a few beats, then turned on her heel and ran back up the stairs.

Ginger turned back to face Stephen. They were relatively alone, but thankfully there were palace guards nearby. Some help, if necessary. "I have no quarrel with your mother and sister, Ginny. I don't mean them any harm. In fact, I think it's wise for them to leave right now."

She gave him a hard stare. *He knows about the bomb.* "The people here tonight are innocent civilians, Stephen."

His eyes flickered, but he looked pleased. "Then you're aware of the imminent danger we're all in."

She lowered her voice. "These are people who you once considered friends. What good will this do? The nationalists have no more desire to be ruled by the Germans than they do by the British."

Stephen gave a shrug. "I have no interest in the plans of nationalists. Or Germany." Taking a meaningful step toward her, he ducked his chin. "For many months now, the only thing that's interested me is returning every favor a certain colonel bestowed upon me."

He reached for her but she stepped back, the heel of her shoe jutting against the bottom step. Her pulse increased. "Noah did nothing to you. You brought everything upon yourself."

Stephen's hand dropped to his side. "I see things differently. And really, what else matters but what people perceive? Truth is a tricky thing. All it takes is a few well-planted lies in the garden of the mind, and ideas sprout. Ideas that grow so tall that they shadow the sun. Until all anyone can remember is the dark. And everything else in that garden is forgotten."

Ginger recoiled from his words. *What is he planning?* As she searched his gaze, Stephen squinted toward the chandeliers throwing light into the staircase. "In fact, because I know you're so worried about these people, I'm going to give you a choice. Go now, to the cellar, and find that device you're worried about. Save them. It's in the wine cellar."

*He must be lying.* Why would he tell her? She caught her breath. "Or?"

"Or find your lover. Tell him I planned it all from the start. That he would be involved in the assault of a British officer. That he would supply a missing lorry of arms to a nationalist group. And tonight, his attempt to blow up Abdin Palace. And then he'll be the traitor."

What was he talking about? She only knew about Captain Young. She furrowed her brow. How did he possibly think he could make Noah culpable of so many crimes? "No one will ever believe you—"

"Won't they?" Stephen adjusted his bow tie, as though it were loose around his neck.

"No, they won't. Whatever Noah has done was for Lord Helton—"

"You mean Lord Reginald Helton, of course? As in the man who freed me from prison just days ago? Who signed papers swearing his knowledge of Noah Benson's intent to frame me for all his own crimes and illicit activities? Helton, a man desperate enough to do anything to free his daughter and angry enough at you for breaking your word to him to be swayed in his loyalties?"

The ground beneath Ginger's feet gave way again.

*It can't be true.*

Would Lord Helton betray Noah like that?

… and her?

But Victoria was free, wasn't she? Where was Lord Helton, exactly?

Stephen smiled cruelly. "Yes, dear girl. I've already won. There's nothing you can do. And now, you can go and try to tell Noah. But if you do, you'll bring these walls down around you. Or I go up there now while you try to save these people. Officials are on their way to arrest Noah, and I plan to make sure he doesn't get away."

The soft strains of violins from upstairs, the gaiety of the laughter and noise, blurred with the pounding of her heart. She willed Noah to come to the doorway to save her from this excruciating choice.

But what could she do if she went to the wine cellar? Stephen did nothing without an ulterior motive. If she went anywhere alone, she was vulnerable to his attack. "But ... I-I don't know how to dismantle a bomb. What am I supposed to do?"

"It's easy enough. Remove the detonation cords from the blasting caps." Stephen shrugged.

As though she knew what that meant.

Did he want her to choose to go upstairs?

Her mouth felt dry, her fingertips trembling. "I'll tell the guards about the bomb. I'll scream. Make your plan known to all who are here. You can't stop everyone."

Stephen's lips pursed. "Then you may seal the fate of all who are here." He leaned toward her. "How do you think I slipped a device in here while I was in prison? I have help, Ginny. There's someone else planning to detonate the device if I am unable or if a scene is made." He pulled out a pocket watch. "Steady now. If you don't choose, I'll have to choose for you. If you don't go to the cellar, then I will. If you go, then I'll go upstairs. Tick-tock."

Bile crept up her throat.

Her family was upstairs. Noah was upstairs.

Everything Stephen was telling her could be a lie.

*But if it isn't?*

If she did nothing to try to save them from the bomb, would they all perish?

She let out a shaky breath, then shouldered her way past Stephen, her head feeling dizzy with uncertainty. Who knew what she would find in the cellar, but what choice did she have?

"Save them, Ginny." Stephen's voice sounded behind her, a soft creepy whisper. "If you can."

## CHAPTER THIRTY-TWO

Inside the stateroom, Noah searched the crowd.

So many people were here tonight. No wonder Victoria and Alastair had so easily concluded that this would be a good moment to strike. *Where the hell is Alastair?* He hadn't turned up here yet.

Noah recognized fellow officers and members of Anglo Cairo, and he nodded stiffly at them as he passed. Much as his job required him to know how to navigate polite conversation with ease, he loathed it. He was not inclined to speak to strangers under most normal circumstances. Even casual acquaintances rarely roused him to conversation if he could avoid it.

At last, Noah stopped, spotting his uncle about thirty feet away.

His jaw clenched, rage snaking its way up his spine. All these people were in imminent danger. And Masry was here *smiling* and *laughing* with them. Before he planned to kill them.

While last night his uncle had looked like the fierce leader of an extremist nationalist group, tonight he looked every bit the part of the refined gentleman in white tie from Egypt's upper class.

Noah's pulse leapt in his throat, as he tried to do everything in his power to keep his fury from controlling him. He needed to find Victoria, tell her to give the signal to Alastair that Masry was here.

"Captain Stephen Fisher, Viscount Huxley."

The announcement of the newest person entering the room slammed into Noah's gut with ferocity. Noah turned. At the entrance stood his enemy, dressed to the nines.

And free.

Fisher held a champagne flute. He lifted it to Noah in a mock toast.

*How? How was he free?* And walking so openly in society.

It meant more than just an escape.

Noah didn't appear to be the only one who had noticed Stephen enter. Masry had left his spot and stalked toward Stephen, a scowl on his face.

As Masry reached Stephen, Stephen bowed his head. Then he whispered something, pointing toward Noah.

The distance between them was far enough that Noah couldn't overhear Stephen's voice. But he knew what he was saying.

Masry's head jerked up, his eyes combing the room.

Whatever hope Noah might have held that Masry wouldn't know him dressed like this faded away. The expression on his uncle's face was a mix of twisted fury and hatred.

The noise of the crowd fell away to a dull din.

Masry started toward the exit.

Where was Ginger? Had she left yet?

Noah pushed his way toward Stephen. As he did, he bumped into a woman holding a champagne glass, spilling it all over them both. "My word!" the woman said.

Excusing himself, Noah sped past her. He'd almost reached Stephen when he nearly slammed into a guard.

"Colonel Noah Benson? Come with us," he said in a heavily accented voice. Another guard joined him.

Masry had descended the stairwell. "What's this about?" Noah asked the guards as one of them gripped him by the elbow. Stephen was only a few feet away, an amused look in his eyes.

Noah was attracting stares from some of the guests.

"You're under arrest," one of them said.

Noah didn't have time to spare. If he allowed them to take him, even the attempt to explain himself might make Masry speed up his timeline. He tried to see where Masry had gone. "There's a bomb," he said to the guard, his eyes narrowing. "I need to go after that man."

"Just as I told you," Stephen said cryptically to a guard. "Take his sidearm. He won't hesitate to use it."

As one guard put his hand on the holster at Noah's waist, Noah moved with speed. He threw his elbow hard into the guard's stomach, then drew his pistol. The man doubled over, but Noah wrapped his arm around his chest, putting a pistol to his head.

The scuffle provoked gasps from the people nearest to him. The other guard held his hands up in surrender and Noah backed away, wrestling the man in his grip to move with him. "Now ... you will let me leave this room."

"Surrender, Benson. You've lost." Stephen's voice carried. Murmurs had spread through the room, the guests falling to silence. He had an audience now.

Other guards began their approach.

Noah backed toward the door. "This man is working with an extreme group of nationalists," Noah shouted to them. "They planted a bomb here tonight. Everyone should proceed to the exits immediately."

His shout unleashed chaos.

A few women cried out, the crowd panicking.

"Still attempting to blame me for your own actions?" Stephen stretched his shoulders, looking broader. Bolder. "The game is over, Benson. We all now know what you are." Something twinkled in his eyes.

As though he was enjoying this.

Noah had only seconds to go after Masry before the exits became too crowded with the panicked crowd. Hauling a hostage through the mess would be impossible. He pushed the guard into the other one, then dashed past them, toward the stairs.

"She's in the wine cellar, Benson. I sent her there myself."

Stephen's shout sounded behind him and Noah risked a look back at him.

He'd cupped his hands around his mouth, to ensure his voice would be heard over the noise.

*She?*

Stephen knew him well enough. He could only mean one person. *Ginger.*

Cold sweat broke out on Noah's neck as he pushed his way forward. By now, the well-dressed ladies and gentlemen of Cairo society had broken into a dash for the doors. They offered one advantage: the guards chasing him wouldn't dare fire into the crowd. Noah shoved his way past the attendees.

"I say. Benson?" one of his friends from the CID called out as he bumped into him.

*No time for apologies.*

Noah had lost all sight of Stephen, not that it mattered. He couldn't hope to catch Stephen under these circumstances.

When he broke free of the throng blocking the door to the

staircase, he skipped the stairs. Then he jumped onto the railing and slid down part of the way, to audible gasps. As his hands slipped on the cold marble, gripping for a handhold, he flung himself over the side.

His hands wrapped against the stone rails, grasping them as his feet searched for a toehold. Finding one, he pushed his weight down. The drop wasn't a long one—far easier than others he'd made. His palms ached with sweat as he let go, falling freely onto the floor below.

His feet hit the floor hard, his knees bending and absorbing the blow.

He was exposed, and the guards from the room were now on the railing, trying to get to him.

Running would leave him vulnerable to being shot in the back. But what choice did he have? He needed to get to the cellar.

Shots rang out, one ricocheting from the floor near him, sending a spray of broken tile onto his shoes.

A servant carrying an empty tray of champagne glasses stood frozen to the spot in the hallway. Noah dove past him as another shot rang out, then grabbed the silver tray, sending the stemware to the floor. The glasses shattered, and Noah held the tray out in front of the servant and himself.

A bullet deflected from it, burying itself in the ceiling above their heads and knocking the tray from Noah's hand.

Grabbing the servant by the front of his shirt, Noah hauled him to his feet, using the servant to shield himself. "Take me to the wine cellar," he ordered in Arabic.

The man trembled, his hands raised in surrender. They raced down the hallway together, Noah half-dragging the man before they headed through an open doorway. Noah kicked the door closed.

"Where's the cellar?" Noah demanded.

The man shielded his face in terror.

"No harm will come to you," Noah added, more gently.

In rapid Egyptian Arabic, the man gave him directions. Then Noah released him and broke into a sprint.

Servants, unaware of the chaos unfolding in the stateroom, carried trays of food and champagne. Noah ran past them. They gave him astonished looks, pushing back against the walls, holding on to their trays tightly to keep them upright.

The aromatic scent of food and smoke told him he was close to the kitchens. He paused, catching his breath, his throat dry.

The cellar wasn't far.

He pushed his legs back into action, despite the exhaustion weighing down his limbs. Why had Ginger gone this way? Then again, Stephen could have lied to him to lure him here. But he couldn't take that chance. As he reached the cellar door, he slowed and drew his gun, wrapping his hands around the handle.

Anything could be behind that door.

He pushed the door open into darkness.

He heard nothing. But that meant nothing either.

The shuffle of a footstep sounded, then the blade of a knife sliced past his face, the tip barely skimming his cheek as he pulled his head back and saw his attacker.

Masry grabbed a fistful of his shirt, hauling him into the dark room, illuminated only by the faintest flicker of an oil lamp on the floor. As the door closed, Noah was blinded by the darkness.

In the dark, the gun was no advantage. Masry had had more time for his eyes to adjust, more time to prepare mentally with a plan. He swung toward Noah again, and Noah jumped back.

Their dance continued, as Noah grappled without a plan. Masry's skill with a knife wasn't something he could take for granted. The blade caught his jacket several times, shredding it, leaving long, thin, excruciating scratches in his skin underneath.

As Masry swung again, Noah kicked at his wrist. His uncle released the knife, and it clattered across the floor.

Then Masry tackled him against a row of wine bottles, hands outstretched.

Noah's head collided with the bottles and his vision danced with spots. Masry's hands closed on Noah's throat, squeezing tightly.

A bottle smashed against his uncle's head and shattered into pieces. Red wine and blood poured down over them both.

Ginger stood there, the remains of the bottle in her hands.

*Oh, thank God.*

Masry fell back with shock and pain. Stumbling to the ground, he collapsed against a wire rack, out of breath.

Noah lifted his gun again, then found the light switch for the cellar. He turned it, and the room was bathed in orange. Towering over Masry, he leveled the gun at him. "Where's the bomb?" Noah demanded.

Masry spat at him, bleeding from a wound at the top of his head. His eyes narrowed with pure hatred. "You son of a whore. I should have known. I should have recognized you. Fatima—"

"Don't you dare speak her name." Noah jabbed the gun at him. "Where is the bomb?"

"I already found it," Ginger said, her face pale. She came toward Noah, a briefcase in her hands. "It's filled with dynamite. I barely had time to hide with it when I heard this man come in."

Noah's heart throbbed at her. His beautiful, noble wife. She'd come down here to stop the bomb. *Of course she did.* He couldn't think of anything more... her.

Unfortunately, it likely meant Stephen had intended it this way.

Masry wiped the blood from his head and attempted to struggle to his feet. Noah shoved him back down again. "You stay there until I tell you to get up."

He found Masry's knife and held it in his left hand. Holding the gun out to Ginger, he motioned for her to come closer. "Take this. And get out of here. Find any exit you can—preferably not the front entrance—and go home."

"But, Noah, you don't understand." Ginger's pupils were wide in the dark. "I saw Stephen. And he told me he'd planned all this. Planned on you attacking Young and delivering some shipment of arms. And this—this bomb. He's trying to have you implicated as a traitor. Come with me. We must leave now ... they're coming to arrest you."

Noah clenched his jaw. If Stephen had planned this, then he would have also planned no escape for Noah. And if Ginger was caught with him, she'd be in more danger. "Ginger, get out of here. Right now."

"But—"

"Now, for God's sake. I love you, now go. Take this damned gun and use it if you need to."

The soft fabric of her gloves brushed against his fingers as she took the gun and set the briefcase beside him. "But, Noah, there's something else—" Her eyes were wide with pain and fear.

"Leave. Now." His voice was strained, and Masry watched her intently. The last thing he wanted was his uncle knowing about her but it couldn't be helped.

Ginger slipped out of the cellar door, giving him one last look before she left.

Noah sucked in a painful breath.

*Please, God, let me see her again soon.*

He hauled Masry to his feet. The tip of the knife swung and stopped at his uncle's neck. "Now walk." Grabbing the briefcase of dynamite, he nodded toward the door. "And while you're at it, tell me what you know of Stephen Fisher."

Masry's lips pressed to a line as he moved forward. Blood trailed down from his head. "You have no power over me, no matter what you may think."

They hadn't made it far down the hallway when the pounding of footsteps headed their way.

Soldiers of the military police and a few palace guards came into view, guns drawn.

"Put down the knife!" they ordered as they saw Noah.

Noah slowly raised his hands. The knife remained in one hand, the briefcase in the other. "Colonel Noah Benson, with Cairo Intelligence. I've been investigating this man, Khaled El-Masry. And he intended to detonate a bomb that I've recovered here."

At his words, more orders were barked at him, from various voices.

"On your knees, Colonel!"

"Put the briefcase down!"

"Both of you, on the floor."

It took only a matter of seconds before Noah found himself face-down on the floor, his cheek pressed to the cold tile. Masry was beside him, panting. Soldiers had descended upon them. They took the knife and the briefcase.

Amidst the scuffle and the disordered garble of voices, a pair of boots paused beside Noah's face. Noah turned his head, looking up from the ground as Lord Helton loomed above him.

Noah's body went rigid.

"That's him. Benson." Lord Helton didn't look Noah in the eye. "Arrest him. For attempting to detonate an explosive here tonight."

Noah closed his eyes, the puzzle pieces clicking into place at long last.

"He's trying to have you implicated as a traitor."

How many people would testify that they'd seen Colonel Noah Benson take a palace guard hostage?

He'd been found with a briefcase of dynamite, condemning him.

After beating a British officer.

After stealing weapons.

After committing the crime of being born the son of an Egyptian woman and Irish man.

He heard running footsteps approaching down the hallway. His heart pounded as his brain scrambled to catch up. "I've only done what I was ordered to do by Lord Helton," Noah said through gritted teeth as a soldier bent over him, restraints in hand.

"Father!" Victoria's voice broke through the noise, echoing in the hallway.

*Victoria.*

Noah snapped his gaze up at Helton. "Was it for her? Did you decide to become a traitor to your country for your daughter's safety? Or before that? How far back in this plan do you go?"

Victoria pushed past the police, then gasped when she saw Noah on the ground.

"What are you doing? Release him!" Victoria dashed to Noah's side, dropping beside him.

"Victoria, get away from him!" Lord Helton sprang toward her.

Victoria was his only chance.

Noah caught the legs of the man about to restrain him between his own, sending him tumbling toward the ground. Snatching Victoria by the arm, Noah pulled her against him. They'd worked together how many years now? He knew her well.

Knew that she kept a gun strapped to her thigh whenever she was likely to be out on the streets after dark.

He found the gun and pulled it from its holster. Cocking it, he held it to her temple. Victoria froze.

"We're going to stand. And then we're going to leave, understood, Helton?" Noah got to his feet, dragging Victoria up with him. Several guns traced his movements. Any man with confidence enough in their shot might attempt something. Noah crouched lower, using as much of Victoria's body as possible to shield his own.

Helton's mouth twitched under his moustache, his face reddening. "You would never actually shoot her."

"Wouldn't I?" Noah dug the barrel of the gun deeper. *Even if he's right, you can't let him know that.* He hardened his face to a mask. "I don't love her. Don't give a damn what happens to her."

Victoria's eyes brimmed with tears, her breath was coming in short gulps.

"Stand down," Lord Helton managed at last. As the guns lowered, Noah heard the exhales that accompanied them, the loss of tension.

Three hostages in one brief span.

He was only racking up the potential charges against him.

"Tell your men to go," Noah ordered. "Take the bomb with you for God's sake."

Lord Helton gave a nod and the men left, dragging Masry away with them.

Victoria didn't struggle, didn't hardly move. And as much as Noah wanted to let her go, he couldn't. Helton wouldn't make the mistake twice of allowing her near him.

When the soldiers were gone, Noah straightened, the gun still pointed at Victoria. "Why?" he demanded of Lord Helton. "Why are you doing this? You're allowing all of Stephen's crimes to be placed on my shoulders."

Victoria gave her father a bewildered look. "Father, no! You can't—"

"I had a choice. My daughter's freedom, and every contact Fisher had in Cairo, or you. Frankly, it was a straightforward decision. You've deliberately disobeyed me, lost your head over that Whitman whore."

"My *wife*," Noah said through gritted teeth.

Victoria choked out a cry.

Lord Helton guffawed. "Yes, yes I know. You were a fool to think there would be no consequences."

"And that was it?" Noah shook his head. "And you really think Fisher will keep any part of his word to you?"

"I've rounded up nearly thirty men in the last two days. His intelligence has not only been accurate and reliable, but it has also saved countless British lives. You're expendable, Benson. You always were. And your usefulness has run its course." Helton stepped toward him. "Now release her."

"No." Noah's hands tightened around Victoria's waist. "You've only taught me just how valuable she is right now."

He backed up, down the hallway, taking Victoria with him. "I'm leaving here with her. And if I'm followed, I promise you the next time you look at her she will be inside a wooden box."

A tear splashed against the back of Noah's hand.

Victoria's.

Struggling to keep his composure, Noah dragged her along with him, backing up slowly so that he continued to face Lord Helton.

They reached an exit at the end of the hallway, and Noah pushed the door open. As they tumbled out into the moonlit night, Noah shut the door with his foot, his pulse pounding in his eardrums.

"Walk," he ordered Victoria, still holding her in front of him. Who knew what else awaited him?

Victoria was silent, tears slipping onto her cheeks, glistening in pale silver light. "You can't flee from him, Noah. You know you can't. My father knows your every friend. Every contact. Every alias. He'll find you."

"Then what's your suggestion? Turn myself over? I'll be hung before the sun rises."

Her breath was broken. "No—"

His grip tightened as they continued out of the grounds of the palace, toward a side street. "Did you know about this? Did you know he'd betrayed me?"

"No, I swear it. I didn't." Victoria's hands trembled as she wiped her tears with the back of her gloves.

As they reached the safety of a row of buildings, Noah pulled her into an alleyway. He pushed her away from him, sickened by her touch. The gun remained in his fist, and he held it close to her, menacing her.

"Did you know Stephen was behind it all?"

"No." Victoria swallowed hard, searching his gaze. "You must believe me, Noah. I didn't know. But the man who kidnapped me was Jahi. He seemed to work mostly alone, but he had some locals who reported to him in the house where he took me. And there was also an Englishman …" She shuddered.

*It must have been Osborne.*

Noah released her slowly, stepping back from her. She shivered, holding her arms over her chest. "Please hide. Go and don't come back. You know what he'll do to you if you do."

"Stephen? Or your father?" Noah raised a brow.

"Both." Victoria's voice broke, and she covered her mouth with one hand. "Noah—" She struggled for breath. "There's one more thing I overheard. The Englishman knew I heard it. He beat me for eavesdropping. I should have told you before but I was selfish and afraid for my father. I wanted you to find him first. I should have told you everything I knew. And I was wrong, Noah—I'm sorry. I'm so sorry. You'll hate me for it..."

White-hot fury shot through Noah's spine. He'd had his doubts about Osborne, disliked him even. But the thought of him beating Victoria made him ill.

But he didn't dare comfort her. They were beyond that part of their friendship now. And he had to leave. "What is it?" he asked, his voice raw.

"I know where Jack is."

## CHAPTER THIRTY-THREE

*E*very light in her home appeared on as Ginger stepped onto the pavement in front of it. She paid the calishe driver, then turned to face the house. Her fingertips were numb, still wrapped around the gun Noah had given her, her shoulders knotted with tension.

The entire ride over from the palace she'd wanted to go back for Noah. But she didn't dare. Not with Stephen on the prowl.

She had to get her family away from here. Away from him.

After letting herself through the gate, she hurried toward the door. She tucked the gun into the folds of her skirt, hesitant to put it away. Stephen could have very well beaten her here.

The door opened before she could reach it. Her mother stood there, her cheeks drained of color. "Oh, thank goodness. You're safe." She pulled Ginger into a fierce hug.

Ginger melted into the warmth of her mother's embrace, taking what comfort she could that her mother was here. The smell of her perfume was sweet and familiar, clinging to the curve of her neck. Ginger pressed a kiss to her cheek, then pulled back. "And Lucy and William? Are you all here?"

"Yes, yes, we're here." Her mother guided her into the house. "I was so worried, though. Lucy came and found us and told us to you wanted us to leave. Then, minutes later, I heard gunshots."

The butler closed the door, and William and Lucy hurried in from the parlor. Lucy's eyes were red-rimmed. And she didn't appear happy to see Ginger.

Ginger turned away, discreetly tucking the gun into her handbag.

"I can't stay long," Ginger said, fear knotting inside her. "None of us can. Stephen Fisher has been released from prison."

"Prison?" Lucy gasped.

"Who is Stephen Fisher?" William asked in a quiet voice.

Her mother lifted her head sharply and then dismissed the servants. After they'd left the foyer, she answered William, "A former friend of the family." She turned her attention to Ginger. "Yes, Lucy said he was there at the dance. But when we were outside, there were rumors of Colonel Benson being involved with what happened tonight."

"That's partially why I can't stay." Ginger tucked a loose strand of hair behind her ear, her fingers shaking. "I must help Noah. And you all must go back home to England. Please, William, take my family home."

Alarm filled William's face. "Ginger, what's happened?"

"You're going to Colonel Benson's side?" Her mother's expression grew frosty. "I thought I told you to stay away from that unscrupulous scoundrel."

"Mama." Ginger drew a calming breath. Telling her family about her marriage would do little to help, but it was necessary at this point. "I simply can't allow you to speak of my husband that way any longer."

Lucy's jaw dropped.

"Ginger ..." Her mother's warning was soft.

Ginger narrowed her gaze. "It's the truth. We married in secret, in the Coptic Church. We haven't been to the consulate yet, but as soon as we do, we'll make it official."

William shifted awkwardly, as if he shouldn't be here. Disappointment was written on his face.

Her mother's hand flew to her throat, and she dropped into a chaise lounge near the stairs. Lucy and William remained near the parlor. While Lucy's reaction was muted, she fidgeted with her gloves.

At last, her mother found her voice. Her eyes flashed with anger. "How dare you?"

"Mama, please, the discussion of whether or not we should have is long past us at this point. We're married," Ginger said in a flat voice.

"No, you're not. Not in the eyes of the law and certainly not in the eyes of God. A papist church?" Her mother shook her head. "Not my daughter. You clearly don't respect me or my opinion, but any delusion you might harbor as to my acceptance of such an illegitimate union is absurd. Noah Benson is directly responsible for the deaths of your father and brother."

"That isn't true." Ginger's jaw clenched. Her mother's continued insistence on blaming Noah for their deaths felt like a stranglehold. Ginger hadn't told her the precise details of their deaths and Lord Helton had manufactured paperwork that claimed they died in service to their country. But perhaps Ginger would have to remedy that. It was time for the truth.

"Lord Helton tasked Benson with investigating Edmund, didn't he?" Her mother's hands tightened to fists. "And Henry considered him a friend."

Lucy was looking frantically from Ginger to her mother, clearly desperate for more information.

"Father and Henry chose their own paths. They cooperated with the crimes of Stephen Fisher. What was Noah supposed to do? Tell the CID that he wouldn't do the job he'd been hired for?" Ginger approached her mother and squatted before her, reaching for her hands. The foyer felt stuffy and claustrophobic, despite its size. "And Stephen is now free in Cairo again. He's been planning something—"

"What about Stephen?" Lucy interrupted, stepping away from William.

*The love letters.* Yes, Lucy would have a hard time understanding the truth about him if she'd truly cared about him.

But Lucy wasn't a girl anymore. Ginger had wanted to protect her from the truth, but at what cost? She didn't believe that he'd been in love with Lucy, not after the obsession he'd had with Ginger for so long. He was cunning enough to have nurtured an infatuation in her younger sister for some other devious purpose.

She hated that Lucy had to find out like this.

"Stephen is a German spy, Lucy." Ginger met her dark, confused gaze. "He used Father's debts to him to manipulate and push him into horrific crimes. Crimes that led to his killing Father in the desert last May. Stephen shot Father while trying to kill me."

Her mother flinched. "What? How? What were you doing there?"

*Tell the entire truth.* Ginger didn't want to remember it herself. How would she ever get the words out? She rubbed the back of her arm with the opposite hand. "When you and Lucy got on that boat to Luxor with Angelica Fisher and I'd run off—I went to deliver something of importance to the government to Noah. But Stephen, Father, and Henry tried to stop us and when they caught up with us, Stephen tried to kill me. Father died saving me."

Lucy steadied herself once again on William's arm, as though she was about to faint. William offered her a comforting arm, drawing her close against him. Two red spots appeared on his pale face.

"Stephen killed Edmund?" Her mother trembled, as though unsure of how to respond.

"Yes, Mama."

The room was quiet and Ginger swallowed, her words tinged with bile.

"But accidentally." Her mother fixed an icy stare at Ginger. "It seems to me Colonel Benson still winds up at fault for many things. And your silence about Henry's death tells me it must have been Benson. I know it was him. I know it in my heart. Henry wasn't mixed up with the crimes Edmund had committed. Henry was a good man, and he never—"

"I killed Henry, Mama!" The words ripped from Ginger's throat in a way she hadn't expected.

Shocked silence filled the room.

Ginger felt unsteady. *She'd actually said it.*

She hated herself for doing this to her family. Telling them the truth about her marriage to Noah under these circumstances was bad enough. Adding to it the knowledge of what she'd done in the spring ... they'd never forgive her now.

The admission spread through the room like a poisoned mist.

Lucy left William's side and rushed to her mother. She stared at Ginger, horrified. She looked beautiful and grown-up in her evening gown, earrings sparkling from her earlobes. "Ginny, what are you saying?"

Her mother's gloved fingertips covering her lips. "Why?"

"I ..." Ginger's throat went dry, what little bravado she'd felt fading. *What did I do?*

Telling them the truth didn't assuage her guilt. She'd only brought the horror of the past back into their lives again. Lucy didn't even know the extent of her father's crimes. She swallowed hard, then managed, "Henry was going to kill Noah. He shot him, multiple times. I was forced to intervene and ... I had to shoot him."

"You *had* to?" Her mother repeated in disbelief. As though she couldn't comprehend what could have possibly induced her daughter to kill her son.

"Mother, you've received a farrago of information about all this. Henry had already thrown his lot in with Stephen and Father. He'd hidden his knowledge of the truth, tried to kill a spy for the British, kidnapped a nurse, and participated in her torture—"

"Ginger, for goodness' sake ..." Her mother's voice held another warning, as though she was saying too much. For her part, Lucy didn't appear to have blinked, transfixed by Ginger's words.

"Henry was far from blameless." Any certainty Ginger had felt that telling her family the truth was vanishing.

"So you destroyed our family?" Lucy managed, her voice in disbelief. "I can't believe it. Why are you saying such cruel and terrible things like this? Stephen told me about your obsession with him. How he'd been forced to put distance between you because of your erratic behavior. I never imagined that it could be true."

Stephen had said what?

Fury seeped through Ginger's skin and she caught the uncertain look in William's face, the shift onto his back leg. Lucy's words made her want to vomit.

At the same time, Lucy didn't understand. She couldn't accept the truth.

Ginger gathered herself together, her jaw clenched. She had to make Lucy believe the truth about Stephen. Her mother sniffled and Ginger refused to look at her. Mama could speak up, tell Lucy what she knew about Stephen. *Why doesn't she?*

"You're wrong, Lucy. You've been lied to. Whatever purpose Stephen had in trying to woo you—I promise you it was malicious. I was never obsessed with Stephen. But he was obsessed with me. He tried to rape me—"

Lucy and her mother gasped.

William paled, stepping further back.

"And he carved his initials into my chest to claim me." Before she could regret it, Ginger tugged back the neckline on her gown, shifting it just enough that her scar was visible.

Tears streaked Lucy's red face, her eyes shifting as she looked at the lines of the scar. Her mother stiffened.

"My actions were the only things that spared us from scandal," Ginger said. "Lord Helton agreed to hush the whole matter up on my behalf. Had the knowledge of Father and Henry's crimes been disseminated, the damage would have been irreparable."

"Thank you." Her mother's voice was brusque. Pain took on a new vigor in her eyes. "I have nothing more to say to you, Ginger. Except that I'd like for you to leave this house. Right now."

"Mama, please! You must listen to me. We could all be in danger—"

"I'm sorry for this humiliating display, William. I apologize." Her mother gave her a withering stare, then rushed from the space.

Lucy looked stricken. She moistened her lips, her mouth opening as she searched Ginger's gaze. The news had been worse for her than for her mother. "Ginny, how could you?" she finally managed. Then she turned and fled after her mother.

William set his hands behind his back. "It seems we all have our secrets."

His words landed like soft blows. *He's right. You've been a hypocrite.* Ginger gave him an apologetic look. "I'm terribly sorry, William. You're perfectly right in condemning me. Would you—my trunk is in my bedroom. Can you have it fetched while I ring for a carriage?"

She would have to send for the rest of her things later. There was no time for it now. If Noah had escaped the palace, maybe he would still meet her at his friend's safe house. She prayed he would be there.

Ginger tried to gather her thoughts, feeling sick. At least no one could ever threaten her again with exposing the truth about Henry's death. But her mother might never see her again either.

William gave her a sympathetic look but stayed rooted in place. "I obviously came into this situation with no understanding of the facts." He gave her a sad smile. "I don't know the details, but I know you're a good woman. You have a kind heart, and I can't think that confessing that to your family was easy. I admire it."

Ginger's throat constricted with tears. At least he had offered some sort of olive branch. She clasped her hands together. "Thank you. I've put you in a terrible position. But, please, take care of my family. Please take them home to England. It isn't safe for them here."

"You have my word."

Ginger started forward. She stopped, then went over and kissed his cheek gently. Considering how disgracefully she'd brushed off his proposal, he was being kind. "I'm grateful for you. You've been an unexpected blessing to us all."

She left him in the foyer, trying to keep her composure. After ringing for a carriage, she went out the door to wait for a servant to come out with her trunk. Ginger glanced back into the house.

"Please forgive me," she whispered. Then she shut the door.

## CHAPTER THIRTY-FOUR

Getting to Alastair's house turned out to be a harder process than Noah had expected. He'd been able to reach the roof of a building about a block away by climbing a tree. He didn't dare go by the street. Victoria knew Noah had been there before Abdin Palace. Given her questionable loyalties and Alastair's failure to appear tonight, there was a chance Alastair had betrayed him also.

But Noah foolishly sent Ginger there. Which meant he had no choice but to go, even if it could be a trap. Lord Helton and Stephen may already be there waiting for him.

He surveyed the remaining roofs between where he stood and Alastair's house. From here he could see the minarets of Sultan Hassan's famed mosque in historic Cairo, shining in the moonlight. Beyond that stood the famed Citadel of Saladin. The medieval fortress was a stark reminder of how very close the British military was to his location—the army used it as a military garrison. He couldn't count the number of times he'd visited the citadel on military business.

And now he was being called the enemy.

Noah's attention shifted back toward Alastair's house, now only one building away.

Would Alastair really have betrayed him? Acid burned his throat, his jaw clenching. After Henry Whitman had shot him, he'd become more wary of friendships. And now Victoria joined Henry's ranks. She'd kept the truth about Jack away from him to manipulate him into saving her father instead.

According to her, Jack was being held captive here in Cairo.

The revelation had only made him doubt Alastair more. How could Alastair, who prided himself on his information networks, get so much wrong about all of this?

Noah pressed forward, reaching the edge of the roof where he stood. He'd been forced to make a few jumps across buildings to reach his intended target. He wasn't comfortable with heights but his recent experiences jumping from buildings brought a new level of dislike. His palms felt slick as he crouched and jumped again. *One more jump.*

One more opportunity to fall.

The chance of being heard was great. It was one thing to crawl quietly from one rooftop to the next. Quite another to take a flying leap. He also had no doubt Alastair had one of his pupils on watch at the roof. He'd have to neutralize the youth.

He didn't dare stand to attempt seeing the street from here.

Was Ginger here? Crawling across buildings had slowed his progress. The chances of her beating him here were high.

For all the trouble he'd given Ginger, he was proud of her ingenuity. He didn't like her involvement; having her in a position to be hurt or killed made him worry more. Lord Helton wasn't wrong about that. Before her, he'd never let his emotions factor into the decisions he made while on an assignment.

God, he loved her.

She'd changed him, but not in the way Lord Helton seemed to think.

Ginger had given him a reason to survive this war. And that was more powerful than any desire for self-preservation. Helton had just been too short-sighted and arrogant to see it.

The building in front of him, made of dark sandstone, seemed to take on a reddish hue in the dark, like blood. His fingers twitched, curling into fists as a molten wave of fury lashed its way through each sinew of his tautly corded muscles. Helton and Victoria's betrayal gave an edge to his movements, a reckless desire to find a way to punish them both for it.

He might be able to forgive Victoria if he managed to save Jack. She'd feared they'd kill her father otherwise.

But Helton was another story altogether.

Noah rubbed his hands on his trousers and adjusted the holster around his waist. This jump seemed wider. He'd have to take a running leap, which could mean he might be seen from the street. He breathed out, trying to prepare himself for it.

He stood, cautiously. The darkness was a double-edged sword, however. In the dark, he normally couldn't see where he was jumping to as clearly. Tonight, the moonlight paved the way in greys and blues and reflected whites. Desert landscapes were fortunately bright on nights with full moons like this. The sandstone glistened. He could see more clearly, but he was also exposed to any eyes on the alert.

He backed up, then pumped his legs into action. He ran across the roof, then took a mighty leap at the edge.

For a split second, he was weightless, his body hurled forward by his momentum. The other roof felt distant. The moment hung … then his fingertips scraped against the ledge of the other roof, followed by his hips slamming against the stone. He caught himself, the impact painful, then hauled himself up onto the roof.

He hadn't been quiet enough.

As he gathered himself, the boy on the roof attacked, wrestling Noah to the ground.

He pinned Noah beneath him, his hands at his neck. Noah scissor-kicked his legs, then swept the youth's feet out from under him, knocking him over.

Noah grabbed the hilt of his knife. He slid it free from its sheath, the blade gleaming before he brought it to the boy's throat. The youth's eyes widened, as though waiting for death.

But he was barely a teenager. No older than fifteen.

Noah's chest heaved and a knife pricked his back. A fatal mistake.

*There were two of them.*

A sudden clatter sounded—the knife at his back falling to the rooftop. Noah swiveled his head and found the familiar face of Khalib.

Khalib stepped forward, the shock on his boyish face transforming to a toothy grin. He'd grown several inches since Noah had last seen him. Less of the baby fat remained on what had been a round face before, and now his cheeks and chin showed angles.

Khalib threw his arms around Noah's neck without warning. The youth who had attacked Noah sighed with relief as Noah pulled his own knife away. Noah's arms wrapped around Khalib's bony shoulder blades. "How are you, my friend? What are you doing up here?

"I watch at night." Khalib indicated the city. "Why do you come by the roof?"

Of course. Khalib was one of Alastair's boys now. Even if Noah had specified he wanted Khalib to take a more scholarly direction, Alastair was still likely to give him the skills necessary to survive the clandestine life.

"The alley was too dangerous." Noah released him, then gave him a frown. "How is your school?"

Wrinkling his nose, Khalib shook his head. "I come with you again, instead?"

"Not yet, Khalib." *Never.* He'd sat the boy down to the conversation months earlier, told him their adventures together were at an end. Khalib had wept, and the tears that had stained his cheeks had damn near done Noah in. But he'd never risk the boy again. The prosthetic hand was more than enough reminder of what Khalib had sacrificed for Noah's recklessness.

As Khalib helped the other youth to his feet, explaining who Noah was, Noah surveyed the roof. Khalib couldn't know he intended to confront Alastair without warning. It was better to have Khalib stay here than to get caught in the middle of something potentially dangerous.

"I'm going inside. I'll come and visit you out here before I leave." Noah set a hand on Khalib's shoulder. "I'll be sure to tell Alastair how you bested me." *And if it hadn't been Khalib, I could be dead now.* The thought chilled him.

Khalib gave a proud nod, and Noah found his way to the rooftop door. He slipped inside. He couldn't compete with the stealth that Alastair taught his protégés, but he'd slinked though enough spaces to hold his own.

It took him a minute to orient himself, then he found the door to Alastair's bedroom. He knocked, then opened it just as Alastair said, "Come in."

Moving quickly, Noah took a few long strides toward Alastair, gun in both hands. He looked down the sights at his friend already in his dressing gown. Alastair raised both hands in surrender. "You came by the roof, then? You'd be dead if you hadn't, you know."

Was that a threat? Or just a statement of fact? Noah narrowed his eyes. "Don't try the mind games with me."

"Oh, come now, Benson. Put the gun down. I put Khalib up there on purpose. You're smart enough to not come in through the alley. Helton's sure to be watching the house. You shouldn't have risked coming here. But I thought you might. Especially when your lovely bride arrived just a half hour ago." Alastair stepped back, lowering his hands.

Ginger was here. *Thank God.*

But it meant leaving would be more difficult. At last, he lowered the gun and put it in its holster. "Why didn't you come to the palace as we discussed?"

"Lord Helton was at CID headquarters. He told me he was heading to the palace with men to handle the matter and ordered me home. I couldn't have known what they were about to do to you. I'm sorry I wasn't there. I've been getting bits and pieces over the wires though. The situation looks grim."

*No wonder.* It must have all been part of Helton's plan. "What's the official story?"

"You're wanted for immediate capture. Apparently, you're the criminal mastermind of the last decade. Maslukha and Aleaqrab leader, all in one. I'm certain the papers will carry the tales tomorrow of how you murdered the Earl of Braddock and his son, framed the innocent Stephen Fisher, and Fisher rotted in prison without a trial for your crimes. Let's not forget your more recent exploits of killing a Captain Harold Young, stealing a lorry of arms from the army, and attempting to blow up Abdin Palace. You've been quite busy."

None of it surprised Noah, but to hear Alastair lay it out like that nauseated him. Everything he'd worked for his whole life would be taken away. He'd been foolish. But how could he have known the way Stephen planned to twist and manipulate everything?

Capturing Lord Helton had most likely been all Stephen needed to finalize his own release. While Noah couldn't imagine how it had come about, he could picture the satisfied smile on Stephen's face, knowing he had pinned his crimes on

Noah's back. "And Masry? They found me with him at the palace."

"I suppose you can feel some relief there. He's been arrested. But I sincerely doubt he'll own his role in the Aleaqrab. The messages I intercepted labeled you as their leader. Still, Masry will most likely be imprisoned, his organization dismantled. I very much doubt it was what your uncle intended when cooperating with Stephen, but apparently Stephen's in the business of hanging his friends on a line. Either that or Lord Helton demanded it."

Whatever satisfaction Noah may have felt at his uncle's arrest and the blow to the Aleaqrab, it was minuscule compared to the shadow of rage curling through him. "Lord Helton can save me from this debacle, but he's been bribed by Fisher. I walked right into the trap Fisher set for me."

"I assumed as much about Lord Helton once I started getting messages. I can't understand what Helton is thinking. He knows the devil he's sold his soul to. Fisher must be in possession of a means to manipulate him and keep him from going back on his word." Alastair's face was sober and sympathetic.

*That's true.* Stephen would have wanted a way to make Helton his puppet. Finding out what that was would be crucial in the future.

Alastair set a hand on Noah's shoulder. "While you're free, you can keep working to out the truth. Just don't let them capture you. They'll hang you before any of us can try to save you."

What truth? He'd seen the deceptive practices his government had employed to get what they wanted.

Noah sank wearily against a wall. "The truth?" His laugh was bitter. "You and I know well how the truth matters. I don't think I can escape this one, Alastair. How can I ever be exonerated or free? I committed half of the crimes they're accusing me of, in shades of grey."

"Do you want my real advice?"

"Do I?" Noah fought the surge of panic that crested in him. He could well imagine Alastair's "real" advice.

"Disappear, Noah. Start a new life. You can ask your wife to go with you, but if she does, she'll have to continue a life running from the law. Not to mention that it's harder to run with another person at your side. I'm going to do everything I can for you, but your chances of living to a ripe old age are better if you simply flee alone."

Noah straightened. The idea had merit and was tempting, but how could he ever ask something like that of Ginger? And he would never abandon her. "I never expected to live to a ripe old age anyway." Noah rubbed his right shoulder with the opposite hand. "I need your help." The familiar stiffness from his wounds earlier in the year made the muscles throb, but he couldn't worry about that now.

"I'm happy to outfit you." Alastair cocked his head to the side and led him out of the room, down the hall. "You're going to need a few disguises."

"I'm going to need two." Noah's voice echoed in the hallway.

Alastair looked over his shoulder with a sharp-eyed squint. "For *la belle femme?*"

"I'm not leaving her."

"I didn't think you would."

Alastair led Noah to a darkened room. "Where are you going?"

Noah blinked as Alastair turned on an electric lamp. The room was filled with shelves, a few wardrobes, and baskets. "I'm not sure yet. I have news of Jack. He's here in Egypt, likely in the outskirts of Cairo."

Alastair appeared stunned, the corners of his eyes squinting. "Who did you learn this from?"

"Victoria. She says he's deathly ill too." Noah rubbed his jaw, the stubble on his face already rough against his palm. Growing facial hair quickly had its benefits but meant having to shave every day when he didn't want it. "The Aleaqrab never had Victoria. Osborne did. And, apparently, Jack was being held where they took her. They even had her confer with Jack about some clue regarding the location of the concession paperwork. My assumption is that Freddy Mortimer was found with it." Noah didn't have time now to explain what Ginger had found out about Mortimer's identity.

Alastair winced. "And Victoria said nothing before now? Why?"

"Because she's Victoria. She's selfish. And she knew if she told me, I'd focus on finding Jack instead of her father."

Alastair shook his head slowly. "It seems to me she may have had other motivations for not telling you. Logically, if they held her where they held Jack, they would have taken Lord Helton there. Unless she knew her father wasn't really being captured."

Tense silence hung between them.

Victoria's sobs replayed in Noah's mind as she told him about Jack. Had that been a performance too? Everything about her seemed like a lie to him now. Irritation pricked his throat. "It's certainly possible."

"Why would they have captured Jack? What was the need?" Alastair searched his eyes.

"Because Jack is the finest cryptologist on this side of the Atlantic Ocean. No doubt they needed someone as familiar with …"

Noah trailed off. Ginger had mentioned that Paul Hanover's wife was an archeologist. And if Paul had left a coded message, it was possible he'd intended it for someone.

*Someone like Paul's wife.*

What if Osborne hadn't needed Ginger to find the concession paperwork for him?

What if he'd needed her to find Sarah Hanover?

Noah's gut instincts gnawed at him as Alastair watched him in silence. "Yes?" Alastair asked at last.

"I need to borrow your motorcar."

Alastair frowned but gave a curt nod. "I thought you might. I had one of the boys park it near Rumayla Square. You do realize I'll have to report it stolen? I'm certain they won't believe me, but that's the minimum I can do to protect myself."

Noah scowled. He needed to go after Sarah Hanover right away. And take Ginger with him. He wasn't about to leave her here in Old Cairo. Who knew how long it would be before Stephen or Lord Helton tried to use her as bait? "You need safe houses that the CID doesn't know of. I may need to leave Ginger with you in the future if I can't clear my name."

"Unfortunately, it's not as easy as all that. They watch me terribly closely, you know." Alastair moved to a wardrobe and opened it. He pulled out a dirty Bedouin *thawb* that was neatly folded with string and set it on a chair. "What sort of outfit does *la belle femme* need?"

"Anything that hides that red hair of hers." Noah crossed his arms.

"Has she considered tinting it? It might be a way to solve the problem if she must hide for a while. Though, to be honest, her nursing costume is a damned good disguise."

Each time Noah drew Ginger further into the treachery that surrounded him, he felt he'd stolen something from her he could never restore. "I shouldn't take her, should I?"

"You love her. You don't trust her with anyone else. Don't look so put out about all this, Benson. You'll have your beautiful, resourceful wife to yourself for a bit. She's willing and loves you. Anyone choosing to stake her future in you is going to need resourcefulness, especially while this war rages." Alastair placed a few bundles of clothing in a sack, then handed it to Noah. "How are you going to find Jack?"

This time Noah couldn't help the angry expression he was certain came to his eyes. "Victoria lied. She doesn't know the precise location, but when they took her from the tomb where they were holding her, she saw the Step Pyramid of Djoser from the lorry."

"Saqqara?" Alastair dropped his chin. "But the whole region is littered with subterranean tombs. You may be searching awhile."

"From what she described, I have a feeling I know where they were keeping her. But I'll have to hurry before they move him."

"That's wise." Alastair cleared his throat, shifting uncomfortably. "Noah, we may have to cut off communications for some time. I value our friendship. But I have quite a few children in my care to think of should something happen to me."

"Of course." Guilt ate at his gut. He'd asked more than enough of Alastair. "I don't think I'll be back here for some time. But I won't forget what you've done for me." Noah slung the sack over his shoulder, then headed out of the room. "Now if you don't mind taking me to my wife."

"I had the servants draw a bath for her. To help settle her nerves." Alastair saw him to the next level of the house. He stopped at a door and then put a hand on Noah's shoulder. "Be careful, old friend. I'll do whatever I can to help."

## CHAPTER THIRTY-FIVE

The water in the tub had long since gone cold, but Ginger remained in it, shivering. Her hand clutched the soap, which had developed a layer of slime on the exposed side. The soap curled against her hand, stuck to it.

Ginger's hair floated in the water behind her as she shifted, numb and cold. She lowered herself slowly, gasping as the water covered her torso, then flooded her neck, her cheeks, her forehead … the tip of her nose.

The water stung her nostrils and she listened to the hollow drips, the strangeness of sound under the surface. She opened her eyes. The hazy light of the moon cascaded through the window, giving the water an achromatic, vespertine glow.

A shadow blocked the light and she jolted. A set of firm hands clasped her elbows and pulled her up. As she broke through the surface amid the slosh and drips, Noah knelt beside her, his face a mask of concern.

*Oh, thank God. He's here.*

She choked back a cry, the emotions she'd been trying to restrain threatening to spew out in a flood of tears.

He released a quick breath. "I thought for a moment you'd drowned."

Her heart pounded. "You scared me." Her skin vibrated against the hammering of her heart, her exposed scar quivering.

"I'm sorry." Noah searched her gaze, then, still fully dressed, he leaned forward and slipped his arm under her legs. She sank into his arms, relieved to be held by him. He lifted her from the tub and set her down gently, then wrapped a towel around her. "Have you given yourself hypothermia?"

Her body quivered, goosebumps breaking across her skin. What had she been doing? She still gripped the soap.

Noah peeled it away, then used a washcloth to remove the residue on her hand. Her fingers had pruned in the water.

Lifting her once again, he carried her back into the bedroom.

The night was chilly, and servants had lit a fire in the fireplace. Ginger blinked at him as he set her down on the bed. Tears filled her eyes. "I was so afraid you might be dead."

"I managed to escape, but they're chasing me. We can't stay here long. They don't know I'm here, but you were likely seen coming here." Stepping back, he removed his soaked shirt and jacket, then hung it off the back of a chair by the fireplace. "Are you all right?"

"I told my family the truth about our marriage and Henry's death." She tucked a wet strand of hair behind her ear, then covered her face with one hand. Ever since she'd arrived here, Stephen's image had floated in her mind like a demon come to haunt her. "And my mother ordered me to leave."

Noah sank onto the bed beside her. He seemed on the verge of saying something, then thought better of it.

She raked her fingers through her hair, bringing her knees up to her chest. Her throat was so tight she could barely get the words out. "Mama hates me. If I were her, I would hate me too."

When had she become so callous? On the train, when she'd had to choose between the Australian and the deserter, the decision had been so cold, so effortless. Allowing a man to die shouldn't be so easy, should it? But she'd let the war numb her to death.

Numb her to the fact that she'd killed her own brother.

Noah gathered her in his arms, the warmth of his body radiating onto her cold skin. In his strong arms, the pain that stabbed her heart felt contained. She didn't care that they needed to flee. She needed him and his strength for a few minutes, even if it was selfish. She was thoroughly spent.

"Don't let me go," she murmured, setting her cheek against his chest. The ache inside her threatened to spill forward, into the churn of her gut and the depths of her blackened soul. Noah's arms tightened reflexively.

His voice was a low rumble. "The first time I killed a man, I told myself I felt nothing. That it could be as simple as stepping on an insect on the ground—a chore that had to be done without a backward glance. But I've never forgotten the face of the first man I killed. The instinct to kill or be killed isn't enough to make it easier. You know what I think of now?"

A strange pressure gripped her. "No." She couldn't possibly think of anything that would make her feel better. Less guilty.

"I think of the people who would die if I don't take that life." Noah's fingers intertwined with hers, and he lifted her hand, brushing a soft kiss to her fingertips. "I know who you saved when you killed Henry. And I will always work to be a better man for it and worthy of the choice you made." He kissed her open palm.

His words did help, more than she'd expected them to. She wiped away a few stray tears, then slid her hands around his neck. "How many times am I going to find you like I did tonight? Running for your life, bloodied? You can't keep insisting that I stay to the side. I'd rather we face these dangers together."

"There's been a marked improvement in my ability to survive accordingly." He grimaced, feeling a cut on his temple.

Ginger was increasingly more aware of how incongruous her state of dress was to the conversation. Her wet towel hung limply around her waist, but, other than that, she wore nothing. And while she should have felt self-conscious, she was strangely comfortable even like this.

Comfortable and now very aware of how much she wanted him.

She moistened her lips, not wanting to end their conversation just yet. She pulled up the towel, covering her breasts.

A warm smile hinted in Noah's gaze. "It's good you did that. I was finding myself increasingly more distracted." He lowered his lips to the soft spot of her neck, just below her earlobe and jaw.

She murmured a lusty response, tilting her cheek away to surrender to the feeling of his lips. "You're already worthy of the choice I made, Noah." Her lips curved upward, her body tingling at his touch. "I never should have let you doubt it. I wanted to return to you immediately and apologize. But the same pride you accused me of stopped me. I kept imagining Victoria in your arms and tormenting myself."

"What must I do to convince you that Victoria means nothing to me?" Drawing his legs onto the bed, Noah tilted her back onto the mattress, sliding one hand over her naked hip.

Something about the movement was unbelievably alluring, revealing the powerful muscles of his torso and arms. His eyes were dark and passionate as he lowered his mouth to hers, catching her mouth in an open kiss. Their tongues collided, and she closed her eyes. She loved his taste, the fullness of his mouth against hers. She melted back against the pillow, the kiss growing in fervor as he cupped her breasts. One of his hands glided to her flat belly, then lower still. His fingertips grazed her hips.

She barely noticed as he unbuttoned his trousers and pushed them from his own hips. He guided himself inside her effortlessly, her desire for him so intense that she gasped, then pulled him closer. "Noah, my love," she moaned, her hips rising to meet him.

"My God, *rohi* ..." His hands slid into hers and he pinned her hands above her head, stretching out over her as he moved within her. His mouth found hers in a breathless kiss, and she moaned against his lips.

She didn't want the moment to end, didn't want him to leave her. Being connected to him intimately was everything she'd needed, especially at a time like this, and an unexpected tear slid from the corner of her eye, down her temple, and pooled in her ear.

"I love you," she murmured, pulling her lips away and kissing his jaw, then his neck. "And you're my life now. My all."

"I love you too, my beautiful wife." Noah's hands were tighter against hers.

She wrapped her legs around his waist, clinging to him as they found a steady rhythm together. As he brought her closer to a climax, she moaned.

At last, she cried out, as her entire body trembled, tingling from her feet to the deepest part of her core. He groaned as he finished, and they stilled together. Then Noah rolled onto the bed at her side.

They lay beside each other, panting. She had been freezing before. Now her entire body felt flushed. She rolled over toward him and kissed his shoulder.

However reckless it might have been to take the time to make love at a moment of urgency like this, she didn't regret it. This moment was all they had. She traced her fingers over his arm. The pruned flesh of her fingertips had faded. "I must admit I was angry with you for sending me away tonight. Not just because I wanted to stay with you. It seemed odd that you were willing to leave me vulnerable."

Noah drew a deep breath, then rolled onto his hip, facing her. "I hired a man to follow you and keep you safe. It made it easier for me to send you away."

How had she never seen the man? She smirked. He *would* have done something like that. The thought only endeared him to her more. "Why did you do that?"

"Because I feel strongly drawn to protect what's mine." He leaned forward and kissed the tip of her nose.

*His.* She looked down at the ring on her finger. She crawled away from him and went to the trunk she'd brought with her. She opened it, squinting at the contents in the darkness. She found the pouch where she'd stored his mother's ring. After placing it on her other hand, she came back to him. He'd watched her silently, but his eyes were warm. "I'm sorry I took it off," she said sheepishly. "I promise I'll never do it again. Now I have two wedding rings."

He stood and went over to the fireplace, where he grabbed a bag and removed a *galabeyah*. "I have a burqa here for you and we should hurry. But there's something I must tell you. Something only a handful of people know about me. You should know before I take you fleeing into the path of danger."

*As though he could tell me something that would make me not want to go with him.* Ginger frowned and took the burqa he offered, then found a simple cotton dress in her trunk to wear under it. "What is it?"

"The Egyptian nationalist I fought with this evening. The

one from the cellar. What I didn't tell you about him yet ... He's my uncle. Khaled El-Masry."

She gave him a confused look. "What do you mean? As in ... your relation?"

Noah came closer to her and interlocked their fingers, staring at their hands together in the darkness. "My mother's brother. My mother was an Egyptian. Her name was Fatima El-Masry."

*Egyptian?*

She turned toward him, studying his profile. No trace of falsehood or teasing hinted at his features. But the corners of his eyes squinted as he awaited her reaction.

He was waiting for her to show her outrage.

She smiled. Why had the thought never occurred to her? It fit perfectly. Though no one would doubt he was English, he blended perfectly with the Arabs as well. He tanned to a glorious gold, but his striking blue eyes had prevented her mind from making the link. She felt ashamed of the fact. She'd met several Egyptians and Turks with blue eyes.

And he spoke Arabic perfectly. He was a chameleon not only because of his skills but also because of his parents. Marrying outside one's race was scandalous. He'd likely been brought up to believe his true background was a thing to be ashamed of. She kept her voice low. "Do you really think I could ever look at you differently because of that?"

"You might. It wouldn't be the first time." A shadow crossed his face.

"Which is why you'd hidden the fact," she said, her brows furrowing. She didn't have to ask why. She knew how anyone perceived to be from another race was viewed in society.

Noah went back to dressing himself. "I've only told a few people. My aunt had advised against it."

She thought of the young orphan boy he'd been, told to deny

who he was and pretend the mother he'd loved had been someone else. "That can't have been easy," she said. She pulled the burqa over her head. "You'll have to do a lot more than that for me to look at you differently, my love. Though, I think I finally understand why you're so perfect for this job you're doing. No wonder Lord Helton wouldn't let you out of his grip for so long. There aren't many men like you."

"He and Victoria know of my family background. Matter of fact, Victoria is half-Egyptian herself."

Despite everything, she felt an irrational stab of jealousy. *Victoria?* There she was again, making inroads into their lives. Ginger pushed the thought of her away. "You know, Jack would probably be furious if he knew I told you, but he said you always kept a photograph of your mother with you. Given what a handsome son she had, I'm certain she was beautiful."

He searched her gaze, then placed his thumb and forefinger on her chin. He lifted his head to hers and kissed her lips with a feather-soft kiss. "She was. I'd like to think she would have liked my exquisite wife."

A warm feeling spread within her. "How did your parents meet?"

"My father came to Egypt in the 1880s to fight in the war with the Sudanese. While he was here in Cairo, he fell in love with the daughter of one of the Egyptian generals. They were hopelessly matched, my father being an Irish Catholic soldier and she a Moslem from a wealthy family. When they ran away together, my mother's father disowned her and threatened to kill my father."

He'd told her before how much his parents had loved each other. They must have, to have risked so much. Even Noah's father had taken a risk: his mother wouldn't have likely been looked at kindly in his world. "You said your mother taught you Irish?"

"She taught me several languages. She had studied French and English besides Arabic. One of my parents' neighbors that she befriended taught her Irish."

Ginger's thoughts grew darker. "Does your uncle know who you are?"

"Stephen made certain of it tonight. According to Alastair, the British government has decided to call me the leader of the Aleaqrab, though. They're hunting me, Ginger. And I want to take you with me, but I'm not certain how easy it will be to get away. But if I leave you here, they may try to use you—"

"To capture you." Osborne's claims about Noah's divided loyalties were now clearer than ever. And given what had transpired this evening at the palace, she was sure Noah's family history would help convict him in the eyes of British society.

Rage crawled into Ginger's chest. "How could Lord Helton allow this?"

"I'm no longer useful to him. And Stephen has offered him intimate knowledge on British enemies. Far more intelligence than I could have produced in years. I must leave here right away."

"I'm going with you, of course. But where are we going?"

"After Sarah Hanover. Then Jack. It won't be easy, though. I can't rely on any of my friends or contacts to help. Not with Lord Helton knowing as much as he does about me."

"Is Sarah in danger?"

Noah set his hand on the back of a chaise. "Victoria confessed earlier that Jack was being held on the outskirts of Cairo, where they had held her. Apparently, Osborne had some sort of coded message about the concession he tried to have Jack decrypt. One that—"

"They need Sarah to decrypt in order to find the concession." *Of course.*

Noah went back to his bags. "Yes, I believe so. I have a

feeling they captured Paul Hanover after he'd returned from Malta. Victoria mentioned Paul had been found with a coded message. But it's likely that the message wasn't intended for Jack and might be something he's not able to decrypt. Victoria mentioned he was sick with one of the tropical illnesses too, which may have hindered him. I think it's likely the message was intended for Sarah."

Ginger clutched the black fabric of the burqa. Noah's deductions seemed accurate—she never would have put it all together the way he had—but they'd also come too late. "We need to hurry then." Sarah was friendly and warm, and her sense of humor, though outrageous, had been welcome. If any harm came to her, Ginger would feel responsible. "What if they've already—"

"Don't worry yet. If they've taken her, she may be on her way to where they're holding Jack."

Ginger went toward her trunk. "I should get my kitbag together. Take some things with me."

They'd have to leave her trunk here since there was no way to lug it around with them. But anything she left she risked never seeing again. With both Stephen and the government hunting Noah, who knew when she could return? "Do you think we'll ever come back here?"

Noah lifted his bag onto his shoulder. "I'm not sure. I won't be able to move with the freedom I'm accustomed to. And they'll likely be looking for you too. We'll have to be careful."

Ginger pulled extra clothes into a kitbag, along with her medical supplies. The way things seemed to go, she would likely have to use it. Her fingers hovered over her folded nursing uniforms, and her heart constricted. She'd spent her entire time in Egypt in these. Then she grabbed two uniforms, unable to bear the thought of leaving them. At the very least they could provide an extra disguise if needed. "If they know I'm here, how do we leave without being seen?"

"The same way I came in—by the roof."

## CHAPTER THIRTY-SIX

The engine of the motorcar thrummed across the bridge, the pale dawn taking shape. The Nile was calm, flowing with a steadiness that Ginger found comforting. Even at this time of the morning the shapes of a few of the traditional Egyptian wooden boats—*feluccas*—with their triangular white canvas sails were silhouetted against the sky. Some were likely getting an early start on the day. Others had occupants who'd paid to watch the sunrise on the river.

Ginger hugged her arms, thankful for the extra warmth the burqa provided in the cool dark. She and Noah hadn't had time to discuss things further, but a low simmer of fury burned inside her. He'd given himself entirely to the British cause, and now everything he'd worked for had been snatched away.

Snatched away, in part, because he'd dared to love her.

The journey to Rumayla Square to find Alastair's waiting motorcar had taken hours, despite its relative proximity to Alastair's house. Crossing rooftops had been terrifying, especially knowing that she had to do so in silence or risk being caught.

She'd never admired Noah's skills more.

Ginger directed Noah to Sarah's house. As they crept closer, Noah turned off the headlights, not wanting to announce their arrival.

Set off from the main road, the house was still, shrouded in dark.

That wouldn't have been unusual, if it weren't for the prone body of an Egyptian man in the courtyard.

Noah brought the car to a stop, and Ginger hurried from her seat to check on the man. His limbs were stiff, jaw and eyes open, lifeless.

A bullet hole in his garment revealed his cause of death.

*We're too late.*

Noah crouched beside her. "Whoever did this might still be here," he whispered, pulling her upright by the elbow.

"He's been dead for at least a couple hours. Probably longer." She stood straighter. She'd been around enough dead bodies to know how long it took for a body to stiffen.

Noah led the way toward the house, where they found the front door broken. Bullet casings littered the ground, along with a trail of dusty footprints.

Whoever had come for Sarah most likely hadn't come alone. Had Osborne done this? Or, worse still, Stephen?

She gritted her teeth as they found an Egyptian woman dead near a staircase. Ginger tightened her grip on her gun, wanting to restore the fallen woman's dignity. The dead servants were innocent. They'd done nothing wrong.

Where was Sarah? Ginger should never have involved her, but how could she have known? Worry crested in her mind as they searched the house. Sarah was nowhere to be found. Ginger hoped she'd fled.

Or had she been captured?

They started down the stairs and Noah paused. His brows furrowed. He leaned toward her and whispered almost inaudibly, "Go down a few steps."

The heels of her boots thudded softly against the wooden steps. Then she stopped, turning to face Noah.

Noah signaled that she should continue, then he moved to the top of the staircase, watching her closely.

She did as he asked.

Noah went to the middle of the staircase. Tapping the risers with the backs of his knuckles, he listened closely. He paused, then ran his fingers over the corners of each step. Finding what he appeared to be looking for, he lifted the flat edge of one stair to reveal a hidden space under the stairs.

There, blinking in the dark, was Sarah. She held a gun out toward Noah, hands steady. "Don't you dare think of touching me, you son of a bitch."

Oh, no—she thought Noah was after her. Ginger rushed to Noah's side. "No! Sarah, wait!"

Sarah looked from Noah to Ginger and lowered the gun.

"What in the hell is going on?" She pushed her way out of the dusty crawl space. Her face was wan, and she wore a thin satin dressing gown. "You're lucky I didn't shoot you."

"Sarah, this is my husband, Noah Benson."

Sarah picked a cobweb from her hair. "Ah. I'm sorry to have greeted you this way. I didn't know."

She must have been terrified.

"How long have you been in there?" Ginger asked.

Sarah rolled her shoulders and winced. "A few hours. Paul built the damned thing. Comes in handy, but there's no way to let yourself out. Not the smartest design. I was counting on one of my ..." She spotted the body of the woman at the bottom of the stairs. *"Oh ..."*

She bolted past Noah and Ginger, taking the stairs two at a

time. "Nenet!" She reached her, then tried lifting the woman into her arms. "No, Nenet!"

Stumbling away, Sarah set her back against the wall and slid down toward the floor. She hugged her knees against her chest, her face stricken with grief and tears. "She died protecting me."

Ginger exchanged a look with Noah, then left his side to go to Sarah's. Crouching beside her, Ginger set a gentle hand on her shoulder. "Sarah, I'm so sorry."

She wiped her cheeks. "I heard shots but didn't know what had happened. I didn't know it was her."

Ginger didn't have the heart to tell her about the others right then. To Ginger, they had been innocent bystanders, which was bad enough. To Sarah, they were no doubt like family.

Sarah clenched her jaw, her lower lip trembling despite the effort. Tears slid onto her cheeks, and she wiped them away with the back of her hands. "Why did you come back?"

"A lot has happened since we parted." Ginger stood, feeling clumsily inadequate to address Sarah's broken heart. After all, she'd brought this on Sarah, even if unintentionally. "The man I took you to meet with yesterday—"

Sarah crossed her arms. "He came here tonight. Nenet barely had time to hide me away." She breathed shakily.

Then it had been Osborne.

Noah put his gun in the holster and offered her an arm, which she accepted. "Are you all right?"

Sarah looked paler now and sat wearily on a nearby chaise. "I'm beginning to understand that Paul was mixed up in something more dangerous than I realized. Would anyone care to explain to me what's going on?"

Ginger felt horrible for having dragged Sarah into this. The archeologist had been relatively safe while her connection to Freddy Mortimer went undiscovered.

Sitting beside Sarah, she fidgeted with her skirt. "My father lost his fortune. I think he must have spent most of it on that concession. He became indebted to a family friend, a man as soulless as they come. His name is Stephen Fisher. He had sympathies to the Germans and used my father's debts against him to pull him into his criminal activities. My brother too, at the end. I discovered it by chance last spring."

Sarah met Ginger's gaze. Her eyes didn't contain fear, just questions. "And the spy—Stephen Fisher—he's on the loose?"

"Yes." Noah crossed the darkened space to the window. He peeked outside the curtain. "Fisher got away when we tried to arrest him in the spring and recently resurfaced and allowed himself to be captured. I believed the whole time he had some plan, but I wasn't certain about the objectives. One was to pin all his crimes on my shoulders. The other was to find you."

Sarah sat straighter. "And Osborne?"

"Osborne appears to be working for him." Ginger gave Sarah a sheepish look. "I didn't know—"

"I'm not angry with you," Sarah said. "But why me? It makes no sense."

Noah straightened. "By any chance, Mrs. Hanover, do you have any experience in cryptography?"

Sarah rubbed the back of her neck. "Some. Why?"

"Is it possible that your husband would have written to you in a code that would have been difficult for anyone but you to decrypt?"

"I ..." She pursed her lips. "The short answer is yes. I've always written my excavation notes in code, one that Paul knew but would be gibberish to most people. Are you telling me that Paul left me a note?"

As the morning moved steadily toward sunrise, the space they were in became more visible. A large hall with a squared staircase. Bookcases lined most of the walls beside them. No wonder Sarah was so bright—she surrounded herself with books.

"That's Noah's theory." Ginger shifted in her seat. "They captured our friend, a man named Jack Darby, who happens to be a cryptologist. We think they hoped he would be able to decrypt the message Paul may have left you. We need to rescue him and then find the concession paperwork, if we can."

"Jack Darby?" Sarah arched a brow. "I might have known he was involved in this mess."

*She knows him?* "You're acquainted?"

"The archeological circle in Cairo is a tight-knit community. And fellow Americans have a way of standing out. Yes, I know him. I haven't seen him for a couple years." Sarah lifted her chin toward Noah, with a quick intake of breath. "No wonder you look familiar to me, Mr. Benson. You're his friend, right? I think we've met before. Years ago on a dig in Aswan. I still went by Sarah Anderson back then."

The revelation wasn't shocking, but Ginger looked at Noah in surprise.

He gave a slow nod. "That was a long time ago, but, yes, I think I recall."

That Sarah had met Jack and Noah before gave her an air of trustworthiness Ginger hadn't expected. "If the community is so tight-knit, how is it that Paul assumed two identities so successfully? Wouldn't someone have recognized him?"

Sarah shook her head. "I think that was part of the fun of it for Paul. He was quite good at his disguise. When he was Freddy, he was an English fop, ran in a circle of high society. Your father may have been the only one who ever saw through it. I'm assuming he told Olivia Hendricks eventually. Even I didn't discover it for a few years, but that's also because he carefully avoided me as Freddy."

Sarah stood, a more determined look to her face. "I suppose it may be helpful for me to get some of my books about Malta, just in case that's where Paul left the concession." She paused and gave Noah a once-over. "You're not actually a criminal, right? You're being framed?"

That she asked as an afterthought made Ginger hold back a smile. The feeling of friendship she felt toward Sarah appeared to be reciprocated.

Noah's eyes hinted at humor. "No, I'm not," he said dryly.

"Then I'm going with you. Five percent is all I have left from that bastard husband of mine. But five percent of a few billion dollars someday might make my life easier. And if Jack Darby needs help, I want to be a part of it." Sarah stood and craned her neck at Ginger. "I have a burqa upstairs—I'll go find it."

She stepped forward, then paled, seeing her servant by the stairs. "I have to inform her family of what's happened." Her fingers shook as she pushed her hair over her shoulder. Her eyes misted. "And Babu. I saw them shoot him in the courtyard before I hid. Are there any others?"

"We didn't see anyone else. Do you have a telephone here, Mrs. Hanover?" Noah asked.

Sarah's hands still appeared shaky. "In the library."

Ginger rose from her seat and put a steadying hand on her elbow.

"Why don't you gather what you need?" Noah said. "I'll make a phone call to a friend of mine who can see to caring for the bodies in your home." His voice was exceedingly gentle. Ginger snuck a glance at him, her heart warming. His ability to be both kind and competent in times of heartbreak was wonderful.

Sarah nodded and left them and went up the stairs.

Ginger went to Noah and tugged at his hand. She interlocked her fingers with his, trying to read his face, which was cast in shadow. "Do you think it's wise to take her with us?"

"I don't know. But she's not safe here. If Osborne came after her, it's because he thinks there's something that only she can offer him." Noah lifted Ginger's hand to his lips and kissed the backs of her fingers. "Taking you both seems risky, to be honest."

Heaviness weighed on Ginger. "It feels as though we're being lured there, doesn't it? And by taking Sarah aren't we taking the piece of the puzzle that they're missing?"

"I don't know of any other option. Only that Jack would go for me if the roles were reversed. And if he's as ill as Victoria says he was, it may be too late already."

Ginger followed him to the library. "Is it safe to make a telephone call?"

Noah nodded. "It should be. This friend isn't connected to the government. Just someone who does me favors occasionally when I need to obtain a respectful burial for someone. I won't identify myself anyway."

Ginger chewed on her lower lip. Intriguing as it was, she wasn't sure she wanted to know more.

Noah's phone call turned out to be in French. As he chatted in low tones, she moved toward the window, gazing over the courtyard of palm trees that surrounded the house. What sort of life had Noah occupied before the war?

Until hours ago, she hadn't even known her new husband was half-Egyptian.

The things she didn't know about him far outnumbered those she knew.

Movement in the courtyard caught her attention. She sucked in a breath, then squinted, trying to distinguish what she'd seen.

She leaned forward, one hand on the glass, searching the courtyard.

A man's face appeared in the window, inches from her own.

Screaming, Ginger dove away from the window. Gunshots

and breaking glass followed. Ginger covered her face with her arms, her ears ringing.

"Ginger, move!" Noah commanded. He'd dropped the phone and fired his gun at the same moment. The man who'd peeked in through the window lay dead, half-sprawled into the broken window.

She scrambled from the floor and rushed toward Noah as another figure came running up behind the dead man. Noah fired toward the window again, pulling Ginger behind him. She peeked out the window.

A second man, dressed identically to the first, twitched on the ground. "Who are they?" Ginger asked.

"Considering that they were holding guns, I wasn't going to wait to find out. Let's get Sarah and go. Who knows how many more are here." Noah dragged her from the room. She ran at his side, hardly able to keep up.

Sarah was already back down the stairs, a rucksack over her shoulder. She hadn't changed into a burqa but held one under her arm. "What happened?"

"More men with guns arrived. Do you have any weapons here? All of mine are in the boot of our motorcar," Noah said.

Sarah led him toward a closet. After unlocking it, she flipped on a light and stepped back. Several rifles were inside. Noah eyed Sarah curiously as he slung them over his shoulder, grabbing ammunition. He lifted his brow at a crate of dynamite and hand grenades.

*What on earth is Sarah doing with all this?*

"You never know when dynamite will come in handy," Sarah deadpanned.

Noah grabbed a bundle of dynamite. He lifted a few grenades. "And these?"

Sarah shrugged. "I'm American, for God's sake. We like being prepared for any scenario."

Noah smirked and pocketed some grenades.

They raced from the house. The car was parked just outside, shrouded by the early morning light that had barely broken through the horizon. A dog nearby barked, adding a sense of urgency to their flight.

Ginger and Sarah climbed in as Noah worked the starting handle.

The roar of a car engine approached. Ginger's heart accelerated as another car pulled up in front of the gated entrance, then blocked it. Several men were inside, all of them with rifles.

British soldiers.

"Noah!" Ginger cried out.

"Keep your head low!" Noah shouted to them. A few shots rang out as he slammed his foot on the gas pedal, speeding the car toward gate.

He was aiming straight toward the other car.

The squeal of tires sounded as the soldiers realized, too late, that Noah would be undeterred. Ginger peeked out from her seat to see the other motorcar pull forward slightly but not enough to avoid being hit.

Sarah hung on, huddling down in the seat as Noah swung toward the wider gap and rammed their motorcar past the gate and the other vehicle. A hideous metallic scrape sounded, the bumper of the assailants' car ripping from the back. Ginger shielded her face.

They continued forward, careening toward the dirt road, bumping across grass and rock to get there. The car jostled and gave a hard bump—one that made her insides feel like they'd dropped—then the smoother road followed.

Ginger tugged at the fabric in front of her face as the wind whipped it. Her black robe billowed, and she held it down with her arms. Would these disguises even help now that they'd been seen?

Thankfully, the British soldiers didn't seem to have Noah's skill at driving and remained far behind them. Noah turned onto the main road. With the dawn breaking, carts and cars clogged the roadway. He sped around one, sending a fruit cart flying. He spun the wheel, then pushed the gas pedal harder.

The British soldiers were quickly gaining on them.

Ginger covered her face with her hands, praying. *Please, God, let us get out of this.* If they captured Noah, who knew what would happen? Would they shoot him? The army might not care to capture him alive. He had to escape.

Sarah appeared to be loading a rifle.

As they turned onto the open stretch of road before the bridge, the soldiers drew closer. Their rifles glinted in the first rays of the sun.

*Oh my God, they're going to kill us all.*

Noah withdrew the bundle of dynamite from his robe. As he flicked a flame with a lighter, he simultaneously slammed on the brakes of the car. The soldiers careened toward them, tires squealing as they tried to stop themselves from slamming into the back of their car. As both cars drew to a halt, Noah lit the fuse on the dynamite, then hurled it into the soldiers' car.

The men in the car gave one horrified look, then went scrambling, diving out headlong as Noah lurched their own car forward.

A *boom* behind them shook the ground. Her heart in her throat, Ginger looked back to see the car a ball of flame and smoke, the soldiers still fleeing from it.

The rush of adrenaline pumping through her filled her with energy, glee, and horror all at once. She tossed her arms around her husband's neck. "That was brilliant."

Noah shrugged. "You were right, Mrs. Hanover. The dynamite was quite handy."

Sarah stared at them both, then burst into the nervous laughter that came with having barely survived certain death. "Under the circumstances, maybe you should start calling me Sarah?" The car barreled forward in the wind and sand of the Egyptian landscape, the red light of sunrise lighting the sky.

# CHAPTER THIRTY-SEVEN

Noah awoke to a light shake of his shoulder. He breathed in sharply, then his hand dug for the pistol under his pillow—but there wasn't a pillow. Or a pistol.

He startled, his eyes opening fully.

"It's me." Ginger sat back from him, a flash in her eyes. "It's been two hours."

Disoriented, Noah tried to shake the fog of sleep from his head. Two hours hadn't been nearly enough, but he'd insisted she wake him. His exhaustion had been so great that the dirt floor beneath him hadn't even been an obstacle to sleep in the ramshackle hut.

He peered around the empty space, which was bereft of any furnishings. "Where's Sarah?"

"Watering the horses. And trying to see if she can bathe them, if possible." They'd disposed of Alastair's motorcar after escaping the soldiers and purchased a few nags from an eager native. The poor animals were coated in dust and flies. Then they'd ridden to Abusir, just a few miles north of the town where Victoria had suggested they were holding Jack.

Noah had taken the first watch, allowing Ginger and Sarah the chance to sleep for a few hours. Then he'd taken a turn, the bare minimum on which to function. He'd thought his anxiety over Jack would keep him tossing all night, but he'd fallen asleep almost immediately.

Standing, Noah stretched his shoulders back. He went to his bag and searched for a new disguise. He'd spent so many days in disguise over the last few weeks that the skin on his face had begun to feel raw from the spirit gum. "When Sarah returns, I need to ask her expertise about Saqqara. And we should hurry. They may have been so distracted by searching for me last night that they haven't moved Jack. But I doubt the situation will remain that way for long. The only advantage we have is that they may be unaware that we know where Jack is."

"Unless Victoria tells them she told you. She may have even given you a false location. Either way, they could be counting on your devotion to Jack to attempt a rescue."

He understood her anger with Victoria and shared some of it, but a betrayal of that level on Victoria's part seemed too vicious. Would he ever trust Victoria again? Doubtful. But her confession at the end had felt genuine.

"Possibly. But I don't think so. If she really wanted to have me captured, there were far easier ways." He pulled a mirror from his bag. "Can you hold this for me?" he asked Ginger. As she took it, he found a bottle of spirit gum and a false beard.

"Where did you learn to do all this?" A smile tipped at the corner of her luscious mouth. He fought the temptation to kiss her, shifting his eyes back to the mirror.

"A book on theatrical makeup by Cavendish Morton." The pungent scent of the spirit gum burned his nostrils as he opened the bottle. He hated the stuff, but these theatrics had saved his life more than once. His eyes burned as he applied it to his face.

Once he'd finished dressing, he put his supplies away. She

watched him warily, her pupils large in the dimly lit hovel. "Noah, I'm worried. I can't help but feel we're walking into a trap."

"Not we, just me. You promised to stay at a distance. And I'm not going to lie, *rohi*. I may not return. If I don't, I left everything of value to me at Alastair's house, including our marriage certificate from the priest. Most of my money is there, but there's some—"

"Noah, stop. You can't talk like that." Tears fringed her lashes.

A crack sounded as Sarah moved the wooden board they'd used to cover the entrance. There wasn't a real door, but it had sufficed.

Sarah pushed her veil from her face as she came in. "I'm sweating," she said, scratching her cheek. "And probably covered with bites." She nodded approvingly at Noah. "Nice costume. You would fool me." She tugged the straps of their canteens from her shoulder. "I filled these up at the well, treated them with bleaching powder. Where in Saqqara are we heading?"

"The Serapeum, I think. Victoria mentioned some rather large sarcophagi. She also said the Step Pyramid wasn't directly within walking distance but that she saw it when they drove past."

Sarah pursed her lips. "That makes sense. They likely wouldn't have driven past it unless they were coming from the south or west side of it." She squinted, as though trying to comb her memory. "Come to think of it, I heard something about the Greater Vaults being closed recently due to sand erosion."

Ginger set her hands on her hips. "And why, exactly, does it make sense?"

Noah strapped a pistol just above one ankle. Sarah had the advantage of knowing the local archeology as well as, or better, than he did. "Saqqara was built as a burial place for the kings of ancient Memphis, the capital of Egypt. But several cults used it as well, including the Apis cult, which buried sacred bulls at a complex known as the Serapeum, hence the large sarcophagi. The site was excavated a half a century ago, but most of it has become inaccessible over the years."

Sarah gave Ginger a sympathetic smile. "Why not just thunk her over the forehead with an encyclopedia on Ancient Egypt?"

Noah crossed his arms and quirked a brow at Sarah. "She understood."

Sarah raised her chin as she met his eyes. "Good man. You don't underestimate her."

They slung their bags over their shoulders and left the hut.

The horses looked better than they had when they'd purchased them, though being forced to load them with their bags added an extra strain to the already-overworked creatures. Noah patted the gelding he'd ridden here, glancing over the top of the saddle at Ginger. She wore an amused expression in her eyes, which was the only part of her face he could see now that she'd donned her face veil. "She isn't wrong," Ginger said.

Noah strapped the bag to the gelding. "I'd be happy to leave the archeological explanations to the expert." He nodded toward Sarah, who had already climbed onto her horse. He helped Ginger onto her mare, then mounted up beside her.

They rode from the hamlet toward the pyramids of Abusir, which took them to the edge of the desert. Like Giza, the cultivation from the Nile was a strong line of demarcation—the fertile expanse of palm trees and other forms of green plants seemed to come to a sudden stop at the edge of the crumbling, dry plain of the desert. It was hard to imagine what these areas must have looked like thousands of years earlier, when the Nile had taken a closer course to where the pyramids lay.

The broken limestone bricks forming the mounds of the pyramids at Abusir were all that remained of those times.

"How long will it take us to get there?" Ginger asked, bringing her horse alongside his. Sweat glistened on her forehead.

"The trip south is about five miles. My guess is that it will take us about an hour," Noah said, swatting a fly away.

"An hour in five miles? Aren't we supposed to be in a hurry?" Sarah's voice was dry.

Noah patted the gelding's neck. The saddle cloth encroaching on its neck was mere tatters and strings. "These horses can't handle much more than a trot for an extended period time. If we need to take them to a gallop later for a quick getaway, we don't need them already exhausted. As it is, one of them will have to take two riders. If Jack is able to ride on his own, I'll take Ginger with me on this gelding on the way back."

"And once we get to this Serapeum?" Ginger looked from Noah to Sarah. "Is there any plan to get Jack?"

What sort of a plan could there be? He didn't want to worry her more than necessary. "I'm hoping they aren't expecting us. Unless Victoria said something—"

"Which I maintain is entirely possible. I have no faith in that woman." Ginger wiped her brow with her fingertips.

"But if she didn't, they won't know to expect us right now. Stephen is likely to be celebrating his triumphant return to society, and Osborne may still be looking for Sarah. Victoria maintained that Osborne was mostly alone there. And Jahi is dead. There may only be a handful of people guarding Jack, especially if he's ill."

A hesitant look crossed Ginger's face. "But if we're seen, they could kill him before we get close, Noah."

"Which is precisely why you'll be staying at a distance. I can't sneak the three of us in anywhere." The gelding's ears pricked back and it stumbled in its steps. Noah surveyed the horizon. Nothing. *The last thing we need is a skittish horse.*

Sarah rode up on his other side. "Have you wondered at all why it is that they're using the site of a major archeological find to hide their captives?" The canteen at her hip bounced lightly with each step of the mare.

"I'm not sure. Stephen and Lord Braddock were deep into the smuggling of antiquities, though. While Stephen's deal with Lord Helton has resulted in the arrest of most of his associates, it wouldn't surprise me if he's still up to his neck in the smuggling trade in some way." He rested his hands on the worn leather horn of the saddle, holding the reins loosely. Much as Sarah appeared to be trustworthy, he hesitated to tell her more than necessary or muse on hypotheses with her.

The heat of the day had started to climb into uncomfortable temperatures, and Noah settled into silence between the two women. Outside of an occasional pack of stray dogs and some flying buzzards, they passed no living creatures, the desolation of the desert giving him too much time to think.

What would it take to prove his innocence?

*You're not innocent.*

But there was that gorgeous woman at his side, his wife. His chance at a future he now wanted so desperately that losing it would be soul-crushing.

Could he ever give her even half of what she deserved?

As they drew closer to the Serapeum, they stopped. Noah retrieved a pair of binoculars from his bag. There was nowhere to hide near here—the flat plain of the desert stretched before them. Their enemies had a similar disadvantage, though. In the wavy lines of heat rising at the horizon, Noah focused his attention on a tent pitched near the entrance to the Serapeum. If they had a guard watching at all, it was possible he took shelter from the sun in there.

He saw no one.

Noah wound the strap around the binoculars. "I'm going to

walk from here. It will be the quietest way to get there." He handed the binoculars to Ginger. "If I need you to ride in and help me, I'll signal. If I'm not in your line of sight, I'll send up two shots. But hopefully I can avoid that."

Ginger nodded, and he wished he could see her beautiful face. But he could read the fear in her eyes easily enough. He wanted to comfort her, tell her all would be well. But a foreboding feeling hung in the stillness of the dry air, of sand and blood … and the ancient drumbeats silenced long ago in this valley of death.

Noah dismounted from the horse and gave Sarah the reins. Then he started forward on foot.

## CHAPTER THIRTY-EIGHT

A strong breeze whipped across Ginger's face, cooling the sweat trails on her face and throwing sand into her eyes. She glanced in the direction Noah had gone, unable to feel settled. She could no longer see him through the binoculars. He'd approached a massive stone wall, then disappeared out of sight.

"You're not entirely comfortable with his line of work, are you?" Sarah said, breaking her train of thought.

As she wiped her face, Ginger noticed the gnats swarming near the eyes of the mare. The poor creature had no way to easily repel them, but it didn't seem to mind either. "It's hard to feel that every time he walks away from me, it could be the last time I see him."

"Yet you married him knowing that about him." Sarah took a swig of water, swished it in her mouth, then spit it out.

Ginger wished she had a hat instead of the veil and shielded her eyes with her hand. The brightness of the sun was blinding. "I did. But I love him. I could hardly have avoided it if I wanted to be with him."

"I suppose." Sarah shrugged and pulled her face veil back into place.

Hadn't Sarah said she was "crazy" about her own husband? Her remark was curious. "Why did you get married?"

Sarah laughed lightly, rolling her neck. Even with the burqa, she had the mannerisms of someone distinctly not native. "Mostly to prove to my father that I knew better than he did." Her eyes glinted. "Turns out he might have been right. But, I don't know. Even despite him being a bastard, I did more exciting things with Paul by my side than I ever dreamed possible."

Ginger chewed on her lower lip. Jane Radford. Sarah Hanover. Even herself. They'd all struck out on their own. The results hadn't been quite what they'd expected, nothing had been easy, and their dreams hadn't been without sacrifice.

And then there were women like Olivia Hendricks and Lucy. Women who sacrificed what they wanted for what was expected and easy.

But they didn't seem happy either. And they hadn't really gotten what they wanted in the long run.

"Sometimes I wonder if we don't all put too much expectation on unpredictable outcomes. If this war has taught me anything, it's that any semblance of control I have is just an illusion," Ginger said. How many times had she heard soldiers making plans one day, only for those plans to go terribly awry the next?

Sarah lifted her canteen in a mock toast. "Hear hear. Which is why I learned to live for myself. Everyone else is too unpredictable." She nodded in the direction Noah had gone. "Including him. He seems like a good guy though. But if you're worried that he's going to disappoint you one day, let it go. He will. That's just the nature of man."

As wise as Sarah's words sounded, a protective feeling curled around Ginger's heart. She and Noah loved each other in a way she had never imagined possible. Wouldn't that help them get through the difficulties too?

"Do you think Jack is still there?" Ginger asked instead.

"I don't know. But if Noah's right, they may not be in a hurry to move him yet. Or think that a man fleeing from the army is more likely to be worried about his own hide than rescuing his friend."

Two gunshots punctured their conversation.

*Noah.*

Ginger lifted a shaky hand, putting the binoculars back up to her eyes. Noah had re-emerged ... and appeared to have Jack slung over his shoulder. Her breath caught. How on earth had Noah found Jack so easily? Noah started running toward them.

About thirty yards behind him, a couple of men were giving chase.

Jack's arms hung limply.

*Oh my God. He's dead.*

"Hurry!" Ginger said, but Sarah had already taken off across the sand. Her horse's hooves pounded against the ground, sending up a trail of dust, and Ginger had to squint to avoid it landing in her eyes.

She followed Sarah, her heart pounding. *Please don't let Jack be dead,* she prayed, her body falling into the rhythmic gallop of the horse. Each fall of the hooves pulsed through her like an electric pulse. How had Noah found him so quickly?

Something must be wrong.

They reached Noah minutes later. He'd continued to run toward them, and his face dripped with sweat, the false beard beginning to curl away. As they reached him, Noah set Jack down on the ground, then ripped the beard from his face, wincing and out of breath.

Ginger scrambled from her horse toward Jack. "What happened? Is he alive?"

As she drew closer to Jack, she saw his chest move with breath and relief poured through her. She rolled him onto his back, the smell of vomit and feces reaching her. His skin was a sickly yellow, and his forehead burned to the touch.

Sarah held the reins to the three horses, who stepped in place nervously. She drew a gun, firing toward the men heading their way.

Jack's eyelids fluttered and then he curled onto his side, moaning. "He has malaria," Ginger said. She met Noah's eyes. "How did you get him—"

"He was under the tent, unguarded." Noah's eyes were dark. "I think they must have moved him outside to be sick. We have to get him on the horse."

"There's more of them, Noah." Sarah's voice held a warning.

Ginger swiveled her gaze toward the Serapeum. Four men were scrambling out from behind the walls, surveying the desert, about a hundred feet away. Another man was bringing horses from a separate direction.

As the sound of more gunshots cracked the atmosphere, the gelding Noah had been riding reared backward and broke away from Sarah's grasp. He took off with a whinny, tearing away from them.

Noah swore. Pulling his gun out, he returned fire toward the men. "Get Jack up on a horse!" he called out.

Ginger and Noah bent down and helped lift Jack onto Sarah's horse. His body was nearly draped across her legs, but Sarah made no complaint, and handed Ginger the reins to the other horse. As Sarah took off at a gallop, Ginger mounted the horse.

More gunshots.

She steadied her breath, praying they wouldn't be hit. A

glance back revealed the men quickly gaining on them, now on their own horses.

Noah swung up onto the horse, behind her, then they started forward. The mare seemed to resist, then stumbled slightly. Ginger's hands tightened on the reins as Noah fired behind them again.

"Osborne is with them," Noah said, his voice a shout near her ear.

Osborne was here? She resisted the urge to look back, but his face flashed in her mind and she shuddered. How many times had the man left her at the hospital in Cairo in the morning and come here? The thought of his duplicity made her skin crawl with disgust.

As the mare seemed to stumble again, Noah reached past her, then drew the horse to a halt. Before she could make sense of his actions, Noah dismounted. "This horse is too weak to carry the both of us."

Her mind took a moment to catch the full meaning of his words.

He meant for her to go on without him.

She twisted her body to face him. "Noah, no!" Another gunshot cracked past.

"You must go." Noah lifted both hands, as though in surrender.

*No. Not this.* There had to be another way.

"I won't leave you." Her mouth felt dry, her fingers shaking. She reached out for him.

"You must, *rohi*. Go, they're getting closer." Noah took her hand in his and squeezed it. "Get out of here. I'm safer if you're not with me. If they don't have you."

The gunshots, it appeared, had stopped. The men chasing them slowed.

Could it be true? Her capture had been used against him before.

Ginger stared at him squarely in the eyes, her brain scrambling for anything that might help. "Tell Osborne I'm coming back tonight with the location of the concession. That he can have it—but only if you're still alive."

"Get out of here!" Noah released her hand, then hit her horse across the backside as hard as he could.

The horse took off at a gallop.

As it carried her away, tears slid from Ginger's eyes onto her cheeks. She looked over her shoulder, terrified as the men descended upon Noah, guns drawn.

Every fiber within her screamed at her to turn back.

Would they kill him?

A sob choked her throat. She hadn't even told him she loved him.

Then she pressed the horse harder, faster, following Jack and Sarah.

# CHAPTER THIRTY-NINE

Ginger lifted her head as Sarah came back into the hotel room Sarah had acquired for them on the outskirts of Abusir. The sun was setting, the sky a dazzling spectacle that she couldn't appreciate. The room wasn't much more than a bed and two simple wooden chairs, but it was better than the hovel where they'd taken shelter in the morning. Especially for someone as sick as Jack.

She could barely think straight. She whispered a prayer for Noah and clutched Jack's hand for strength. She'd been sitting beside him while Sarah was gone.

"Did you burn it?" Ginger asked as Sarah sat in the chair.

The trace of ash on her trousers confirmed it. "I found a rubbish bin. Lit it all on fire." She sank down further against the back of the chair, kicking her shoes off.

"Good. I don't think we could have salvaged them." Ginger had removed all of Jack's clothing and shaved his face and head since he appeared to have been afflicted with lice on top of the malaria.

While Sarah had been gone, she'd washed Jack and dressed

him in Noah's clothes. They'd managed to catch the gelding eventually, which had been a stroke of luck as it had Noah's bags strapped to it. Jack slept now, looking younger and sicker with his head and face shaved.

She wished Jack was awake. He'd offer his teasing smiles and jokes.

And hope. Without him they had no way of finding the concession.

But malaria could be deadly serious, especially when a patient was left untreated. She'd seen too many patients die of malaria to not be worried. His lack of awareness was a sign of how far he'd succumbed to the disease. She doubted they'd administered any form of medical care, given the state she had found him in. Ginger had given him a three-grain dose of quinine as soon as they'd stopped the horse. She'd given him three more doses since then.

Thank goodness she'd brought her medical kit.

Swallowing the tears in her throat, she said, "Should we make a plan to go back for Noah?"

Sarah had closed her eyes and was half asleep. *She must be exhausted.* Yawning, she said, "And if we show up without the location for the concession?"

Ginger raked her fingers through her hair. "I don't know. All I know is I have to try to help my husband."

Sarah stood and approached Jack. She sat on the bed beside him and shook his shoulder. Jack grunted, then blinked toward her. "Jack, we need you. Noah said they gave you a code of some sort. Do you remember it?"

Jack mumbled and flopped onto his stomach.

Sarah went over to their bags. She lifted her canteen and poured some water onto her hand. Then she splashed it onto Jack's face and patted his cheek. "Get up, Darby. We need you."

Ginger frowned. The familiarity with which Sarah seemed

to address Jack was curious. But, then again, she'd admitted freely to knowing Jack. Not everything had to be a secret or a mystery, but Ginger had spent so many months surrounded by events shrouded in deception that her mind seemed to go there naturally.

Sarah shook Jack again. "You want to save Noah Benson, don't you? I need the code Osborne gave you."

Blinking blearily, Jack opened one eye, just barely. "Notepad."

Would Jack remember anything with accuracy in this state? His fever seemed to have improved since she'd started him on quinine—but enough for something this important?

Ginger dug through Noah's belongings and found a notepad and pencil. She handed these to Sarah, who set the pencil in Jack's hand. She slid the notepad under his palm.

Jack made a few scribbles, then the pencil jerked downward, uselessly.

*This is hopeless.*

"Can we use smelling salts? Anything that will wake him more?" Sarah asked hopefully.

"I can try." Ginger found a container in her medical kit. "I can't remember the last time I needed these." She uncapped it and held the bottle under Jack's nostrils.

He drew in a sharp breath, then opened his reddened eyes more fully. He looked at Ginger, then Sarah, then closed his eyes. "What?" he asked.

"The code, Jack." Ginger put the salts under his nose once again.

He opened his eyes, drawing his face back. "Stop it," he said through gritted teeth. Then he lifted the pencil. Scribbling once again, he wrote a few lines of text, then set the pencil down. It rolled off the notepad and onto the floor.

Ginger's heart fell. What he'd written looked like complete gibberish.

Sarah lifted the notepad, then stiffened. She lowered the paper to her side.

"What is it?" Ginger asked. Jack let out a soft snore.

"It's my code." Sarah's eyes were wide as she dropped back into the chair with a dazed expression.

Ginger bent beside her. "And you can read what it says?"

"Yes—they're Greek letters written in Egyptian Coptic. From that translation, it's a standard Playfair cipher. I always used the same key. Hopefully Paul did the same. Otherwise, I might face a bit of a battle." She brushed her fingertips over the writing as though indulging in a sentimental moment.

No wonder they had needed Jack. A cipher written in an ancient text? He was a known expert in that sort of thing. "You know Coptic?" Ginger gave her an impressed look.

"I started studying it as a young girl. It fascinated me. I always dreamed of being an Egyptologist, so the language, both past and present, was a part of my studies from the start. I taught Paul after we'd married. Do you think Paul intended this cipher for me?"

Ginger weighed her words. Despite Sarah's attempts at stoicism, she had a feeling that her outward indifference to Paul's fate was an act. Paul had scorned her, after all. "Noah said they caught him with a cipher. Perhaps he knew he was being followed and wanted to send you some message so that you could find the paperwork."

"That makes sense. Otherwise, why write anything down?" Sarah drummed her fingertips against the paper. "Let me get a pencil. I can work my way through this."

"Red." Jack murmured his nickname for Ginger and she left Sarah's side to feel Jack's forehead.

Jack barely opened his eyes to look at her. "I didn't dream you up."

She smiled, the sound of his voice so welcome that her eyes grew teary. "No, I'm right here, Jack."

"And Noah?"

A lump formed in her throat. "We're working to get him here too. Osborne has him."

Jack moistened his lips, closing his eyes as he struggled. "Not here..."

Ginger pulled up another chair beside Jack. She slipped her hand into his as he grew silent again. Even though she hadn't known Jack for long, she loved him dearly. And she knew how much Noah loved him. If anything happened to him, Noah would never forgive himself for not having gone back for him weeks earlier.

Ginger struggled to stay awake. Even if Sarah figured out where the concession paperwork was hidden, she doubted Osborne would simply exchange Noah for it. Most likely, he'd try to kill them all, once their usefulness was at an end.

And, according to what he'd hinted at during their conversations, he had every reason to want to kill Noah.

Why, oh why, had Noah offered himself up? And what condition would Noah be in when they went tonight? There were so many things Osborne could do beside kill him.

She shuddered, unable to continue the line of thought. Her imagination was too vivid, aided by gruesome injuries she'd seen during the war.

Sarah's voice cut into Ginger's thoughts. "The text says, 'In the hidden tombs in the city of sand, wind, and stone, where the lady once slept. I lie beneath.'"

Ginger looked over at Sarah and raised a brow. "Do you know what that means?"

"It honestly could be several cities, but given that Paul was in

Malta before he was captured, Valletta makes sense as the location." Sarah's face was drawn as she set down her pencil.

Tense silence crept into the room.

Valletta was several days' journey from here and by sea. They wouldn't be able to simply hand over the concession. Or confirm its location. Which meant that Osborne would be reluctant to release Noah.

Ginger moistened her lips with the lip of her tongue. "And the tomb?"

"Just outside Valletta there's a famed hypogeum—an ancient underground tomb. The one at Hal Saflieni is one of the best preserved from prehistoric times. It's an archeologist's dream, purportedly." She pulled a few books from her rucksack. "I have a suspicion I know what it is. Fortunately, I brought those books with me from home. They might help us with the last part."

She sat once again, flicking through pages.

Ginger glanced at Jack's face. "I imagine as he got sicker it was probably harder for him to keep his silence about what he'd deciphered."

Sarah pressed her lips together. "Keeping silent while being so sick would have been damn near impossible. He did a good job. And now we know why they needed to kidnap me. And, if I'm right, Jack wouldn't have been able to find the paperwork to the concession even if he'd told them the truth."

Sarah lifted the book in her hand and turned it to Ginger, waving it. "These are the excavation notes of Father Emmanuel Magri—he was the archeologist in charge of the initial excavations at the Hypogeum in Malta. He was Paul's friend for many years and sent these notes to Paul long ago. And they're not in English either."

Ginger laughed. "Are all archeologists so particular with their excavation notes?"

Sarah twirled a strand of hair around her finger. "Only the good ones. The rest are too busy trying to find out what the others have learned. Ah, here it is." Sarah held her book open to a crude drawing made in pencil. "The Sleeping Lady was an artifact discovered by Father Magri in 1905. It was moved, of course, so few people know exactly where he found it, but Paul apparently did. And now I do too." She pointed to the text, which Ginger couldn't read.

Trying to think clearly, Ginger peered at the text. "So we need this artifact? I'm confused."

"No, no—" Sarah rubbed her face. "Sorry, I'm not making much sense. We don't need the artifact. Only the location where it was found. The code said, 'where the lady once slept.' It's referring to the place where she used to be, not where she's located now. 'I lie beneath …' must be a reference to some feature under where the artifact was found. Paul probably buried the concession paperwork there."

"In the Hypogeum? In Malta?" Ginger asked, still unsure if she was understanding Sarah correctly.

"Yes. That's where the Sleeping Lady was found." Sarah studied the text again. "Paul must have chosen the location because of how difficult it would be to pinpoint without Father Magri's notes. I don't think he expected to die and leave me as the key to the puzzle though. He probably thought he was being terribly clever." She breathed out, her eyes red-rimmed. "Stupid man."

"Then you can find the location where this artifact was found?" Ginger was too worried about Noah to be relieved.

"I think so. But I can't be certain until I go into the Hypogeum." Sarah lowered her gaze, staring at the text again. "But you realize that if I tell Osborne the location to the concession, he's going to want to take me with him to Malta. He might not release Noah at all. And your family—and I—will lose everything. Without that paperwork, what hope can we have of proving ownership of the concession or the Arab Anglo Oil Company?"

Ginger's pulse was slow. What Sarah said was true. "What choice do I have? Go to the authorities? The army? If I involve anyone official, Noah will be arrested." Ginger felt sick. "I have to save my husband."

"You're certain he's worth it? We may all die trying to save him. And I've learned the hard way that there aren't many men worth dying for." Sarah gave her a grim look.

*Oh.* That's where this was coming from.

A defensive feeling rose in her. Sarah didn't love Noah like she did. She had no reason to sacrifice her life or safety for him.

But this wasn't about Noah.

*This is about Paul.*

Ginger took the excavation notebook from Sarah's hands and held hers tightly. They hadn't had a long time to form a friendship. But despite not knowing each other well, Ginger could see the black and blue of Sarah's battered heart. "I know it's not much, but they had captured Paul for a couple months, Sarah. They probably found him with this cipher. And, if I'm honest, they probably tortured him."

A sob broke from Sarah and she shook, her fingers tightening around Ginger's.

"He was a terrible husband. He didn't deserve you. But he loved you enough to protect you until the end. They never got him to tell them about his name, or what this damned cipher meant, or how to get to the only thing he'd left you with. He gave them the name Freddy Mortimer, a name that led them back to Olivia Hendricks. But he loved you so much that he probably died instead of giving them anything that could lead them to you."

Sarah pulled back, then wiped her eyes. "We both need sleep, don't we?" She laughed at herself humorlessly. "Thank you, Ginger. That's a kind way of thinking about it."

Rising from her seat, Ginger went to the window of the hotel room. The moon had already risen. They were running out of time. She'd promised to return with that damned oil concession—the oil concession that the government would have stolen from her regardless. Sarah was wrong about that. No matter what, it never would have been theirs. Her government would go to any extreme to have oil.

She set her fingertips on the cool glass, leaning closer to it.

*All* governments seemed to be willing to go to extremes to have oil, though, didn't they? Including the Germans and the Turks.

She turned and put her hands behind her back. "Stephen can't get his hands on that paperwork, Sarah."

Sarah ducked her chin. "Didn't you just say that you didn't have a choice? That you had to do it to save your husband?"

"Yes, but Stephen was, and I'm certain he continues to be, a German spy. Whatever he's been doing, he's desperate to get his hands on this paperwork. What if it's to help the Germans and the Turks?"

"But oil hasn't been discovered at the concession site, has it? Paul and your father didn't even begin an exploration for it." Sarah searched Ginger's eyes. "At least that I know of."

A strange feeling, like a mixture of excitement and dread, grew in her. "But we don't know. We don't know how far my father got with it all. And it wouldn't take Stephen long to mobilize the exploration, at any rate. He has the money for it. What he needed was the freedom, which he took back by framing Noah for his own crimes."

"And the concession paperwork, of course."

Ginger stepped away. "You see?" Her throat felt thicker. "Stephen can never get his hands on that paperwork. However he plans to do it, the details don't really matter. I'm sure he can't mean this as a help to the British. This is about so much more than you and me and the potential money to be made."

Sarah rose to her feet. "Well, we're two intelligent women. I say we outsmart these men, how about you?"

*Intelligent women.*

*"A woman in Intelligence,"* Dr. Radford had said when she met Ginger.

Ginger had laughed at the thought of herself as being a woman in Intelligence.

Lord Helton had told her she'd interfered and made her feel as though she didn't belong in this world of men.

She'd blamed herself for everything that had happened in the spring, lived with the guilt, and been crippled by it.

*No more.*

She turned to Sarah. "What weapons do we have?"

Sarah came over to her and sat on the floor. She upended her rucksack, and a few pistols tumbled out, along with a bandolier of ammunition. Beside them a replica of an Egyptian statuette landed with a loud *thunk*. Smirking, Sarah picked up the statuette. "Anubis, how did you get in there?"

Ginger arched a brow at Sarah's affectionate tone. "Friend of yours?"

Chuckling, Sarah shrugged. "I seem to have a hundred of these things floating around my house."

It reminded Ginger of the bracelet she'd found in her father's study. She'd stashed the bracelet in her trunk, which now sat in Alastair's house. Focusing back at the task at hand, Ginger found the bag Noah had brought full of weapons: a pair of rifles, two bandoliers of ammunition, a pistol … and the grenades he had taken from Sarah's house.

She lifted a grenade, rolling her fingertips over the deep

grooves of the surface. They reminded her of Private Emerson and nursing and Alexandria. That time seemed so long ago.

What was it Emerson had said?

"*. . . the hand bombs. They have a pin you pull at the top. But you can continue to hold them so long as you grip the lever on the side.*"

Ginger glanced from the hand grenade to the statuette of Anubis, her eyes widening.

"I have an idea."

## CHAPTER FORTY

Noah woke with a start. He'd dozed off, despite his best efforts. Two nights of the barest minimum of sleep had been more than he could manage.

His arms ached. Osborne had tied his arms behind his back, binding his wrists tightly. At this angle, the circulation to his shoulders was constricted, numbing his fingers. He wiggled his fingertips, and they scraped the stone wall behind him. The wall had provided him a place to sag against.

He tried to gather his thoughts and get his bearings. Osborne had brought him inside the Greater Vaults of the Serapeum, a long underground corridor of enormous curved ceilings and vaults containing smooth granite sarcophagi. The ancient Egyptians had built this as a necropolis for their sacred bulls, and the sight of it was breathtaking.

He didn't know what time it was. Even at midday, the chambers had to be lit with candlelight: without them, they'd be left in pitch darkness.

Though Noah had been here before, he would have appreciated the Serapeum's spectacular architecture, if not for

Peter Osborne, who sat across from him. A pistol sat lazily on his lap, pointed at Noah. They appeared to be otherwise alone.

Osborne watched him thoughtfully. "You were asleep for a few minutes that time."

Noah shifted, shooting pains traveling down his legs from sitting in one position for so long. "How clumsy of me." He didn't mean to sound as though he was mocking Osborne, but he couldn't quite help it either. The dry, unaffected tone of voice that he'd gotten accustomed to using in situations like these would only enrage Osborne further. Given his position in government, Osborne's inability to keep a stiff upper lip about his emotions either displayed a man who teetered on the edge or who lacked control. Both could prove dangerous when provoked.

Osborne pulled a coiled, polished black rope from his rucksack. Noah blinked at it. *No, not a rope. A whip.* "Do you know what this is?"

Noah studied the object. "A kurbash."

A wicked gleam came to Osborne's eyes. "Good."

The kurbash wasn't any ordinary whip. The weapon was made of hippopotamus hide, used as a symbol of Ottoman oppression over Egyptian slaves for centuries and recently outlawed in Egypt because of British objections. Osborne caressed the braided leather base. No doubt he intended to use the damn thing on Noah.

"I'm curious. Why you? Fisher has more than enough reason to want to see me dead himself. Wouldn't he rather see it done than send a lackey? Or you could have returned me to the military. Made a public spectacle of my death and brought yourself glory." Noah was parched, his lips cracking, but he wasn't about to ask Osborne for water.

"Oh, dear fellow, don't worry. I won't kill you." The tips of

Osborne's teeth showed as he sneered. "Not on purpose, at any rate."

Just torture him, then. Noah's jaw clenched at the thought. Noah's death was too merciful for Stephen. Probably for Osborne too. But he was certain Osborne had no intention of letting him go.

"Won't Fisher be angry that you haven't turned me over to him?"

Osborne shrugged. "I will. Eventually. But I made a deal with Fisher. If I helped him, then I got you. I don't need his permission to do what I want with you."

Osborne's vitriol toward Noah was dumbfounding. They must have crossed paths before. Noah stared him down. "I have no memory of you."

Osborne's cheeks reddened. "No, you wouldn't, would you? I was nothing to you when we met. At least that was what you said to me. Your precise words were 'you don't matter.'"

*You don't matter.* Noah leaned his head back against the wall, racking his memory. A man like Osborne, who acted from a place of revenge, could often be more dangerous than a man who simply knew his soul to be black. But what could Noah have done?

The answer had to be in Kut. Osborne had indicated as much.

Noah had been there twice. Once with the delegation sent to offer a bribe to General Pasha, and before then, when he'd visited the commanding officers during the height of the siege, tried to advise them against their mad actions. He'd barely escaped with his life going in and out of the besieged city. He'd snuck one of his fellow intelligence mates out of the city, and there had been an officer clinging to his leg, weeping, begging to come with him.

Noah lifted his gaze to Osborne's face. *Could it be?*

The memory of the man's face was faint in his mind, but the grey eyes … they had once been filled with desperation. The back of Noah's throat itched. "It was you—you who grabbed me as I tried to leave."

Osborne leveled his chin. "You punched me instead. Left me in a pile of excrement."

Any remorse Noah may have felt for his actions would have evaporated because of Osborne's threats. Though there wasn't much to feel sorry for. "You wanted to abandon your men. And you were making so much noise and were so unfit. You would have caused not only my capture and death but the death of my companion. I had no choice but to leave you."

With a grunt, Osborne rose to his feet, pistol in one hand, kurbash in the other. He stalked closer to Noah. "Yes. And I was left instead to watch those men die of starvation. To see us abandoned by the weak, pathetic representatives of the insipid Crown. To march across the deserts at the end of a whip." Osborne brushed the coiled whip against Noah's cheek.

Noah stiffened.

*And Osborne blames me.*

"I imagined you out there, drinking your tea and getting fat while I wasted away on mule meat and stale biscuits so hard that when the Turkish officers gave them to us, almost a hundred men died overnight from eating them." Osborne leaned down, sniffing Noah's hair, the barrel of the gun digging into Noah's neck. The action was strange and intimate, igniting his nerves. Osborne squatted to Noah's eye level.

"And after rotting away in prison for a year, whom should I meet but a German officer who hated you as much as I do."

*Fisher.*

"You met Fisher after he escaped to the German side last May?"

"Fate, it seems, brought us together. When the British

wanted to arrange a prisoner exchange, Fisher arranged to have me be part of it. And it was easy from there. I came back a hero." He set the kurbash down, then tugged at the laces of Noah's boots.

Noah pulled his feet back reflexively. "What are you doing?"

Without answering, Osborne pulled off one boot, then the other. "Have you ever felt the kiss of the kurbash, Benson? It's quite a thing to watch. To see the very life beaten from a man. Observe them reduced from a living, fully formed being to a bloody lump of clay."

As Osborne exposed Noah's bare feet to the air, he couldn't help the gooseflesh that broke out on his arms, the shiver that ran down his spine. Whatever Osborne had planned, he imagined it involved a maximum amount of pain. "If I'm found that way tonight, you won't have much leverage to convince Lady Virginia or Mrs. Hanover to negotiate with you. Give you those precious concession papers."

Though he'd hated to tell Osborne about Ginger's offer, he hadn't had much choice. Osborne needed a reason to keep him alive. His attempt to capture Sarah had shown just how badly he, or Stephen, wanted the concession paperwork.

He hoped Ginger would stay away, even if he knew she wouldn't.

Maybe this was what Lord Helton meant. About love driving people to do the irrational.

"Don't worry. Your injuries won't be visible. Besides which, if you think those women will have much room for negotiation this evening, you're underestimating me. There's only one way in here." Osborne went back to his bag and grabbed rope. Kneeling once again before Noah, he tied Noah's ankles together. He waved the pistol at Noah. "Now, onto your stomach."

A sense of caution pounded through his body as Noah did

what Osborne asked. He was thoroughly depleted, his brain exhausted. "What about the women?" Noah asked, closing his eyes. He doubted Osborne intended to let him live. "What will become of them?"

Osborne sneered. "Fisher wants your whore unharmed. She's an English rose—spoilt, I'll admit. There's nothing more reprehensible than women who choose to throw themselves at your kind. How Fisher could still want to marry her after you seduced her is beyond my comprehension, but who am I to deny him his chosen wife?"

The thought of Stephen near Ginger made him ill. Noah's diaphragm ached as he struggled to breathe. Osborne bent his knees back and used another rope to bind his legs in that position by attaching the rope to his bound hands—a hog-tie position.

Osborne had stopped speaking to him and removed his uniform jacket. Noah turned his cheek, breathing into the dust. A rock poked into his cheek. His fingers were already numb with the strain of being tied behind his back.

Osborne unrolled the kurbash. "There was a German officer in one camp I was in. He introduced me to this method of discipline." Before Noah could imagine what that might mean, Osborne struck Noah with the whip, hard, across the soles of his feet.

Pain exploded through Noah, his body jerking with the limited motion allowed by his position. Noah grunted, squeezing his eyes shut. He'd experienced various beatings, been shot, broken bones.

Nothing had ever hurt so much.

Spots flashed in his eyes as the whip cut through the air again, whistling before it snapped once more against his feet.

The agony of it was blinding, and a scream curled in his throat and hung in his mouth. He didn't want to give Osborne the satisfaction of hearing him cry out. Of seeing him broken. With his chest to the ground, he felt suffocated, dizzy.

Another strike.

*Good God ... how will I survive this?* He focused on the ground beside him. It wasn't enough to distract from the torment, the searing pain that ripped up his nerves.

*Whistle ... snap.*

The rhythm of the whip was like a song, a cadence to the torture. He prayed, letting his mind drop further inward, away from Osborne's teeth bared in concentration. Away from the kurbash.

In the throes of agony, Noah thought of Neal.

His brother had been a few years younger than him. A better person in every way. Kinder. More generous. Beloved by everyone.

They'd fought as boys, as all brothers did. Competed while their tutor watched over their shoulders.

And Noah had taken a fair share of punishments on Neal's behalf.

A sharper blow brought him out of the train of thought, as though Osborne was enraged that his blows hadn't caused Noah to cry out. Noah held his breath, grinding his teeth so hard that he thought they would break.

He tried to imagine Neal as he might look like now.

They'd looked the same, really. Noah was taller and Neal fairer.

The whip cracked again, the pain tearing through him like a knife. Any hope that he had that subsequent blows would grow less painful had disappeared. They only got worse.

*"Noah! Help me!"* The image he'd conjured of Neal dissolved in his mind's eye, the flesh flaying and falling away from his handsome face, revealing a skeleton below the skin and muscle.

Bones in a grave in Gallipoli.

"Neal!" Noah's hands uncurled from fists, reaching for the brother that wasn't there.

The pain from his feet felt like molten lava flowing through his blood, thick and fiery.

*"I'm going after him."* Noah was a man possessed with a singular mission, all his other tasks be damned. Neal was missing. He would find him and bring him home.

Another strike. His breath was stolen away once more, his mind reeling with the memories of a few years earlier.

*"A man like you is a weapon, Benson."* Lord Helton's voice rang in his mind. *"Your brother is dead. I confirmed it this morning. And you're better off for it. The more attachments you have, the less effective a weapon you become. And make no mistake—you're a weapon. Mine."*

A knife sawed through the rope holding his feet upright. Noah blinked, barely registering his boots as Osborne threw them into the dirt beside his face. "Sit up. Put them back on."

Osborne's face was unusually blank. Noah gave an involuntary shudder, rolling to his side. His entire body felt unsteady as he attempted to sit. Whatever willpower he'd used to keep himself from showing a vocal reaction to the pain was gone. His hands shook violently as he tried to pull the boots back onto his swollen, bloodied feet. They were a strange shade of red and black, and the mere act of putting the shoes on was another punishment.

After Noah had managed the task, Osborne approached him. "Stand up. We have a short walk ahead of us, further into the tombs. You'd better hope your bitch returns tonight."

Noah struggled to his hands and knees. His stomach was too weak—vomit spewed from his mouth before he could stop it, onto Osborne's shoes.

Osborne leapt back, disgust on his face and Noah felt a

twinge of satisfaction. He wiped his mouth with the back of his hand, but the scene around him grew blurry.

* * *

When Noah woke, he didn't know where he was. He had been moved and lay slumped against hard, flat stone. His arms had been tied behind his back once again.

He coughed, his mouth so dry that his lips stuck together. His feet throbbed. He appeared to be in another underground chamber. Oil lamps lit the dark space, throwing an eerie glow into the ancient tomb.

The structure appeared only partially excavated, but the stone pathways were well cut. Wooden beams had been brought into the site of excavation, used to bolster the sides of the tunnel.

Footsteps approached. Osborne came into view, followed by three other men. He stopped short when he saw Noah. "You're awake." He came up behind Noah and grabbed his wrists. "I didn't intend to put you to sleep, but perhaps I chose the wrong punishment."

Noah held back a smile. At least he hadn't given Osborne the satisfaction of knowing how much the whipping with the kurbash had hurt him.

"I've thought of another punishment for you, Benson. Inspired by the Aleaqrab itself." He tossed the end of a rope over one of the wooden beams near the tall ceiling, and it fell to the other side. "The Palestinian hanging technique—or scorpion position. Name's a befitting punishment for you. Once Lady Virginia arrives, one pull of this rope and you'll know pain. Pain you won't ever forget."

Noah tensed, his eyes going to the rope. He knew the torture technique Osborne referred to and had the misfortune of seeing it done before. When Noah had witnessed it, the man who'd received it as punishment had lasted thirty minutes before death. Thirty agonizing minutes of being hung with his arms behind his back and over his head, shoulders dislocated.

The man's screams had haunted Noah for days.

The Strappado.

## CHAPTER FORTY-ONE

Riding beside Sarah in the dark, Ginger listened to the soft crunch of the camels striding through the desert. They'd procured the animals with the help of the owner at the hotel, preferring to leave the exhausted horses at the stable there rather than force them to make another long trip. The owner didn't ask questions—he was getting handsomely paid—and the two women had started toward the Serapeum.

Had Noah given Osborne her message about returning tonight?

She prayed that he had. Noah was stubborn, and he had to know the odds were stacked against them. How else would he survive this?

The gun at Ginger's waistband weighed heavily.

As they drew closer to the necropolis, sickness curdled in Ginger's throat. Her exhaustion made her feel sluggish, but she had to press forward. She had dealt with less sleep than this before.

They'd been forced to leave Jack, who was still fading in and out of consciousness, though his fever had improved remarkably.

Near the Serapeum, Sarah gave Ginger a sidelong glance. "Are you ready?" They dismounted the camels, then found a stump of a pillar to tie them to. From there, they approached the entrance to the Serapeum, a large doorway that would lead them underground.

Ginger sucked in a breath. She reached into her medical bag slung over one shoulder. Her fingers brushed against the cold metal.

The entrance seemed unremarkable, as though they were heading into a cellar. Sarah had explained that, like so many archeological discoveries, the locals had paid little attention to the treasure beneath their feet until a French archeologist had blasted through with dynamite, causing irreversible damage to the site.

A few men waited by building the entrance, along with Osborne. Their faces were in shadow, lit only by the glow of an oil lamp held by a man further inside.

Ginger's heart beat faster. Noah had given Osborne her message, it seemed.

*Please be alive, Noah.*

Osborne stepped out toward them. "Both hands where I can see them, Lady Virginia. I'll have to take those pistols, of course."

Ginger's hand tightened, fisting around the hand grenade in her medical bag. She pulled it out and lifted her chin. As she leveled her gaze with Osborne, his eyes widened.

She slipped her finger into the ring and pulled the pin, the metal of the ring tugging into the back of her pointer finger as she pulled.

Osborne's men dropped back, one covering his head.

The slightest hint of a smile touched Sarah's lips.

Ginger's hand was tight around the grenade, holding down the lever. She drew closer to him. Somehow her hand remained steady, despite the pounding of her heart in her ears. "I don't trust you, Osborne. So we've made our own plans. We're going inside, and once Noah Benson is released safely we will give you the concession paperwork. Shoot Sarah and you won't get your paperwork. Shoot me and this grenade will fall with me. We'll all die."

Osborne stepped toward her, and she held her hand up. "Or I could throw this at you and your men now, if you'd like."

"Do that and you risk trapping your lover underground."

He was right. But digging Noah out was a possibility she'd had to consider when they'd come up with this mad plan. "As long as it kills you, I'll take that chance."

"And Mrs. Hanover? How do you know I won't shoot her?"

Ginger shrugged. "Shoot her and you won't get the concession papers. Jack Darby remembered the cipher you gave her and let her have a try with it. As it turns out, she's the only one who knows how to find the papers. And they're right here in the Serapeum."

Osborne's eyes narrowed. At last, he nodded. As he turned toward his frightened men, the yellow lamp light gave her a glimpse of the redness on his face.

*He's furious.*

She held back a smile.

Osborne's men shifted nervously. Osborne barked an order at them, then led them inside the ancient temple.

The cool temperatures of the underground structure in the desert did little to stop Ginger's shivers. The lever of the grenade dug into her hand, a hard-edged reminder of how little lay between her and certain death. A slight slip of her hand would cause detonation. In a tunnel like this, the fragmentation and explosion would kill them all.

Their footsteps echoed, but with only the men's torches for light, she couldn't see far into the carved walkways of stone. Sarah had explained that archeologists believed the structure had been intended by the Apis cult as a burial place, but that all the tombs had been empty.

While normally that would fascinate Ginger, right now she found it terrifying. They were surrounded by death.

Deep in the labyrinth, the reverberation of their footsteps filled the chambers. Bile tinged her throat as Noah came into view. Ginger's heart lurched.

He was alive. His hands were tied behind his back, attached to a rope that had been thrown over and tied to a large wooden beam, forcing his arms up behind his back—at an uncomfortable angle.

*Thank God he's alive.*

She wanted to run to him, free him from the ropes. The grenade in her hand, the only thing keeping her safe, felt more slippery than ever.

Osborne had forced him to step onto three rickety wooden crates, and Noah appeared to be completely still. What would happen if he fell off those crates?

Ginger's eyes followed the rope behind his head.

A fall would mean Noah's arms would go over his head —backward.

She let out a choked cry. His shoulders would dislocate, the tendons tear. Her palms ached intensely. "Let him go." Her voice sounded hoarse from the strain.

Osborne came out of the shadows. "Get the concession first. Once you have Benson, I have no assurance that you'll give it to me."

"I will." Ginger's voice shook. She met Noah's eyes. His pupils were large in the dim light, his lids unblinking. Having him so close by but unable to reach him or help him made her feel weak.

Then he saw the grenade in her hand. His brows furrowed, sudden understanding dawning in his eyes.

With a callous shrug, Osborne inspected her. "Call me a skeptic. You know what a kick to those crates will do to Benson. Just because you may have the advantage now, it doesn't mean I'll leave him unharmed if you don't keep your side of the agreement. Let's take care of first things first, Lady Virginia. Mrs. Hanover gets the concession, then I release Benson."

Sarah released a slow, tense breath beside her. "I need a torch."

Osborne handed one to Sarah. She drifted it around the space, trying to find her way. She directed the light down a path. "That way."

"I'm going," Osborne said. "I don't trust either of you."

"You stay here." Ginger's voice was calm and in control. Osborne couldn't know how sweat had broken out on her back, or how her hand ached from gripping the grenade. "But you can send one of your men if you're worried."

Osborne's hands clenched. "Only if she gives me any weapons she has."

Ginger and Sarah's eyes met. Would Sarah feel safe walking alone with one of Osborne's men and no way to protect herself?

Sarah seemed to understand Ginger's questioning look. She pulled her gun out of its holster, then turned over a knife. Osborne smirked. "Don't think of trying to be heroic, Mrs. Hanover. My men are under strict orders. If they suspect even the slightest betrayal, they will put a bullet in Benson's head."

"And then Ginger will throw the grenade," Sarah remarked dryly, clearly unimpressed by Osborne's threats. He scowled at Sarah and Ginger felt a flare of pride at her poise.

Sarah went down a stone path. The longer Ginger held the

grenade, the more she wanted to shift it in her hand, relieve the pressure of the lever pushing into her palm. The ring attached to the pin remained on her other forefinger, and she squeezed the pin into her fist.

*Please hurry, Sarah.*

After a few minutes, Sarah returned, her face troubled.

"Well?" Osborne stepped toward her. "Where is it? Did you find it?"

"I found this." Sarah showed him a small broken Egyptian figurine. "In a crevice right where the cipher said to look." She muttered a swear word and stared at it in confusion.

Ginger bit the insides of her cheeks to keep her expression even. Sarah was so convincing that she nearly believed her.

Osborne snatched the figurine. "This is all you found?" He lifted the figurine toward Sarah. "What is this?" His voice was a snarl of anger.

"It appears to be another clue." A shadow crossed Sarah's face. "Two summers ago, Paul and I worked at an excavation near the Pyramid of Djoser, just south of here. The statue of Ramesses II was discovered there at the Great Temple of Ptah, broken in six pieces over a hundred years ago. This appears to be just the head of the statue." Her eyes glimmered. "My guess is that Paul hid the paperwork for the concession under the head of the statue in Memphis."

Ginger held her breath. *Would Osborne believe it?* She didn't dare look at Noah for fear that her reactions would be less controlled if she did.

A few beats passed. Osborne's men had steadily moved back while they'd been speaking, more than likely afraid of the grenade.

Sweat beaded on Peter Osborne's tired, dusty face. "Then you're telling me it's not here?"

"We came for another clue, apparently. Archeologists have an interesting sense of humor." Sarah smiled.

Ginger held her breath, counting the moments as comprehension dawned on Osborne's face. He scowled. "If I'm going to Memphis, you're coming with me, Mrs. Hanover."

"That wasn't our deal, Mr. Osborne." Ginger glared. How her hand had remained steady on the grenade this whole time, she wasn't sure. The aching in her hand had turned to a cramp.

"You don't believe I have the power in this situation, Lady Virginia. And that's unfortunate." Osborne stalked up to Noah, placed his foot on top of one crate, then kicked it out from under Noah's feet.

Ginger gasped, stretching her free hand toward him.

Noah fell about a foot, his feet barely finding the next crate, which swayed precariously. Osborne's men, panicked at Ginger's sudden movement, fled. Sarah jolted, then stopped as Osborne pointed a gun at her.

The grenade, which had felt like safety, now kept Ginger from reaching for the gun at her own waist.

Noah's arms had risen, tied behind him, just slightly above his head. His face strained, the position obviously already painful. Men rarely had the flexibility for that sort of movement. A further fall would do permanent damage to his arms.

"Now, when I kick out this next crate, the pain Colonel Benson will feel will be excruciating. His screams will fill these caves." Osborne was sweating now, a sheen across his forehead. Was he worried? "You can't save them both, Lady Virginia. Put the pin back in the grenade. Your hand has started to shake. You can't hold it much longer, can you? But with your hands free, you can try to help him once I flee with Mrs. Hanover."

"Don't listen to him, Ginger. He'll shoot you as soon as he has the opportunity." Noah's voice was tight, and he wheezed.

His arms shook, the movement causing the crates beneath him to quiver and wobble.

*Hold steady. Think.* Despite the tightness of her chest, she managed a suffocated breath. He had to be bluffing.

Ginger gave Osborne a contemptuous glare. "No."

"No?" Osborne's eyes bulged.

She shook her head slowly. "Because I don't believe you'll shoot Mrs. Hanover. We lied to you. That statue? It's not Ramesses II. You underestimated us, Mr. Osborne. And you still don't know where that concession paperwork is. Only she does. Shoot her, and you will never find it." She lifted the grenade. "Your men have abandoned you. And you still can't kill me because you'll die if you do. You've lost."

Osborne blinked at her, his face darkening to a deep shade of red.

Stunned silence counted the seconds.

Then, with a yell, Osborne kicked the rest of the crates away. Sarah threw herself at Noah's legs, catching them as he fell.

Osborne fled.

"Ginger, help me!" Sarah cried out. Her face was strained, blood vessels in her forehead bulging as she struggled to keep Noah from falling further.

Time seemed to slow as Ginger lifted her gaze at the darkened tunnel. Would Osborne come back? If she put the grenade down, he could overpower her, though she still had her gun.

If she didn't put the grenade down, she couldn't help Sarah.

Her left hand shook violently, both from the strain of holding the grenade and from the terror clawing at her as she tried to replace the pin.

One try—the pin slipped past the hole clumsily, metal scraping against metal.

Another attempt. The scraping of the head of the pin sounded like mockery.

*Steady.*

She pictured herself suturing a patient in a field, bombs screaming nearby.

*Steady now.*

The pin was safely in. Ginger thrust the grenade back into her bag, then turned toward Sarah.

The crates had broken with Osborne's kick and lay smashed against a stone wall. Diving beside Sarah, Ginger wrapped her arms around Noah's legs, helping Sarah support his weight as he dangled.

"Cut the rope," Noah managed, writhing with pain. The tendons in his neck were taut, stretched as he ground his teeth, jaw clenched.

"I have a knife under my pant leg," Sarah said to Ginger. "If I let go, can you hold him long enough for me to cut the rope?"

Ginger shook her head. There wasn't any way she could hold Noah alone. She didn't know how Sarah had managed it for so long. "Noah, I'm going to crouch underneath you. Put your feet on my shoulders."

Noah couldn't argue with her. Ginger stooped beneath him, and Sarah helped guide his feet to her shoulders. As Sarah released him, his weight crushed the tops of her shoulders, bruising her, digging deeply. She gritted her teeth, crying out despite her best efforts.

She could do this. She could hold him.

She would hold him until Sarah cut the rope.

Sarah was behind her, where Ginger couldn't see. She heard the sawing of the blade against the rope and she prayed.

*Hurry, Sarah, please hurry.*

She could do this.

The pain in her shoulders was blinding. She struggled for breath, trying to concentrate, seconds turning to minutes.

Noah breathed with equal strain.

She had to do this for him.

"I'm nearly there," Sarah called out. "When I get to three, let him go, Ginger. Or he'll fall on top of you. One ... two ... *three!*"

Ginger dove out from under Noah. He fell, free of the rope, landing on her legs and pinning her down. Her hips slammed into the stone, bruising painfully, and she cried out, gasping.

But he was free.

Noah rolled off her, and she crawled to him where he lay, his chest heaving. His face was streaked with sweat and grime. His body shook, and she kissed his lips gently. "Thank God," she whispered, unable to hold the tears back now.

Sarah helped Noah cut the rope from his wrists. He sat, stretching his shoulders, his face marked with pain. He took Ginger's face in his hands, then kissed her again. "I love you," he said.

She returned his kiss, her heart still constricted by the fear she'd had for him. He was safe. *He's safe.*

A gunshot rang out in the distance and they all looked up.

*Osborne?*

Ginger handed her gun to Noah. Even if his arms hurt, he was still likely to be a better shot than her. "What just happened?" Noah managed, his voice tight.

"We'll explain the whole thing later." Sarah grinned. "But, really, it was your wife who thought up the entire plan."

Ginger felt too numb with the events she'd witnessed to feel any pleasure in the plan having worked. She never wanted to see Noah like that again. She gave him a wan smile. "It wasn't the best plan."

"Don't be modest. As you Brits say—it was 'bloody' brilliant." Sarah winked, then lifted an oil lamp as footsteps approached.

Ginger reached into her bag for the grenade again, trying to prepare herself for another confrontation.

As a figure came closer, her eyes widened. *Jack.*

Jack held a gun. "Am I late?" His voice was hoarse, and he still looked as sick as when they'd left him. He scratched his fingertips over his chest. "I … uh … killed Osborne. Near the entrance. You can thank me later." As though feeling a sudden wave of malaise, he reached out blindly toward the stone wall beside him, steadying himself.

Ginger's mouth dropped open. She exchanged an astonished look with Noah.

She didn't know what shocked her more: the news he had killed Osborne or the fact that he was here.

She rose to her feet, and unexpected laughter bubbled up and choked her throat. Tears stung her eyes.

Osborne could never threaten them again.

"Jack Darby, I've never been happier to see you in my life."

## CHAPTER FORTY-TWO
### VALLETTA, MALTA

"You have that distracted look in your eye again," Ginger said as she leaned into Noah's arm at the café. They sat on an open square with Jack and Sarah in Valletta, drinking tea and coffee with sandwiches and pastizzi—Maltese pastry filled with cheese.

To an outside observer, the group would probably have looked relaxed, like tourists enjoying the perfect weather. The city emerged from the crystal sea like a giant sandcastle perched on a cliff. The sandstone carried over to the buildings that rose on each side of the narrow streets. A perfect place for a holiday.

But Ginger was close enough that Noah was certain she felt his tension and saw his concern. He'd feel better once they'd recovered the concession paperwork from the Hypogeum of Ħal Saflieni. They'd stopped for food after disembarking from their ship just a couple of hours earlier—it was irrational to think anything could happen to the paperwork in the meantime.

"I'm fine." He gave her a patient smile. She wanted to ask more than she did, that much was obvious to him. But he appreciated her understanding how much he didn't want to discuss the darkness of his thoughts.

Osborne had awoken something in him. A dark shadow that crossed through his mind. He rarely felt as calm as he acted. Every time he went out, he examined his surroundings for potential threats.

The beggar on the corner.

A woman pushing a baby's pram.

Two soldiers playing cards and smoking a few tables down.

Noah scooted his chair closer to Ginger's, his knee brushing against hers. At least he was free to love her in public now. And the value of that benefit wasn't lost on him.

Across from them, Jack stared at him a beat too long, then shook his head. "Disgusting. Stop dangling your love in front of those of us less lucky at it." He winked at Sarah. "Unless you're interested in strolling arm in arm with me to see the view."

Days of quinine treatment had Jack on his feet once again, but the jaundice hadn't completely faded from his skin. Even though Sarah claimed she wanted to come to Malta to see about getting the concession paperwork, Noah wondered if Sarah had come, in part, because Jack was coming. Sarah had been at his side since they'd rescued him at Saqqara.

Sarah laughed. "No, but I'm interested in grabbing a few things from the market before we make our way to the Hypogeum. Do you want to go with me, Ginger?"

Ginger squeezed Noah's hand. "Can I have some money?"

Noah pulled out a few bills. "Enjoy. But don't take long. The man we hired to take us to the Hypogeum should be here in twenty minutes."

She pressed a kiss to his cheek, then rose. "We'll be back soon."

As Noah watched Ginger and Sarah disappear around the

corner, he straightened under the weight of Jack's gaze. "What?" He sipped his coffee.

"What do you think the chances are of Sarah being an American spy?"

Trust Jack to have noticed. "I'd say about a hundred and ten percent." Noah had suspected it immediately. "She made a mistake. Claimed she'd met me with you in Aswan. She may have been testing me, to see what I knew. Then she casually showed me her collection of hand grenades and dynamite."

"You think her husband was too?"

"Most likely." Noah paused as the waiter came by and poured another cup of coffee. "That's not to say I don't believe her husband's business dealings with Lord Braddock weren't legitimate. God knows how many archeologists they have drafted into Intelligence. I don't think she was expecting to get pulled into any of this."

Jack shifted back into his seat. "But you think she'll probably tell the US government about the concession and paperwork. Maybe even try to take them?"

"I think …" The distant blues and whites of the harbor were dazzlingly bright, and Noah squinted. "I think I'm not willing to trust anyone with the ease I used to. Save for you and Ginger. And maybe Alastair. He gave me the documents to get me this far, at any rate."

"The question is, have you told Ginger your suspicions about Sarah?" Jack smirked, then watched as the waiter poured steaming black coffee from a carafe into his cup.

"She needs a friend." Noah adjusted the hat on his head. "What difference does it make? Planting seeds of doubt about her won't help. We'll find out soon enough what her interest in that oil concession is."

Jack's expression sobered. "Just be careful. I don't know a lot about women, but I know Red won't like it if she finds out you lied to her."

Noah sighed. He hated to add anything to the list of things that Ginger might learn of later and be angry about. But it was also the safest decision for all involved, including Sarah, if she really was a spy. The Americans were their allies, after all. "I know. But right now Sarah Hanover is barely a concern of mine. I must decide how I'm going to survive the next few weeks. The money I brought with me won't last forever."

"You know I'll loan you some." With a shake of his head, Jack said, "Just don't be tempted to go back to Cairo. Go … live in America. Make up a new name, a new life. Take Red with you. She'll go with you anywhere." Jack clasped his hands together. "Love like that, that's luck. You don't need anything else."

"I don't. And maybe we can go to America until the war is over." Noah stared in the direction Ginger had gone. "But Ginger has lost everything because of me, including her family. The day will come when she wants to make things right with them. And I worry if I deny her that, she'll always look back at our marriage with regret."

Jack sucked a breath in between his teeth. "You should have shot Stephen in the desert when you had a chance."

Noah let out a sardonic laugh. "And that's what *I* have to regret." Noah held his gaze. "I'll be fine, Jack. Just focus on getting your health back for now. And enjoy your time with Sarah. She may not be Kit, but I think she'd make you happy." The great love of Jack's life wasn't a name he dared to mention often. But Jack seemed to take it in stride.

"People like Sarah and me—we don't get to pick that sort of happy. But I think we'll enjoy our time together regardless." Jack's eyes gleamed. "You're the lucky son of a bitch."

Noah sat back in his chair, the weight of his discussion with Jack hanging over him.

Jack couldn't know the darkness of his thoughts, the blackness his soul had felt recently. And Noah wouldn't tell him, either. Even Jack couldn't help him there.

Then Noah thought of the woman who'd literally borne his weight on her shoulders, to save him, to keep him safe.

A smile curled Noah's lips. "I can't argue with that."

* * *

AT THE ENTRANCE to the Hypogeum, they disembarked, and Jack paid the driver extra to wait for them to return. Ginger turned toward the entrance, which seemed almost unremarkable compared to the structures she'd grown accustomed to seeing in Egypt. The way to the Hypogeum was marked with wooden signs, and a few other tourists milled about in the area.

"Will we be able to access the area where Paul left the paperwork?" Ginger asked Sarah. There were a few guards posted, but nothing looked very official.

Sarah shrugged. "I don't know. But I'm sure we can come up with something if not."

They stepped through a roughly hewn entrance cut into stone. It revealed another doorway beyond that, with curved stone ceilings and remarkably straight pylons on either side of the open doorway. Ginger arched a brow at Jack. "This reminds me a bit of the Serapeum."

"I didn't choose that by accident, Red. When I guessed the cipher would lead here, I decided I'd rather not be stuck in Malta. Of course, I assumed my best friend was trying to break me out of prison." He gave Noah a teasing smirk.

The stone pathways were straight and flat, resembling a prehistoric temple of squared archways and chambers. Swirls in red ochre decorated some walls, and skeletal remains jutted out amongst the stones.

"I had every intention of going back for you right away," Noah said to Jack.

"But you didn't." Jack raised both hands with a shrug.

"Keep your voice down," Ginger hissed, even though she noticed the twitch in Noah's smile. "You've forgotten how to behave in public, Lieutenant Darby."

"I haven't forgotten anything, Red." Jack's eyes shot to Noah. "Least of all how I rotted in a prison trying decipher Greek codes while dying of malaria while my friend was busy getting married and rescuing some other girl."

The sarcastic tease was in form for Jack, but Ginger winced inwardly. Didn't he know how guilty Noah felt about that? She'd have to tell him later, if not.

"Coptic," Sarah corrected with a lift of her brow.

"Whatever. It's all Greek. You're a genius or insane. Either way, marry me." Jack gave her a wink as they moved further underground.

"I'm never getting married again." Sarah pulled her notes from her bag, checking them against the light of an oil lamp set on the pathway. "I think we're close. But we may draw less attention to ourselves if I go on my own. In case someone comes by and wonders why I'm inspecting the crevices in the stone."

"I'll go with you," Jack said. Sarah offered no argument and they pressed onward, as Ginger and Noah hung back.

Ginger watched as their shadows faded. "Do you think Jack cares for her?"

"Maybe. He's had his heart set on someone unobtainable for years."

Ginger's heart squeezed with sadness for him. Jack deserved to be happy.

Noah's gaze fixed on the ochre paintings on a wall. "This is one of the oldest known manmade structures ever discovered.

Likely built almost two thousand years before the pyramids at Giza."

She studied his profile. "Do you think you'll ever go back to archeology?"

Noah's jaw tightened, and he didn't meet her gaze. "Truth is a blunt instrument. I was fooled into believing my importance, manipulated into actions I can't take back. The man I was is dead, Ginger."

His words brought her chills. She touched his cheek, gently, drawing his face to the side so that she could meet his eyes. "He's not dead to me. Or Jack. Or even Sarah, for that matter."

Noah's lips parted as though to reassure her, then he paused. He gave the hint of a sad smile, then nodded. They stood in silence, the air around them still and cool.

How would they ever be able to clear Noah's name?

Noah seemed to be standing better today, after she had insisted he rest as much as possible on the sea voyage. The swelling in his feet had lessened, but his physical injuries worried her the least.

For three nights in a row she'd had to shake him awake from nightmares, finding him coated in sweat. He'd told her little of what had terrified him, but she was concerned. Cuts and scrapes she knew how to treat. But Osborne had opened some wound in him that she hadn't even begun to understand.

Ginger slipped her hand into Noah's as they waited. He'd let his beard start to grow and she'd tinted her hair, but would it be enough to keep them safe? Along with the concession paperwork, Malta had offered the hope of escape that hadn't existed in Egypt.

She hoped William had kept his promise to take her family home to England. It seemed hard to believe it had been over a week since she'd been with them. Her life had taken such a strange direction since then, tossed into the chaos that Stephen had created.

Whenever she thought of the destruction Stephen had wreaked upon her life, she felt physically ill, hardly able to breathe. And the thought of Stephen being free ...

Footsteps, announcing Sarah and Jack's return, did her the favor of breaking her line of thought. Sarah held up a thin leather pouch, about the length of a sheet of paper.

*She found it.*

Ginger's heart thumped. She didn't know whether to be nervous or glad.

Sarah came closer, then opened the pouch, handing the contents to Ginger. Inside were several documents, including the agreement between Ibn Saud and her father and all the paperwork for the Arab Anglo Oil Company.

Ginger felt the hair on her arms stand up and her heart slow at the sight of her father's familiar script.

And Stephen Fisher's signature.

She edged the concession agreement closer to the lamp light, peering at the text. "This says that Stephen owns forty-five percent of the company."

Ginger met Sarah's eyes, her stomach sinking. No wonder he'd been so desperate to get his hands on it. He wasn't simply trying to steal something. He wanted what was rightfully his.

But he would also use this to twist, manipulate ... who knew what else?

The papers in her hand shook. So much had been destroyed for these.

Jack glanced over her shoulder. "You're officially in business with Fisher, then?" He eyed Noah. "I don't have to ask Noah's opinion to tell you that's not the best idea."

Noah took the papers from her, scanning them. "It explains

Fisher's obsession with getting the papers. And he won't lose interest in them either."

"So much greed." Ginger felt disgusted with herself. Even she'd been captivated with the promise the oil concession had provided. She'd seen it as the solution to her troubles and those of her family.

In the end, it had only done more harm. Brought her more trials and tribulations. She'd been used as a pawn in Stephen's game—one that had cost Noah almost everything.

Sarah crossed her arms. "Well. That's that, I suppose. I'm not even sure it feels worth the trouble of having found this. We can't do anything with this paperwork without the British government and Stephen Fisher getting involved, right?"

"Probably not," Ginger admitted.

And much as she didn't want Stephen to get his hands on this paperwork, she didn't want the government getting it either. She ran her fingers over the dried ink of her father's signature on the document.

This had destroyed him too.

She glanced at Noah. "Do you care if your wife is completely penniless?"

Noah chuckled, folding the papers. He handed them to her once again. "I knew your father had lost his fortune even before we first spoke."

Lifting the papers toward Sarah, Ginger found her hands remarkably calm. "Will you be able to survive without that five percent?"

A light dawned in Sarah's eyes as her gaze flicked from Ginger's face to the papers. After a moment, she nodded. "I can survive. I always have."

Ginger bent down toward the oil lamp nearest them, then tipped the corner of the paperwork toward the flame.

"You sure about this, Red?" Jack asked. His face didn't reveal his opinion.

She didn't have to answer. She held the paper steady, watching as the yellow flames curled around the corner. Then the paper gave a bright burst, the whooshing sound of fire crawling quickly up the sides. The charred edge crept inward, glowing, leaving ash in its wake.

Ginger blew on the flames, to help them spread, and the ashes lifted into the air like the winds of the sirocco that had swirled through her life, bearing her here. The concession would join the dust and the sands on the ancient stone and she would never be beholden to it again.

# EPILOGUE

Strolling hand in hand with Noah through the Upper Barrakka Gardens of Valletta, Ginger glanced at the couples seated at the restaurant they'd just left. They dined outdoors, to the gentle balm of piano music and the birdsong from the surrounding trees. Warm with the flush of the red wine they'd shared, Ginger leaned against Noah's arm, feeling peaceful.

"Have I told you today how handsome you look with that beard?" She grinned up at him.

"Once or twice." Noah tugged her through the arcades—a series of graceful, sweeping arches—toward the view of the harbor that lay just beyond them.

The views of the city and the Mediterranean from this vantage point were breathtaking. The waters sparkled in the twilight, beneath a cluster of clouds tinged with pinks and yellows from the light of the fading sun. A cool breeze whipped past them, and she scooted closer to Noah. In response, he slipped his arms around her, drawing her back against his chest as they faced the harbor.

The weather here was perfection.

Despite the naval ships in the harbor, she could imagine this being their honeymoon. Instead, they were hiding here like escaped convicts, and the ships in the harbor carried soldiers and wounded, more signs of a war whose pulse continued, however faintly.

Even with the reminder of war and death, all her fears of Stephen were easy to keep at bay while here on the island of Malta. Even as awful as the encounter with Osborne had been, he didn't hold a candle to the fear Stephen inspired in her. Here, they seemed to be beyond the reach of the dangerous winds of war they'd faced in Egypt, but were they really?

As Noah's lips skimmed her temple and then grazed her jaw, she murmured a low, satisfied groan only he could hear. "Don't tempt me while we're still in public."

His chuckle was deep in his chest. "You'll find the temptation isn't at all one-sided."

Church bells tolled the hour, a peaceful interruption to their conversation. Noah's eyes shifted toward the skyline. She reached for his hand. His fingers encircled hers. On the levels below the area where they stood, cannons faced the sea.

"We should get back to the hotel," she said regretfully. "You've been on your feet far too long today. And I should check to see how Jack is feeling before he retires for the night."

"And you pretend you're not a nurse anymore." Noah didn't move or release her. "You can leave Jack to Sarah, though."

"I know. But I'm tired too." It was a fib, but he wouldn't protest if she said that. Truthfully, she wanted to stay here. Their dinner al fresco had been intimate and wonderful. The locals were charming when they learned they'd just been married, bringing bottles of wine to the table and desserts like Ħelwa tat-tork—a delicious nut fudge. "Let's stay here on Malta.

We can find a small house that overlooks the sea and have a few children running barefoot in the grass."

His smile was charmingly sweet as he dipped a soft kiss to her lips. "Sounds like heaven."

She thought of her father's house here. While they had decided it was too dangerous to go there, she understood his purchase more. Had her father loved this island? It wouldn't have surprised her. He'd loved the sea.

The turquoise-blue waters of the bay shimmered in the sunset. Beyond that, the sandstone city seemed to come to life as the glow from lamps spilled through windows in the houses.

Sighing, she leaned back against Noah, listening to his heartbeat. They swayed together, the soft trill of piano music drifting from the restaurant. Then she remembered the present she'd brought for him in her handbag and startled.

"What is it?" Noah looked down at her, concern in his eyes.

"No, no, nothing bad. I've just remembered something." She opened her bag and dug out a pouch. "I bought this for you a few days ago at the market with Sarah, but the man at the store said he may need to size it." She held the pouch out to him.

Noah gave her a curious look. He tugged at the strings, then emptied the contents into the palm of his hand: a silver ring, with a filigree Maltese cross stamped into it—a cross-like shape with eight points. A thistle was engraved in the center of the cross.

She'd never given him anything before and couldn't help the jitter of nerves in her stomach. "It's a wedding ring. For you." She took it out of his palm and slipped it onto his finger. "Some soldiers I treated had them, and I always thought it was sweet. Since you've given me two, I thought I might get you one. What do you think?"

His eyes darted to hers, then he looked down again at the

ring on his hand. Moistening his lips, he seemed at a loss for words.

*He hates it.*

Then he lifted his gaze to hers again.

His eyes were red-rimmed, glassy. A glad cry choked in her throat. "Do you like it, then?"

Rather than answer, he bent and lowered his lips to hers, kissing her as though they were alone. Her heart thudded, her senses alive at the touch of his lips.

When he broke away, she was breathless. "You can't kiss me like that here."

"Do you really think I care if anyone suspects I'm going to take you back to our room and make love to you until neither of us can move?" His voice was deep and sensual.

Her lips parted. Ginger shot him a mock glare. "You are terrible."

"Terrible?" He looked up, and a smile hinted at the corners of his mouth. "Then I might need to practice."

*Scoundrel.* She laughed and kissed his cheek, then stepped back, holding his hand.

He watched her with a look that made her feel beautiful. "One moment." He left her standing there, heading back toward the restaurant. Had he left something behind?

When he returned, he tugged her back by the elbow under the arches, the glow of the lights in the city deepening the yellows and oranges in the indigo-hued sky. The pianist played the song "Let Me Call You Sweetheart," and Noah held out a hand. "Will you dance with me?"

"Here?" She smiled. He must have requested the song.

"I've always promised myself that I'd have a dance with you. And I can't think of any place more perfect than this."

As he swept her into his arms, she closed her eyes, his

masculine scent mixing with the sweetness of the windy breezes from the sea. "You're right. This is perfect."

His lips grazed her ear. "You don't know how beautiful you are. And while I may not have intended to leave the army like this, I fully intend to spend every second doing everything I've dreamed of doing with you. And, apparently, I need to practice."

Her eyes flew open at his boldness. Then, unable to find the words to argue, she laughed and pulled his head down into a kiss. The promise of hope swirled in the breeze that wrapped around them.

For today, that was enough.

\* \* \*

CONTINUE the journey with Ginger and Noah with the rest of the Windswept WWI Saga:

Whisper in the Tempest: Book 3

...OR SEE where it all started with:

A ZEPHYR RISING: A Windswept Prequel Novella

IF YOU'D LIKE to keep in touch or find out the latest about my new releases, please sign up for my newsletter or join my Facebook Reader's group! I love hearing from readers and have some great offers and giveaways lined up for my subscribers.

## AUTHOR'S NOTE

Thank you so much for reading and joining Ginger and Noah for another adventure!

The further I get into researching the Middle Eastern front of the First World War, the more fascinating nuggets I find to explore with this story. While some of the names mentioned in this book are very real and became major players on the international stage, this is obviously a work of fiction so I took some liberty with the facts for the sake of my narrative.

One of the things that I wanted to highlight in this book was how big a factor oil domination really was in the entire war, which was labeled one of the most important war aims of the British. In fact, there were some historical accounts that I found that went so far as to suggest that the disastrous Gallipoli campaign was mostly about oil.

I made a quick reference to oil near Kirkuk and Gertrude Bell (who I really wish I could have included more of in this book, but she was assigned to Baghdad and actually sick in the hospital during the period in which this book is set), but it is interesting to note that toward the end of the war, the British

Army made a mad dash to capture Mosul (fifteen days *after* the Mudros Armistice) and then reneged on the boundaries they had delineated in the Sykes-Picot Agreement with the French. That region came under the control of the British after the war as Iraq and, ten years later, oil was discovered at nearby Kirkuk.

Also of note, the British weren't the only ones out there searching for oil: for example, up until the United States entered the war, the Standard Oil Company of New York had employees conducting oil explorations in the Middle East. One of those men, William Yale, went on to work for the U.S. State Department during the war *while still on payroll* for Standard Oil.

That said, I'm not trying to make a political statement. The truth was that *all* the world powers involved in the war were looking for oil and hoping to control it. They were dependent on it already. Pointing out how one government went about it doesn't mean that other governments were making a more honest job of it.

In less controversial notes, throughout my research, I stumbled across inconsistencies in spellings and place names between now and the early 1900s. As much as possible, I aimed for consistency with what was known to the British in 1917, (thus Abdeen Palace is written Abdin Palace). Likewise, modern-day Tahrir Square is written as Ismailia Square, as it was known back then. There are several instances of this throughout the book.

I found some interesting tidbits about architectural elements in Cairo that I was eager to include, since some of them were really fascinating. For example, the tunnels at Café Riche are real and the basement was used by nationalists for their meetings. And, fortunately for history, the nationalists that did use these spaces were much more peaceful than the fictional El-Masry.

One last little thing, for those who might take issue: the word "petrichor" wasn't coined until the 1960s. But because it's so lovely, such a precise term, and used in the context of prose, I went ahead and used it anyway!

Thank you again for reading and I hope you join me (and Ginger and Noah) for the final installment of the Windswept WWI Saga, *Whispers in the Tempest*, which will be released in September 2023! You can preorder now or join my newsletter for updates as they're available. If you enjoyed this book, I'd love for you to leave a review or rating—they go a long way to help me be able to write more books!

# ACKNOWLEDGMENTS

This book wouldn't be here without the hard work of so many people who have been integral to my process and helped bring out the best version. The first draft of this book was probably my favorite thing I've ever written (even though it wasn't what it needed to be) and having a friend like Andie Burke who gobbled up each chapter as I wrote it was absolutely brilliant. (Thank you, thank you.) It's hard to imagine ever writing anything so fun again.

Thank you to my wonderful editor, Susanne Lakin, who always gives me the most amazing feedback when I'm heading in the wrong direction and helps straighten me out! Your edits were invaluable to getting things flowing the way they needed to be and I can't thank you enough!

Many thanks to my brilliant (as we defined it, haha) copyeditor, Robin Seavill, who polished this to a shine and helped me find all those pesky Americanisms. I truly enjoy our chats and your wonderful advice.

A huge thanks to my proofreader Amanda Coleman for her dedication to this and to my sister, Christi, for taking the time to look at early drafts and steered me away from whiplash and toward better character development, haha.

I think everyone will probably want to thank my writing bestie, Lisa Boyle, for saving them from the cliffhanger ending I had originally envisioned for this book. It would have been mean. It would have been bad. And she had a lot to do with it not happening.

Thank you to my beta readers and reviewers and everyone who told me they were anxiously awaiting the second book. Each drop of encouragement helped!

Lastly, to my husband Patrick for his patience and pocketbook (thank you George Jetson, I truly appreciate it) and to my children who cheered me on with every word I wrote.

# ABOUT THE AUTHOR

Annabelle McCormack writes to bring under-explored periods of history to life. She is a graduate of the Johns Hopkins University's M.A. in Writing Program. She lives in Maryland with her name-that-tune-champion husband, where she forgets to move the laundry to the dryer for her (mildew-scented) five children.

Visit her at www.annabellemccormack.com or http://instagram.com/annabellemccormack to follow her daily adventures.

Printed in Great Britain
by Amazon